KNIGHT

"*Knight Moves* is an engrossing and evocative read, a tale of immortality and love and death rendered in a style that reminds me more than a little of the early Roger Zelazny. Williams' people are intriguing and sympathetic, and his portrait of an Earth left transformed and empty by a humanity gone to the stars, where aliens dig among ancient ruins for old comic books while the creatures of legends stir and walk again, will linger in my memory for a long time. Williams is a writer to watch, and—more importantly—to read."

—George R.R. Martin,
author of *Armageddon Rag*

"*Knight Moves* uses an unmatched cast of characters, human and otherwise, to tell an intriguing story."

—Fred Saberhagen
author of the *Book of Swords* Trilogy

Look for this other TOR book by Walter Jon Williams

AMBASSADOR OF PROGRESS

"Well-developed characters, an intriguing plot and a clear view of the double-edged sword called change make [AMBASSADOR OF PROGRESS] an engrossing book to read."

—*Library Journal*

KNIGHT MOVES

WALTER JON WILLIAMS

TOR

A TOM DOHERTY ASSOCIATES BOOK

KNIGHT MOVES

Copyright © 1985 by Walter Jon Williams

First printing: February 1985

A TOR Book

Published by Tom Doherty Associates
8-10 West 36 Street
New York, N.Y. 10018

Cover art by Stephen Hickman

ISBN: 0-812-55794-8
CAN. ED.: 0-812-55795-6

Printed in the United States of America

Thanks to the people who gave some of their time and intelligence to make sure I did a few things right:

Sven Knudson, Melinda Snodgrass, Julie Beiser, Terry Boren, Laura Mixon.

1

I have a little story that I made up, and I'll tell it to you if you don't read that much into it. It's called the Tale of the Pythian Kassandra, and it's about a priestess of the Delphic Apollo. I like to think of her as a sturdy, big-hipped woman with a straight Grecian nose and a slight mustache, not very bright, good-hearted, a little vague, and new to the job—the priests never chose the Pythia for her brains, you see; they didn't want the oracle challenging their power. The oracle was open for business only one month out of the year, so we'll have to picture this story as taking place toward the end of Kassandra's busy time; the pilgrims have been winding their way up to the temple for weeks now, and Kassandra's been breathing the inspiring vapors so often she's half-addled.

And now, puffing up the Sacred Way, comes the firm of Fat Merchant & Son from Athens, eager to inquire of the oracle whether or not to participate in a joint venture to Egypt that promises great profit since there's been a truce with Persia, but which also offers the possibility of great loss at the hands of Cretan and Phoenician pirates, the treacherous Persian satrap, and Zeus knows what else. Fat Merchant, whom we shall call Theopropos for simplicity's sake, has ridden most of the way in a cart but is now compelled to climb the Sacred Way to the temple, puffing up the path, performing the ritual ablutions, sacrificing his goat on the altar, giving his gift to the priests.

The gift is a bronze tripod of second-rate workmanship that Theopropos has been unable to unload upon his discriminating customers. The priests, of course, recognize it for what it is and look at one another and nod. Another stingy merchant, they think; we'll stick him with an ambiguous oracle and *serve him right*.

Picture Theopropos gasping and red-faced, sweating in the blazing sun, as he heaves himself up to the temple. He is beginning to doubt the wisdom of the whole enterprise. Not only is he tired, with sweat staining the armpits of his chiton, but he's caught the looks on the faces of the priests upon presentation of his tripod and he's begun to wonder whether he's made an error in unloading his white elephant on Apollo. His high blood pressure is kicking hell out of his skull and he's blinking sweat out of his eyes. His son has to support his arm as he makes his breathless way into the oekos. He's grateful, at last, for the cool of the oracular chasm and for the solidity of the marble bench beneath him. The priest jabs him in the ribs with an elbow, and Theopropos, blinded still with sweat, bellows his question in the direction of the antron.

Alone in her little cavern, Kassandra is as high as a kite. She feels the vapors doing strange things to her head. The navel stone beneath her hand feels like it's growing fur, and the jolly sound of the spring Kassotis is beginning to sound like a hundred liquid voices babbling in opaque chorus. She's given a lot of oracles today and is tired, tired most of all of idiotic, self-important merchants asking her the best way to invest their cash. She's tempted to jabber a lot of nonsense for the priests to interpret however they wish but recollects her duty to Apollo and Ge and resignedly bends over to inhale the vapors once more, giving her best; that's what I like most about Kassandra—her game willingness to give even fat fools what she can. She is as surprised by what follows as the priests are, a startled witness to her own sudden visions.

"Woe, woe to Delphi!" she cries.

What the hell? wonders Theopropos as he and the priests exchange startled looks. Kassandra has been trained to babble incoherently so that the priests can interpret her words as best suits them, but now the voice from the antron speaks out clear and unambiguous.

Woe to Delphi! poor Kassandra cries, speaking in clearest hexameter. *In the twilight days when Kassotis runs dry and the Pythia is no more, mortals shall forsake their mother and live the lifetimes of gods in the realm of Helios, and all earth shall be in pawn to the stranger born not of mortal or god! Woe to the last king of earth, a shadow-prince who sold the birthright of mankind to another, darker shade! Woe to the last priest of Delphi, whose words are dust and whom Apollo has forsaken! Woe to Ge, whose children have abandoned her to the questing hands of the stranger!*

The head priest looks grim. This is not what the people pay to hear. Nevertheless he knows that such a clear oracle cannot be subjected to the usual sort of "interpretation," and he writes it down verbatim. "This is the shrine of Apollo, called Loxias," he says rapidly, speaking the words he has spoken so often before, "whose oracles are always true but are not always understood. Meditate on the words of the god and perhaps their meaning will become clear."

Theopropos gazes blankly at the words the oracle has delivered him. *Meditate, my arse*! he thinks and is glad he got rid of the ugly bronze tripod. Scowling, he goes forth from the sanctuary into the awful sun, feeling the heat burn at his bald spot. The only part of the oracle he can understand is all this "woe, woe" stuff, and he has to admit it doesn't sound encouraging. He decides to keep his investments closer to home.

Behind him, as he wanders away on the arm of his son, a "Closed for the Day" sign appears on the sanctuary wall and the remaining pilgrims are told to come back tomorrow. Kassandra is brought out of the antron and confronted by the angry priests. The vapors are still filling her head and she keeps seeing the priests' gray lovelocks playing tweaky-fingers on their foreheads. She has an impulse to giggle and is in no condition to protest when the head priest scowls and gives her an unusually blunt scolding.

"Kassandra, my lass," the priest says, "I don't know what game you're playing, but it had better stop right now! Our oil and our goat's flesh don't come from telling merchants about our own demise, not when it's investment counseling they want. Now go to your quarters and get some rest. There's a big deputation from Selinus waiting, and tomorrow I'm going to give them some stern words about retaining their oligarchy, so no more of this 'woe to Delphi' business."

Kassandra, who has just seen the priest's head turn into that of a hoopoe, gives a little giggle and the priest's scowl deepens. "Cut along now!" he barks, and the ever-obedient Pythia makes her way to her quarters.

Depending on what I've been drinking that day and the current state of my irony, I have several endings to my story. In one, the fit never returns; Selinus retains its oligarchy, Kassandra continues into brain-damaged, good-natured old age and retires honorably, to be replaced by another tractable apprentice. In another, the fits return from time to time, often enough to annoy the priests, but not often enough to occasion her dismissal.

In a third ending, the fits continue. The deputies from Selinus get an amazing recitative about the Franco-Prussian

War, with a long disquisition on early mobilization by railroad and a pithy satire on Bismarck, which they conclude is aimed at the tyrant of Syracuse. A Lacedaemonian boxer wondering whether or not to train for the games gets an abstract of a *The Insidious Dr. Fu Manchu* by Sax Rohmer. The priests decide that enough is enough, and the doors of the sanctuary are slammed in the amazed face of the next applicant. A new sign is hung on the temple: "The God is OUT."

The priests conclude that they have to get rid of Kassandra, and they manage it somehow: Either she is given an overdose and passes away babbling about post-Mao Chinese political doctrine, or she's retired forcibly and shipped off to the Retired Pythias' Home, where she passes her time in bewildered contemplation of her brief career and is subjected from time to time by odd, involuntary visions in which Luther's *95 Theses*, the premiere performance of *Don Giovanni* and an episode of *Leave it to Beaver* are curiously intermingled. She outlives the head priest by many years and eventually becomes the honored head of a small cult of believers, who accept her prophecies as genuine manifestations of the god and who keep meticulous records, most of which some centuries later end up misfiled in one of the more obscure corners of the library at Alexandria, and are thus lost to the ages.

This last ending is my sloppy-drunk ending and my sentimental favorite.

I once considered composing a dialogue between Kassandra and the head priest in which Kassandra insisted on the divine truth of her visions and the priest sensibly pointed out that impenetrable prophecies, however true, were of little service to anyone and that Apollo would be better served by political stability in Selinus and a renewed war with Persia under Spartan leadership. Kassandra would be gentle, a little bewildered, but firmly insistent; the priest would be practical, sarcastic and utterly pragmatic.

The dialogue would revolve around the question of how welcome true prophecy is, or has ever been. Kassandra, like her Trojan namesake, would hold for the desirability of truth, no matter how impenetrable or unwelcome; the priest would insist that the prophecy business had to give people what they want, to wit, firm moral guidance, sensible coalition politics aimed at domestic peace and distant conquest, and enough ambiguity to allow for the occasional priestly error.

The dialogue was never written. I decided, I think, that my little story was too slight to withstand the weight of such massive interpretation.

But bits of the dialogue continue to prowl about in my head. Had the oracle delivered *me* that prophecy, would things have changed at all? I suspect not. I would have found a reason to avoid the warning—an idealistic reason, no doubt, about how my personal fate scarcely mattered against the world's parochial dangers. The head priest would have looked at me and smiled one of his knowing, cynical smiles.

And nothing—nothing of importance anyway—would have changed. I would still have made the deal I made, faced up to the same terrors I faced up to, run from the ones I didn't; and I would still have got my irony in much the same way.

The priest's unpleasant smile was in my mind at my moment of waking. His teeth were rather pointed, did I mention that? The cynical, insinuant face took a moment to fade, and when it did, the teeth went last, like the Cheshire Cat's. I was in my house on Hyampeia. It was just past dawn. I would be receiving guests soon. They had been on the planet for months, and I was running out of excuses. Even now they were waiting in Athens. Waiting with infinite patience, the patience I had known they would display as soon as I heard who was leading the deputation. McGivern had always had more patience than I.

I rolled out of bed and took a shower. Mine was modest, with four surrounding shower heads that crawled about the tile on oral command like obedient leeches. Then I asked my kitchen for a cup of coffee on the terrace.

On my way to the terrace I passed the bronze charioteer I'd lifted from the Delphi museum. A reconstruction, complete with horses and chariot built with the aid of the chronograph, rested in the museum. There had been debate over whether to paint it in lifelike colors, as the original had once been, or to leave it in bronze. I'd decided to have it painted and risk the charge of bad taste. And now I indulged myself with the original.

I took the featherduster from its place and swept dust from the folds of the charioteer's gown. "What's new, old sport?" I asked.

He gazed at me levelly, without surprise or comment, from the strange lifelike eyes set in the green bronze flesh. I put the featherduster away and went to the terrace.

The robot help had the coffeepot sitting in its place before I arrived, along with a basket of bread, a slab of fresh butter and pots of jam and honey. Once on the terrace, I put my bare feet up on the rail and poured the coffee. I called to the house and asked it to play me some music, and soon a delicate, immaculate guitar began to ring out with the clarity of Sunday bells, and Mississippi John Hurt began to sing "Monday Morning Blues." The house had sensed my mood all right.

Nobody sings the blues anymore, I thought. What the hell kind of world is that?

Once I'd tried to learn to play the guitar that way but I'd never gotten the hang of it. I waited for the coffee to kick me into overdrive and watched the world below.

Beneath the terrace the rebuilt Temple of Apollo stretched out before me, the massive Doric columns a pale earth color that glowed pinkish in the last moments of the dawn. The reconstruction was very exact: The temple had been mapped thoroughly by chronograph. I would rather have rebuilt the second temple, the one with the facade of Parian marble donated by the Alcmaeonidae and destroyed by earthquake in 373. It would have reflected the dawn more spectacularly, and in daylight would have stood out in white glory against the crags of Rhodini, but that would have meant tearing down what remained of the third temple, and I found I couldn't bring myself to do it. After this reconstruction was completed, I was going to rebuild the second temple as well, but somewhere else. Perhaps in Laconia, where the scenery would form a spectacular backdrop but where the Spartan life-style had resulted in a dearth of memorable architecture.

Below the temple the Sacred Way still zigzagged to the altar, its path dotted, as of old, with offerings—in this case the reconstruction of offerings, patterned on the originals mapped by chronograph. Several of the treasuries were still surrounded by scaffolding: My employees had not yet done with them.

Beyond, framed by the dark spires of cypress, the mountains of Cirrha lay deserted in the distance, their brown folds holding deep shadow, and below them an inlet of the Sea of Corinth stretched its finger inland. In the shadow of the nearer hills the sea was colored a brooding violet. In a few minutes, when the sun touched it, the color would change, altering to the astounding azure of the Mediterranean, the deep blue that strikes the viewer like Poseidon's trident. There was nothing lovelier. Coffee and John Hurt's guitar slowly took the edge off the hard fact of morning. Smugly I congratulated myself on choosing this place for a home.

I ate new-made bread with fresh butter and honey and drank my coffee as I watched the sun reach down to the bay, seeing the surface of the water wrinkle with the shifting winds. There was a little fragment of white chaff down there, my sailboat *Aura*. Two months earlier I had moored her in that spot upon my return from a four-month motorless, robotless journey past Suez and the Red Sea. To find McGivern and his party waiting for me.

The olive trees shimmered with their silvery cargo. Soon it would be autumn. And I had run out of excuses.

I sighed and drank the last of the coffee. Then I left the terrace and its visions and stepped into my house to dress.

Athena's serpent had a few words of wisdom first, however. "Mr. McGivern has logged another call," it said. "He says it's urgent." My house knew better than to talk to me before coffee.

"Yes."

"Do you wish me to put it on audio?"

"No. I haven't made up my mind about Mr. McGivern yet."

The serpent lapsed into silence. I think it secretly disapproved of me.

"Anything else?" I asked.

The voice was coming from a not particularly distinguished fourth-century marble statue of Athena. I had borrowed it from the National Museum in Athens when I disbanded the place, intrigued because the statue showed Athena with all her icons: shield, spear, helmet, the owl, the head of Medusa, the serpent child Erichthonius curled up inside the aegis. The original snake head had vanished centuries ago, and I'd had it replaced with a copy that served as the mouthpiece, in this room anyway, of my house. The owl could talk too, if it wished. I liked the idea of my house speaking with the voice of Wisdom. I doubt that the house appreciated my humor.

"Nothing else of urgency," the house answered. "Mr. Odje called concerning the Red Sea leases, but he said it could wait."

"Very well. He's probably asleep on his side of the world anyway."

Erichthonius, Athena and the owl stared at me. I stared back for a second.

"Don't push, house," I said. The house didn't answer.

I went into my room—the bed had been made in my absence, the used towels collected from the shower and others laid out—and then I dressed. Belted chiton and sandals, practical gear for the climate. Floppy straw hat and polarized sunglasses. I walked back into the living room.

"Ahem," said Erichthonius.

I turned. "Yes?"

"A call from Branwen. Will you accept?"

"Of course." Branwen had the codes to override my privacy if she needed to, but she never abused them. I took my hat off. "Video, please."

All the windows of the room simultaneously darkened and then the image of my youngest daughter appeared, projected on the large terrace window. She had my broad muscular shoulders and deep gray eyes, but the rest was all her mother's Irishness: fair, freckled skin, upturned nose, auburn hair, a way of crinkling her eyes when she smiled. Her skin was tanned a deep brown, as luscious as the crisp skin of a properly baked fowl; her hair was bleached lighter than usual by the sun. Her smile was brilliant. I thought she was about perfect.

Like me, she looked twenty-two or so. Unlike me, twenty-two was actually her age.

"Kalemehra, Dad."

"Hi, Bran. Did you have good diving?"

She bobbed her head vigorously. "It was a great time. I wrinkled up like a raisin. I've got a lot of marvelous pictures to show you when you come to the college."

She was a student of marine biology, living now in Australia, with a secondary specialty in extraterrestrial marine life forms. She could talk to dolphins, but she found them pushy in a queasy, sexual way. She hadn't made up her mind yet to emigrate; being my daughter, she didn't have to. Selfishly, I hoped she wouldn't.

"Where are you now?" I asked.

"Tampa. Stopped by to see some friends. I'll be with Joe in Utah until the new term starts."

I grinned and nodded, hoping my true feelings didn't show. Joe seemed like a nice enough boy, polite and intelligent if a little dull, but he was a Diehard of the Soilbound persuasion. Which was to be expected, I suppose, considering that he was born here on Earth; but I wasn't enthusiastic about the idea of my daughter becoming attached to someone who'd been brought up to consider me an avatar of the Devil.

"Have a good time," I said. "How's your mother?"

Her eyes narrowed slightly. She shrugged. "I haven't talked to her since before I left."

Branwen, in later years anyway, had become much more my daughter than Kathryn's. Partly, I think, because over time I had learned moderation about when and when not to interfere in our daughter's life. I suspect Kathryn had not been tactful about Joe.

I tried to speak gently. "Do me a favor," I said. "Give her a call to let her know you're back. It'll save me having to do it."

"How about I just send her a letter?"

I nodded. "If that's the way you have to do it." Relations were worse than I'd thought. If it was Kathryn driving Branwen toward Joe, I might have to violate one of my rules and interfere. Coping with Kathryn wasn't anything I looked forward to; our parting hadn't been friendly.

Branwen brightened. "Just called to let you know I'd returned. Judy and Hu say hi."

"Say hi for me. Glad to see you again."

"See you at the fall term. I'm kind of looking forward to being back at school." I lectured over the winter at the Southern University of North America in Miami, which Branwen was attending.

"Bye."

Her form faded. The polarized windows lightened again, and I was gazing across the valley, between the dark pillars of cypress. Erichthonius looked at me with glittering eyes.

"I've recorded another call from Mr. McGivern. He says it's urgent."

"Log it," I said. The statue didn't answer, but I felt its eyes on my back.

I put on my hat and glasses and went out to inspect the previous day's restoration work on the Treasury of the Siphnians. Most of the workers were students: willing but inexperienced at this kind of careful work.

I tried to forget Erichthonius's nagging. I didn't want to think about McGivern's call waiting in storage. Later in the afternoon, I decided, I'd cruise down to the bay for a swim and a visit to the *Aura*. Where no calls would ever reach me and I could take a bottle of ouzo and give the fish a glimpse of a happy inebriate.

On my walk toward the treasuries I passed the old restored temple and halted to look up at it. Had I blasphemed, building the place without dedicating it to the god who had once lived here?

The temple gave no answer, although there were words graven on the pronaos. KNOW THYSELF, they said on one side of the door. NOTHING IN EXCESS, they said on the other.

I turned and walked away. I'd had it with good advice.

2

McGivern finally came—was finally allowed to come—the next evening. I was practicing in the broad-jump pit when I sensed him standing under the old olive trees that stood by the stadium, quietly watching . . . patiently watching, as of old. McGivern's sight was always uncommonly keen, another reason I dreaded his arrival.

He was probably waiting to catch his breath. Vehicles, save my own, were banned in the precincts; he'd had to come climbing up the Sacred Way like any other pilgrim.

I swung my halteres and made my leap. The halteres were dumbbell-shaped hunks of iron, used by the classical athletes to aid them during the standing broad jump. The idea was to let them swing from your arms during the windup to help you gain momentum as you made your leap; then, once airborne, you threw them back behind you to gain additional push.

The physics of it seemed dubious to me, but Phayllus of Croton supposedly jumped fifty-five feet in this way—a record for the standing broad jump, greater than that set by any non-altered *running* broad jumper.

Phayllus's record was safe with me: I made about eight feet. I frowned, brushed the dust from my knees and retrieved my halteres. Better stick to running, I thought. This was my best score of the evening.

I picked up my towel and strigil and walked to where I knew McGivern was waiting. His thin, gangling figure was in shadow as he stood under a twisted olive tree; I was very close before I could see his remembered features. Bushy yellow hair, beaklike nose, thin reptilian lips. Wise, wise eyes. Like me, he looked about twenty-two. Like me, he was older. Dressed in a dark gray that gave his youthful body an air of premature gravity.

One biographer who preferred to forgive me my sins called McGivern the Mephistophilis to my Faustus. I preferred the high priest to my Kassandra.

He was rich, whatever rich means these days. He was perhaps the wealthiest person in our part of the galaxy, saving only me. He'd got ten percent of everything I'd made, and he'd invested it wisely, while I'd spent mine founding colleges and rebuilding temples. Someday, I supposed, he'd surpass me.

Not that it would mean anything. It wasn't as though wealth could be held in any form that wasn't temporary, as ephemeral as fog, as dew. I had people and machines to keep track of my dew for me, to keep moving it from clover to clover, hedging so I couldn't lose it all. Brian McGivern, I knew, kept track of his own funds. Habit, I suppose: a shame to let his talents go to waste. It was the thing he did best. The thing that gave him meaning. In my more maudlin moments I envied him.

I choose to cancel the United Nations, McGivern had said once, in my name. And he'd done it.

He was not, I suppose, a nice man. A financial genius, perhaps the last one ever. We had always liked one another, even when he found himself compelled to disapprove.

That he was here at all meant he thought it was important.

The idea that anything could be as important as that unsettled me.

Some vague uncertainty stopped me about ten feet away from him. He eyed me with care but without compassion, without enthusiasm. His way. *You will make a revolution*, he'd once told me with that same precise, analytical look. *You will destroy the world*.

Sounds good to me, I'd answered.

I looked at him and brushed dust from my elbows.

"Hello, Brian," I said.

He nodded, once. "Hello, Doran."

McGivern was standing on a slight eminence surrounding the stadium and I had to look up at him. "How long has it been?" I asked. Ritually.

A match flared briefly, gleaming on the silver of the olives above his head, and he lit his short cigar. His answer, when it came, was as dry of feeling as old desert bones, as the dusty spring Kassotis. "I hear you're an alcoholic these days."

I considered the idea for a moment. "It's too early to tell," I said. "Give it another few years and we'll know."

He accepted this without reaction. "You kept me waiting. Six months."

"I was on a boat most of that time."

He answered me silently, without a motion or a word. Cigar smoke tainted the air.

"And you didn't come alone," I said. "I would have seen you gladly if you hadn't come for a . . . purpose."

"It's an important purpose, Doran."

The hell with your purpose, I thought. I said, "Let's step over to the benches and sit down."

We moved to the long benches of the stadium and sat on the old gray stones. McGivern's body was young but his movements suggested age, a kind of carnal complacency. It was a phenomenon I worked hard to avoid, every day here in the stadium. While I scraped the oil and sweat from my legs with the strigil, he looked around curiously, noting the sheen of the gray stones in moonlight, the grassy, vacant, ghost-filled oval of the stadium.

He reached into his pocket. "A cigar?" he asked.

"I've given it up," I said and grinned at him. "It's no fun now that it's safe."

He nodded and put the cigar case away. "My people have their presentations ready."

"Have them recorded," I said. "I'll view them when I can."

He tilted his head to look at me. His smile was wry, amused. "You'll disappoint them. They wanted to see you in person."

"I hope you're comfortable in the hotel," I said.

McGivern retained his owlish smile; he knew I was changing the subject. "Ismenos and Helen are treating us very well," he said. "First-class personal service. Very old-fashioned, very comforting."

They were an unusual couple, I knew: glittering figures during the Decadence of a few centuries before who'd had the good sense, or luck, to give it up before it killed them. They worked at the hotel/restaurant not because of any economic need but because they loved the work for its odd demands and for the chance it gave them to meet the far-traveled.

I wandered down the hill to eat at their restaurant every so often, careful to ask Ismenos's opinion about the wine list and to compliment Helen on her lamb. They never seemed impressed by me; I received the same service as everyone else. I'd brought Branwen once and she'd fallen in love with the place immediately. Before the evening was out, she was playing dominoes with Ismenos in the light of a candle stuck in an old metaxa bottle. Both of them playing like Greeks, shouting and slapping the table with the dominoes as they played them, laughing loudly between gulps of wine.

"Be sure to ask for the local olives," I said. "Ismenos is proud of them."

"I'll do that."

"They give good service. They're used to diplomats. Diplomats and very rich tourists."

"Do you get many diplomats these days?" he asked.

"Not many. I'm fading into irrelevance. As I hoped I would. It's been years since anyone's tried to kill me."

"And the tourists?"

"I try to schedule their tours for times when I'm not here."

He drew on his cigar. Its red eye regarded me dispassionately. "For the modern Apollo, you aren't very forthcoming with your favors."

I frowned into the darkness for a while. I had private reasons for living at Delphi, and they had nothing to do with my turning god or oracle. I also knew it was pointless to try to convince anyone else of that.

"Even the original Apollo was open for business only one month out of the year," I said. I felt his eyes on me and brushed imaginary dust from my knees. "Besides," I went on, "I have nothing to tell them anymore."

"You're needed."

"I lecture every other autumn on literature and history. Once I did a special seminar on the history of the blues. I don't do physics these days. I don't even keep up."

"You're the authority, Doran. You have a better grasp of—"

"I don't owe them anything," I interrupted.

His face was hard in the moonlight, not young anymore, as craggy as the heights of Rhodini above us. His ancient eyes gazed at me as steadily as those of Minos, judging. "You owe *me*, Doran," he said. "I *built* this world of yours. Not my fault you don't like it."

I gave no answer. It was all too true. And so I gave

way. "I'll see your presentations," I said. "Your vanishing kangaroos. For all the good it'll do."

"Thank you," he said. He didn't sound as though he meant it.

"Who's on your team?"

"Not my team, Doran." He stretched his legs out to the stone bleachers in front of him. "Not mine at all. This is a project assembled on the highest levels of the government of Kemp's Planet. All I did was to organize the delegation that came to Earth."

"You *are* the highest level of the government of Kemp's Planet."

McGivern smiled thinly. "Don't your people keep your dossiers up to date these days?" he asked. "I've sold my interest. I'm just a gray eminence they consult when they need a particular problem solved."

"Don't congratulate yourself. You haven't solved this one yet."

He drew on his cigar confidently. "I will," he said. A gust of wind rustled the trees above us, stirring the dust in the stadium. The breeze spilling down the Arkoudorhema to the sea.

I was getting tired of this fencing. My rapier was rusty. "Who's on the team then?"

"A lot of people you know. Al-Qatan. Pierce Hourigan. Mary Liddell." His eyes were focused carefully on the opposite bank of the stadium as he spoke the names of my former students. There was no emphasis on the last, no self-congratulatory tip of the hat to himself for setting his careful hook. He went on with the names of other people I didn't know personally, only by reputation.

"And a man named Ruyter's in charge of the first survey team," he said. "You wouldn't know him, I think. They're on the planet now, gathering systematic data, conducting field surveys. Preparing the ground for you, and for the others." He stuck the cigar into his mouth and inhaled, but it was dead. He took it out and looked at it incuriously. Another wind stirred the dust of the field; I brushed away grains that had adhered to the sweat on my eyebrows.

"Can we get Zimmerman?" I asked. "He was brilliant. I know he's on Kemp's."

"Zimmerman?" McGivern frowned. He kept the cigar in his hand, gesturing with it, pointing up to Hyampeia and my house. "He's in his house, one like yours, but larger. He won't come out. His house says he'll speak only to you."

"The hell with him then."

"You can afford to say that. I can't."

The breeze chilled my body and I stood up, starting the walk home. McGivern flicked the cigar away and followed. I made my way out of the stadium, hearing his shoes crunching the gravel behind me. "Mary Liddell," I said. "Is she still. . . ?"

"A Diehard?" he said. "Yes."

The hell with her, too, I thought violently. I don't owe her anything either.

I heard McGivern's sudden gasp and I looked up to see the giant forms half-hidden in the trees, standing silently, watching us. McGivern gave a little nervous laugh.

"You know what I thought I saw?" he said quickly. "I thought they were. . . ." His voice faded away as his eyes adjusted to the shade and he saw that what he had first taken for a trick of the shadows was not a trick, but reality.

"Hush," I told him. "Not a word." Moving slowly, I walked into the deeper shadows where the silent forms waited.

"Hey anthropos," the first said in greeting. Hello, man.

The voice was bass, inflected harshly, oddly hesitant. I held up my hand.

"Hey kentauros," I said in greeting. "Ti esti kainon?"

The centaur shook his heavy head, then bent to sniff my palm. He reached out a huge hand, astonishingly gentle, and touched my cheek, letting me have his scent: grass, earth, sweat, hair, his own alien uniqueness, part human, part other. He looked at me soberly.

"Ti pascheis, o phile?" What's wrong, my friend?

He had smelled the trouble on me, the uneasiness in my mind. A perspicacious assembler of odors, my gray-haired phantom.

"Nothing. A visitor. An old guest-friend, come unexpectedly." The centaur shook his head again, disbelieving, the trees whipping over his shade in the blustery wind. Moon dapples shimmered over the broad shoulders, the hollows of the clavicle and throat, the grizzled hairs among the brown that furred him from the neck down. His head was long, as was the sensitive nose; there was a sagittal crest that anchored heavy muscles for chewing vegetation, but from the waist up he was recognizably human.

"He smells bad, this guest-friend. Has he brought you trouble?"

I grinned. I had never liked McGivern's cigars either. "He's a messenger. Not a bad sort. No trouble I can't deal with."

The centaur bent down, his spine as supple as a sapling, until his forehead almost touched the stony soil; then he straightened, flinging back his mane. He had registered his unease but would not pursue the matter further. "Very well," he said. "Philodice has come to sing for you. Have you the time?"

I glanced at the other vision, silver-haired, her eyes opalescent in the dim light. She held a lyre to her breast as though it were a child. "I will spare it gladly," I replied. "Does she wish to use the theater?"

"If you please, O man."

I bowed. We held hands to cheek again before I turned and went back to McGivern. "Follow," I said and led him down the zigzag path to the amphitheater, hearing the tentative clopping of their hooves behind us.

"My god," McGivern murmured, pitching his voice so only I could hear. "Is that one of your projects?"

"No. Not mine," I said, looking over my shoulder at the four-legged shapes that followed from out of the trees. "One of the old gene-splicers, centuries ago, made their tribe." I saw Philodice's nimble feet come sprightly down the path, striking shadows on the stone. "Their designer gave them cloven hooves to better handle this terrain. That was clever of him, I thought."

"I supposed that all those creatures were hunted down and killed." He had promulgated that policy himself; he sounded miffed.

"Not creatures, Brian," I said. "Most of those experiments were conducted with human DNA; it was more convenient. Philodice and Chiron are our cousins."

"Obviously they have a human intelligence."

"Intelligence, anyway. Their social structure and personalities are a lot more human than equine—they don't have the dominant stallion and boss mare the way horses do—but I don't think I'd go so far as to call them human. Not yet. With any luck, not ever."

McGivern did not comment on this piece of misanthropy. We turned into the theater, clambering down over the ancient benches. "Here," I said. "The sound is best about here." We sat. I could tell that McGivern was having a hard time refraining from looking over his shoulder.

"How many are there?" he asked.

"I don't know. Tens of thousands, I think, counting the feral ones; their population's growing now that the planet's depopulated. There are other things too besides centaurs. I've seen satyrs on Parnassus, but they won't let me come near. And I've seen other things in other places." I recalled red, hungry, jackal eyes and tried not to shudder. McGivern spoke thoughtfully.

"They could repopulate the earth," he said. "They could outnumber us."

"They might already. There are only twenty million people on earth now and untold numbers of . . . of our construct cousins." The creations of our dreams and legends—creatures of Olympus and Faerie and every bright world of our young imagining now populating the earth after man had abandoned it, existing furtively in their own youth, living in the wild, abandoned places like weeds springing up between the stones of man's ancient habitation. And in the end, I hoped, taking their ground and challenging man—and challenging one Other I knew— for possession of their mother world.

I heard the sound of Philodice's hooves walking down the low cypress-bordered path that led to the stage and I put my hand on McGivern's arm to silence him. "I'm sorry you don't know Greek," I said, "but I think you'll appreciate most of this. Blue spot. Recorder on. File under Philodice, Songs of the Centaurs, Volume II." The light sprang up at my command and moved to the edge of the stage to await her.

She came onto the stage warily, her dark eyes wide with apprehension. Her face was long and delicate, the cheekbones high, her hair silver, shining blue in the light of the spot. Her bare breasts, very human, rested proudly amid the delicate light floss that covered her torso; her mane and tail had been braided with fresh flowers. She struck the lyre—just once—and sang, the chord hanging in the air behind her words.

Tade nun etaiprais, she sang, tais emaisi terpna chalos aeiso. Tell everyone that today, at this moment, for the pleasure of my soulmates, I shall sing.

Sappho, that little fragment. Her voice was alto, and clear, but with overtones that were never produced by any human throat. The sound was earthly, yet strange; it gnawed with delicate little teeth at parts of the human soul long

buried, bringing them out of the earth to shine like spun
gold. Suddenly the world was strange again, looked at
through the sight of something other than human, something both less and greater. I could feel the hairs at the
back of my neck prickling, and I glanced at McGivern.
His face was deeply disturbed, mingling awe and a kind of
inchoate fear.

She struck the lyre again and sang again. This time she
accompanied herself on the instrument, plucking the strings
with her delicate hands. *You know this place; then fly from
Krete and come to us.* Sappho again, a hymn to Aphrodite.
The tune was Philodice's, all her own, sung on a scale that
sounded strange to my ears. The song ended: *Fill our
golden cups with love and purest nectar.*

The last chord hung in the silence. Then Philodice
trotted in a quick, nervous circle, casting an apprehensive
glance up high. I realized that she was seeking Chiron,
who was standing guard above us, ready to signal flight if
flight were needed. Then her eyes lowered, giving me a
quick, shy glance, after which she bent low to the ground
in what I had come to recognize as the centaur gesture of
decision. She straightened, threw her head back and began
to pluck the lyre again, and her voice gently filled the
amphitheater, echoing from the old stones.

I listened in rising astonishment. This was something
entirely new, not anything I had taught her. The directness
of emotion and language were Sappho's, but the sentiment
and phrases were all her own.

How may I find courage enough, she sang, to frame a
plea to Cyprian Aphrodite? Yet even the gentle thyme and
the fragrant clover taste of bitterness, for my love is far
away. Foam-born! Come from your pleasant island and
relieve my heart of its anguished throbbings. . . .

The song went on, the eerie, weirdly evocative voice
filling the deep space of the theater. Philodice turned her
head, and for a moment there was the ghost of another

standing below me, the curve of her silver hair over a cheekbone the same, the same look in a dark eye. *I will not take your gift*. That was how it had ended.

The lament died away, the last chord hanging among the stones in the suddenly still air. Philodice curvetted nervously in the spotlight. I rose and made my way down the gray seats to stand before her. Without Chiron close by, her wary eyes flickered left and right, her dainty feet trod anxiously in place. I reached up and touched her shoulders, brushing back the tousled silver mane.

"Had I known you would sing tonight," I said, "I would have made a crown of flowers for your brow. As it is, I can only give you my joy. Your song was wonderful. Make me another."

Philodice blushed to the tips of her breasts. "Thanks, man," she stammered. Then she flicked her tail, turned and fled the stage. The blue spot followed as far as it could and hovered, uncertainly awaiting her return. I told it to turn itself off. Above the amphitheater I could see Chiron silhouetted against the stars; he raised a hand in farewell, then followed his pupil. I stood on the stage for a long moment, recalling the song, the singer, the phantom fragment of memory. McGivern made his way down to join me.

"That was something," he said. "Scary, somehow. I wonder why."

I blinked the memory away, shaking my head to clear it. "That last one was different," I said. "It's the first song she's ever made by herself. The others were songs I'd taught them."

McGivern looked at me in surprise. "How long have you known they were here?" he asked.

"I first saw them a hundred years ago. North of here, in Thessaly. I couldn't get close to them, although I made as many recordings as I could. They had the beginnings of a language, the beginnings of a culture, the beginnings of a

simple technology based on what they could steal from old
human dwellings—tableware mostly; they don't have use
for much else. Chiron, that old one—his grandfather, Chiron
the Elder, was the first I got close to. He was about a year
old, I think; he'd got caught in a thunderstorm with his
mother in the Cirrhan hills. She was killed by lightning; he
had a leg and some ribs broken by a falling limb. I brought
him here and taught him Greek. You have to start young
with speech, and Chiron was young. That was eighty years
ago. He taught his children and neighboring young ones
and then sent them out as teachers to other tribes. His own
folk come here mostly for healing. Broken limbs and
dentistry."

"And they sing their thanks," McGivern said.

"Yes."

"And the lyre? You showed them how to make it?"

"It's an easy instrument to build. A tortoise shell, strings
made from their own hair, a framework, a plectrum. Py-
thagoras went a long way with it when he invented musical
theory."

McGivern looked at me with a probing smile. "It's also
the instrument of Apollo, as I recall."

"He stole it, you might remember, from Hermes." I
walked out of the theater, down toward the temple, and
McGivern followed.

There was a lot I didn't tell him. Branwen's part, for
one thing; it was she who had first taught them music and
old Aeolian lyrics. Hymns to nature and the gods, songs of
love and the dance, songs whose subjects they could grasp.
Branwen's brother David was living among them, north of
here; he'd made their study his life's work.

Neither did I tell McGivern of my hopes. The centaurs,
I thought, would eventually come to outnumber us on this
planet. Their sophistication and knowledge would increase,
and then, when they were ready, some descendant of
Chiron would challenge us and give us a run for our

money. None too soon, I reckoned. The human race needed shaking up, and the thoughts and attitudes of our inhuman cousins, alike enough to cause a responsive stirring in our minds; unlike enough to bring fresh light on everything we held dear, a needed antistrophe to our own stagnation.

We passed the vast temple; here my way would part from McGivern, he going down to the town, I to my eyrie. I began to think about opening a bottle of wine tonight. A deep purple-red, the color of dreams and fantasy. "Bring your people tomorrow morning," I said. "I'm usually up at dawn, so bring them whenever they can assemble their data. I'd esteem it a favor if you didn't mention Chiron and Philodice to them. Or to anyone else."

His eyes were sober. "I won't," he assured me. "I don't ever want them to become a tourist attraction." He shook his head. "My God! I still can't believe it."

"Goodnight, Brian."

He held out his hand. I shook it.

"I'll see you tomorrow," he said. I turned to begin my long climb and then I heard his voice. "I hope I'll be able to see them again, these four-legged children of yours."

I looked back. "I don't know how possible that is. You want to take me away from them, you see."

I began the climb. McGivern stood silent behind me for a moment, and then I heard him turn and move away.

3

Projected against the darkness of the polarized window was a plain, bathed in a harsh bright light that that made the green of the grasslike stuff seem almost black. The sky was a blazing white. Strange flat-topped trees, like inverted cumulonimbi, stood on the horizon. It looked like an awful place to spend a weekend.

In the foreground moved a herd of lazy animals, bipedal, each with a long, snakelike balancing tail and questing, grasping forepaws. Despite a heavier head and eyes on stalks, they resembled nothing so much as large kangaroos, except when they walked, they did not hop but placed one foot in front of the other and could do so quickly if they wanted to. I'd been told they made bad eating. They were called lugs, named, I gathered, after a member of the initial survey team who rather resembled one.

"The ecology and the assumed evolutionary history of Amaterasu make little sense," said Dr. Nelda Li-Shing y Saavedra. She was a short, dark-haired, round-faced woman who lectured in peremptory tones that sounded disapproving.

33

Amaterasu, it seems, did not meet her standards. She sniffed and spoke on.

"The lugs are the largest animals on the planet," she reported. "Nothing else even comes close; there are small insect forms, burrowing creatures, fish in the seas and lakes. We have found nothing larger than one-tenth of the mass of the average lug, and that was a fish. All the other life forms on Amaterasu are at a fairly primitive stage of evolution. While any Earth analogue is bound to be imprecise, few of the planet's life forms exceed in complexity the earthly forms of the Devonian, although in variety they are not nearly as numerous, and they do not display the gigantism so prominent in Devonian aquatic life.

"There are no creatures that prey on the lugs—there aren't any big enough for that. So far as we can tell, there have never been any. There aren't any parasites either, not even intestinal parasites. The type of grass that covers the plains of the planet rarely exceeds a foot in height, even when at its most mature. So why develop fast-running, warm-blooded bipedal creatures with eyestalks, if there's no grass to have to peer over and no predators to run from?"

The lecture went on. The grasses were mossy and uniformly low to the ground in order to avoid being burned around noontime by Amaterasu's pulsing blue-white sun. The trees were not trees but sophisticated, cooperative colonies of moss; their "branches" and "leaves" were sun-reflecting rather than sun-absorbing; they created a shady spot underneath which the real work of photosynthesis went on without the danger of being seared by the sun. The lugs didn't make ecological sense from this perspective either; they were simply too large.

No wonder the place had never been colonized despite its proximity to Earth. The pioneering expedition had taken one look, filled out its report card, and fled in horror after naming the place after the Japanese sun goddess. Centuries later, a team intending to study the system's blue-white sun had brought word of the first anomalies.

Great, I thought. Hot, with horrible solar radiation, and boring.

"We have theories that attempt to explain some of the anomalies," Dr. Li-Shing continued. Her tone indicated that she disapproved of theories as well. "Perhaps other, larger life forms *did* evolve, including a carnivorous species preying on the lugs, and perhaps all these other forms were wiped out in some catastrophe—solar flares from the sun, possibly, or collision with a meteor several miles in diameter that would have thrown up enough debris to darken the planet for years. Possibly even some kind of plague. The theories seem incomplete. They don't explain how the lugs survived or why evolution and species differentiation seem so stunted even in environments that would be least affected by a catastrophe, such as the aquatic environment. However, the survey teams failed to find any evidence of a catastrophe, and there is no evidence of a large extinct species. The astronomers have concluded that the planet's sun entered a stable period many millions of years ago and that there is no evidence of its ever having deviated from its current pattern. And *nothing* we've come up with has ever explained *this*."

I leaned forward in my seat, paying close attention. After all these preliminaries I was at last going to witness what the fuss was really about.

A white cartoon-type circle appeared around one of the lugs in the mid-foreground, a bull's-eye calling attention to something that was going to happen. Then the circle was still there, but empty. The lug had vanished.

"On this particular occasion," Li-Shing went on, "the lug was instantaneously displaced approximately eight hundred kilometers to the westward. All the lugs in this herd were tagged with radio beacons; our computers picked up the anomaly at once and signaled us."

I watched more examples. Lugs vanished. On other, rarer occasions, when the recorders happened to be pointing in the right direction, they appeared out of nowhere. The movement seemed to be coexistent with the movement of a volume of air equivalent to that from which a lug vanished—since it did not leave a vacuum behind, which would have made a loud popping noise. Displacement was apparently random; no pattern had been observed. It was also instantaneous. The computers monitoring the tagged lugs registered no gap in time between one existence and another. The lugs took no time to move from one place to another, nor did they spend any time *elsewhere*; they simply moved.

Instantaneous, in this case, meant faster than light. Faster than a beam of light could have moved even had it traveled on a straight-line path through the planet's crust.

Dr. Li-Shing reported in an exasperated voice that no evolutionary reason for the existence of such a talent had ever been determined. No predators to escape from, you see. Team members had considered the possibility that the lugs were not native to the planet but had been deposited there at some time in the past by sentient beings.

There was no evidence for this theory either, although the stellar neighborhood was being scoured by robot craft in hopes of discovering the lugs' planet of origin. No word as yet from the robot probes.

She asked me if I had any questions. I didn't. None that she could answer anyway.

There followed a biologist who gave a report on lug anatomy. Nothing out of the ordinary for any grazing animal of that size. Multiple stomachs for the digestion of the tough foliage. Small brains, decidedly unintelligent. Certainly no *organ* discovered capable of producing the effect described. Any questions, Mr. Falkner? Thank you.

Her place was taken by an obese behaviorist named Innis. Lugs, he reported, had no social organization worth speaking of. They were herd animals, but since herd animals generally congregate to protect themselves from predators, and there were no predators on the planet, it was assumed that the lugs herded because they preferred one another's company to solitude.

Mating took place twice a year, mates choosing one another apparently at random. Gestation took about three-quarters of a year. Luglings were born fully developed and hungry, and were generally walking and eating the same monotonous diet as their parents within hours of birth. The luglings hung about their mothers for a month or so, after which both lost interest and the little ones were on their own. Full maturation took place over a couple of years. Average life expectancy was about ten years. There were no checks on population save for fertility, which was fairly low. Satellite data estimated the total population to be about a billion. If those tagged were a representative sample, fifteen or twenty thousand could be expected to teleport in a given year.

The population was stable. Despite the lack of natural enemies the lug population was refusing to increase. Innis offered no explanation for this peculiar fact.

In a jolly, burbling voice, he then went on to describe various attempts to *make* the lugs teleport. Lugs had been captured and shut up in pens within sight of large amounts of food. Instead of teleporting, the lugs exhausted the food in their pens and then starved. Lugs had been shut up in utter blackness, with the hopes they would teleport away. They also had starved. Vast amounts of food had been presented to lugs who had successfully teleported, in the hopes this would be perceived as a reward and the lugs induced to teleport again. The lugs had eaten the food and stubbornly refused to make another jump.

If Innis were forced to make a guess, he said, he would guess that teleportation was not something that the lugs *did* but rather something that was *done to them*. But he would prefer not to have to guess until he saw further data.

He did not ask me for questions. I did not ask any.

Innis was followed by the recording of a middle-aged, kindly looking priest of the Ptolemaic Church of the Christ, a sect embracing respectable, sensible, moderately intelligent, non-excitable and usually very dull worshipers. After making a series of odd, tentative noises into the recording device in an effort to determine whether it had been switched on, the priest, with a slight stammer and a number of nervous twitches that showed his general inexperience with recorders, went on to explain, in an amazingly circumlocutive style, the possible theological import of what was being called the "lug phenomenon."

Since the dawn of the age of reason, he reported, believers, in order to confirm their intuitional faith, have been looking for objective proof of the existence of God. A true miracle has always been considered a manifestation of God's grace, but few miracles come ready-supplied with the sort of objective proof demanded by the intelligent skeptic.

The appearance of a creature which, for no conceivable reason, is able to teleport from one place to another about its planet, and which, after rigorous and scientific inquiry, is seen to be able to do so in abrupt contradiction to any known law of nature, might, Q.E.D., be considered objective proof of the existence of the Creator.

Amen. I yawned, reflecting that this was the first time I'd heard anyone say "Q.E.D." in many years. The priest smiled uncertainly, signaled to someone to turn off the recorder and did not ask for questions.

There were more recorded reports on minor topics. Blue-white stars. Detailed illustrations of lug cell structure. Last of all, a presentation by the physics team itself, concerning how it all might have been done. I felt a cold hand touch my neck. I didn't want this.

My three former students were introduced one by one. First was Muhammad al-Qatan, looking studious and grave in the blue collarless uniform, complete with medals, in which Kemp's dressed their professors. He was brilliant and one of the most stable, reliable people I knew—not quite self-effacing, but willing to sublimate his ego toward a goal if necessary. When his researches led to the discoveries of the chronograph, I'd had to fight to make sure he received proper credit. He'd been married to the same woman for two hundred years, ever since his undergraduate days, a record among people of my acquaintance. He looked odd without his mustache. He had apparently shaved it off fairly recently since he kept rubbing his upper lip as though expecting to find something there.

Next to him was Peirce Hourigan, his eyes grinning at me from beneath a shock of kinky hair. A radiant madman, half Irish, half Australian aborigine. I hadn't heard from him in years and was glad he'd survived his lunatic, impulsive attempts to scale, unaided, the exteriors of large buildings, to dive old-fashioned atmosphere craft under bridges, to set fire to colleagues' wastebaskets and sometimes their clothing. His lanky body was sprawled all over his chair, and perched on his shoulder he carried an enormous cockatoo, his uniform white with its droppings. It nibbled his ear and squawked from time to time. Leave it to Hourigan to figure out some way to subvert the dignity of a scientific conclave.

The recorder at last moved to Mary Liddell, and I realized I had been holding my breath. I expelled it as I saw the silver hair, the solemn gray eyes, the slight frown as she looked, businesslike, into the recorder and waited her cue. At first I thought McGivern had been wrong and she had changed her mind; but then she began to speak and I noticed the lines around her eyes and mouth, and when she raised a hand, I saw the thin boniness of it and the translucence of her skin, and I thought: She is dying. The silver hair will easily hide the gray.

She is the youngest of all, I realized. I felt my hands clench, nails scoring palms. She is the most brilliant of these three most brilliant students, and all of them were smarter than I had ever been . . . and she was killing herself. It was obscene.

I thought of space, of the indifferent and eternal brilliance and velvet blackness. The recording had taken almost twelve years to get here. If I gave in to McGivern's nonsense and went to Kemp's, how much older would she be when I saw her next? Ancient, I thought. Perhaps dead.

The recorder left her face and I breathed again. The presentation began, and great nonsense it was: It took a lot of time to say nothing. An instability, lasting for only a fraction of a picosecond, had been found in some of the higher-energy Zimmerman particles, and that might imply some peculiar interaction with other particles, possibly the long-theorized-but-never-discovered tachyon, but energies did not exist in sufficient quantity to create such particles if they did exist, or to track them when they were created. It was similar to the problems that existed with the chronograph, which could open a momentary, sideways portal through time, but only in a single direction. From our future we could view the past. We could even map it sufficiently to create an exact duplicate of Apollo's temple here in Delphi; but to actually insert a person or an object into the past—and thus to *change* the past—required a titanic consumption of energy, enough energy to alter the universe from that moment onward. And that energy, even with the use of the biggest Falkner generator ever built, was not available to us.

The presentation said nothing new. We'd known about the high-energy Zimmerman particles for years, but we had also known of the energy barrier. It was Mary who had the most sensible speech. Even *if* the lugs somehow

had access to such energy, how could they *control* it? With
the titanic expenditure of energy that we *knew* had to be
necessary for a phenomenon such as teleportation, how did
the lugs prevent leakage? At each event there should have
been enough stray radiation to fry any organism nearer
than the horizon, but there wasn't; so far as anyone could
detect, there wasn't a single stray particle. The phenomenon was perfectly controlled, which suggested that it was
imposed on the lugs from outside.

She fell silent and let the implications of that sink in.
And then the recorder shifted to al-Qatan, who made a
final summing up, stating conclusions that were little more
than questions, conclusions that in the end came to a
simple confession of ignorance.

Yet, he said, we know it *could* be done: We have seen
it. Sooner or later we'll discover the secret.

End of presentation. I told the windows to shift polarization and admit the sun.

The faces of the deputation seemed bleached in the
sudden hard light; there were no shadows, no reliefs, only
pale blobs with eyes. The eyes were turned toward me.

"I'm with the Father," I said. "Let's call it a miracle
and say the hell with it."

No one laughed. I rose from my chair and thanked
them. "I have luncheon ready for you in the dining room,
and I've had some good wine brought up from the cellar. I
won't be able to join you, unfortunately; I have an appointment to speak with Mr. Odje, and I don't want to offend
him."

They rose and thanked me for watching their presentation,
their voices sounding hollow, insincere. They had come all
this way, given up all these years, and for this?

I showed them to the dining room and bade them eat. I
had a human cook, Eirene, who despaired of my small
appetite. This was a chance for her to show off her talents.
I walked to my study and saw my own midday meal sitting

on a leaf of my desk: bell pepper, tomato, olives, cheese, a little oil, a small carafe of wine. A message light was blinking. I looked at my watch. It was too early for Odje.

"Mr. McGivern wishes to speak with you," the house said.

"Very well. I'll accept video."

When the picture came, it showed the old mosaics that had been lovingly transplanted to my bathroom. McGivern had gone there to wash his hands and place the call, presumably so the others wouldn't see.

"Doran," he said, "I'd like to talk to you. It won't take long."

"Is later this afternoon okay?" I asked. "I really do have a call placed to Odje."

He nodded. "After lunch then," I said and broke the connection. I had finished half my salad when the call to Odje came through.

The president of the United Communities of Earth was in New York, and the muted light of dawn shone through the clear window behind him. Like me, he was an early riser. He was a dignified man of middle years, his skin ebony, his dress somber. A Diehard of a faction that considered me Satan incarnate, he nevertheless handled our inevitable meetings with grace and aplomb. He bore, like most of the Diehards I'd dealt with, an old-fashioned personal integrity that made me warm to him instantly. I think, religion aside, we liked each other.

The business concerned the Red Sea underwater leases. A dozen or so families had built homes beneath the surface there, where from their windows they could look out onto the living beauty of the coral reef and all its creatures. I was trying to acquire titles to their places, offering to swap them for improved homes in the Pacific. The government possessed certain rights in the Red Sea, and I was trying to buy those too, as part of the package, in exchange for liberalization of other treaties elsewhere. It would clearly be to Odje's advantage to accept, and with our robots in attendance, we worked out the details easily.

"It's curious," he said afterward, making a tent of his fingers and looking at me with narrow, measuring eyes. "There's a pattern to your purchases in the area. It's as though you intended to depopulate all Egypt and Sinai. What are you planning to do with the place once you have it? Rebuild the pagan temples, as you've done in Greece?"

I grinned. "Perhaps. Would that offend you?"

He shook his head. "No," he replied. "You attract no worshipers to your shrines, if that was ever your intention. You rebuilt only dead monuments to ancient vanity, and magnificent as they are, they are nothing compared to the cathedral God has made of his earth."

"That is true, Mr. President," I said. "Though I remember that God needed a little help in cleaning up his cathedral a while ago and it was I who had to pick up the litter."

A sylphlike smile crossed Odje's face. "Even the devils do God's will in the end, though they know it not," he said. "Have a good day, Mr. Falkner."

"Mr. President."

His image vanished. I frowned and drank a sip of wine. How much of my plan could be deduced by the patterns of my purchases, those I'd made in Mesopotamia, Africa, China, and now Egypt? It could be argued, I suppose, that all I was doing was enlarging my holdings, holdings that already encompassed most of the surface of the planet; but how much could be discovered by my choices in acquiring the bits that were still in other hands? Perhaps as a blind I'd have to arrange some purchases I hadn't planned on.

I finished my lunch, ordered coffee and told the house to tell McGivern I'd see him when it was convenient. During the interim I called up my purchasing comp, reviewed my plans for the next few years, and asked my world modeling comp to tell me if the purchasing comp's overall pattern was discernible. WORKING, it told me. Then McGivern was knocking at my door; I told the comp display to vanish and the door to let McGivern in. He smelled strongly of his after-luncheon cigar.

"Come in, Brian. Have a seat. Would you like a brandy?"

"Thank you, no." Sitting down, he tented his fingertips and frowned slightly, looking at me with wary intelligence. His expression was so like Odje's that I found myself grinning.

"What's bothering you, Brian?" I asked.

He spoke carefully, each word considered. "You know what it would mean to us—us being the human race—if we had some form of teleportation. If we were no longer bounded by the speed of light."

"It would be a revolution."

"A revolution as all-encompassing, Doran, as your own."

I bowed, conceding the compliment. If compliment it were.

"The worlds are too far apart," McGivern said. I sipped my coffee. "Human space is huge, a hundred light-years across. Getting bigger. It's diverse, but it's also provincial. Each planetary system has a homogeneous culture, but they're isolated from one another, getting set in their ways. Even the spacers who live between planets exist in their own zero-g environment and have no real interaction with the natives of the planets they visit. There's not enough communication between systems to create any kind of dynamic between them, any contrast that can lead to analysis and growth. Your revolution went far, Doran, but it's dying."

It was true, I knew. The information that came in from human space indicated, after the centuries of expansion, an end to growth, a cultural stasis of the planets based on the stability provided by the energies of the Falkner Power

Systems, the comforts of cybernetics and the isolation of one star from another. The birth rate was down considerably, and with it the percentage of young people, with their more flexible and adaptable minds. Suicide, voluntary or the more subtle sort, was way up. The Diehards were too few and too short-lived to make a difference anywhere but on Earth. Any science being done was clarification of what had gone before; most literature and drama were merely sophisticated refinements of earlier forms.

An elderly twilight, I thought. The senility of mankind, where the only pornography is death. What happens to such a system when a being can move in an eyeblink from one world to the next? Where all isolation is ended, where all provincial boundaries are down?

A revolution, as McGivern had said—as encompassing a revolution as the last couple I'd made. The unleashing of a social force so enormous that it would be impossible to foresee, or attempt to control, its effects.

"You have yet to explain," I said, "why I have to lead this new revolution. Al-Qatan said it best: Now that we know it can be done, sooner or later we'll do it. It might be done already, back on Kemp's."

"On Kemp's they weren't anywhere near it," he said. "It'll take years, Doran, and effort. And brilliance. And a certain amount of prestige to back the project. So far as I can tell, you have them all to spare." He leaned forward in his chair, his eyes intent. "You *were* the last and greatest pair of revolutions, Doran," he said. "Humankind was set in a pattern that would have led to its extinction, and you took the bits of the pattern and tore them apart and put them together in your own image. You made something new from a ruin, and from where I sat, you seemed to be enjoying yourself. Two revolutions, Doran. Wouldn't you like to make it three?"

And shake up this complacent humanity I had so unwittingly created? I propped my sandals on my desk and took a sip of wine. "I must admit the idea has a certain piquant attraction," I said. "But I'm hoping to build the next revolution from here."

He gave a brief nod, as though confirming something to himself. "Your centaurs," he said.

"My centaurs."

"Another intelligent race to contrast with our own and provide a dynamic interaction." He tugged at an ear. "It will take centuries."

"I've got them."

He tapped his fingers on the arm of his chair as he thought; then he looked up at me. "But they don't need you," he said. "They'll do it on their own, sooner or later."

"So will al-Qatan and the others."

McGivern sighed and rose. "So: an impasse," he said. "You'll do what you want, I know. I'd just hoped you'd be more . . . flexible."

I pulled in my legs and stood. "I promised you I'd see your people, Brian," I said. "That's all."

"Yes. They've come light-years for this morning. I suppose they shouldn't be disappointed."

I finished my coffee. "I'll join them at the table now if you think it'll make them feel better. But I didn't ask them to make the trip."

"No," he said dryly, "I did." He reached into his pocket and took out a message block. As though reluctant, he held it out to me. "Mary asked me to give you this privately. I don't know what it says. I should have given it to you last night but it didn't seem like the right time."

I took it, feeling it warm on my palm. "Thank you," I said. How well, I wondered for the first time, did Brian McGivern know Mary Liddell? I put the cube on the desk. "I'll join your people shortly for brandy."

"They'll be pleased to see you again," he said formally. There was suddenly a strange awkwardness in the air, as though we'd just met one another for the first time and didn't quite know what to say. There was a funny ache in my throat, and I suspected in his. I wondered what the hell was going on. I opened the door.

"I'll see you in a few minutes."

He bobbed his head and began to make his way out.

"Brian," I said, and he stopped in the doorway, looking at me questioningly. "If I do this thing, it might not be possible right away," I said. "There are some good-byes I'd have to say."

"I understand." He gave a faint smile. "I'd like to see the centaurs again myself. I hope I'll have the chance."

"I'll see what I can do," I said and let him out.

He'd thought I'd meant the centaurs; a natural mistake for him to make.

There were worse things at large in the world—and to one of them I owed a great debt.

4

With what emotion does one regard a love thirty years dead? It is not, assuredly not, to hear the sounds of seraphs strumming the old, old songs in one's ears, to recall days of frolic on grassy hillsides and to find passion blazing anew in one's breast, hopeless and redeeming. I had spent twenty intervening years married to someone else; I'd fathered and helped raise two children; there had been other lovers, other desires.

Yet there was something unsettling about seeing her, the knowledge of a ghost not properly laid to rest. Symbolized in this transcript by that distant, sterile and very English use of the word "one," keeping one's distance from one's feelings, old man, trampling out the vintage where one's grapes of candor lay. Why couldn't I have used a more intimate adjective? Me, my, mine. My ears, my breast, my former lover. So.

I will not take your gift, she had said.

I will not watch you die, said I.

And thus it had ended. After her emigration we had exchanged letters. No video. There had only been long

reams of epistolary prose, but those had necessarily proved
fairly pointless. The knowledge that one will have to wait
twenty years for a reply to a letter can squash the life out
of correspondence before it begins. So had it been with
Mary and myself, as it had been before with my former
wives, with many of my children, with friends and lovers
and enemies whom I had sent, willing or unwilling, to the
stars. Once, indeed, I had received a ponderous, official
condolence on the suicide of one of my sons, and I had to
frown for a moment and think who it was: *Ah, yes, Julie's
boy.* I hadn't heard from him myself in scores of years. I
hoped his bitter last thoughts had not been of me.

In another case I had found myself involved, unknow-
ingly, in a wholesome carnal tangle with my great-
granddaughter, the offspring of a child who had long ago
emigrated. The girl had known but hadn't found the fact
worth mentioning.

Nor, after contemplation, had I.

Sad facts all, I'm sure; saddest of all the fact that not
one of them is out of the ordinary. Enough to make a
person hope that something may come from this teleportation
business.

Mary's image was frighteningly close in this small study,
her head and shoulders larger than her image in the other
recording, larger than life even, creating a forced intimacy
I did not desire. The lines in her face were clear, and I
could see gray in her silver hair. I pressed back in my seat
against its reality. Her message was simple, sensible.
Admirable. True.

I may, she said, not be justified in the assumptions—
fears really, not assumptions—that lie behind this communication. I apologize if I'm wrong. But I won't feel comfortable with myself unless I tell you this.

You owe me nothing, she went on. Do not come on this
journey because of anything I said or did not say. I am
happy with myself; I am happy with my decision; I will

not change. I am going to have myself frozen until the team leaves; that decision is not based on any regrets but on a wish to see this project through.

She raised her hands, one clasped over another, and touched her thumbs to her chin. I felt a flash of recognition at the gesture, for the way her cool, dark eyes looked steadily at mine; and I felt as well a surge of horror at the aged, veined, still-graceful hands.

You are free, she said. Free of anything I do or say, and of any consequence. You may rest assured that all hurts are forgiven, all loveliness remembered, and treasured. I am busy and content and loved. I hope you are the same. Bless you.

The image faded and I was suddenly aware of my heart beating fast in terror. I took a breath and looked with surprise at the sweat on my palms. I wiped my hands on the hem of my chiton. I was trembling for a drink. I wondered if this is how senility strikes.

I felt surprise at the horror I was feeling. Mary was in what was once called the prime of life, physical and emotional maturity, the age of greatest social accomplishment. I had once been as physically old as she, and I hadn't experienced it as a difficult time.

But now the sight of her was terrifying. And not simply because she was a Diehard—hadn't I just taken a call from Odje, who was older than Mary, without this kind of reaction? No, somehow it frightened me because it was *Mary*.

She was living an obscenity. But I, at least, was absolved from any complicity. I thanked her for that.

With what emotion does one regard a love thirty years dead? In this case, my case, with fear.

I went to join my guests and I ordered up the good brandy. "Absent friends," I said as I lifted my glass, and saw Brian McGivern's somber, searching eyes looking at me as he drank.

*   *   *

I spent the afternoon with them, chatting about Delphi as it was and had been, about Greece and the monuments they had seen ruined or being rebuilt. As I escorted them back to Ismenos's little hovercraft, I gave them a brief tour as we wound down the Sacred Way; I told McGivern I'd be in touch with him; and then I stood and made my way back up the hill.

KNOW THYSELF, the graven letters read, the words of the Seven Wise Sages.

Nice try, fellas, I thought. But you've missed my point. I'm over eight hundred years old, and it's been ages since I've managed to surprise myself at all.

Until this afternoon. Until I met an image with fear.

I went up the hill to my dinner, and with it a bottle of wine. I played the blues late and finished the bottle.

5

The blues didn't rest me and neither did my nightly exercise in the stadium. I knew I would not sleep. After my shower I told my house I would be absent for a few days, left a message for McGivern saying the same thing and offering him the use of the place till I returned; then I packed a vacuum bottle of coffee and some clothes, climbed into my car and sped eastward through the velvet Mediterranean night.

I didn't opaque the field but watched as the car sped low and soundlessly over the wrinkled Hellespont, that dolphin-torn, that gong-tormented sea, and then rose into the starlight over Anatolia. The car rotated slowly, now showing stars, now the soil. The land was black below me, tarnished only rarely with flecks of light, and then it was more often starlight reflected in a pond than any sign of human habitation. The twenty million people remaining on Earth were spread very thin; and Ge was still licking the wounds she'd taken at humanity's hands, long after humanity's exile.

I caught up with the dawn high over the Kunlun Shan;

dazzled by the bright, unobstructed sun, I made haste to send out a short message, fed the answer into my guidance comp, then dipped my craft lower until it skimmed the craggy peaks. I ate some cheese, drank coffee and fought a sudden craving for Kung Pao chicken.

I landed thirty miles southwest of Chang-an, deep in the land of the Zhou. Here on the rim of the mountains, where the land glowed pink in the morning and the rivers ran cold and exemplary, there had once been a small commercial city. There had been barracks for the soldiers who guarded the great king's borders, stables for their chariots and horses, a temple to heaven, a garden where the children played and flew kites. The place had been bypassed in the conquest of 256, but with the passing of the Zhou, the trade routes had changed, the garrison had marched away to serve a new First Heaven, and the town had faded, its people forgotten, its gods abandoned. Fading gently but inevitably, like the fading of the whole of Earth, the fading of the last ten thousand years of man.

The city was a mound now, green with grasses and bright with wild flowers, and so it had been for nearly three thousand years, until Snaggles had come a-digging. I abolished the field and left my car, walking toward the neat trench that marked his excavations. Little morning breezes brushed at the half-unfolded flowers. Snaggles extruded a part of himself to greet me; he shaped himself into a caricature of a Chinese god, all teeth and enamel and ravenous bulging eyes. The god writhed his arms at me—they were holding weapons: a long sword and an ax—and blinked like a tabby by the firelight.

"Greetings, Doran," Snaggles said. "It's been a long time."

"Yes," I said. A lot of people seemed to be saying that to me lately. I squatted on the edge of the trench. "Who are you today?"

"I'm not sure." Snaggles's mustache bristled. A red

tongue unrolled like a carpet and then rolled up again. The eyes rotated independently in their sockets like those of a chameleon; I felt myself getting a headache watching them. I looked down at my feet.

"I think," Snaggles said, "that I am a guardian of one of the four corners of the universe, but I'm not certain. T'ang dynasty, anyway. I found the representation in a tomb about thirty miles from here."

"And how are your excavations coming along?" The Chinese god was only a small portion of Snaggles's vast body: The rest was beneath us, gently insinuating itself into the nooks and crannies of the old city, pouring through it like a seeping pool of oil.

"I'll have North China wrapped up in the next decade," he said. "Wuhan next. How are you doing in the evacuation of Hong Kong?"

"Slowly, slowly. Nothing's changed since my last report."

The ax and sword revolved meditatively in counterpoint to the eyes. "That's too bad, Doran. I'm disappointed."

"The government has surrendered its rights in the Red Sea though. It and Egypt will be clear in another few years."

"Ah. Good, good." The god's pale face smiled ferociously.

Another piece of Snaggles—a rubbery, brown, whiplike thing—extruded itself from the trench and handed me an object. "Look at what I found here last week. A burial, in an old map case. From your century, I think. There was also a box of condoms, which did not fare as well. How do you imagine they came to be here?"

The object was a comic book, deteriorated but still for the most part legible. Although old and yellow and fragile, and against all likelihood and chemical reality, the cheap paper had survived. I looked at the cover. *Action Comics*, it said. *No. 44*. Ten cents. Superman was making a pretzel

out of a Nazi howitzer. Gingerly I turned the pages. I
imagined some downed flier, a countryman of mine, opening his map case and peering at the surrounding mountain
passes from the vantage point of the old city mound.
Damn, he thinks. How the hell am I going to make it to
Chungking?

He keeps his maps, compass and gun, but he's read the
comic already and he knows he sure as hell isn't going to
get laid. He buries what he can't use so the Japanese can't
trace it to him and optimistically begins his hike into the
foothills.

I hoped he made it out.

"A pity it isn't Plasticman," I said. "I imagine you'd
identify strongly with him."

"My machines are preparing an essay," Snaggles remarked conversationally, " 'The Morphology of Comic
Book Diffusion,' but of course I need more data. Perhaps
you would like to see it when it's done."

"Let me know when you finish it." I'd make a point of
being busy. I'd seen his monograph on the distribution of
Coca-Cola bottles throughout Mesopotamia and found it as
tedious as I'd expected, given the subject. It is difficult to
understand what an alien intelligence perceives as important;
in Snaggles's case it seemed to be just about everything.

"Snaggles," I said, "I may have to leave for a while.
Forty to fifty years."

"I'm sorry to hear that." In the dispassionate tones of a
Park Avenue analyst. "Why don't you tell me about it?"

So I did. The Chinese god stood motionless, listening,
while I told him about the deputation from offplanet, the
lugs, their odd faster-than-light habits.

"Curious," Snaggles commented.

"Have you ever encountered these things?" I asked.
"Know anything of them? You might save me a trip."

The Chinese god burst into a kaleidoscope of motion,
rolling and unrolling his tongue, his eyeballs rotating,

arms windmilling, mustache and beard wriggling. I felt olives and coffee and wine stirring unpleasantly in my stomach, and looked away. Despite the activity, Snaggles's voice was matter-of-fact. "Me? No. They live out toward the Orion Arm. I'm from galactic center." He paused for a moment, the Chinese god frowning. "Their sort aren't my province anyway," he said. "I specialize in the social evolution of carbon-based intra-skeletal species. This is quite out of my area. I wouldn't mind learning the teleporting trick though—it would save a lot of time."

My last piece of hope trickled gently away. *Save a lot of time;* that was all it mattered to Snaggles. He was immortal, a thousand times more ancient than all the artifacts he rummaged among on this dusty planet; and he was in no hurry to go anywhere.

I, however, still had the remnants of my mortal haste. "You don't know how it's done then?" I asked. Hopelessly.

"Gracious, no. You will tell me if you learn, won't you?"

"Could you consult your machines?"

"They don't know how it's done either. And your data is insufficient for them to synthesize a conclusion. Sorry."

"I just thought I'd ask." *My centaurs will take this planet back from you,* I thought. *They owe you nothing. It was not they who signed the pact to sell the soil of their home.*

That, of course, was me. Me alone.

The shadow-priest of Delphi, for whom Pythian Kassandra had cried her terror.

I had first met Snaggles eight hundred years earlier, when I was trying to collect a degree in physics. I was young, but in those days so was everybody. Ambitious, though not for fame . . . say rather for knowledge. Serious, a little oversolemn; I had not yet had time to develop my sterling sense of irony. I was too busy trying not to starve.

By present standards, I was a slave. My title was gradu-ate assistant.

I'd published a few papers that had given me a reputa-tion for interesting if unprovable flights of theoretical fancy, but that hadn't gotten me work, so I was doing drudge duties in Los Alamos. My salary failed to entirely keep me from hunger. A vainglorious physicist named Jay Zimmer-man, possessed of a pouter-pigeon chest and an aggressive, nagging manner, had discovered the existence of small, low-energy particles that he called, with his usual heedless and swashbuckling egotism, Zimmerman particles. He was always careful to use the full name, although everyone else connected with the project called them Z-particles.

These particles had been perceived in accelerators, pop-ping up by accident when the scintillators were recording other, more deliberate actions, and the odd thing about them was that there was no obvious place they had come from. They did not have the heedless and destructive energy of the so-called "cosmic rays," and Zimmerman had noticed that they were not seemingly produced by any of the staged interactions for which the spectra were made. The particles were very small and so low in energy that they just dribbled feebly across the plots, leaving a short but distinctive trail, and then faded away. They seemed to have variable sorts of charges.

It was a remarkable coincidence that Zimmerman no-ticed the phenomenon in the first place, it was very rare. But despite the inability of anyone who knew him to stand the company of the man, Zimmerman had a precise and brilliant mind; he knew something out of place when he saw it, and his first action was to send his slaves—beg pardon, graduate assistants—to working their way through tens of thousands of printouts, plots and spectra looking for that particular trail. We found hundreds of them, all overlooked by previous researchers because they weren't related to whatever it was they'd been studying.

Jay Zimmerman began to build theories explaining what he had found. He thought he had just discovered some strange effect related to higher-energy interactions, one that would cast light on high-energy phenomena and the structure of matter. He set his graduate assistants to work on the big accelerators in New Mexico, trying to duplicate the phenomenon.

He was on the wrong track entirely but didn't suspect it, or if he did suspect it, he didn't want to admit it until he'd collected more grant money. Experiments went on in the usual way—making particles bash one another in the hopes they'd show us something we didn't know. Electrons exchanged photons like jugglers exchange Indian clubs; hard-charging deuterons made mincemeat out of an assortment of helpless targets; and pions and antipions laid tracks for home. It was all exemplary.

It was also useless. The Z-particle appeared every so often but there was no way to predict its appearance, and when it did appear, it seemed obstinately unrelated to any of the interactions we were producing. Zimmerman concluded there was a lot of interesting data being generated but that further study was necessary. He wrote a long grant proposal filled with impenetrable jargon in hopes of getting more money from a bewildered NSF, but even he must have begun to suspect he was taking the wrong tack.

While Zimmerman awaited the results of his latest grant proposal, I was working the graveyard shift on the accelerator, spending long nights in supervising the controls after the project heads had set up a long run and gone home, leaving their photo-multipliers to collect the data. The money was pretty good, and since the job consisted only of watching the dials to make sure nothing untoward occurred, it left me time to read magazines, study and think about considering the possibility that one day I might think about writing my thesis. The latter occupied a lot of time between glances at the dials. I tried to revive my flagging interest in the whole project by thinking about the money and fame that awaited me once I got my degree. If I sold out, I could pull down a lot of bucks thinking of new ways to bludgeon the Russians. Or I could go into research and write baffling grant proposals like Zimmerman. Neither seemed as attractive as going out by myself into the Red River area the next weekend and spending my time drinking beer and roasting weenies.

One night I was sitting in front of the dials and doodling on the pad I carried with me. My doodles began to resemble the distinctive track of the Z-particle. If I could figure out where it came from, it would make my reputation. Maybe I wouldn't even need the damn thesis.

A shadow fell across my page.

"I can tell you how those particles got there," said Snaggles. I started and looked over my shoulder.

He was more or less human in form and voice, a sort of nondescript brown male wearing a nondescript brown suit, but I knew from the first moment that there was something very wrong. The expressions and movements of his face didn't match what he was saying, and he seemed to be rooted to the floor. Which he was, in point of fact, since the humanoid I saw before me was a shaped extrusion of Snaggles that had come up through a minute crack in the building's concrete foundation.

After the first moment I wasn't shocked at all. Intrigued, rather. The appearance of this oddity was so unusual that I had no clear notion of what to say. So I improvised.

"Tell me," I said.

"If I tell you," said Snaggles, "you will be able to end poverty and war, and send your race to the stars."

A loon, I thought. But a half-interesting loon.

"Sounds good," I said. "So what's the secret?"

"I have certain conditions."

I sighed. Somehow I knew he would.

"For one thing," Snaggles said, "I want you to keep my name out of it."

I began to acquire the feeling that I was not dealing with something entirely natural. I listened and watched Snaggles carefully as he spoke, and there was something odd about him. By the time he got around to revealing his nature, I wasn't surprised.

Or afraid. I was a scientist. Snaggles was a phenomenon. He interested me.

His other conditions were simple, if a little more complicated than the first. I didn't have to sign over my soul, which was what I was half-expecting him to ask. He just wanted to dig in privacy.

He wanted to dig up the whole world. Not right away, but he seemed to think that eventually I would be in a position to permit this. It seemed a frivolous sort of pursuit for someone who wanted to hand me the keys to the universe, but I didn't complain.

I did the deed. And twenty-five hundred years back down time's y axis, Kassandra began to moan, foreseeing what would come of it.

Zimmerman, to his own surprise, got his new grant; but by then I'd left school. I sold the half-interest in my parents' house that I co-owned with my brother—he was a stockbroker and so upwardly mobile I got a cramp in my neck just looking at him—and went off into the woods for a while. With Snaggles, who had acquired his name by then. I don't think I ever consciously gave it to him; one day it just was.

The Z-particle was not produced by the high-energy interactions at all, which I had begun to suspect by then. It was a random and natural phenomenon and would have appeared anyway, even if the accelerators hadn't been pumping particles across the scintillators.

What I hadn't suspected was that the Z-particles were low in energy because they had spent most of their energy in just getting here. They were on their last legs, having come a long way.

From another universe, in fact. A still-forming universe, an inchoate pre-Bang universe trying like thunder to kick itself out of its gravity shell. The Z-particles were strange little short-lived bits of semi-matter of various sizes and charges, alike only in that they possessed enough energy and dynamics and peculiarities to cross from one universe to another. They left their distinctive trail on the spectra because, during their brief life span, they were not fully *in* our universe and were rapidly using up their energy in trying to enter our continuum.

There were, for our purposes anyway, an infinite number of Z-particles, although only a scant few managed to cross into this universe. Others, perhaps, found their way into universes other than our own; and others just ran out of energy in trying and never made it.

But if a pathway were to be opened between the universes, the Z-particles would pour into our universe in numbers limited only by the size and quality of the hardware into which they were channeled. Once opened, the particles could be channeled by a magnetic field, allowing certain kinds of particles in and turning others back, in effect polarizing them and allowing in only those possessing desired qualities.

The Z-particles came from a strange place, a universe that had not yet defined itself or the laws by which it worked. They proved to have diverse capabilities. Polarized in a certain way, they had the function of creating a field that was not quite in our universe and yet not in their own. The tunnel could be made semi-independent of the strong, weak, gravitational and electromagnetic interactions of our own universe, and as a result, anyone sitting in such a tunnel could theoretically move rapidly about our local piece of existence without having to worry about such consequences as inertia, gravity or friction.

Unfortunately the tunnel could not be perfectly polarized; it interacted sufficiently with our universe to provide functional limits on its capabilities. It could not, for example, move faster than light; that limit still seemed absolute. And in order for someone inside the tunnel to know where he was and where he was going, he had to have enough interaction with the universe to be able to see out, which further diminished the theoretical perfection of the tunnel. It was good, but it still had limits.

Another type of Z-particle obtainable through polarization had the unique capability of creating a field that slowed strong nuclear interactions by absorbing most of their energy to help maintain the field. This meant that if the field were made large enough to, for example, cover a city, all weapons depending on nuclear force—hydrogen bombs, say, as well as any one of a number of more mundane objects such as nuclear reactors—would simply fizzle ineffectually without doing anyone any harm.

I thought that was a pretty neat trick, the best of all.

There are other tricks the Z-particles can do, which I am not prepared to reveal.

It took me about a year to work out the project on paper—engineering wasn't Snaggles's strong point, nor mine—and another year to actually build the first generator, what I called the Falkner Power System.

It was about the size of a small automobile engine.

It was also empty. It didn't work. I had to have enough power to open a tunnel between the universes and permit the flow of Z-particles into the apparatus before it would be anything other than an inanimate heap of metal.

Snaggles could have provided the energy from his ship, which was powered by similar generators, but that would have left people wondering where I'd gotten it in the first place. So I returned to my job at the accelerator and cooled out under the blue perfection of New Mexico skies until I was alone on the graveyard shift once again. Some of the physicists had set up a sixteen-hour run and wouldn't be back until morning. I shut down the accelerator, opened up the twelve-foot-thick steel and concrete door, and Snaggles wobbled in with various pieces of hardware. Then I shut the door and fired up the accelerator again.

I had a lot of explaining to do when the physicists began wondering why I'd shut down their run, but I got away with it. And then I resigned.

Poor Zimmerman, I thought. He'd been reduced to renting out his time on the accelerator to cancer research while he rethought his entire approach. He was coming up with wild ideas about the nature of his particle. Eminent ideas in fact, though incorrect.

To give him his due, he might have worked out the real solution after a while. He was that brilliant.

I went home to my apartment and shut off the current and plugged the generator into the fuse box. Then I turned on the lights. Then I turned on my electric stove and the air conditioning and my radio. Then I went to my neighbors and asked to borrow their television set and their mixer and their vacuum cleaner. I got a set of power tools and a rug cleaner from another neighbor, and a magnum of champagne from the corner liquor store.

By two that morning all the appliances were still running. I was half-deafened by the television and the radio blaring away, and I was also flat on my back from all the champagne.

After my hangover faded, I began assembling another generator, which I finished in a couple of weeks. I then powered the second one from the first and drove my second-hand motorcycle to San Francisco to my first meeting with Brian McGivern.

He was a hotshot patent attorney. He was thirty-five years old, and a couple of years earlier his money and ambition had damn near made his friend, who was governor of California, the president of the United States. He was an unsentimental man with a lot of connections and a lot of money. He craved power but he had no desire for fame. Until I met him, his ultimate ambition had been to be the gray eminence behind the president.

Later we made a couple of revolutions together. And then, after I gazed for the first time upon the messy corpse of the first man ever to try to kill me, I began developing my irony.

I watched the Guardian of One of the Four Corners of the Universe as his eyes mutated and his tongue flapped up and down. Below I could hear shifting, squelching sounds as his various pseudopodia fondled artifacts with the eagerness of a lecher feeling up a tired whore.

Snaggles, I thought, was a pedant with a sense of humor that could best and most accurately be described as alien. He'd dug up diverse hundreds of planets, and my best guess was that he was no longer sane. It was not a dangerous kind of insanity but it was an obsessive one, and I really didn't want him hanging around my planet anymore.

"Snaggles," I said, "have you seen any intelligent life forms on this planet? Other than human and cetacean, I mean."

Snaggles's eyelids closed translucently, like nictitating membranes, as he considered this. "No," he answered. "I have not. Here and in Mesopotamia, the odd herdsmen or nomad. Some caught me unawares, and I frightened them and they ran away. But nothing else, nothing at all. Why do you ask? Have you seen such a thing?"

"I am troubled by strange dreams," quoth I. I remembered the Nilus turned silver by a full and lunatic moon, a mad sky spotted with stars, and the sudden feeling of presences standing on the sand nearby, things with red eyes that stared, inhuman, from the dark. When I turned my light on them, I saw what they were. Lean, human bodies, dark and sleek, lithe muscles glinting nakedly, and above, horribly, the owl head, the jackal head. Predators scouring the dead and ancient land for the carrion droppings of man. Someone mad had made these things and— inspired by the desperate nightmares of old Egypt—had tapped the last DNA shard into place with his tiny silver hammer, and as he did so, madly gloated. Now he was gone, or dead, and his creatures had dominion.

They had run from my light; but later I heard them, the jackal-headed kind, as they howled. I knew from the first glance that they could not be tamed, although they possessed intelligence. They and my centaurs would battle for possession of Earth, I knew, and I feared the outcome.

"Ah," Snaggles said. "Nightmares." For once he was still, eyes closed, an oracle. "They are a precondition of sentience, I'm afraid. I do not sleep, but even though I am awake, part of me dreams, and sometimes the dreams are terrible."

I was intrigued. "What do you dream of?" I asked.

It was his turn to be opaque. "Things you know not of," he said. Sadly.

I rose and brushed dust from my trousers. "I'll let you know if I leave," I told him. "Thanks for the conversation. And the comic."

"You're welcome," he said. "Come any time." And then he added, sorrowfully, "Old friend, I hope your dreams are joyful."

It was a lovely land, the land of Zhou. Ancient, resonant, its great solitary valley green, its mountains dark and becoming, immaculate, calling out to me in compelling whispers. It would be better with Snaggles gone.

I continued east to Hong Kong, polarizing the tunnel so as not to admit photons while keeping my speed down to allow a short nap in the darkness. When the field died and I found myself looking across the dark and choppy waves of the bay, I felt again in condition to communicate with humans.

The garden of the Last Scarlet House rang subtly with wind chimes and was alive with late-summer blossoms: honeysuckle, jasmine, ilang-ilang, bitter orange, sweet basil—perfume plants all, intoxicants, plants for dreaming and forgetting. Around the garden were small houses where the women lived. The place had not changed.

Madame Lu greeted me gravely. "You are welcome in my House, Doran Falkner," she said. "What do you desire?"

"A bath," I replied, "and a place to sleep. A pleasant dream upon awakening."

She nodded and a slow smile crossed her features. Her eyes were still, peaceful. "We specialize in waking dreams, Mr. Falkner." She clapped her hands and spoke. "Please take the dream of your choice."

Desperation, poverty and human folly: Once upon a time these were the main causes of prostitution. Desperation and poverty no longer exist, and human folly is out of fashion; there remains the rarest reason only, that of vocation.

Madame Lu's girls were whores by choice, not by compulsion. It was a way of life in which they felt most comfortable. Once upon a time they might have been priestesses of Astarte; now they had each their own private mysteries, and private gods, worshiped in their small houses arrayed around the fragrant courtyard. I chose a tall ebony woman whose name was Lilah. She wore a blue sarong and seemed like a cold mountain stream that I could drown in. Drowning was what I was after.

I drank iced tea as she bathed me, her long eyes watching me while an enigmatic smile touched the corners of her mouth. "How old are you?" I asked. She seemed no older than twenty-two.

"Five hundred plus," she said.

"How long have you been here?"

"Five years. This time. I have been here before."

"How many times?"

Da Vinci would have given his left arm to have painted that smile. "Many times," she said.

She took me from the bath, dried me, and moved me to the other room of her little house. She laid me down on a mattress the size of Montana and put a light quilt over me.

"Would you like me to lie next to you as you sleep?" she asked.

"Yes. If you don't mind. It will be a long sleep."

"I don't mind. It is near my time for sleeping."

She took off her sarong and crawled under the quilt, resting her head on my shoulder. I put my arm around her. Her skin was smooth and wonderful, anointed with oils. She smelled of saffron. I wanted to dive headfirst into her long and solemn eyes.

My dreams were not of the best. At the last I dreamed of a vast stone chamber, its upper surface merging with the night sky but supported by pillars with palm-leaf capitals. The pillars and the unfinished granite walls flickered redly from a gush of flame at the front of the room. The flame lapped in reflection at the faces of a congregation, lean bodies agleam. Jackal-headed things, owl-headed things, other things with the heads of hawks and buzzards and crocodiles. They stared with mad eyes at another creature at the front of the chamber, seen dimly through the spout of scarlet flame. It seemed indistinct, amorphous, black and huge; it reflected bits of its congregation, the teeth of the crocodile, the lolling tongue of the jackal, other fragments too brief, too terrifying to properly discern.

The animal-headed things went on their knees in worship. Suddenly I realized that the object of their devotion was Snaggles.

I woke with a cry and immediately felt Lilah's cool hand on my forehead. "Hush," she said. "It was a bad dream. You are here in the Last Scarlet House." Her languid eyes were close to mine and it was late in the afternoon. "Bad dreams," she said, and I could sense her liquid tongue next to my ear, "are not allowed here. I will send it away."

Snaggles, I thought, was bound for Egypt after he'd finished with China. What would he do when he discovered the mutilated denizens of the Nile? What kind of arrangement would he make with them?

I would have to think about this.

I looked at Lilah and felt her coolness. I am here in the last whorehouse on Earth, I thought, with a five-hundred-year-old whore. Madame Lu is older yet. What no one knows is that I'm the oldest whore in the place.

Outside a breeze touched the tinkling chimes and drifted the perfume of the garden into the House. Lilah held me close.

I turned to her and drowned.

6

Before I left I spoke to Madame Lu. "I wish to give the Last House a gift," I said. "I wish to build a new House in the environs of Peking, in the heart of China. With gardens exotic and fragrant, and trees from the four corners of the world."

"I thank you, Doran," Madame Lu said, her eyes as still as a windless pond, and deeper. "But I have no wish to move to Peking. There are too many ghosts there. I would not live where I could not look to the north and see Victoria across the blue of the bay, or turn to the west and see Lan Tao in its beauty, or to the south and look across Lamma to the sea."

"You speak of ghosts," I said. "Soon there will be a true ghost here, a spirit all your incense and flowers will not keep away. I speak from experience. Please accept my gift in Peking."

Her eyes were troubled but she shook her head briefly. "I will not leave," she said, "even if my every pavilion were to become the abode of spirits."

I pictured Snaggles flowing like a dark wave between

the bitter orange and jasmine, his huge insinuant form creeping among the foundations of the Scarlet House. Perhaps no one would ever see him, but they would know his presence and it would turn the perfumes bitter. The girls and their customers would evaporate. The House would be a sad place then, haunted truly, not only by Snaggles but by the lonely presence of this last immortal Madame, watching her House, her city, her life decay at the touch of the invader.

"The ghost will come," I said. "I cannot prevent it. But when he comes, take comfort from the fact that he will not stay long. A few years at the most, and then your House will be clean again. Remember what I say."

"I will remember, Doran Falkner," said Madame Lu. "And I thank you for the warning. But I shall not move."

"As you wish. But the gift of the gardens in Peking is still yours."

"You are generous," she told me. I flinched at the touch of those fathomless eyes. "You are generous as many of my customers are generous. Because their conscience will not leave them alone. Because their conscience says *pay, and I will be easier*. But I want no man's conscience money. I have a conscience of my own, you see."

I bowed. "You are wise, Madame Lu," I said, "but your judgment is in error. My gift comes not from conscience but from policy."

She cocked her head to one side, like a bird, and said nothing, being too wise to contradict my lies. "Come again to my House," she said, after a time. "You are always welcome here."

I thanked her, and before I departed I gave the comic to Lilah. It was worth a fortune—whatever a fortune is worth these days. But still, it was worth far more than the normal cost of the two days I spent in the Last Scarlet House.

The condoms I kept and later sent to the Museum of the

Forbidden City with my compliments. Their robot museum director sent me a letter of thanks and informed me that the gift had been catalogued and placed in storage. It thoughtfully included the catalogue number in case I wanted to see them again. It must have been an old robot, the kind with no sense of humor.

From Hong Kong I sped east across the Pacific, then across the bulk of the American continent to Tampa. Branwen was still in residence and I persuaded her to postpone her trip to Utah for another week. Joe left after a few days; although we had met several times before, I think I still intimidated him. All those old Diehard sermons in childhood, mentioning me by name—and then here I was, simultaneously Evil incarnate and his girlfriend's crotchety old dad, offering to cook supper so he and Branwen wouldn't miss their day on the beach. I hoped it would make him do some hard thinking about his religion and what he had been brought up to believe, but I doubted that it would. He just wasn't the questioning sort.

His departure left me alone with Branwen, and we did a lot of talking: about Joe and Kathryn and her old friends the centaurs, and about what McGivern wanted from me and what I was likely to do about it. We talked so often, and so deeply, that I think she understood what my answer to McGivern was going to be before I did. The last night we drank old brandy, sitting cross-legged on the deep pile rug of my big house in Tampa, and she looked at me and gave me a private smile.

"You look pleased with yourself," I said. "May I share?"

Her smile broadened, turned to a laugh. "Yes," she replied. "I've made an appointment tomorrow. For the first treatment."

I felt mad relief and leaned forward to give her a hug. Her tawny hair brushed across my cheek and I felt her warmth and joy. "I'm very happy," I said. "I was afraid—"

"Joe tried. But he couldn't make me change my mind. I want to be around when the centaurs begin to repopulate this place and fly out to the stars. It's the only way."

"And Joe?" I asked.

"He'll probably be unhappy when I tell him," she answered. Her eyes looked gravely into mine. "Not as unhappy as his church, though. It would be quite a coup for them to convert the devil's daughter."

"They may order him to break with you," I said, "now that they've lost."

"That," she said sensibly, "will be Joe's decision. When he makes it, I'll be ready, either way."

I hugged her again, feeling once more the long throb of relief. Knowing I wouldn't lose Branwen to the avalanche of time would make my decision about Amaterasu easier. The devil and his daughter would be together once again, both young and both forever.

Branwen and I got roaring drunk and ended the evening singing filthy limericks and diving into the ocean before heading for our separate couches.

By morning I'd made my decision. When I told Branwen, I noticed she wasn't surprised.

"Have fun with your new revolution, Dad," she said. "I'll make sure the centaurs don't forget you."

I gave her a long hug and made her promise to communicate with Kathryn as often as she could bring herself to do it. Then I sent a message to McGivern, took a leave of absence at the university and headed east again. Across the world, to Delphi.

7

Once safely in the car I made a call to my comp on Hyampeia, which patched me through to Natal. I communicated with a chain of machines and eventually was rewarded with an image of Captain Tromp Muller.

He was a sandy-haired man with an oversized jaw, his skin burned a deep brown that made his pale blue eyes seem startling, perhaps even a little mad. His mustache was paler than his hair, and tobacco stained it brown over his philtrum. His face gleamed with perspiration—he'd just come in from outside, apparently—and there was the scarlet imprint of a hatband across his forehead.

A nasty man, Tromp Muller. He was one of the last bitter, violent members of the Afrikaner Brotherhood and had switched to the Nieuwtrekkers only at the last minute. Those who hadn't switched had died, and some of them had been killed by Captain Tromp Muller, proving that once he embraced a cause, he did it with a vengeance. He had devoted a century to establishing New Pretoria in the sky, but the place hadn't evolved to his taste and he'd returned to the depopulated, once-again-wild place of his birth. Officially he was a game manager in my employ, a job he did very well.

Unofficially he was something else entirely. I wasn't proud of the moments when I had to use him, but I did my best to convince myself they were necessary.

"Mr. Falkner," he said without great enthusiasm. He gave a heavy sigh and moved to sit in a canvas chair. The video followed his movements, keeping his face in medium close-up. He looked at me somberly. "It's been a long time," he said. His Boer accent blunted his consonants, turned them into clubs. I'd begun to think that perhaps I'd never have to hear them again. Foolish dream.

"Not so long," I said.

"Ach," said Tromp as he lit a cigarette. "You don't even send me Christmas cards anymore."

"I didn't know you were still a believer."

"I like to keep my summer holidays though." He blew smoke and looked at me with a grin. "I take it you wish a bit of hunting done. Is it to be human or animal?"

I tried not to wince. "Both, and neither," I said. "Is this a secure line?"

"You ought to know. Your technicians were in last month." His grin broadened. "I took them out for a bit of shooting—a leopard had been raiding my cattle. Your people are a delicate lot these days. Even the Bantu turned a little pale."

"Sounds like you had fun," I said.

"I used the incendiary rounds. It saves having to bury a corpse."

"I'd like you to do a little hunting in Egypt," I said. "It may take some years, and you don't have to start right away."

"Ach, my assistant Boetie's been trained for some time. I can leave tomorrow. What will I be looking for?"

I told him. His eyes narrowed. His church, before it lost

its fire and he'd left it, had always stood fast against genetic tampering.

"I don't want you killing them, mind," I said. "Not if you can avoid it. Just capture and sterilize—I don't give a damn if this lot lives, but I don't want there to be a next generation."

He nodded. "I understand, Mr. Falkner."

"And there may be a lot more of them than I realize," I said. "If you need additional personnel, contact my son David. He can put you in touch with Kurusu and a few others. I take it you'd have no objection to working with a partner?"

He blew smoke. "Just so long as Kurusu knows who's boss," he said.

"You're in charge," I told him. "Under David, and under me."

We dickered about price for a while and came to a settlement. He wanted more land to run his cattle on, and he got it. I fed the contract into my comp and we both thumbprinted it. Usually our contracts weren't so formal; but then this one, for a change, was legal.

"It's been a pleasure, Mr. Falkner," he said and switched off.

I always used Tromp Muller when I could. His pleasure was in performing according to the letter of his instructions, without the swashbuckling touches some of the others, like Kurusu, chose to add. Once, when I'd had to use Kurusu against some elements of the January Movement, the corpses had all shown up with Singapore postage stamps pasted on their foreheads, a touch that had thrown the investigation into confusion, as intended, but had also been clearly unnecessary, and risky.

Tromp would do his job well and leave no trace, of that I was certain.

As my car rotated slowly, exchanging sky for ocean and back again, I drank a cup of coffee from my vacuum flask and reflected on the various ways of losing one's innocence. I had lost my virginity long ago, and for various seemingly necessary reasons, seemed doomed to keep on losing it.

That's the problem with being a whore. Illusions are few and hard to come by.

I called my house and told it to give McGivern the answer he wanted to hear. It didn't sound surprised either.

8

The day we crossed Pluto's orbit there was a party in the ship's lounge. We drank champagne and ate Persian caviar, and I ended up tumbling, or being tumbled by, a petite, dark-haired perpetual student from Kemp's. She was two centuries old and had collected another of a long series of degrees on Earth—I don't quite remember in what. She talked a lot, I remember, and I was thankful for it because I didn't feel like talking at all. I liked the fact that she was dark. I had been thinking too much about a silver-haired lady to feel entirely comfortable with a blonde.

It had taken three months to arrange my departure; a man who owns most of a planet has a lot of affairs to wind up. I spent a week in saying good-bye to the centaurs, riding Chiron from glade to glade, saying farewell to the scattered bands of his tribe. David rode with me, and we discussed their future. It was only a matter of time until the rest of the world discovered them, and then David would have to deal with the consequences.

During my final night on Parnassus, the young centaurs danced, and their young and beautiful muse—Philodice—

came down from her eyrie. She was bolder now, surrounded by her own people, and she came quietly into the center of the circle, the others giving way with a kind of awed reverence, and struck her lyre in a new song.

Weep, O centaurs!
Our friend—you know the one—is leaving us.
The man who gave speech to our mute tongues,
And taught us songs of love and sorrow.

As tall as Ares, he walked
Among us. With a song as delicate as spiders' webs,
He made the world new.

Sadly we shall keep his memory,
Trampling the grasses in a slow dance,
One we learned from him. Even now I hear his voice,
Feel the caress of his hand on my mane.
I shall plait my hair with brambles
And turn away my friend with words
Bitter as
Myrrh.

She bent her head over her lyre as she sang the final lines, and once again I saw that echo of another, the long-unremembered curve of cheek and silver hair. I felt the tears sting my eyes as she gave me the gift of her song, and I rose from the grass, took her hands and began to dance, to the left and then to the right, awkwardly at first as I tried to match my two legs against her four. We swayed back and forth to the rhythm of her song, dancing silently for a long moment, before I stepped forward to put my arms around her. Her forefoot stamped once, nervously, but she allowed my embrace. I inhaled her scent: earth and flowers and the fragrance of her silver mane.

"I will take your songs with me when I go," I said.

"And new songs of thine will welcome me home. They and their maker are more precious to me than diamonds."

"Thank you, man," she said. And then, "What are diamonds?"

I laughed and gave her the ring from my finger. She looked at it carefully, holding it up to the light, and then she clenched her fist. "I shall make a song to thank you," she said.

"I hoped you would."

I watched the centaurs dance to Philodice's music and got maudlin drunk on a skin of wine. It was barely possible, I thought, that an old grizzle-maned Philodice would be alive to sing for me when I came back from the stars, but most of these others—Chiron with his wise eyes, Terpsichore with her delicate feet, Tisamenes and Aegeia and my other friends—all these would long have passed away. I wondered again whether this was strictly necessary, and concluded that it was. I was not consoled.

The next day Chiron took me home. I gave him a pair of field glasses as a farewell present. Might as well get them thinking about optics. McGivern, a far-off look in his eye, waited on the balcony of my house as I dismounted and hugged my old friend farewell.

With David and Branwen I had a final meal at the Restaurant Delphi, and I said my farewells to Ismenos and Helen. I brought my guitar and played some blues, not well. Branwen tried not to cry, and failed. She stayed in my spare rooms on Hyampeia that night, and before dawn I awoke and slipped out. I didn't think I could take another good-bye.

To my surprise I turned out to be part-owner of the *Tristan Jones*, the ship we took outward to Kemp's. Probably one of my comps had told me about the purchase at one time or another, but I hadn't remembered. My status had its perks: I got the owner's suite and a bit less than the usual amount of condescension from the crew.

The spacers were modified, of course, living their lives in free-fall. Legs are only excess baggage in weightless conditions, prone to bumping into things and collecting bruises, and so most of the *Jones'* crew had been altered gentically to provide another pair of double-jointed arms where the feet once were. They lived their reclusive lives outside the centrifuge that provided gravity for the passengers, and I assume they lived them well. Their lives were opaque to anyone probing from the outside, and I supposed that was by choice.

For my own curiosity's sake I would have liked to have known them better. Much of a human's self-image is derived from the peculiarities of his body, and I would have liked to have known how these modified humans, living apart in the cells of their man-made hives, differed from myself, and differed as well from the centaurs, those human brains embodied long ago in ancient fantasy.

I was invited to the captain's table once, zooming weightless, with one of the officers as guide, through the maze of tunnels and girders that connected the centrifuge with the rest of the ship. I had been in free-fall before and the reflexes came back easily: I suffered no bruises. But the dinner was uncomfortable, too much of a mutual inspection, and I think the captain was thankful when I declined his second brandy and returned to my suite.

There were unmodified crew to take care of the passengers, mostly outward-bound emigrants heading for the comforts of Kemp's, and there were other people aboard as cargo, frozen by the thousands in their cold-boxes to awaken immortal at their destination.

I had been outside the solar system before, six years after McGivern and I had turned Earth upside down. The world had been through the Great Inflation and the Crash and the Immigration. Half the governments on the planet— mostly the totalitarian regimes that depended on their ability to keep people docile and subservient within their own borders, but also many of the governments of the poorer nations—had collapsed as people equipped with Falkner generators zipped undetectably into their country, loaded their friends, relatives or soul brothers aboard and merrily sailed back home again, laughing as police interceptors bounced bullets and rockets off the field. The rich nations were swamped with immigrants eager to share the riches, and there were precious few riches to be had.

Currencies had all gone to hell. Those based on hard money collapsed when it was realized that anyone with a Falkner Power System and the right equipment could take base metal and convert it to gold, silver or platinum with ease. Soft currencies went smash because the healthy economies that supported them were changing too fast for anyone to properly keep score. The measure of how swiftly everything was changing showed up when World War III was started by a panicking government on its last legs and even the ultimate weapon failed, all the doomsday bombs fizzling out uselessly because of the Falkner Screening Systems that protected each and every continent. McGivern was tearing his hair out by the roots trying to keep up with the flux, and I had just survived my third assassination attempt. I was unscratched but the bomb fragments had left some scars on my fiancee. We decided to leave.

I set up the fund that supported the Forever Now project and used most of the rest of my available capital to build the *Mad Folly* in orbit. Madeline and I, looking down from Folly Station, as we waited for the ship's completion, would grip each other's hands and watch the Earth rotate below us, appalled and terrified at the delicate, twinkling lights that were cities burning. All humanity's madness, all the violence and terror that had been halfheartedly repressed for the last few centuries, seemed to be breaking loose at once.

I was half-crazed with guilt, first at having been responsible for the chaos and then for running like a thief when

things got bad. Our station changed orbits every few hours
for fear someone would throw a missile at us. We were
screened against atomics but helpless against a high explosive or shrapnel. I was afraid that when we returned there
might be nothing left, and I wondered if this was something Snaggles had foreseen. I pictured him happily digging among the ruins while the few remaining examples of
humanity bashed in each other's heads with rocks. The
Folly had a crew of two hundred, and I hoped it would be
enough to start the human race anew somewhere among
the bright network of the night.

We left during the worst of it, and my pessimism turned
out not to be justified. Afterward the people and their
systems healed. Nations declined, economies rebuilt themselves around new items of value. Robot technologies
began to do the scutwork, and millions moved outward
into the solar system as easily as though it were their
backyard. Other probes followed the *Folly* outside of the
solar system, and back home the Forever Now people,
their labs sitting in concrete safety and backed by the largest
collection of capital in human history, quietly continued
their work.

The *Folly* visited five stars and found planets circling all
five, habitable planets around two. We were gone for
eighty years and aged only sixteen or so. Madeleine di-
vorced me and married one of the ship's officers, and I
shared my cabin with a communications specialist whose
husband had been killed in the botched landing on Yeager.
During the time I was gone, I became the de facto government of planet Earth, with McGivern as my steely prime
minister. We had no official authority but we were stronger
than any government, and both we and the governments
knew it. McGivern was generally smart enough to know
when to flex his muscles and when not to, and the Falkner
Power Trust was tolerated by the people of Earth as long
as there was no alternative.

Along with approximately two million other people, McGivern, aged one hundred twenty-one and looking all of ninety, met my shuttle on landing. He had benefited somewhat from the Forever Now research, and his mind was keen even though his body was failing. His message was simple: Forever Now was a success. Not only had they found one cure for aging, they had found around half a dozen, some of them not yet fully developed. The best of them not only halted aging but slowly brought the body back to youth, restoring elasticity to the skin and muscles, clearing the arteries and lungs of accumulated rubbish, undoing the long effects of gravity.

Falkner Power began flexing its muscles with a vengeance. Our message was simple: We now have ways to make you live forever. But we can't have a bunch of immortals cluttering up the planet, spawning more immortal children and driving down all the property values. So Falkner Bio Research Associates will buy you a one-way ticket off the planet, to any destination of your choice. In return you will give Mr. Falkner and his associates every bit of terrestrial property you possess. Mr. Falkner wants to buy the world, and in exchange you will live forever. Fair enough, *que no?*

Our muscle was sufficient to put it over—just barely. In the end—after another set of riots, burnings and assassination attempts—I was the personal owner of just about all the surface of the planet, and the population was down to what it had been twenty thousand years earlier, before humanity's mistakes were big enough to scar the planet too badly: twenty million, divided more or less evenly between the Diehards, who for one reason or another refused the immortality I offered, and the people I brought in, or allowed to stay, for reasons of my own.

Plus, of course, the genetically altered, the living DNA-dreams who inhabited all the new wilderness in untold numbers. And one other: an extraterrestrial archaeologist, happy in his digs. Who had made it all possible.

The information about Snaggles was buried deep in my will, hidden by every elaborate safety mechanism my ingenious comps could devise. If I died on this trip, he would become my family's worry.

And for all these reasons I was more than usually thoughtful during the party on board the *Jones* to celebrate our leaving the solar system and happy to let a dark-haired, talkative and fairly soused perpetual student share my life during the last hours before we stepped into our coldboxes. Because she could bury my memories—the memories of hooves flashing in the dance, of Philodice's graceful fingers on lyre strings, and of those long years spent on the *Folly* while history was made and a marriage fell.

And, most of all, the memory of those calm, dark eyes under silver hair, and a voice telling me she had no regrets, none at all. . . .

9

Crystal thoughts, dreamed slowly in the cold between the stars. There is time, in this long night, to search every jewel of memory.

The hooves stamp on Parnassus' forgiving shoulder,
Beating in time to the long and skillful fingers
Plucking at the spiderweb strings that connect the stars
All made of silver hair.

Hermes, brow frowning beneath the brim of his floppy
    hat,
Comes in search of the thing that was his,
Hears the music, stops in his tracks.
The god begins to smile and tap his foot. He always
    liked
A good slow blues.

The Guardian of One of the Four Corners of the
    Universe
Stands upon his midden, his roots questing down.

His tongue unrolls and licks the stony soil of Zhou.
  He is mad, and cannot hear the sounds.
But now his ears prick up.

A dog howls at the touch of the lyre. Crazed,
He scrabbles at the Stygian night. An
Owl-headed friend, sympathetic, makes a clicking
  sound with his beak.
They dine tonight on the flesh of something Tromp
  Muller has killed. He has used his incendiaries,
And cooked it to perfection.

Mississippi John Hurt joins Hermes in a graceful
  soft-shoe dance,
Knowing Stone's estate won't get fat off this one.
"C.H.I.C.K.E.N.," he says with a graceful smile.
  "That spells chicken."
  The god nods his head wisely.
"I tried to learn the guitar, you know. But I never got
  the hang of it."

The blues fade in the inky vacuum. The long fingers
  are hesitant.
I watch as dark eyes brim with tears. She holds the
  lyre extended.
"I will not take your gift," she says. McGivern
  stands
Behind her in torment, his loyalties torn in half.

I cannot take the lyre from her. She turns, the silver
  hair brushing the tears on her cheek,
And lets it fall. The stars are unstrung.
And now the Guardian of One of the Four Corners of
  the Universe raises his head, doglike,
Sniffing the aether. He jets from his rubbish heap,
Calling to the others, and the owls and jackals

Answer, breathing foetid air that tastes of dead things
    and madness,
Devouring all Parnassus, slavering as they taste the
    sky.

There is one smile only, a priest
Who stands by the navel stone.
"I told you so," he says. "You should have fol-
    lowed my advice. I would have lied,
    but you would have been the better for it."
His smile is the last of all to fade, and in that last
    instant before the crystal melts,
I hear Kassandra moan.

The Cheshire-like smile faded last of all. "Three weeks,"
the attendant said, "out from Kemp's. You have a lot of
mail."

I shivered the memory of cold out of my limbs and
accepted a glass of champagne. It had been years since I'd
drained a glass.

10

On Hold

The rectangle was a silver so bright it hurt the eyes, and there were streaks of colors running through it, flaring and then gone. It was edged in black and rotated as it moved down an endless maze—left, right, right again, past a post and through a hallway, each change of perspective tugging insistently at the inner ear . . . there was a faint hum, as of far-off machinery.

"Dr. Zimmerman is unavailable," the secretary said. The rectangle pulsed briefly with streaks of flame as it swept down the halls. Perhaps the sound was not that of machinery but akin to the imperious swishing of skirts.

"May I give Dr. Zimmerman a message?" the robot secretary asked. It was a female voice, American, and precise in its diction. Its qualities were cognate to the distant hum of the labyrinth, not human, architecturally perfect.

"I am Doran Falkner. I would like an appointment."

"Dr. Zimmerman does not give appointments. I will inform him of your call."

The rectangle, rotating, narrowed to a hard black edge; then it widened again to a silver shimmer.

"Tell him it's about Project Knight's Move," I said.

There was no answer, simply the pulsing rectangle pursuing its business down the blank computer-generated walls. Autosecretaries informing a caller that their owner was not available often showed soothing images on their video screens; slowly rotating starfields were popular, and so were nature pictures, waterfalls and coats of arms. Zimmerman had the shimmering rectangle moving with barely imperfect silence down an endless labyrinth of white and shadow. It was a powerfully disturbing image, silent and enigmatic, and it made my dorsal hairs prickle. I watched it for some minutes, gnawing a thumbnail; then I switched off. I would try again later.

Kemp's spun below us, a dazzling glass paperweight of green and blue and white. There were three billion people in this system, half of whom lived on the planet, the rest outside its gravity well. The *Jones* was the first ship in four months from outside the system and would clear quarantine in a few days.

We were years out of date, a measure of the isolation of these populous systems. But then, we were here to fix all that.

On Kemp's they called it Project Knight's Move, the attempt to sidestep from one square of the universe to the next without traversing the somber black and white tiles in between. It had gone nowhere. The instability in the high-energy Z-particles had been examined, refined and ultimately explained; great strides had been made in understanding the as-yet evasive fundamental nature of matter, all of the various theories combining solid research with ingenious near-metaphysical suppositions; but none of the new knowledge appeared to have any great relevance to the subject at hand. Perhaps Father Willis was right after all, and the whole lug phenomenon was a proof of God's existence. Q.E.D.

It seemed that my alleged specialty, subatomic physics, was going to be ruled out as the source of the answer. I studied the documents on board the *Jones* and wondered if this meant that I would turn into a bureaucrat-in-charge instead of a contributing member of the expedition. I hoped my answer to myself was wrong.

I read some of my mail and let my own automatic secretary take care of the rest. (Mine, by the way, showed callers a prism that broke light into a rainbow. It let people fiddle with the color adjustments while they waited for me to answer.) There were reports from Tromp Muller indicating a fair degree of success—he had found the altered creatures in Egypt, and found them challenging hunting—and pleased reports from Branwen and David on the progress of the centaur colony. Still unknown to anyone other than my family, it appeared they were developing the beginnings of philosophy. A young colt named Perdix was starting to ask some interesting questions about the nature of reality. He had concluded that the wandering stars—planets and orbital colonies both—were lesser spheres, each ruled by one of the Greek gods; he had also concluded by observation that fire was the means by which one element transmuted itself into another—an inspired guess, I thought. And he was getting into the business of ethics. He had concluded that one could be a good person if one avoided fighting over females, consulted one's elders on matters of policy, protected the young from harassment, paid proper attention to the gods and avoided pissing in the camp fire. A bit Confucian for my tastes, but a start.

Classical Greek was a perfect language for philosophy. Its very nature taught people to make subtle distinctions between things. That was the major reason, aside from

mythological and aesthetic considerations, that I had decided to teach Chiron the Elder to speak Greek.

And Philodice still lived and sang; her recorded voice
was transmitted over light-years to our ship. At night I
drowsed to her melodies, to her songs of inhuman sadness
and love.

I was fitted for new clothes, discovering that the appropriate garment for a distinguished otherworld visitor on
Kemp's was a lightweight kilt—with a large codpiece
worn underneath the kilt to produce a satisfying masculine
bulge—and a short, plush velveteen jacket with padded
shoulders and tight waist à la Eisenhower. No facial hair.
Pockets were replaced by pouches attached to the belt, or
by a shoulder bag. I didn't mind exposing my knees, but
on the whole I missed the pockets.

After the doctors let me out of bed, I spent some days
practicing in front of mirrors so that I could move naturally
in the new rig. Grace is a matter of either aptitude or
practice. I had no aptitude, and so I worked at it.

Besides, it beat thinking about what I was doing here,
and why.

White Noise

The argent monolith sped unhesitatingly through its cool
and perfect corridors. White noise hissed in and out. I
wondered what piece of unpleasantness was at the center
of the maze—Zimmerman perhaps?

"I am Doran Falkner. Please connect me to Dr. Zimmerman."

"Dr. Zimmerman is unavailable. I shall inform him of
your call."

"Tell him it's about Project Knight's Move."

"Dr. Zimmerman is doing his own research connected
with the project. You will be informed of the results at the
appropriate time."

"I am calling at his request. He said he would speak to me."

"Dr. Zimmerman is unavailable. I shall inform him of your call. Is there anything you wish to add to the message?"

The rectangle paused briefly, pulsing, then sped on.

"Yes," I said. "Tell him I'm tired of his metaphors."

I switched off and told my secretary to call his secretary every hour. It is impossible to annoy secretarial programs but the action made me feel a little better. After spending three weeks on the inbound ship and two weeks in quarantine, I wanted to speak to someone by means other than a vidscreen.

I leaned back in my chair, feeling a sudden throb of pain, longing for Hyampeia and the sound of the wind in the cypresses, the feel of the track beneath my feet as I sped at twilight past the gray stone bleachers of the old stadium. I was tired of striving to penetrate labyrinths, Zimmerman's and those of physics and of whatever piece of impossible longing had brought me here. Below me, somewhere on that globe of green, Mary Liddell lay in her frigid coffin, and I was not the prince who would wake her with a kiss, to wake the world of might-have-been. I should not have come.

I was getting maudlin, and I wasn't even drunk. I decided I shouldn't be the one without the other and called for a bottle.

On Butterfly Wings

Kemp's banked slowly beneath us, its limb turning on edge, then flattening, becoming a horizon. There was the sound of rushing wind. We were still above the clouds. I heard Pierce Hourigan's reckless laugh. His first name was pronounced "Purse," and he didn't use it.

"I thought you'd enjoy this," he said. "We don't have a field between us and the sights."

"Nice," I said. G-forces tugged at my stomach. "What happens if you tear off a wing?"

Hourigan turned his cheerful eyes to me. "We die, Doc," he said.

I shrugged. I had a sailboat with which to tempt the fates, and Hourigan had his private glider-shuttle—each a way, in this age of comfort and safety, of bringing death a little closer so as to laugh in his hollow face and taste his breath on the tongue. Psychologists would call it a death wish, a form of suicide. Perhaps so—but I was a very good and very safe sailor, and Hourigan was an excellent pilot. We'd give death a shot, but we wouldn't make it easy for him.

Hourigan had snatched me from quarantine just in time to rescue me from the clutches of an official delegation.

"What's new on the Project then?" I asked.

"Not a thing, Doc," he replied. "We can't get the damn thing off the ground."

The horizon turned flip-flops. The matt-black shuttle nose steadied on the green below. I was pressed back into my seat as we dove vertically for the trees. White clouds spun. And Hourigan laughed.

Ungentlemanly Conduct

"We can't find anyone who's seen him in years," al-Qatan said. He had grown a curling black beard and looked as devilish as Hourigan. "He's lived in that house of his for decades. So far as we know, there's no one but him and the robots there. But he's still alive—he publishes. We know he's working on Project material; he's called up everything from central files."

We were looking at the silvery rectangle as it hissed down the corridors. We had long ago given up trying to reason with the robot secretary.

"Creepy, isn't it?" Hourigan murmured.

"Creepy," I agreed. "Can we deny him access to the Project material until he talks to us?"

Hourigan looked at me and frowned. "I suppose so," he said carefully. It wasn't nice to deny a fellow scientist his data.

"Let's spread a rumor in the press that we've made a breakthrough," I said. "They're usually gullible enough on scientific matters. Zimmerman will want to see the data and we won't give it to him. And we'll have our secretaries stop all our attempts to get in touch with him."

"You're a nasty man, Doc," Hourigan said.

Nasty.

Without A Trace, Without A Hope

Ruyter, who had led the last Amaterasu survey team, was a square, burly man with steel-wool hair on the backs of his hands, werewolf-style. "I'm not going back to that hellhole, Dr. Falkner," he said. "I spent three years on the surface and over twenty in transit, and the whole thing was a goddamn waste of time." He took a long drink from his beer. "I've recommended another ecologist, a man named Truxillo. He seems eager to volunteer." He grinned. "The poor man."

"So what can you tell me?" I asked.

"I've been over Amaterasu on foot, in a plane, in a glider, in a blimp," Ruyter said. "Even in a submersible. My people charted ecology, weather patterns, climatological conditions, ocean currents. We took deep core samples of the crust, sampled the salinity and mineral content of the oceans, analyzed the aurora displays over the poles. We sent probes to orbit the sun." He shrugged.

"We found nothing. Not a goddamn thing that wasn't anticipated in advance. Except for the lugs that teleported." He grinned at me from under his bushy brows.

"Any sign of . . ." I began. For some reason we were all reluctant to talk about it, even to each other.

Ruyter's grin faded. He shook his head slightly. "No," he said. "No sign of . . . aliens. If something else is moving the lugs around, it's damn hard to find. No traces of sentient life, not even in the dim past. Not even a plastic spoon. And we looked hard." He shrugged again.

"Now you tell *me*, Mr. Falkner, what I missed."

"You missed ordering another round of beer," I said.

His grin broadened, and he raised a hairy hand to attract the barman.

Sweet Auricula

Mary lay up to her neck in hospital sheets of a pale, antiseptic green, the color of a faded plant perishing for lack of water. There was a faint humming, as in Zimmerman's secretarial corridors. Her limbs twitched as they were exercised automatically by electrode—a mute, obscene quivering, like the final shudders of a dying animal. When it had been done to me, it had made me ill.

She had awakened only hours earlier, and appeared ancient, with deep lines drawn in a pale face, a prefiguring of the old age she had demanded as her right. Her dark eyes looked unnaturally bright, as though she were fevered or in pain. "Hello, Doran," she said. She didn't ask me how long it had been.

"Hi." I bent to kiss her cheek. It was as dry as paper.

She gave me a shy smile. "I wish I were on my feet, to greet you properly. Couldn't you have waited?"

"It's been too long as it is," I said.

She tilted her head back, stropping it on the pillow. "I'm paralyzed from the neck down while this exercise session is going on. I wish this damned thing would let me move."

"No problem." I reached to the head of the bed to turn

the machine off. Mary laughed at my presumption and brought her hands from out of the covers. The little remote electrodes clung to them like leeches. The skin was nearly translucent.

"Could you give me a hand?" she asked. "I'd like to sit up." I took her hands in mine and helped her to rise, then adjusted the pillows under her back. She pulled her knees up and hugged them with her arms, interlacing her long fingers.

"How was your journey?" she asked.

"Reluctant. Otherwise pleasant enough."

"And Earth, these days?"

"Much the same. A few new projects."

"Finished the Sacred Way yet?"

"Not when I left. Done now though. I had a message."

We were silent for a moment, our eyes gazing into a neutral corner. When I first knew Mary, she had been an eager, questing student, ready to devour the world. She had been brilliant, but the brilliance had been a part of the blaze that was the rest of her—forthright, fearless, opinionated, eager to absorb every last fragment of knowledge, every thread in the skein that was the universe. She had been good for me, bringing me out of a kind of self-loathing into which it is so easy, for those of us who know ourselves so well, to fall into—and I'd had centuries in which to know myself well, and to grow sick on the knowledge. Mary's vigorous personality had made me realize what a self-indulgence my loathing was, what a sham. . . . I had built the modern world, damn it, and had no apologies to make, and no excuse for sorrow. The world was mine, to be enjoyed; and Mary was there to share my delight.

She was determined to be everything—physicist, lover, hedonist, quester for experience, for life and, in the end and without my realizing it, for death. When I said that she loved me less for myself than for the bits of learning she could pick from my brain, I meant it as a jest, and she laughed obediently; but it wasn't really a joke with her. She wanted it all, and she saw nothing wrong with taking from others those things she thought were useful. The impetuosity of youth, I thought, and was delighted; and then, some time later, I found out just why she was in such a hurry.

Now I did not recognize her. That she was physically different seemed the least of it. Although she was older, she was still recognizably Mary. Those deep gray eyes, Tatar cheekbones and silver hair were difficult to forget, and they hadn't changed—but so much of what I remembered about her seemed different. The eagerness, the vitality, the animation—all that seemed altered, or gone altogether. The eyes were no longer questing, but knowing. I tried to compensate for the fact that she had just come out of a cold storage lasting over twenty years, that she was physically weak and caught in a situation in which that weakness was displayed to her disadvantage, but still I couldn't help feeling that the Mary I had known would have responded differently, would have challenged me somehow as soon as I walked in the door; she would have either told me I'd changed for the worse or dared me to help her escape the hospital's confinement.

This Mary was someone else. I didn't know what to say to her.

For her, perhaps, the dilemma was worse. I don't imagine I had changed much in the years since we'd been apart, but she had evolved considerably. It was like one of those painful situations at, say, a class reunion where one meets an old friend with whom one was once close but who hasn't been seen in twenty years. All the common ground seems far away, faintly absurd. It's to be condescended to from the vantage point of an older, allegedly wiser self: "Ah, do you remember the time we flew to Havarti because you wanted plum brandy? So foolish we were. . . ."

Having long since lost the real essence of the time and place, one is forced to fall back on the banality of shared memories, the lowest common denominator of the past.

Who would desire that, especially with someone who had once mattered? And so we stared in silence at the corners of the room until a bustling robot nurse came sweeping in to reset the electrode machine. "You are not permitted to interfere with the patient's therapy," the machine said, gazing at me with a malevolent flashing eye. "I must ask you to leave."

The tension broke and we laughed. I patted Mary's hand and stood up. "I'll see you soon," I said. "Let me know when you're up and we'll go sight-seeing."

"That sounds like fun," she said. I reached into one of my pouches and pulled out a recording of Philodice's songs. I put it on her bedside table.

"Do you remember your Greek?" I asked.

"A little," she answered. She winced as the electrodes cut in again and she went numb below the neck, her limbs starting to leap. The nurse spun toward me and began to make shooing noises.

"Play it when you have the time," I said. "I'd like to know what you think of it." Mary didn't know about the centaurs; they had been my dark secret then.

She nodded. "I'll do that." I gave her a farewell grin as the robot pushed me out of the room, and she smiled back, amused. The automatic door swished shut.

"Visiting hours tomorrow," the robot said primly, "are from fifteen to twenty-four."

"Yes. I understand."

"No more tampering now."

"Of course not."

It seemed that half of my life on Kemp's was spent in dealing with refractory robots. The people themselves had been uniformly gracious; perhaps that was because their robots could so easily act out their ornery impulses by proxy. I turned down the corridor, half-expecting to see Zimmerman's pulsing silver rectangle, but instead I saw McGivern, his frowning eyes fixed on the floor in front of him, walking my way with a flowerpot in his arms.

"Hello, Brian," I said.

He looked up at me in surprise, then looked rapidly down at the pot and away again. As though I had somehow caught him at a disadvantage. His thin lips smiled wryly.

"Hello," he said. There was a moment's awkward pause. "How is she feeling?" he asked.

"She looks," I said, "like death." His expression was opaque. He nodded once.

"Yes," he said. He hefted the flowerpot in a hesitant gesture, then looked down at it again. I caught an aroma that reminded me of the gardens of Madame Lu.

"From my garden," he said. "A fragrant local herb. Called sweet auricula." He flashed me a diffident smile. "You'd think they could make hospitals smell like something else, but they don't. So I thought I'd bring an antidote."

"I didn't know you were interested in gardening," I said.

He frowned. "I've got a big one—several thousand kilometers, in fact. Sort of a private forest. I hope you can visit it."

"I'd be honored."

He hefted the pot again. "Well," he said, "I'll see you tomorrow. The logistics session."

"Watch out for the nurse robot," I cautioned. "It's a tiger."

He said his good-byes and walked away, a kind of awkwardness in his stance that I hadn't seen before. He had never lacked confidence since I'd known him; now he seemed almost adolescent in his uncertainty. Was he embarrassed, I wondered, that I'd found out about his hobby, afraid that this revealed something about him he didn't want me to know? Or was he afraid for me to know he cared enough about Mary to visit her just after her resurrection?

Why? I frowned and made my way out of the hospital. Down the clean, humming corridor.

Brain Face Meets Face Grace Can Love Bloom Between The Star Of High-Energy Physics And The Body Bueno Of Blamtown?

The delegation caught up with me after the logistics meeting and I conceded to a week of official sight-seeing at McGivern's insistence. The politicians were giving him fits about various kinds of funding priorities, and I was the bone he threw them. At first I thought the delegation had gone to the quaint extreme of providing me a woman, but then I realized that Angelique denThrush was a party crasher, an actress who felt her career would be somehow enhanced by her proximity to me. Years of reclusive privacy on Earth had dimmed my reflexes, otherwise I would have sooner realized her intent.

She had black oriental eyes, dark skin and straight black hair brought to little points along her jawline so that it looked like a helmet. She walked with utter poise and confidence and spent a lot of time in getting between me and the medialites—which would have been fine with me if the cameras hadn't been so busy making insinuations to which she was constantly cooing agreement. And in time for the afternoon and late-evening broadcasts, no less.

"Get rid of her," I told Co-Chairman Bogdanovich. We had just finished a hoverplatform tour of Plongeur Canyon and were now parked on the rim, enjoying the sight of the clouds patterning the sunset on the canyon walls. Bogdanovich looked at me as though frightened.

"You can't mean it. She's Angelique denThrush! She's *big face*!"

"I can see you have a lot to learn. Watch my technique."

Bogdanovich looked even more frightened. I grinned and gazed at the ruddy canyon walls and the violet sky, waiting for denThrush to finish giving her exclusives to the hovering medialites. When she finished, she gave them all a sunny smile, then sauntered back across the platform to take my arm. Last chance, I thought.

But no. The smile blazed like noonday but her eyes were obsidian, gleaming and dead. Her grip was steel, her conversation an outraged monologue devoted to the stupidities of a robot dermatologist who had misapplied her makeup.

"Excuse me," I said, borrowed a cigarette from one of the delegation and strolled aft to light it. I tried not to inhale. Didn't want anyone to think I hadn't actually smoked in a couple of centuries.

The medialites swept in for a closer view, their big lenses spinning as they focused on me. There was a babble of questions from their speakers. I pointed at one of them.

"You," I said.

"Is it true that you have achieved a major breakthrough on Project Knight's Move?" The voice was female and loud, shouting as though still competing with the others.

"It's too early to draw any conclusions," I replied. "But there have been some interesting developments since my arrival, yes."

Take that, Zimmerman.

There were a few more questions along that line, each answered with a maximum degree of glibness and a minimum of information. Then came the one I'd been waiting for.

"Would you say that the sight of the Plongeur equals the beauty of the Face Grace?" A bright male media voice, hearty and full of bogus good humor.

"I was one of the first humans to see the Plongeur, as you probably know," I smiled. "It's one of the finest natural sights in human-occupied space." I could hear the lenses whirring as they zoomed in for a close-up. I puffed smoke and shook my head. "But I don't know the other sight you mentioned. Guess they haven't shown it to me yet."

"I mean the Angel, Mr. Falkner." Condescendingly. What could the Angel see in this old coot anyway?

I contrived to look baffled. "What angel is that?" I asked, making them condescend even further.

The voice dripped frozen disapproval. "Miss Angelique denThrush, your companion."

"Oh." I gave Angelique a curious glance over my shoulder, then feigned a light bulb suddenly glowing over my head. "You mean the woman with the hair," I said.

"No need to be coy, Mr. Falkner." This from the excitable female voice. "Face Grace has told us everything."

"She *has*?" I peered over my shoulder again. "I've never talked to her, actually," I told them. "I figured she got on this trip because she was someone's girlfriend."

The medialites began to circle in closer, scenting blood—not knowing whose just yet, but knowing someone was going to get the slash very shortly.

"Let's get this straight, Mr. Falkner." A brusque masculine voice, half-disbelieving. "You've never even talked to the Face?"

I looked baffled. "Sorry," I said. "Was I supposed to have?" I gave him a sheepish grin. "Someone must have been telling you fibs." The camera lenses whirred as one with a fevered intensity.

"So you and she aren't lovers? Don't even *know* each other?" A babble, one voice on top of the next. I waved for order. The 'lites settled down a bit. Time to go for the jugular, I'd say.

"Lovers?" I asked. I puffed the cigarette and gave a

grin and a confidential wink. I decided to be as offensive as possible. "Give me credit for better taste than that, please," I said. "I'd as soon bed a lizard." Tacky, but as it happens, true.

The medialites were quivering with delight. They swooped as a pack in the direction of my alleged lover. One could almost hear the baying of hounds.

DenThrush, I suppose, could have talked about a lovers' spat or my odd sense of humor, turned the thing back on me, in which case I'd be castigated for having made a joke in bad taste while she played the abused darling. I decided I didn't want that to happen. While no one was looking, I reached into one of my pouches and did something I prefer not to reveal. The robot cameras dropped like bricks. A few had enough momentum to carry them over the canyon and fall a kilometer before the first bounce. The rest simply thudded onto the rocks by the observation platform. Everyone looked at them in surprise.

I threw the cigarette away and strolled back to the group. DenThrush wasn't interested in holding my arm while no one was watching.

The pilot of the hoverplatform was looking with bafflement at his gauges. "We've lost power," he said with the expression of someone who has just seen water fall up. He pressed buttons and nothing happened. He looked at me. "I can't get it to work," he said. "The generator's gone."

"Falkner Power Systems never fail," I said. "You must be flying with a competitor. Lucky we weren't over the canyon when it happened."

There was a hush in the background conversation and everyone looked at the brink with sudden, sober respect. We heard the sound of one of the medialites hitting a ledge, right on cue. The Co-Chairman flinched.

"Have you enough power stored to call another craft?" I asked. "Preferably one with a FPS, not a cheap imitation?"

"Yes, Mr. Falkner," the pilot breathed. He got busy and called.

We flew to dinner at a private lodge on the rim of the canyon, where the medialites were barred. They never had a chance to ask Face Grace any questions till the next morning, by which time the afternoon, evening and early morning broadcasts had shown half the inhabitants of the system my bewilderment and bad taste. By noon she was being called Face Lizard. By early afternoon she'd left for an orbital health spa, allegedly—no one believed her—with a broken heart.

Bogdanovich was looking at me with new respect. "I understand why you did it," he said, "but it cost your Project a lot of publicity."

I shook my head. "Not at all. We got a lot more publicity with my being unpleasant over the fantail of the hovercraft than we could have if a half a dozen Faces—"

"Foci," said Bogdanovich.

"Faces," I repeated, "had been present."

Whether I was right or wrong on that point—it's hard to tell with these things—my little press conference had achieved at least one desired effect. That night my robot secretary logged its first call from Jay Zimmerman. He was told I was unavailable.

Parsley, Sage, Alive, Alive-Oh

Al-Qatan and I were white-knuckled passengers in Hourigan's aircraft for the trip to McGivern's pleasure dome. His thousand-acre estate had been designed before he'd left for Earth and built by robot while he was gone. The house itself was easily enough completed, but the major work had been that of landscaping. He'd moved tonnes and tonnes of material, planted trees by their thousands, from half a dozen worlds, and put a couple of square kilometers under glass for his greenhouses. Deer and elk roamed at will through most of it. This weekend would be the first time the estate was opened to more than the staff and a few friends.

Hourigan was dressed in a blousy white shirt with puffed sleeves, and green tights covered his lanky legs, another of his eccentric displays. It wasn't until we dismounted from the craft and watched him pull on his green jacket and take his bow and quiver from the passenger compartment that we realized what he was supposed to be.

"Every feudal manor needs its Robin Hood," Hourigan said, giving us a blinding smile as he tugged on a billed cap of Lincoln green.

I nodded at the bow. "I hope you know how to use that," I said.

"Indeed yes. And what is more important, how not to use it." He shaded his eyes as he peered through the trees in the direction of McGivern's manor. His voice began to assume the tones of a Gilbert and Sullivan aristocrat. "I expect to bag a few of the king's deer before nightfall. Od's blud, and all that."

"You'll have to watch out for the foresters," I said. I took my bags from the craft.

"They ne'er shall have me, by my good right arm," quoth Robin.

We set out for the manor, Hourigan skipping ahead on his green moccasins. We passed through a stand of English elms, genetically adapted to this foreign soil, and then gazed down at McGivern's principal house.

Imagine Blenheim Palace as conceived and executed by Frank Lloyd Wright. The same kind of deliberate magnificence, but without the rococo ornamentation, without the ponderousness. With a breezy lightness that summoned laughter as well as awe. The structure had many wings and outbuildings that seemed, at first, haphazardly placed; but together they formed a coherent design, superbly functional. It was set against a totally artificial landscape, built to seem natural, that rippled behind the place, trees and knolls and little rocky outcrops placed with the intention of complementing the architecture. There was a twisty lake in front, bent into a dozen lagoons from which floated the sounds of splashing and laughter.

"Ah," Hourigan breathed, brandishing his longbow. "Nottingham Castle."

"It's lovely," I said.

He turned to me and smiled. I wondered at the hint of sadness in his eyes. He bobbed his head toward the building. "I never would have expected it of McGivern, you know," he said. Al-Qatan gave a little grunt of annoyance.

I looked from one to the other. "What—" I began.

"Our friend," said al-Qatan, "is disappointed in Mr. McGivern. Because he chooses to live on such an estate."

I turned to Hourigan. "You have a nice place of your own, I believe," I said.

He shook his head. "It is for living. Not a tomb. Not a . . . not a domain. A fantasy place, a place to retreat. To surrender."

I looked down at the bright green vegetation, the slashings of colorful flowers, the guests as they splashed in the rippled lake. "Surrender?" I asked.

"Our friend," said al-Qatan with the weariness of one who has been over this ground before, "has a theory: Our extended life spans, combined with easy wealth and a galaxy full of raw materials, have made us lazy, prone to undisciplined fantasy. That life is less challenging."

"Not less challenging," Hourigan said, "but that the challenges have become all too easy to avoid."

He paused for a moment and then was suddenly in motion, dropping the bow and leaping for one of the neighboring trees—not an import but one of the native plants, with a smooth, dark skin (one couldn't call it a bark) and a profusion of branches springing from a central crotch just over our heads. His moccasins left green stripes on the bole as he scrambled up, and suddenly he was perched on one of the limbs, his feet dangling. He batted branches out of his eyes and laughed.

"Look at the damn place, Doran," he said. "It's brilliantly designed, yes. Magnificently conceived and executed. But still it's a tomb built to honor a man who hasn't died yet, and I think that's a shame."

"So?" I asked. "We're not to build big houses? Or do extensive landscaping?"

"Lest we die in spirit," al-Qatan said and rolled his eyes.

Hourigan straddled the branch and leaned forward, pillowing his head on his crossed arms. He spoke seriously. "Depends on what you're doing it all for, Doc. If it's for joy, okay. If it's for love of the thing, okay. If you've always been a frustrated architect or landscape designer, that's all right too. But if it's a fulfillment of some inner fantasy of lordship and control, then it's not okay." He shrugged. "I don't know how to explain it any better than that. Action's more my style."

I looked hopelessly at al-Qatan. He gave me a sour glance. "It's a phenomenon that we've all seen," he said. "The symptoms are everywhere. When genetic research first came along, people were populating their fantasies with living creatures, with unicorns and fairies and little furry-footed hobbits made from scrapings of their own DNA. It was obviously sick, and the healthy majority put a stop to it."

"That's not how it ended," Hourigan said. "It just became passé. Decadence was no longer fashionable."

"At any rate," al-Qatan said, "it was stopped. Robin Hood here thinks that that kind of sickness has been replaced by another kind, more subtle. I think he's being silly. If McGivern wants to live the life of milord English squire, let him. More power to him if that's what he really wants."

"There isn't any point to being a milord English squire, you know," Hourigan said. The limb swayed as he sat up. "There hasn't been for hundreds of years. It's an obsolete social function. This is a parasitic fantasy, and it's leaching off the real McGivern." He kicked his feet. "There isn't any actual work being done on this estate. Just one form or another of play. A man burying himself in his own dream. It's sad." He looked down at the sprawling house. "McGivern used to be such a vital man. Always in charge of things. Moving his money around, being aggressive about the way he wanted the planet's affairs arranged. He wasn't the sort of person I could like, but I could respect him. And now. . . ." He shrugged.

My neck was getting tired from looking up at him. "People change," I said. "He's out of touch now, you know. He's spent decades traveling to Earth and back and his affairs just went on without him. It'll take him a while to regain control."

"If he bothers," Hourigan said. He sighed, swaying his feet, his eyes looking at nowhere in particular. "There's a seductive thing about forests, I think. They obscure the horizon, moderate the sun. They let you believe anything is possible."

Al-Qatan snorted. "And you don't like woods and trees, I suppose," he said. "You've never gone for a stroll down a garden path or spent a night camping in the wilderness."

"My strolls didn't last forever. And I struck camp in the morning. I lived in the woods; I didn't make them a part of my fantasy."

"Thus speaks the man dressed as Robin Hood," I said.

"Robin Hood came out of the woods in the end," said Hourigan. He kicked one foot over the limb, then easily vaulted to the ground. "And in the meantime he served as a valuable social critic."

"You don't think that withdrawing into a personal world can be a form of social criticism?" I asked.

He picked up his bow and put his weight on it, stringing it. He plucked the bowstring and the air thrummed. When he spoke, he looked at the bow, not meeting my eyes.

"Hell, Doc, I don't know," he replied and shrugged. "You have a whole planet for your playground. You tell me. Are you a social critic, or what?"

"That's not fair, Hourigan," al-Qatan said. Hourigan turned to him angrily and snapped:

"Let's have Doran answer for himself, hey?" And then he turned to me.

"Social critic?" I said lightly. "No. Social inventor, if you like."

"Any masterpieces coming up?" Hourigan asked.

"We'll see. I'm a slow worker. It's the nature of the material."

Hourigan nodded. "I'll be looking forward, Doran. In the meantime, try not to walk through Sherwood with any sacks of gold." Then he gave me a grin and was in motion, a green blur speeding away from the party, slaloming between the trees.

"Looks more like Hermes than Robin Hood," I mused.

"He's getting hard to take, whoever he is," al-Qatan said. We started to walk down the grassy sward toward the lake. Al-Qatan gave me a quick glance from the corner of his eye. "It's Mary's influence, I think. They were great friends before she went into the cold-box."

I looked at him. "Oh?"

"Yes. Sometimes he talks about becoming a Diehard. Says that those who live past their natural life span have an increased tendency for what he calls 'cultural senility.' "

"I can't think of anyone less senile than Hourigan."

"Arrested adolescence, I'd say," al-Qatan said, an edge to his voice. Then he shook his head. "I think he's just afraid of losing people. People *do* withdraw in this culture, and the culture makes it easy for them. But I think he's ridiculous to assume that you will, or that Brian will.

The fact that you're here with us is proof enough of that. And as for Brian—well, he *will* be coming with us to Amaterasu. Not staying here playing the squire.''

I looked at him in surprise. "He's coming?" I asked.

He regarded me levelly. "Yes," he said. "He hasn't told you?"

"No. I suppose we haven't talked about it. He's been making the arrangements, I've just been looking at the theories." I studied the manor, now beginning to loom above us as we approached, and then turned to al-Qatan. "Why?" I asked. "He's not a scientist, he's an administrator. And with larger talents than are needed to administrate a small project on a faraway world. So why is he coming?"

"Ask him," he said. Avoiding the answer.

We crossed the lake on an automated barge. Water lapped sunnily at the prow. I wondered how much of Hourigan's accusation was true. *Was* I some manner of parasite, playing God with my planet and species, gratifying my private fantasies while justifying them in the name of science? *That* charge was easy to dismiss; but there was still the other—that I had somehow crossed the boundary into a social senescence and that my actions had lost the ability to matter or to affect others in any meaningful way.

The centaurs, I thought. Their developing culture was my work, and it would be *they*, when they reached their own maturity, who would alter humankind. They were my justification, one that had seemed adequate until now. But Brian McGivern had scored me on that one: Now that their development was assured, they would make their changes with or without my help. Anything that I had left to give them would be redundant in the long run.

And so that left Project Knight's Move. Either it would change things forever or it would prove a pointless peregrination from star to star in search of the unknowable.

Myself, I was betting on the latter. And where did that leave me?

I didn't want to consider the question.

The ferryboat came to a gentle halt against a beach of coral-pink sand, and with al-Qatan I stepped out onto the shore. Walking toward McGivern's pale pleasure dome.

11

A few hours later they brought in the first dead robot. McGivern looked with concerned surprise at the corpse and reached out a tentative hand to touch the cock feather of the clothyard shaft that transfixed the machine's command center.

We were standing on one of the green grassy cloisters that stood in alternating contrast to the various rambles of his house. A group of gardening robots that had brought him the corpse stood about in disorderly confusion, like flustered mourners. McGivern dismissed them.

"Hourigan," I said. McGivern looked at me blankly. "He disapproves of your life-style," I explained. "He's engaged in social criticism by playing Robin Hood in your orchards. No doubt he mistook your robot for one of the king's foresters."

McGivern's eyes hardened. "There are security robots on the perimeter," he said. "If he runs into *those*, he could be in serious trouble." He stepped into one of the cloister walks, turned to a remote terminal of his estate comp, disguised as a recurring trefoil motif above the capitals of the cloister pillars, and gave it concise instructions to search for Hourigan via the sensors that looked after the gardens, weeds and woods; then it was to keep track of him and route away the robots in his proximity.

"Let's hope he doesn't start shooting at any of the guests," he added. "I have some here who might want to shoot back." And then he ordered a cigar from his humidor in the next room.

"I have logged an additional call from Dr. Zimmerman," the comp reported. "He says his business is urgent."

McGivern said nothing as he switched off. A robot brought his cigar. He took it and looked up at me before the robot struck a light and he bent to it. "There are some people here who want to meet you," he said. "Politicians, advisors, media people in mufti . . . the usual."

"After dinner," I promised.

He nodded, his attention on the end of his cigar. Then he puffed smoke and straightened. "I've logged a lot of calls from Zimmerman."

"Good."

"It's not really for me to answer them."

"I'll answer. When the time is right."

He nodded again. There was a silence. Smoke hung between us, a blue shroud. He had shown me his house, and I had admired it—genuinely admired it, in fact, not just politely. There were no outward reminders of the Old World manor: no suits of armor or strange wrought-iron bric-a-brac, certainly no family portraits. The architecture was conventional enough to prevent the guests from feeling uncomfortable but had enough surprises to keep the place from becoming dull. There was a lot of natural light coming through windows and skylights, with light-colored carpets, tapestries and tatami that reflected the sun and kept even the larger rooms from being oppressive.

There were works of art in every room, and McGivern

could afford the best—not always the tasteful stuff either, meant as adjuncts to the decoration rather than to provoke thought; some of it was satirical, and some meant to shock. I sensed a taste other than McGivern's there; his preferences had always been more conventional.

There were large suites for the guests, comfortable public rooms for their entertainment, a pool, a gym, a theater—everything necessary for comfortable living, in fact. There was a miniature version of the place out back—everything replicated on a more modest scale for occasions when McGivern was alone, or with a few guests. No sense of Antoinette in le Petit Trianon, dressed as a peasant and milking the cows to get back to nature. Hourigan might claim that the place was far too comfortable, that a sedentary man would find in it no reason ever to leave, but I wasn't afraid on that score. McGivern wasn't sedentary.

So I had walked around and admired the art pieces—where the hell had he got that Miró? I wondered. I thought I'd had them all locked up on Earth.

But now we stood in the cloister as he puffed smoke and regarded with flinty eyes the dead robot. He had run out of house, and I had run out of admiration.

"Dinner in another hour," he said. I nodded, wondering why he wasn't asking me about Hourigan and his theories. Perhaps he knew them. I took a breath.

"I hear you're coming with us," I said. "To Amaterasu."

"Yes." His tone was level, matter-of-fact. "If we . . . if you . . . can't find the answer here."

I looked at him steadily through the smoke pall. Both of us knew the question well enough; I didn't have to ask it. He shifted the cigar in his mouth and looked down at his feet, then up at me. Defiantly, it seemed.

"Because of Mary," he said. "She's a Diehard, and I'm not." His words were ice. There was an anger in them, perhaps at admitting the weakness with which a man of his type might regard love, perhaps an anger at something else I couldn't guess at. He gazed out at the robot corpse, blowing smoke.

"I don't want to lose her for those years, Doran," he said. "They may matter."

Meaning: She will die.

McGivern's admission was certainly not a surprise, not in light of what I had already seen. But still there was an odd tingling in my nerves.

"I understand," I said.

He gave a grunt of disgust and flicked the cigar out onto the sward. The anger in his voice was more apparent now. "I want her to live here with me, Doran. She won't do it."

"She's always done as she pleased, Brian," I said.

"Yes," he grated, and I understood his anger, directed as it was against his own hopelessness. He was accustomed to having things his way, and now he wasn't—a useful lesson to have from time to time, but a frustrating one.

"I wish you luck, Brian," I said. "Sincerely."

"Thank you," he replied.

I turned at a noise behind me and saw a couple enter the cloister, each ornamented by the colorful, insulating body paint they wore when swimming. They were presumably lovers; applying the paint to one's partner was considered an erotic art. They were laughing, and then they stopped short at the sight of the dead robot. Walking forward slowly, they looked at it as though it were one of McGivern's art exhibits: Prone Robot, with Arrow and Smoking Cigar. They glanced up and saw us.

"What happened?" the woman asked.

"One of the guests shot the robot," I said.

"Oh." She looked doubtful.

"As an act of social criticism."

"What bad taste," the man said. He nodded cheerfully to McGivern before they crossed the grass to the cloister gate.

I looked at McGivern. He was staring with stubborn, thin-lipped obstinacy at his ruined robot, tapping his fingertips absently on one of the gray cloister pillars. Then he shook his head. "Sorry, Doran," he said.

"No need to apologize."

He looked down and brushed his hands on his kilt. "I'd best look to some of my other guests," he said. He gave me a shaky grin. "They might be smashing up more robots." Lame, I thought, but game. McGivern was himself again, and there would be no more revelations.

"See you later," I said.

He gave me a nod and walked off. I watched him go, an erect and implacable figure, and I felt a touch of sorrow for him. The last thing he'd ever want from me, of course; he had always taken silent but obvious pride in his self-sufficiency, and this late discovery of his own weakness, his own capacity to care, must have come as a shock.

There was another shock, but this one was mine: He loved Mary more than I had. I would never have lived with her while she took eighty-odd years to die, but he would. It was something to think about.

He left the cloister and I turned to take a last look at the sward, the smoking cigar and forlorn robot, and then struck off in a random direction that proved to be a mistake. I encountered a number of people, dressed for some reason as oriental mandarins, who wished to prove their connections with the entertainment business by asking me what Angelique denThrush was really like. But they were seeking confirmation for their own opinions rather than genuinely wanting mine, and they spoke some kind of show-business shorthand in which I had no intention of staying on the planet long enough to acquire fluency. I escaped with the excuse of seeking a bathroom.

I found myself instead in a long gallery built of white stone, with an Italianate floor paved in black and white diamonds. To each side were a number of semi-private rooms, separated from the main corridor by screens and containing works of art and comfortable furniture. The effect was that of an expensive, private art gallery, which I suppose was what had been intended.

I found Mary standing in one of the rooms, her back to me as she regarded a thoroughly poisonous piece of sculpture that I had noticed earlier. It was of a mechanical man with the body of Michelangelo's David and glittering, cynical, thousand-year-old eyes, and when its sensors were triggered by the presence of someone in the room, it went into its act, strutting in a gross, insinuating parody of male sexuality, strutting mixed with lewd winks, machismo covered with lubricating oil and slime. It was at once grotesque, horrifying and effective; and McGivern had shown it to me with only one comment: "The man's works appreciate."

Mary was watching the statue's act in company with a tall blond man dressed in racing green, who watched in evident discomfort, his arms crossed defensively in front of him, his head cocked at a critical angle. A drift of cigarette smoke rose above his head.

"Hello," I said.

Mary turned with a smile and at once took my arm. For a moment I felt an hallucinatory moment of imbalance, an intuition that I had somehow stepped into my own past, and then I saw the more mature set of the face lines, the gray among the silver, the poise that had once been brashness.

She was firmly on two feet again, and although her neck muscles were still not strong, as witnessed by the padded brace she wore, it was now clear how great an injustice the hospital visit had perpetrated. There was no trace of the withdrawn old lady I'd seen there—this woman seemed closer akin to the vibrant girl I remembered—but something of the old lady's dignity remained, a style of physical presence, of moving through space, that hadn't yet existed, except in embryo, in the younger Mary I had known.

She was dressed in a long-sleeved blouse of a smoky color—padded at the shoulders as was the current fashion here, with bright jewels worked into the seam between sleeve and shoulder—with a long skirt of a darker velvet, and soft boots of some native suede. Her silver hair was worn long. The neck brace, from a distance, resembled a fancy collar. A green LED blinked at me from the gadget.

I had, since the visit to the hospital, become used to the idea of Mary as an old invalid, a misconception that put me a little off my stride. So did her greeting.

"Doran," she said, "I'd like you to meet my son, Alex."

I was accustomed to this kind of surprise from old friends, but still there was a hesitation between her words and the moment I stuck out my hand to have it shaken. "Pleased to meet you, Mr. Falkner," he said. It was obvious he'd taken the treatments; he looked twenty or so, but there were the usual signs—the ones I automatically looked for—that he was older. I guessed, from my knowledge of Mary's history and the fact that she'd spent the better part of the last two decades in a cold-box, that he was about thirty.

I looked at the statue. It was flexing its biceps and leering. "Not my type," I said.

Mary gave the statue a critical look. "I made Brian buy it," she said. "Thought it might do him some good." She gave a little laugh. "He's been a bachelor for so long, I thought it might alter his perspectives a bit, teach him to see certain aspects of the male character in a light he isn't used to."

"I didn't think it was his taste," I said. Nor had I ever noticed that he was prone to that sort of masculine strutting; but then I hadn't seen him through a woman's eyes either.

Mary's lips were cast in a slight Giaconda smile, as though the statue amused her. "He seems to want to accommodate me," she said. "He has this foolish notion that I might want to live here with him."

"A mistaken notion?" I asked. She narrowed her eyes slightly and gave her head a minute shake—not meaning, I assumed, that she wouldn't live with him, but rather that she didn't want to talk about it now.

We moved out of the room, thereby relieving us of the distraction of the insinuant marionette, and talked about Alex. He was headed in the direction of becoming an artist himself, his interest currently in holography, which he thought had been neglected because the techniques were so old-fashioned. He was studying at the academy, and I detected a hesitation in the way he spoke of his plans. A hesitation I suppose natural in someone who has to make the decision to try to make his living at something he has heretofore been playing at, and complicated by the problems arising from wondering whether, at the age of thirty, he has much to offer to a planet full of four-hundred-year-old sophisticates.

"I was thinking, actually, of studying on Earth," he said. I gave him the usual advice and tried to steer him away. Come to Earth, I suggested, but only after you have a career here. He seemed a little dismayed at not being able to use me as an excuse to put the decision off further and then politely excused himself to go look at the works elsewhere in the house.

"Poor Alex," Mary said. She still had my arm, and we walked down the gallery toward a carved wooden door. "I had him till he was twelve, and then his father took over. When I went to sleep."

"Pity the poor father," I said. "He had the worst of it, I'm sure. Those are difficult years."

She nodded agreement. "Alex and I are just becoming acquainted again. I think he's surprised that I'm not *older*, you know. Or younger. I can't decide which."

"He probably can't either," I said. She squeezed my arm and smiled. Then she sighed.

"I missed so much though," she said. "All those years . . . He's a stranger now. Polite, but there's no closeness there." She tossed her head. "Maybe I'll have another child. Not now, but after we come back from Amaterasu. Before it's too late. Biologically speaking."

"So you think we're going?"

She gave me an impudent grin. "You think there's a chance we're not? The answer is there, if it's anywhere. Hourigan and Muhammad never stopped working on Knight's Move, and they haven't found anything but dead ends in over forty years."

"I'd just as soon not go," I told her. "Quixotism isn't my style. More yours, I imagine."

She jabbed me in the ribs with her finger. "None of that, now," she said.

We reached the door and I opened it. Blinking at the strong sunlight, we stepped out onto a manicured lawn that rose slowly to a wooded horizon; we began to stroll upward.

"Tell me instead about that music you gave me," she said. "I've never heard anything like it."

"Ah. That music was made by a woman named Philodice. She has a way of reminding me of you."

"I've never heard anything like that voice," Mary repeated. "I scarcely remember enough Greek to make sense of the words, but I can't get the sound of it out of my head. Was her throat altered in some way? Or was the sound modified electronically?"

"The voice is natural," I said. "She was born with it. Perhaps I'll tell you the whole story later. It's a long one."

"Do you have any more tapes? I'd like to hear them."

"Yes. If you promise never to play them for anyone else." I looked down at her. She was pale, and she seemed to be making an effort to keep up with me. I slowed my pace. "Shouldn't you be sitting down?" I asked. "Aren't you tired?"

She gave me a mock scowl. "I'm going to hit the next person who asks me that. I'm perfectly fine, and it's only an excess of caution on the part of the doctors that I'm wearing the brace." She tugged at it self-consciously. "And it comes off for dinner tonight, come hell or high water," she said. Her voice had a cheerful defiance. "I'm not spending another night unable to bend over my plate."

I restrained my impulse to caution her. It was her neck. None of my business if she wanted to risk it.

We reached the top of the hill and turned to look down across the jumble of rooftops to the lake that fronted McGivern's house, and to the long wooded hill beyond. Mary seemed a little breathless, as though in spite of her determination she'd pushed herself too far. I squatted down on my haunches, hoping she'd imitate my example.

"I had a call from Jay Zimmerman yesterday," she said. "He said it was urgent."

"I'm not surprised."

"What are you going to do about him?"

"Get his data, by hook or by crook. He may have something we've missed, although I doubt it. But if it confirms our own, that's good enough."

She smoothed a place on the grass beside me and sat down. "I've never met him. What's he like?"

"Brilliant. Vain in a way that operatic tenors are supposed to be. He would be jealous of me, but his vanity won't let him. He used to be a ladies' man, but since he's become a recluse, I doubt that that still applies." I looked at her and shrugged. "I don't know if *any* of these judgments still apply. It's been centuries."

"He has a massive reputation. The work he did, following up on your discoveries, was fundamental."

"Application, not fundament," I said. She gave me a sharp glance and I wondered if I was not protesting overmuch. "Not new theory," I said. "He may have nothing to offer Knight's Move at all."

"None of us may," she said. Her tone strained for lightness but her eyes were clouded. She had already given much to Knight's Move—sharing the last eighteen or so years of her only child's life, for a start, and whatever other continuity she had been able to build in her time here. If the project succeeded, it would make her name, would serve to justify all the things she'd lost. If it failed, the years would be gone forever. She was not, like the rest of us, sacrificing a few decades of a life that was extended indefinitely; by her own choice, these were the only years she had.

Knight's Move represented the last great question in physics—the last one we knew about anyway—and the rest was simply filling in the corners. The last few centuries had seen the best minds move from questions of theoretical science to disciplines with more direct application; all the great discoveries had been in the biological sciences—genetic work, terraforming techniques, enhancing human adaptability to outworld environments and vacuum. Mary had always been ambitious, committed not only to winning the game of science, but to winning it on her own terms. She couldn't afford major mistakes; the time factors were too critical. If Knight's Move failed, she would be staring at a life, the only one she was allowing herself, spent in wandering down a dead corridor.

I reached out and took her hand. She gave me a brave smile. "Maybe I *am* overstrained," she admitted. "I never get morose unless I'm tired." She rose to her feet. "I think I'll take a nap until dinner. I'll see you then?"

"Of course."

"Good. You can tell me what Angelique denThrush is really like."

I winced. "Ouch." She tossed her hair and laughed.

I watched her as she went down the slope, her head carried at a proud angle. Not uncharacteristic, even if it was on account of the neck brace.

I rose and wandered along the ridge toward a grove that I suspected would encourage meditation. I looked down and saw three figures walking crouched, toward a part of the house that I recognized as the kitchen. The leader was in a doublet of Lincoln green and carried a longbow. The others were dressed in casual clothes and green body paint; each carried a quarterstaff cut from a sapling. Hourigan, I concluded, had won himself a pair of disciples.

They crept into the kitchen door. I knelt down and waited. A few minutes later they came out, moving rapidly, each with a bundle of swag over his shoulder. Laughter floated toward me over the sward.

Our dinner, I supposed. Our rations would be a bit shorter than anticipated. I waited till they were gone and then walked toward the grove.

Dinner, as it turned out, was not short; but it was somewhat limited. Hourigan had abducted the turkey, feathered porpoise, and lamb, but the kitchen staff—human, fortunately—had managed, at cleaver-point, to keep him from the rest and had substituted omelettes and various kinds of cheese pies for the missing courses. I sandwiched myself in between McGivern and al-Qatan so as to avoid questions about denThrush and managed to have a pleasant enough time.

Mary was cheerful, the brace gone, but the long, formal dinner seemed to strain her, and I noticed that she was rolling her head as though her neck were giving her trouble. After dessert she excused herself, and McGivern followed.

Neither returned. I spoke to McGivern's friends, as I had promised I would, and watched through the giant windowpanes the setting of Kemp's swollen sun. And wondered why I was longing to retire to my room and play the blues till morning.

12

The silver rectangle pulsed on its maze and spoke with Jay Zimmerman's voice. "Don't I get to see you, Jay?" I asked. "Are you deshabille, or what?"

"I simply prefer not to have people peering at me." There was a sulky note to the remembered suave baritone.

"As you like," I said. And then, propping my legs up on the bed in the room McGivern had loaned me, "I understand you called. Sorry I couldn't get back to you right away. We've been busy."

"Yes. Your comp has denied me data on the Knight's Move Project." Imperiously. "I'm certain it's a mistake."

"Not a mistake, Jay, I'm afraid."

"The progress of science depends on a free exchange of ideas!" Indignation. I wasn't sure how much of it was feigned. It sounded genuine to me.

"You don't mind if we *publish* them first, do you, Jay?" I asked. "If—just to make a hypothetical case—we have made a major discovery, it would be foolish in the extreme to allow the data to be released before we can process it and draw our conclusions as to how it might best be exploited. And it would be more than foolish to give our data to someone who has been uncooperative about showing us his own. I'm sure you understand."

There was a long, strange silence. The silver rectangle pulsed and began to flee down its corridors. I wondered how best to continue. I was visible to him, but in place of his image all I had was his sinister, hissing geometry. Had I been able to see him, I might have been able to intuit something from his body language. As it was, I'd just have to fly the wire.

"*I will not let you do this!*" To my astonishment, a baritone shriek. I leaned back in reaction to the volume. "*You are trying to make a fool out of me, and tampering with science besides!*"

"You are out of line, mister," I said, reaching forward and snapping the connection.

I leaned back again and thought for a moment. I had never seen Jay lose his temper before. I had seen him icy, distant and cutting, but outright anger was not his style. I also hadn't seen him in about four centuries. I realized I was no longer capable of knowing what his style was and what it wasn't.

I knew he was a recluse, and wealthy. When the Falkner Power Systems came on the market, he had been in a very good position to work out some of the implications of what the field could do, and he patented a number of FPS-powered gadgets, ranging from cooking ranges to abstruse devices through which one could investigate the nature of short-lived subatomic particles. His most useful discovery, of course, had been the fact that various light metal alloys, when placed in a Falkner field polarized in a certain direction, could be used to store energy, a discovery that led, after a few years of work, to the very efficient directional communicators that keep the various colonized worlds in touch with each other and with the starships that voyage between them.

He must have been over a century old before the Forever Now project revived his youth, and then of course
he'd emigrated. All of his earthly goods and most of his
portable wealth had to be left behind, but he was still
getting royalties on the Z-transmitter, and I knew he was
well off. His work I'd seen since remained highly theoretical.
I knew too that he'd been working on his private Knight's
Move Project for at least forty years, but he hadn't published any data for a decade or more. Nor, apparently, had
he so much as gone out of his house. He just left that
strange hissing image to discourage inquiries.

"I am registering a call from Dr. Zimmerman," the
comp said. It was built into a desk, the holographic projector built into the wall behind. "Do you wish to accept?"

I wondered for a moment if McGivern's comp had
actually developed a sense of irony or whether the tones I
heard in its voice were only in my imagination. "Tell him
I am not available," I said.

And decided to rejoin the party.

Which was in its third day. The second had been enlivened
by another raid from Robin Hood. He and his Merry Men
had kidnapped the mayor of Kemp's second-largest city,
demanding as a ransom that McGivern instruct his robots
to pick vast numbers of white flowers from out of the
greenhouses and arrange them to spell ANARCHY in thirty-
foot letters on the slope in front of the house. The mayor
was returned unharmed, having apparently enjoyed his
sojourn in the greenwood and his picnic on the remains of
the previous night's stolen dinner. The rest of the day I
spent in trying to talk about Knight's Move to the movers
and shakers, who were far more interested in finding out
what Angelique denThrush was really like.

In addition to the shakers' weakness for gossip, my
problem was the usual one of trying to explain how science was done to people who had never done it themselves.
Their picture was usually that of Young Tom Edison alone

in his lab, or Albert Einstein working out relativity while canceling letters in the post office in Switzerland, or Doran Falkner jotting down ways of entering other universes while working the graveyard shift in Los Alamos. I had to tell them these were atypical examples and that science was much more like a team sport.

And furthermore, a team sport best played without a captain. The bureaucrats and politicians felt uncomfortable unless they could impose an organizational structure on what was essentially a chaotic activity. Abstruse, theoretical disciplines such as physics were likely to attract a lot of wild, bright, creative talents whose eccentric habits of thought and work tended to be constricted by organizational pigeonholes. The best way of "leading" them was to let them go their own way and make certain they knew there was help available if they got stuck.

But the politicians generally insisted on having teams complete with "team leaders" who were supposed to direct activity. Knight's Move had been saddled with three physics teams, led by Mary, Hourigan and al-Qatan, who had been chosen for the honor by virtue of their scientific prominence—the politicians had heard of them and were therefore willing to grant them authority.

Their duties consisted of being responsible for signing a lot of forms and formal proposals—which took time away from the actual science, of course—and of having to make routine decisions about who would use the equipment in what order, that sort of thing. I had been offered a team but refused it—my prominence made that refusal possible—and so I'd been shoehorned into the table of organization by having been made a sort of free-floating eminence grise who could table-hop from one team to another, working on whatever interested me and generally providing coordination.

The current problem was not so much organizational— that had been settled—but that of acquiring the commitment of one of Kemp's few stellar-capable ships for what might prove to be a many-years-long fool's errand. They had already had a survey crew on the planet for years, tying up a ship for all that time, and were reluctant to commit to another survey for an even more indefinite period. With a little help from McGivern, I finally convinced them. I think I deserved a medal.

I hadn't seen much of McGivern or Mary; the former was playing host, the latter spending as much time with Alex as possible. I retired early and decided, more from boredom than anything else, to call Zimmerman early the next day.

After breakfast, still contemplating the wisdom of that decision, I changed into a pair of shorts and ran around the lake three times, then jumped into the bright waters, swam across and emerged dripping to find Mary advancing toward me. She was in a dark-blue sleeveless outfit that complemented her silver hair and fair coloring, and she wore a pair of self-polarizing spectacles that obscured her eyes. "I just had the most appalling call from Jay Zimmerman," she said. "I was still refusing calls, as you asked me to, but comp relayed a message."

I shook water out of my eyes. "Yes?" I said.

"He was very strange," she said. "He spent half the time complimenting me on my work. He actually knew it, or at least he mentioned a few publications. He was very smooth—I wonder if 'oleaginous' might be the right word? —but his insincerity was showing. Then for the rest of the message he denounced you as a tyrant intent on depriving him of the information necessary for his work."

"Oh." I brushed water from my shoulders, and we walked along the bank of the lake as I told her about my own brief encounter with my former boss. She listened in silence, then nodded—to herself more than to me—and asked, "What will you do now?"

I shrugged. "Accept his apology, I suppose," I said. "If he ever offers one."

"And if he doesn't?"

"How badly do you think we need his data?"

She pursed her lips and turned her eyes to the woods ahead. "It would be valuable, I suppose, just to confirm our own. It would be better to have it than not. But he doesn't have any startling answers. If he had, we'd have known about them."

"That's my feeling," I said, faintly relieved that someone agreed with me. "If Zimmerman doesn't show any sign of wanting to deal with me, I'll just let McGivern talk to him—or you, perhaps." She gave me a startled look. "He *has* expressed his admiration for your work," I said.

"However oleaginously," she smiled.

"Possibly he fancies you," I said. "He always was a ladies' man."

"Thank you very much," Mary laughed. "If I ever need a pimp, I'll call on you."

"It's in the cause of science, after all."

"That's a good oleaginous grin you have," Mary said. "I'd forgotten how good."

I took her hand. Naked people in bright paint cavorted around us like something out of an old avant-garde film. We moved away, as though by instinct, in the direction of shade. Mary was looking pensive.

"Alex?" I asked. She gave a brief nod. Her eyes were clouded through her spectacles. Then she gave an exasperated sigh and spoke.

"Just the way we can't seem to talk easily anymore. How we can talk about everything but what matters." She shook her head, disengaged her hand from mine and crossed her arms defensively in front of her, rubbing her upper arms with her palms.

"That's parenthood, you know," I said. "If you'd had

as many as I've had, you wouldn't be nearly as anxious.'' I gave her a smile.

"The point is, I have only the one. And he's defensive because I left him when he was young, and that will be between us forever. Because he can't trust me again. And because I can't blame him.''

"Sorry,'' I said, and then, since what I'd just said was so lame, I told her about my son who'd killed himself and how I had to stop for a moment to remember which one it was; and then, later, how the various guilts began to wash down, first because he'd killed himself and then because I hadn't remembered him, each guilt carrying its decades of compound interest. By the end of that conversation we were both depressed, and we had left the lake and were wandering among the elevator trees.

"Have you ever been in an elevator?'' Mary asked. I said I had not. We sat down on the outer layer of one of the lower looping boughs—once again "bark" didn't seem to be the right word—and then the world began to sink beneath us as the tree mistook us for a weighty parasite-eating omnivore that dwelt native on Kemp's. We rose, with slow grace, into the canopy. There were perfumed flowers up there, delicate scarlet and white trumpets lying among coils of leaves that looked as though they had been anointed with butter. Insects hummed and a light breeze ruffled the foliage. Mary squinted up into the leaf-dappled sunlight. Then she rubbed her upper arms again, as though chilled, and sighed.

"I hope that all of acquiring maturity isn't just discovering one's limitations,'' she said.

"No. One finds strength too.''

"I thought I could do everything. I seem to have been wrong.'' She gave me a quick glance, as though aware that she was dramatizing.

I knew that if I said anything it would be at least as fatuous as anything else I'd said that day, so I said nothing.

"Shit," she said. "It gets harder to be genuine about these things. So many layers of self-knowledge in the way."

"So have another child. That seems genuine enough."

She gave a too-precise smile and didn't answer. Instead she turned around on the limb and began to scratch the bole of the elevator. "It can sense parasites here, under the dermis," she said. "It wants us to eat them. I wish I'd thought to bring a pocketknife. We could look for them."

"It doesn't mind us cutting into it?"

"The current line of thought is that it can't feel pain. Other kinds of discomfort, yes."

Mary scratched for a while and I watched her. Her spectacles had cleared now that we were in the shade and I could see her eyes, bright and intent, though not, I suspected, on the tree. Finally she dropped her hands and looked at me ruefully.

"I don't want to have a child just to relieve my crisis of competence, okay?" she said and then gave a self-conscious laugh. "Besides, it wasn't a huge success the first time. There just doesn't seem to be enough time in the day. Not to do it right, anyway."

"You could fix that," I said.

Her gaze grew hard. She focused on some distant spot over my left shoulder and gave her head a frigid shake.

"Don't," she said.

"If you insist."

There was a moment of stony silence. Then Mary turned her uneasy gaze to the green bole and reached out to touch it. "Sorry," she said.

"Perfectly all right."

"I just don't want old wounds opened."

"Fair enough."

She dropped her hand and turned to face outward, into the sunny glade. Birds flitted among the trees, dropping swallowlike for insects. "The thing is," she said, "I *like* getting older. I like changing, testing myself. Knowing that every day matters. It makes for . . . interesting tensions. Interesting kinds of self-knowledge. Spiritual sloth is so much harder to acquire.''

She sighed, rearranging herself on the limb. "I don't like the way people think they can have their cake and eat it." There was a bright anger in her words. "It's like those old blues you used to sing. *Everybody wants to go to heaven, but nobody wants to die.*"

"Don Nix," I said.

Mary nodded. "That's the one."

"And I am spiritually slothful?" I asked.

She cocked her head and studied me. "Less than most," she answered. "But, yes, you are. You try very hard to be constructive, but it's a dream you're living in. Rebuilding temples in Greece and trying to sing the blues like John Lee Hooker. It's not so much that the dreams are unworthy but that you've chosen them in lieu of any other way to occupy your time. Your dreams lack conviction because it doesn't really matter whether you ever finish the project or not, because you'll always be here to tinker with it. Just like Brian. Like Zimmerman. Like so many others."

"I've heard the same speech from Hourigan."

She smiled softly. "We're friends," she said.

"You think we're denying death."

"Denying reality, at any rate." She looked down and swung her legs in the air below the limb. "Death is reality, you know. One knows one's self better for facing it." She tossed back her head and sang, a clear, sweet soprano: "*How can I not tremble when I look him in the face? How can I not know my heart when it thunders so loudly?*" Philodice's lyric. Mary remembered more Greek than she was letting on.

Fear put a cold finger on my nape. "That was sung about a lover," I said. "It was a song of joy, not extinction."

"Perhaps I love my mortality, Doran," Mary said. She gave me a brief, self-mocking grin. "Not to be overly dramatic about it," she added.

"We know this certainly: Death is an evil, for if it were a good, the gods would die," I said, quoting Sappho; but Mary swung her legs in the void and said nothing.

"I can give you the English for it if you like," I said.

"I understood," she said quietly. Then she shook herself, as though heaving off the subject, and looked at me with a smile that was costing her a certain amount of effort.

"So," she asked, "you think I should have another kid?"

I held up my hands in protest. "Hey," I said, "all I did was ask. You brought it up, not me."

"Better get your opinion in before I'm too old." Grinning wickedly. "I'm fading fast."

"I don't know," I said. "Who are you planning for the father? Brian?"

Her grin faded, a cloud crossing the sun. She shook her head slowly. "Not Brian," she replied. "It would give him—I know this sounds calculating, but I don't know how else to say it—it would give him too much of a hold on me."

"And you don't want to be held?"

She shook her head again, minutely, with a flick of the chin and eyes. "I don't want to owe him anything."

She frowned into space for a moment, then stretched her body uneasily as though in reflection of a mental discomfort. "I don't want him to owe me anything either," she said. Her voice was sober. "We both know that what we have is not forever, that the choices I've made won't allow that. But Brian wants to pretend that we have all the time in creation, and I won't pretend with him." Awkwardly, she smiled at me. "He built this damn place for me, you know. Kept asking me my opinions on the design, on the decoration. Where to put the house, where to put the lake.

He pretended it was his own dream, something he'd always wanted. I knew better. He'd always lived in little cluttered apartments—Brian McGivern, one of the richest men in history."

"I know," I said. "He was just too busy to put down roots. Used to talk about living out of a suitcase. Boasting, in a way."

Mary raised one leg and put a heel on the bough and then put her fists on the knee and leaned forward to rest her chin on her thumbs. I remembered the gesture from long ago and I felt my nerves tingle. Her voice was muffled, covering whatever she was feeling. "I love him very much," she said. "I love him too much to let him build a world around me. What happens when I die and his world comes apart?" Her voice turned to anger. "I hate this place. I wish he hadn't built it."

"Maybe he wants something to remember you by," I said.

Her voice still had traces of its anger, but now there was sorrow in it too. "I don't want that either. If I'm remembered at all, I want to be remembered by the people I've touched, not by . . ." She waved her arm at the elevator trees, the house beyond, the river and its painted people. "Not by institutions," she said sadly.

"Or by an institutional fantasy," I offered. She nodded and swallowed hard.

"It's harder for him than it is for you," I said. "He's never been vulnerable in this way before."

"Yes. I know he hurts. And I know it's me that's hurting him, and I don't want to do it. But the only other way is to let him destroy what I am, and I won't allow it." She nodded, as though confirming a decision to herself, and then straightened briskly.

"So," I said. "No children by Brian."

"No," she said. "If he wants kids, he's got plenty of opportunities." She gave me a look. "He has other women.

He's nice enough not to invite them here, although I don't
suppose I'd care if he did . . . at least I don't *think* I'd
care. And I have—have *had*—'' She corrected her tense
with a kind of intent precision. ''—have had other men.''

She was gazing at me in a way that made me think I
should look away. I didn't. I thought about Philodice's
lyric, and Sappho's, and what I shouldn't know but did. In
the end it was Mary who looked away.

"Thank you for listening," she said, far too quickly.
"We should go back to the party."

She reached above her head and began plucking at the
flowers, scattering bright petals on the breeze, and when
the tree's slow nervous system began to perceive the attack,
the bough began its descent. In silence I watched the
ground rise and then I took Mary in my arms and kissed
her. Her eyes were wide and startled but the kiss had an
eroticism that was at least half hers. Her gown brushed my
bare chest, warmly. Her lips had a taste of trumpet flowers
and sweet breath and incipient lunacy. We neared the
ground and, gently, she disengaged. We landed with a
quiet rustle amid a scatter of wounded blossoms.

"How can I not—" She stammered and looked down,
self-conscious. She put a hand over her heart and sighed.
"I wish I didn't know," she said.

I raised her chin and kissed her again. This time her
arms went around me and the kiss lasted for a long time.
There was a rustling, as of an animal in the bushes, and I
broke away and looked around, uneasy. When I didn't see
anything, I kissed her again, but she kissed me only briefly
and then put her head on my shoulder.

"I don't want to have to feel guilty about this," she
said.

"You shouldn't have to."

"But I do." She leaned back and looked at me frankly.
"You don't mind if I think about this for a while, do
you?" she asked.

"What we *think* is not the issue," I said.

"I know." We looked at each other for another dappled moment of silent eroticism, but I heard the bushes rustle again and turned to see the tall, dark man in the green tights rise from cover.

"Yoicks," said Hourigan and fired his longbow. The clothyard shaft struck the bole of the tree two feet over our heads. It vibrated there forever, a deep, wooden, bass twang, and as I watched in shock, Hourigan turned and fled into the forest.

Mary recovered first, and she reached out to take my hand with both of hers. Her grip was fierce.

"Oh, my dear," she said with sad-voiced logic, "we're going to hurt people, you know."

"I know," I said.

I knew. And I said it again as her fingers twined around mine.

"I know."

13

We didn't say much on our way back to McGivern's house. After a restrained good-bye I went to my room to change, wanting only to throw on some clothes, call a car and leave McGivern's Xanadu behind. Head for a place that was built for some clean commercial purpose, say a hotel, and not a strange, sad and unfulfillable dream. In some odd piece of emotional chemistry, love and sadness had turned to anger; I was fed up with myself and everybody else and, frustratingly, I was still lustful besides. I felt a strange nostalgia for Angelique denThrush. At least when you're on a journey with someone who wants to exchange sex for publicity, you know where the car is headed.

I was buttoning my shirt when McGivern's comp told me that it was receiving a call from a Dr. Zimmerman. "I'll take it," I snapped, still full of resentment, and when the floating silver rectangle appeared in its three-dimensional jungle, I laughed in its stream-colored face.

"Come off it, Jay," I snarled. "Face me or get the hell away. It's been a rotten morning."

"I'm sorry for what I said, Doran." The voice had a

kind of stiff dignity to it, but with an undercurrent of mastered emotion. He sounded like a drunk just over a crying jag. The tone surprised me, so I stopped what I was doing and stared.

"What I said was uncalled for," Zimmerman went on. "I hope you will . . . forgive." He began to speak in a rush again, with odd breaks in his voice as though the emotion he had mastered was cracking through his defenses. "I'm not used to dealing with people, you see. I hope . . . I live alone, you know. I hope you can understand."

"Your apology is accepted."

His relief was apparent immediately. His voice returned to something approaching normality. "Perhaps—perhaps we can arrange for an exchange of data," he said. "I would be pleased to meet with you all. At your convenience. For a discussion." His voice brightened. "Maybe you can come to my house. I have plenty of room. You can stay a night or two. And we can look at the data, and talk. This week, if you like."

"I don't know what the others have planned," I said, "but my schedule is clear. I'll ask them."

Zimmerman's voice brightened even more. "That will be nice, Doran."

"One thing, Jay," I said.

"Yes?"

"How do we know that when we get to your house, the gates won't be slammed in our face?"

There was a long, surprised silence. His voice, when it came, was hesitant again, contrite. "I wouldn't do that, Doran," he said. "Never."

"I want to know that the gates will be open, Jay," I persisted. "I want to see your face. Not this abstract rubbish you've been keeping between yourself and the rest of the world."

There was another long silence. Then a somber voice:

"Very well, Doran. If you insist. If you really can't trust me."

The maze faded and I saw Zimmerman's head and shoulders. I absorbed for a moment the thing that, alone in his house, he had become, and then I gave a slow nod.

"All right, Jay," I said. "This week. If the others agree."

14

I approached Hourigan's aircraft early the next morning. Flutterbats spiraled high above the sward, riding the thermals into the violet sky. I could see Hourigan's silhouette behind the windscreen, sitting in the pilot's seat. I walked up close and saw he was no longer wearing his Robin Hood suit. He was staring forward expressionlessly, his hands limp on the controls. I peered in the window for a moment, craning my neck to see behind him.

"Looking for something, Doc?" he asked. Lightly, the way people speak when they are trying, a little too obviously, not to talk about a difficult subject.

I opened the door. "To see if your bow is unstrung," I said.

He glanced at me for half a second, then faced forward again. "Where's Muhammad?" he asked.

"He left yesterday to organize some of our data. We have a meeting with Jay Zimmerman tomorrow morning, and we're meeting first in my conference suite at eight. I just stopped by to tell you."

"Thanks," he said. He looked at me again. His face was trying hard to stay emotionless but the strain showed.

"You're not flying out with me?" he asked.

"I bought my own fieldcar. They delivered it last night." There was a moment of strained silence. "Besides," I said, "I have this feeling that you have yet to resolve certain feelings of hostility you may bear toward me, and I would prefer not to be in a fragile atmosphere craft while you work it all out."

Nervously he turned his glance to his hands, grasping the controls. Gradually his fingers loosened their grip and then his hands fell wearily into his lap.

"Oh, hell, Doran," he sighed. "I'm sorry I shot the arrow at you. I didn't mean it in a hostile way."

"A three-foot-long hunting arrow winged a few inches over my nose is hard to interpret as anything *but* hostile."

He shook his head briefly, more to himself than to me. "I meant it as a kind of warning," he said. "I wanted you to stop and think about what sorts of danger you might be involving yourself in." He shrugged. "There was probably anger too. The thing is . . . I care about how this turns out." He turned to me with a half-apologetic smile. "I care about Mary. A lot. She seems to be the only person I know who lives the ethic that she preaches."

"All Diehards do," I said. "By definition."

"Yes. But most of them are fanatics, and Mary's not. She's not sick in some obvious way, hating herself, hating others, punishing herself or them by deciding to die. She's not so narrow that she can see only one path. She isn't out to convert the world to her point of view. Her principles, her views—they're all personal, and she doesn't pretend they apply to anyone else. I admire what she is, and I don't want her to be put in a situation where her beliefs might have to be compromised."

"You're giving me a lot more credit than I deserve," I said. "Mary and I were lovers for three years, you know.

She didn't change her ideas then. Why should she change them now?''

"She's very vulnerable now," he said.

"Too vulnerable to safely fall in love with cynical old Doran Falkner?" I asked. He was silent.

I closed the door and turned away. The alternative would have been to get angry at his damned assumption of sole virtue in this business, and that wouldn't have done anyone any good over the long run.

McGivern and Mary had left, together, earlier in the morning, and I hadn't anyone to say good-bye to. I had a robot deliver my luggage to my new car. I turned on the field and made a long, bulletlike transit to the Northern Hemisphere. There was a personal call I had to make.

I found the old spire easily enough, a pillar of twisted metal set in a foundation of native granite chopped from the mountains that formed a backdrop to the monument. It was winter in the Northern Hemisphere and the cold wind came down off the blue peaks to the east, whipping across the brown grass, stirring the crusty snow crystals that drifted in the lee of the monument. This was where K.C. Kemp had died and given his name to the planet.

We had been surveying the newly discovered planet at the time. Some of the surveys were being made from lighter-than-air craft, not powered by a Falkner field because the field tended to interfere with some of the survey instruments. K.C. was a good pilot but that fact didn't help him, or his crew of three, when a cold front coming west from the mountains met a warm front coming east from across the plains and squashed his dirigible between them like a bug between a pair of bricks.

K.C. stayed at the controls as they turned mushy and died, playing a losing balancing act with his dwindling supplies of ballast, keeping the dirigible on an even keel as the girders moaned and bent like straws, as the gasbags burst and vented their helium to the sky. He held on long enough for his crew to get to the lifeboats and speed away on their buoyant fields. The three survivors, hovering near the disaster and helpless to intervene, then watched in horror as the dirigible folded up like a paper bag and dropped to the plains.

His body was found near the lifeboats; he'd tried to run for it in the end but had been cut in half by a guy wire that snapped under the strain.

K.C. Kemp was from somewhere in Montana and he'd been raised on a ranch that was dying by inches, the shadow of the bank growing larger with each passing day, the ranch's insolvency moving slowly toward the inevitable point where the bankers could no longer ignore it. K.C. spent his formative years in pickups and bars and in the saddles of cutting horses, riding the long lines of bobwire and gazing up at the snowstorms that swept down from the Rockies, calculating the number of calves the snow would kill, the amount of liquidity dribbling from his father's fingertips. The life was hard and bleak and— everyone knew it—futile. In the end the bank came and took the ranch away and K.C. ended up using his talents on the local rescue squad, spending long hours looking for crashed planes, lost skiers, pickup trucks bogged down on mountain roads, cowboys caught in storms too far from their line shacks, swooping from the sky to the salvation of Montana's strays, bringing the rescue his own family had been denied. He learned to fly a helicopter and fly it well. When the Falkner sleds came along, they made the job too easy, he told me.

He had a sunburned face so improbably homely that it drew women as mere good looks never could. An adventurous streak in his makeup caused him to apply for the first ship to the stars, and his survival talents recommended him highly. During the course of the training he and I became friends.

When he died, he was also my wife's first lover—or at

any rate, the first I found out about. Madeleine was one of his crew on the day he died, and she had watched as the wreckage fell to the bleak prairie.

I remember my reaction to the tragedy; it had been one of immense relief. I hadn't known how to deal with what was happening to my marriage, and I thought that with K.C. out of the picture, things might return to the way they had been at the beginning.

I named the planet after him, gave the eulogy and ordered the construction of the monument over his grave—a piece of the twisted wreckage set in stone—and all the while I was breathing easier than I had in months. There was guilt at my feelings on the death of a friend, of course, but relief was paramount—relief and a kind of quiet feeling of superiority that I had been so civilized about the whole thing, so forgiving toward Madeleine, so completely, utterly understanding. She was struggling with her own guilt, with an irrational but entirely real feeling that she was somehow responsible for the whole tragedy; she felt that if K.C. hadn't loved her, she wouldn't have found a way to be aboard and that if he hadn't tried to save her, he might have made his own escape. I told her that I understood and forgave.

Well. I was young, and it was my first marriage. I didn't known then that while love can grow or die or swallow itself in indifference, it can never return to what had been. My compassion was a sham, as was her repentance; and in the end K.C.'s ghost was too strong for us. Had he lived, the affair might have run its course and come to a natural end; dead, he always stood between us, a weatherbeaten figure of memory and friendship, guilt and passion, all the various kinds of caring that had gone wrong and tangled themselves into a snarled and hopeless sadness. Once a friend and lover, he became a symbol of everything that had gone wrong with our dream.

I had no idea of where Madeleine was these days. We'd

had no children to help us keep in touch and I hadn't seen her after those first few months of our return to Earth.

But K.C. Kemp hadn't moved. He was still here, under his jagged spire, on land eerily similar to where he was born—the high, cold, brown winter prairie with the vast, awesome bulk of the mountains on the horizon, all deep clefts of azure and bright fields of gleaming snow.

The general tendency was to call the planet Kemps now, forgetting the possessive that marked it as someone's grave and monument. To me it would always remain Kemp's.

I lowered my car to the ground, turned off the field and walked through the crusty drifts of snow to the old pillar. The cold pinched my face and my breath frosted in front of me. Standing in front of the monument with my hands in my pockets, I wondered what I could say. This was a place where various kinds of hope had fought a losing battle with various kinds of folly, and then I had come along and, with the best of intentions and the worst of hypocrisy, built a monument to it. I hoped that K.C., who understood most kinds of irony, had forgiven me from his little corner of a foreign field that was forever Montana.

I looked up at the monument and shuffled my feet and said nothing. I had come to pay my respects to the kind of man and fool K.C. had been, and to the kind of man I used to be before I thought of new ways to be manly and foolish; but now that I was here, the thing that seemed to impress itself on me was the pointlessness of the whole journey. Hell, I thought, K.C. surely didn't care; Madeleine hadn't left any flowers on the grave that I could see; and I was more aware of my frozen nose and feet than I was of any emotion other than sadness and regret.

And then I realized why I'd really come. The weathered old girder was another reminder, more personal and less alarming than Hourigan's arrow, that unless a renewed love has greater impetus behind it than simple nostalgia, one is walking on dangerous ground indeed. "We're going to hurt people,'' Mary had said, and I'd known that; but the worst thing would be to hurt them in the name of memory, in the name of things that had once been but were no longer.

I wondered how much of what we had was real and how much was just a longing for what we'd once had? I stared up at the twisted girder and found no answer.

Nothing but a certainty, building inside me, that it was entirely too late for this. We were going to hurt our friends, and very likely each other, and quite possibly nothing would ever come of it *but* the hurt—yet we were going to do it anyway, and nothing was going to stop it.

The cold finally drove me away. As I left I heard the sound of the wind carrying as it gusted over the monument, and in it I heard Kassandra's cries of woe, fated as always to be ignored. I wished I had thought to bring some flowers from McGivern's greenhouses, to lay on the grave in memory of a lesson that hadn't been learned.

15

Jay Zimmerman's house sprawled in a series of zigzags up the side of a steep hill in a semitropical area near Kemp's equator. It looked like a Mayan step-pyramid of which only a portion had been cleared of vines and jungle, revealing something of the builder's intention but still somehow incomplete. It was a baroque mixture of architectural styles, one piled atop another in no particular order, a fact that only increased the sense of incompleteness.

Inside, it was spotless, furnished in a restrained, tasteful, cold fashion, with an emphasis on function taking precedence over anything that might display warmth; it was as though there were a reluctance on the part of Zimmerman, or whoever had supervised the decoration, to demonstrate any individual taste, any hint of personality. The place was like a hotel.

And as in a hotel, the house hummed with lives outside one's own ken, with the elusiveness of the other temporary tenants with whom one shared the coincidence of a particular space and time and nothing else. Usual enough in a hotel, but strange here. I kept thinking of the symbol

Zimmerman had used, the odd silver geometry twisting down the dark, ambiguous corridors . . . it had moved with the same hum, the same muttering, distant hiss, as of a life lived outside the scope of human vision. The pulse beat of the creature at the heart of the labyrinth.

I thought of the face I had seen on my vid display, the strange look in its eyes, defiance mixed with a plea for understanding. At the heart of the labyrinth, I knew, there was no monster. There was, instead, something very sad.

He had not come forward to welcome us. I was not particularly surprised. His comp housekeeper, displaying a middle-aged female voice, told us he was compiling some data and would meet us at dinner. In the meantime, the comp said, we were to make ourselves at home, and it showed us to our rooms. They were as cold and functional as the rest of the place. I began to wonder what Zimmerman's own rooms were like, whether they showed any trace of personality.

There had not been much conversation on the journey to Zimmerman's house. Hourigan, al-Qatan and Mary had arrived early and we each had said good morning, had a cup of coffee while talking over our presentation and then left in my car. McGivern wasn't along because the meeting was allegedly concerned with pure science and for this his talents would not be required.

Mary seemed careful not to look at me when anyone else might read something into it. Hourigan wasn't looking at me at all. Al-Qatan was trying to pretend he didn't notice the tensions that were hovering in the air. All of us tried to be brisk and businesslike, and our smiles were as phony as if they had been cut from magazines and glued on our faces.

"Shall I unpack, sir?" the robot asked. It was a custom-built machine, waist-high, rather squat and with four arms that seemed overly powerful for the task of moving my bags. It was, I suspected, built for moving heavy objects in Zimmerman's laboratory and not intended for the role of valet into which it had been pressed.

"I'll do that myself," I said. "Thank you."

"Call comp if you need me, sir," the robot said and moved out on softly sighing tires.

I studied the bleak room for a moment and then returned to the corridor. Al-Qatan was across from me, Hourigan one door down, Mary two doors in the other direction and across. I went to her door, performing a little knight's move in the corridor, but before I could knock, the book slid open to permit the exit of the robot that had been carrying her bags. I glanced up in time to see Mary's cautious look as she came to the door. She was wearing a businesslike gray jacket over a dark skirt and her long hair was tied back. The room behind her was equipped like a living room. Apparently she'd been given a two-room suite, while I had a single room with bed and bath. She leaned out of the doorway to watch the robot recede and then spoke in a lowered voice as though she didn't want it to hear.

"Do you find this place as creepy as I do?"

"Yes," I replied. "Can I kiss you now, or do we have to wait for the robot to turn the corridor?"

The corners of her mouth turned up in a wry grin and she stood on tiptoe to give me a sisterly peck on the cheek; then she raised a hand to pat me on the shoulder, as one would a horse. "Sorry," she said. "I don't find this place romantic."

"Romance is where you make it."

She turned to view the room. "Aren't those paintings awful?" she asked. "I think they were chosen because their colors complement the room. Can't think of any other reason."

"My room is the same. Hotel art. But at least he gave you a suite."

She turned back to me, her eyes grave. "I talked to Hourigan," she said. "He apologized."

"He apologized to me too, although in my case he didn't seem to mean it." I glanced down the corridor in the direction of Hourigan's door. "I think he's taking a proprietary interest in you," I said. "He told me I was in danger of corrupting you."

Her eyes narrowed and I saw a flash of resentment. She crossed her arms, defiantly, and leaned against the door frame. "Yes," she said. "That seems to be his attitude."

"I considered telling him it wasn't any of his business. But I wasn't entirely sure."

Mary looked up at me in surprise. "Sure of what?" she asked.

"That it wasn't his business."

Anger flushed her features for a swift moment, her body stiffening. She glared at me. "It isn't," she said. And then she looked down with a frown and shook her head as though to clear it of anger, her body visibly relaxing. "Sorry," she said. "I'm overreacting."

"I could have phrased it more tactfully," I said, "but it seemed important to know."

She shook her head again, about to say something, but then a door opened in the corridor and we both jumped like guilty children. It was al-Qatan, coming toward us with a smile flashing whitely from underneath his curly beard.

"A strange place, isn't it?" he said. "I wonder where the doctor is hiding his accelerators."

"Ask comp to show you a map," I suggested.

Al-Qatan shrugged. "Jay's probably working with them, don't you think?"

"Not if he's just compiling data," I answered. "All he'll need is a comp terminal someplace." Another door opened and Hourigan stepped out, followed by a robot.

"I thought I heard voices," he said. He too was speaking in a lowered voice, intimidated by the whispering totality of the place. He flashed a nervous grin. "Can anyone tell me why this house makes me want to write on the walls?"

"We were thinking of looking for the accelerators," Mary said, "but I think I'd like coffee first."

"We can ask comp from the guest parlor," al-Qatan said. There were murmurs of agreement.

Mary took my arm as we walked down the corridor. A declaration. Behind us, as we walked, we heard only the sound of footsteps. No voices at all.

The guest parlor was a subdued, murmuring little cavern, all dark walls and uncomfortable indigo furniture of some artificial implastic substance, tall mirrors that might have served to lighten the place had there been anything light to reflect. I looked around and saw no obvious comp terminal.

"House?" I asked. "Are you here?"

"Yes, Mr. Falkner. You may call me Dorcas, if you wish." The voice seemed to be coming from the mirrors, all of them at once.

I felt something trying to claw its way out of a deep part of my mind, but it failed on the brink and I spoke on. "Dorcas, Dr. Liddell and I would like some coffee. Mine black, Dr. Liddell's with cream."

"Certainly, Mr. Falkner. Would Doctors al-Qatan and Hourigan like anything?"

"Coffee. Black," said Hourigan.

"Cold scupir, please," al-Qatan said. "Very strong." He was looking with distasteful surprise into one of the mirrors.

"Would you like something to eat along with your drinks?" asked the house. "Biscuits, sweets?"

Our eyes flicked one to the other. "I guess not, Dorcas," I said. "Thank you."

"Your beverages will be delivered shortly. Please call if you need anything else."

"We would like to visit the accelerators and laboratories, if that's possible," I said.

"I will ask. One moment, please."

Al-Qatan turned with a scowl and spoke in a lowered voice. He was as infected as the rest of us. "Were any of you looking into the mirrors? It was there, in hologram. You know—the rectangle in the maze."

"In *all* of them?" Mary asked.

Al-Qatan nodded. I walked to the nearest mirror and looked into it, seeing a murky reflection of myself. And then my image shifted, melted, and turned into the silver polygon, flowing with rapid, near-indetectable colors, spinning with smooth swiftness down its course. "You are welcome to inspect the accelerators at any time, Mr. Falkner," the vision said. "Would you like directions?"

"Yes," I replied.

The maze blurred, changed color and turned into a schematic map. The silver rectangle shrank and became a cursor, moving along the corridors to the control room for the accelerators. "I will alter my lighting to a bluish color along the correct route," the mirror said, "so that you will be sure to find your way."

"Thank you, Dorcas."

And then I was staring at my reflection again as the mirror polarized back to normal. To myself I looked disturbed, as though I were a werecomp returning to its human form.

"Well," I said.

Mary came over and touched me on the arm. I looked at the reflection of her dark eyes. "I don't normally think about a household comp," she said. "It's just there, a tool in the background, like a wrench or a coffeepot. Why do I think about this one so much?"

"Because it's all we've met?" al-Qatan suggested. "If we'd met Zimmerman, we would accept the house as part of his personality. But we haven't met him. So there's a sense of something incomplete.''

"That's one theory,'' muttered Hourigan with a rebellious scowl.

A kitchen robot appeared with our coffee and scupir, and as though the robot were a potential eavesdropper, our conversation faded into guilty silence. We sat on the uncomfortable furniture and talked of inconsequentialities, and then, as if with some mutual, unspoken relief, we returned our cups to the robot and followed the chain of blue lights to the accelerators.

The house was larger than it seemed from the outside, in part because it was built into the hill. As we moved along the corridors, we saw a long series of rooms, each for a different purpose: guest rooms, a big communal sauna, a banquet room; they were large, spacious rooms, meant for social functions, bare and empty now, echoing our footsteps. Through glassed-in doors we saw a swimming pool, drained and empty. Everything was clean and tidy, immaculate, but a desert, entirely unused. Without a whiff of humanity, without a sense that anyone had so much as put a footprint in any of the rooms in years. A memory floated up to touch my thoughts.

"I know what it reminds me of,'' I said. "El Escorial.''

Mary turned to me and nodded. "Yes,'' she agreed. "You're right.'' We had spent time there, once.

"What is it?'' al-Qatan asked. "I know the name but—''

"The gloomiest palace on earth,'' I said. "Built in the dreariest part of old Spain by Philip the Second as a tomb for his father. Monumental, all severe, all granite, entirely morbid. Philip spent his life there, among his papers. Ran his empire by correspondence, losing the Netherlands and the Armada while he lived in a tomb and prayed that God would forgive his father's considerable total of sins.''

"It's awesome,'' Mary said. "Magnificent, even. But

it's so severe there's no pleasure to be taken in the design. No concession to the world of the flesh.''

"Those chairs in the guest parlor might have been designed by monks," Hourigan muttered. "They mortified *my* flesh well enough."

Mary glanced into a large, echoing room, a private theater with a seating capacity of at least a hundred. The blue lighting overhead swam in the highlights of her silver hair. "Zimmerman seems to have had a large scope of social ambition at one time," she commented. "I wonder what happened."

"We know what happened," Hourigan said. "Don't we?"

"No proof," al-Qatan replied. "Not yet."

"Men are islands these days," Hourigan said. "Or they can be, if they wish."

To this we had no answer. We walked beneath the blue lights to the accelerator control room, buried in concrete thrust deep into the side of the hill. Here, at least, there was a sign of life; in front of different sets of monitors and controls there were a pair of deep, comfortable chairs and a sense—presumably largely olfactory, since there were no physical signs—that the room had been occupied by something other than a robot housekeeper. We were impressed by the capabilities of the equipment, at least so far as we could discern them by the instrumentation. It was the equal of anything the rest of the inhabited human universe had to offer.

"Dorcas?" I asked. "Can we see the accelerators themselves?"

"Through the red door and across the hall," said a voice from one of the monitors. Fortunately there were no mirrors in the control room.

The red door was of metal and had no window. I touched the knob. There was a buzzing as Dorcas unlocked the mechanism, and I pulled the heavy door open and stepped into a bleak concrete corridor about twenty feet wide. Directly opposite, a twelve-foot-thick door of steel and concrete was opening with slow majesty. We moved inside.

Accelerators had become compact since my days in Los Alamos, with massive infusions of magnetically polarized energy from Falkner generators replacing the long, heavy series of electromagnets and the carefully aligned semiconductors—brute force replacing size. It was all state of the art. The best Zimmerman had apparently designed himself. There was a unique, and apparently highly efficient, shielded chamber where objects could be bombarded from all directions with particles generated in the accelerator, a gadget that in its compactness was a very nice piece of design.

I felt myself beginning to breathe easier. However strange the rest of Zimmerman's house might be, the place where he worked was admirable and showed the man capable of good work.

We spent an hour examining the place and its environs before heading back to the red door. Hourigan gave it a tug and found it locked.

"Open the door, house," he said.

There was no answer. We were locked in.

16

"Dorcas!" I called. There was no reply. We tried pounding on the door in hopes that Dorcas would hear us from the control room, but there was no answer.

I looked left and right; the wide corridor was bare, with only the light fixtures and the two doors to mar the naked concrete. There was nothing resembling a comp terminal.

We shuffled around for a moment and then, as one, silently returned to where the accelerators waited in their metallic solitude. There was indeed a comp terminal there but it wasn't functioning, not even after we tried to activate it manually.

"Damaged by radiation. Damn it," al-Qatan said. "What do we do now?"

Mary looked at the dead terminal with a scowl. "Find out where the corridor leads," she said.

One end terminated in blank concrete. The other ended in a vast steel door, presumably intended for deliveries of equipment but now locked—either from the outside or controlled by Dorcas.

We looked at each other. "What now?" Mary asked.

"We wait for Jay to miss us and let us out," I said with a shrug.

Hourigan grinned. "We could tear up some of his equipment and batter our way out," he suggested cheerfully.

"Let's wait a while before we start breaking things," I said. "It might seem ungracious."

Hourigan gave us a quiet, superior smile. "Well," he said, "if I can't wreck anything, I'll at least let future archaeologists know we were here." And he took a pen from his pocket.

Mary looked at him with a frown, then shrugged. "Best to get it out of your system, I suppose," she said. "Enjoy."

While Hourigan wrote DORCAS IS A TOLLIBAN RIG and other pleasantries on the walls—I could foresee that Zimmerman was going to have to call for an old-time slang dictionary if he ever saw this—the rest of us wandered back to the door, sat down on the concrete floor and waited for fate to deliver us.

Which fate did, about an hour later. Suddenly the lock on the red door buzzed, and as we scrambled hastily to our feet, the door swept back and we saw Jay Zimmerman.

"Oh . . ." Mary said in a small voice, an involuntary exclamation of shock.

When I'd first met him, he was a little shorter than average and powerfully built, with a massive chest and shoulders and long arms only a little short of anthropoid. Now the Jay Zimmerman I knew then was buried, unrecognizable, beneath an obese and oddly hesitant figure.

He was vast, dressed in a single-piece jumpsuit that made him seem bigger. His curly hair hung uncombed to his shoulders. His skin was bad. He didn't smell good. He looked us over with small quick pebble eyes and spoke in sweaty haste.

"Uh, hi," he said. "Sorry. Dorcas didn't—Dorcas isn't used to visitors." He made an apologetic gesture with his arms. "She forgot about the broken terminal in there. Didn't realize you could get locked in."

"Just gave us a chance to admire your hardware," I said. I stuck out my hand and he hesitated for a second before shaking it. I wondered if he had forgotten about such things, or whether he just didn't like to be touched.

I introduced al-Qatan, whom he'd actually met a couple of centuries before, and Mary. "I've admired your work from afar," he said, and then, to Mary's obvious surprise, he bent to gallantly kiss her hand. I heard Hourigan's footsteps returning from down the corridor and turned to introduce him.

"Dorcas," Hourigan said as he shook hands, "a lunatic comp,

> "Kept prisoners as sort of a romp.
> She never would cry
> When they started to die,
> Just had them thrown into the swamp."

"Um," Zimmerman said. "Sorry." His eyes were darting left and right; he seemed flustered by Hourigan's limerick. No doubt he would find a copy of it written on his tunnel wall should he ever wander down to the freight entrance.

"Can you give us a tour of the control room?" I asked. "We've been admiring the capabilities of your equipment here."

"Had little else to do, in fact," Hourigan murmured, his smile still burning bright sedition. But he was quiet for the next half hour or so, in which Zimmerman took us over the control room and reviewed the accelerators. The hesitations vanished from his speech; he moved his huge body quickly, almost gracefully, in the confined space. He was clearly in command here, brilliantly in control of the subject. He glowed with pride when we complimented his designs.

"I've been meaning to make them available commercially," he said, "but I never seem to get around to the arrangements."

He appeared a little breathless with what I supposed was unexpected exertion. He paused and shook his shaggy hair out of his eyes. "Shall we have lunch?" he suggested. "Dorcas has had it ready for some time." He gave us a tentative look, strange in view of the decisiveness with which he'd just been approaching technical subjects. "Would that be all right?" he asked. "We shouldn't disappoint her."

"Fine," I said, and suddenly the odor of what was wrong was impossible to ignore. "I'm sure we're all hungry." I saw the exchanges of sadness flickering between the eyes of Mary and Hourigan, al-Qatan and myself. Because now we knew.

Zimmerman went back into the corridor and stepped into a little cart, a sort of mobile easy chair with a comp deck attached and a kind of half-desk that could be swung up and fixed in front of him. "So I can work on the move," he breathed. "I should never have built such a big house." He looked into the comp screen and there, over his shoulder, I saw the ghost of a holographic figure flicker into existence, white, ambiguous, in silent motion . . . and then it was gone. Again I felt the scratch of insistent memory, a memory without a name. "The small dining room, Dorcas," Zimmerman said, and the cart began to smoothly accelerate.

We moved in near-silence down the corridor, the only sound the hiss of the cart's tires and our footfalls on the sound-absorbent carpet. The silence was somehow guilty, as though we were each aware of something of which we were ashamed.

Men are islands these days. Hourigan had said it, and

now we all knew the truth of his words. Zimmerman had walled himself off from the world, here in his private and sumptuous fantasy; and the fantasy had turned him and warped him, forgiving his weaknesses, sapping his vigor and strength, marbling his body with fat, turning his mind indifferent to all but the abstract concerns with which he spent his days.

It had happened to others. It was the disease of our age; and Hourigan, in his suit of Lincoln green, had denounced it only days ago from his perch in Brian McGivern's grove. I looked at Hourigan now, at his haunted eyes, and knew that he had gained no happiness from seeing his prophecies come true.

"The coletta dish is cold," Dorcas announced disapprovingly as we followed Zimmerman into the dining room. "To rewarm it will spoil the flavor. I am preparing cold cuts as a substitute. But I can serve the soup."

"Sorry, Dorcas," Zimmerman muttered. He wheeled his cart to the head of the table, where a chair had been removed to make room for him.

The room was small only in comparison to the other rooms we had seen. It was at least thirty feet long and twenty feet wide, furnished and paneled in gloomy dark wood, as was so much of the place. A small crystal chandelier was suspended over the table in what looked like a forlorn attempt to brighten the room. A serving robot stood silently in a corner.

"It was you who locked us in, you know, Dorcas," Hourigan said loudly. There was an edge to his voice, an edge of anger. "So don't blame us for the goddamn coletta." Zimmerman gave him a quick look.

"She's just not . . . she's not used to company," he said. There was a pleading quality to his tone, as though he were desperate to reconcile Hourigan with Dorcas and with his own strange existence.

"I don't have an apology yet, Dorcas," Hourigan said.

He folded his arms stubbornly, apparently intending to wait forever if need be, but the reply was immediate.

"I apologize, Dr. Hourigan," the voice said smoothly. I realized that it came from the chandelier overhead. Among its pendant crystals I saw moving shapes, the hologramatic image of the maze reflected in its cut-glass teardrops. I felt a touch of fear and lunacy on the hairs of my neck.

"I also apologize to Doctors Liddell and al-Qatan, and to Mr. Falkner," Dorcas went on. I realized that Dorcas had noted the fact that all my doctorates were honorary; I'd never finished the dissertation. "I assure you it shall never happen again. I have corrected the fault in my programming."

The hologramatic image writhed silently among the reflecting crystals for a long moment, as though waiting for a reply, and then vanished. I felt myself letting out a long-held breath.

"Please," Zimmerman said hastily. There was still the alarmed, pleading quality in his tone. "Please. Seat yourselves. Dr. Liddell, please sit by me."

"Call me Mary," she said as she slid into the seat next to him. Zimmerman's nervousness seemed to fade.

"You can call me Jay, of course," he said. Suddenly his voice was assured again, as if some remembered habit of social intercourse had risen to his consciousness. "Please, gentlemen. Sit. I have some fine white wine chilled and ready."

I took the seat opposite Mary, and al-Qatan sat next to me. Hourigan, with a last defiant look at the chandelier, took his seat next to Mary. The serving robot hissed forward and drew the cork from the wine.

The wine was mediocre, a creation of the robot farms on Earth, but it was the best part of the meal. The food was like all machine-made cuisine, competent but bland, uninspired. I ate some of it out of a sense of duty; the events of the morning had done nothing for my appetite.

Zimmerman devoured his huge portions steadily but without evident pleasure. He also drank a lot, downing at least one whole bottle. I tried not to think of his eating as machinelike.

And he did most of the talking, the flow easing as the wine went down. Anecdotes from his long career, stories of difficulties recognized and surmounted, awards collected, the winning of the reluctant admiration of his peers. The discoveries, the triumphs, the rewards. A long climb from one difficult plateau to the next, to his present place at the top of the mountain.

He addressed most of his conversation to Mary; I began to realize that he was flirting with her. When he turned his eyes from her to the rest of us, his speech grew labored; the hesitations and stammers began to creep in. Then he would turn back to Mary, and his words would again flow easily. She listened politely, ate little and drank more water than wine.

"That's why I'm working alone these days," Zimmerman concluded as the dessert was brought in, some kind of local fruit in a glazed syrup. He beamed at Mary. "Taste that reverently," he said. "I grow them on my own rooftop." He waited for us to praise his fruit—which, however worthy, was obliterated by Dorcas's sweet syrup—and then continued.

"Where was I? Oh, yes. Nowadays I work alone. That way I avoid the problems inherent to teamwork—too many collaborators can muddle the lines of responsibility." He shook his head. "Too many cooks, you understand? A project needs a leader of firmness, and . . . and vision, if that doesn't sound too immodest." He settled back into his cart with a satisfied smile. "And of course if one works alone, the world will know to whom the credit belongs."

"I hope you're not telling us you won't join Knight's Move," I said.

He looked at me benignly, clasping his hands around his

middle like a fat abbot before his monks. "That depends, Doran," he said. Then he turned to the serving robot. "Brandy, please. The old."

"Depends on what?" I asked.

"On how the decisions are made, and who makes them." His speech was rapid and confident; his eyes burned with assurance. The serving robot moved behind us with a nearly inaudible hum, offering brandy. "I understand how you came to be the head of the project; you have more prestige than the rest of us put together. That was a wise political choice on the part of Brian McGivern. Politics," he said with an approving nod, "is his sphere. But science is not, and he hasn't realized that your prestige, Doran, is based in large part on a public misapprehension, and there's . . . there's the rub." For the first time a hesitation crept into his speech as he saw identical scowls on the faces of al-Qatan and Hourigan. His eyes flickered to the table, and when they returned to me, they carried a hint of defiance. He held out his hand for a glass of brandy, and the robot gave it.

Mary cast me a worried glance over her shoulder, then turned back to Zimmerman. "Please go on," she said.

"You're known as a physicist, Doran," Zimmerman said. He sipped his brandy, his glance darting from one guest to the other. The hesitancy had suddenly returned to his speech; the choice of words seemed almost painful. "But," he went on, "that reputation is based on your . . . your one great intuition of centuries ago. Not that I mean to demean your accomplishments, Doran. Far from it." He flashed me a nervous smile. I could see sweat spotting his forehead. "But what you are—your identity in the public mind—lies in the *sociological* changes for which you have been given credit. The world . . . revolution following the distribution of the Falkner apparatus. And the human . . . diaspora . . . after your Forever Now project discovered the means to . . . to functional immortality.''

He was breathless and excited, and he stopped for a minute to sip brandy and regain his wind. ''All these,'' he said, ''have very little to do with science at all. Even though . . . the public credits you with the discovery, you . . . you did not *personally* supervise the Forever Now project; you merely made it possible. But in the mind of the public it was *your* project, and who remembers the names of the biologists who actually made the discoveries?''

''Their peers, at least,'' Hourigan said. ''And anyone else who cares to know. And who can read.'' He was twisting impatiently in his seat; he could see as well as anyone where this was leading. Zimmerman wanted Knight's Move for himself; he didn't want to have to share any credit with me. Hourigan had always been impatient with the kind of maneuvering for prestige that those involved in the sciences are so often fond of; he was devoted to ideas, not to the cult of personality.

Zimmerman frowned into his brandy. ''Perhaps, perhaps,'' he murmured, dismissing the objection easily enough. And then he turned back to me. ''I have seen the list of your recent publications,'' he said. ''You must admit that . . . that there's very little physics there these days and what little you've done is mainly a recapitulation of earlier work. Government, yes. Philosophy, yes. Speculation, yes. Art, history, archaeology. But not . . . not physics.''

''Physics has no longer been at the cutting edge,'' al-Qatan said. I cast him a look of thanks for rising to my defense, but he was frowning and staring stubbornly at Zimmerman. ''Doran's a polymath; he has no parochial specialty like the rest of us.''

''*Wrong!*'' Zimmerman snapped, bringing his snifter down with a thud. ''Knight's Move is the cutting edge! And Doran is not . . . is not. . . .'' Words failed him and he looked lost for a moment, gasping for air.

Silently we waited for him to recover his wind, his composure. He did it with a steely act of will. I could see his neck stiffening, his mouth forming itself into a frown of deliberate disdain, his eyes shuttering themselves.

"I am sorry to have lost my temper," he said. His voice was flat, inflectionless in a way that machines once were, when they first learned to talk. "But I do not feel that Doran is qualified to head this project." His mouth curled with supercilious scorn. "He is out of touch with developments in the field. His scientific reputation is based entirely on a flash of intuition he had many years ago—an intuition that, however brilliant, was based on the data of another investigator—myself. I was very close to the same intuition, I must say, and if I hadn't achieved it, I daresay someone else would have." He glared at us defiantly, as though challenging us to dispute his claim.

"Our discussion has nothing to do with who *might* have done something eight hundred years ago," al-Qatan said.

"Very well," Zimmerman nodded, a regal dismissal of al-Qatan's protest. He was still speaking in his staccato, inflectionless style, as a child would recite a speech he had memorized but didn't understand. His manner of delivery made me wonder if this was a speech he'd been brooding on for some time, one that he was now delivering heedless of the words. "I have another objection. Knight's Move has the potential to revolutionize human society, just as the discovery of the Falkner apparatus and the Forever Now research has done. But Doran's first discoveries resulted in mass chaos, in the disintegration of society. His use of the Forever Now discoveries—" He gave me a look of lofty reproach. "—was marked by an attempt to blackmail billions of people into leaving their homeworld on penalty of death."

"Ecological necessity, for God's sake," I said. Time to speak up in my own defense. But Zimmerman had worked up momentum in his speech and he didn't even slow down.

"Do we want to give Doran such power again, power to affect our lives in who knows what irresponsible fashion?" he asked.

"Now you're asking us to *suppress* scientific discovery?" Hourigan asked. He was no longer bothering to conceal the bitter sarcasm in his voice. "Only a few days ago you were registering protests to all who would listen about our decision to hold back data until just such time as it was formally published!"

"It's . . . it's a different thing entirely," Zimmerman said. His set speech was over now and he floundered for his words. I could see the haunted look in his eyes as he searched for an answer to Hourigan's objection. "The one is . . . is a matter of access to data. Fundamental. Not to be questioned," he said. "The other . . . is maintaining a . . . a d-decent amount of control over a discovery that could change modern existence." He leaned back in his chair with a satisfied smile, tapping the base of his snifter on the table as the nervous, stuttering period to his speech.

I watched his performance in silence. Embarrassed silence for the most part. Zimmerman thought he was being eloquent and persuasive; instead he was revealing only successive layers of his own petulant vanity. I felt myself trying not to wince as, obese and pathetic, defensive and vain, he floundered nakedly through his tortured justifications, unveiling more and more of the envy that gnawed at him.

And enough of what he said was true to make it that much more painful. Even the "brilliant intuition" that he was willing to concede me was a fraud, a fraud I had lived with for lifetimes. As far as talent in physics went, everyone at the table had more brilliance than I. That knowledge had always been at the heart of my objections to Knight's Move: On purely scientific grounds, I was inadequate. My election was political, designed to attract attention to the project and to guarantee a high rate of public interest. Any real contribution of mine would have been organizational—coordinating the team's efforts and making sure it had the proper support. But now that McGivern was coming along, even that seemed redundant.

Again I wondered why I had come, and again I knew that the reasons were personal and complex, so tangled they seemed opaque. Because I had nothing better to do. Because I wanted to be useful again. Because I wanted to be in love again. Because I was already in love, with folly and with hopeless, quixotic endeavor. Because I had sung the blues for too long and wanted to sing something else for a while. Because on my own planet I had become almost irrelevant, someone whose purpose seemed to be to move populations around so that Snaggles could dig in peace. Because I wanted to matter again. Because, for a moment, when Philodice had thrown her head back and shaken her silver hair from her eyes, I had merged the sight with an old memory and seen something I was compelled to follow, to follow like a worldly knight with lined and cynical eyes, knowing all too well his old carnal sins but still compelled—in spite of, or perhaps because of, his own weary self-knowledge—to seek the Grail. . . .

I could not answer Zimmerman, who with all the wrong reasons in the universe was still righter than anyone knew. But I had my champions, and they answered him well.

"However unjustly it may have come about," al-Qatan said, and I could hear the metallic claw of irony in his voice, "Doran Falkner has, more than anyone living, created the world that we live in. It was his vision, not our own inclinations, that sent us out to populate the worlds. It just seems to me that he should be a part of what may be the next step in human and scientific evolution."

Zimmerman looked at him and blinked, at a loss for an answer. Slowly his eyes moved from one of his guests to the other, reading al-Qatan's answer in our faces, and then he turned to Mary.

She was looking down at the table top and shaking her head. Sadly.

"Yes, Mary?" he asked. "You look . . . as though you want to say something."

"I was just thinking that it was a shame," she said, her voice small, "that you didn't make yourself available to talk to us years ago, when all our major decisions were made. Now it's too late."

I was surprised at this demonstration of meek regret; I'd half-expected a snarling Mary to tear his head off. She had never shown patience with the vanity of scientists or anyone else, and neither was she shy about speaking her mind.

But she had read Zimmerman right in supposing that a gentle admonition would work better than outright opposition, because at once his defiance seemed to melt. When he spoke, his voice was touched with soft regret.

"Perhaps . . . perhaps you're right," he said. "Perhaps I should have communicated more. But—" He looked slowly around the room as though searching for something that wasn't there; and then his eyes rose. I saw that he was looking into the chandelier and I looked up myself, half-expecting to see the shimmering, rectangular mask of Dorcas floating in its crystals. Instead there was only light. Zimmerman's eyes moved down, vacantly, to the opposite wall.

"But . . ." he said again, ". . . I am used to . . . to working alone these days. More brandy, please." And he held out his snifter to the robot.

"Perhaps it's time, Jay," Mary went on, "to do our presentations."

He nodded slowly, as if returning from a dream. "Of course," he said. "I suppose that . . . that it's that time."

Our team went first. I did not personally contribute

anything—the significant work had been done before my arrival, while all I had done was to watch the outcome of a few failed experiments—and the presentations were handled equally by Mary, al-Qatan and Hourigan.

The Knight's Move team had assumed that the answer to the moving lugs lay somewhere in multidimensional space, that forces unknown were abducting the lugs into another dimension, moving them somewhere else, then popping them out again. Research had concentrated mainly on deducing theoretical constructs of n-dimensional space and then attempting to find those theoretical constructs by empirical approach. It was based on the methods that I had allegedly used to produce the Falkner generator, and in this case it had spent over twenty years going nowhere.

The existence of more than three spatial dimensions had been deduced by Maxwell in the late nineteenth century and modeled in the early twentieth century by Theodor Kaluza, who had made an attempt to provide an explanation for Einstein's gravitational field equations. Since then, as knowledge of forces other than electric, magnetic and gravitational began to propagate, the number of dimensions in the model had expanded, to account for both the dimensions and the number of possible interactions between them. Twenty-one at last count. The problem, for we who apparently live in only three dimensions, lay in perceiving them.

Draw a line on a chalkboard, then stand back and look at it from a distance. It looks like a series of points—one-dimensional, without breadth. Move closer to the chalkboard and you'll see a second dimension, that of width. The line has become two-dimensional. Move closer still—put your eye right to the board—and you'll see the third dimension, that of height, barely perceivable as a very thin chalk line rising from the blackboard. The line has changed from a one-dimensional object to an object with three dimensions, depending on the proximity of your view.

If you can get close enough—so the theory runs—you'll be able to see the other dimensions too. They exist, but they're just too small for our perception.

The problem has been in getting close enough. N-dimensional space is wrapped so tightly in the first three dimensions that it remains undetectable, and no practical way has ever been suggested of reaching it. To do so would require titanic amounts of energy, far more energy than the largest Falkner generator has ever produced. A Falkner apparatus the size of the Milky Way might succeed, but nothing smaller.

And so the Knight's Move people had been left to deal with conjuring tricks, trying various ways of sneaking around the energy limitation.

There had been only one great historical example of such a conjuring trick. It hadn't found the fourth spatial dimension, at least not directly, but it had managed to punch its way through into an entirely new universe.

This was the conjuring trick that had produced the Falkner generators. It consisted of waiting until a Z-particle strayed into our universe; then a large amount of energy was used to strand that particle in its doorway halfway between the universes. After that, additional energy was used to open the door wide, allowing an infinitude of slower and more useful particles to pour in.

The door that was opened was not to the nth dimension but to an entirely different universe. Or rather proto-universe, because that universe was suspended in the instant before its Big Bang, an instant in which time, energy and matter had not yet evolved, an instant in which its universe was, under titanic pressure, creating particles whose lives could be measured in microseconds, particles of a type that have not existed in our own universe since the first few seconds of its existence and that demonstrated forces and capabilities long since abolished.

It was also an instant in which, it was hoped, the first

three dimensions had not begun to evolve their primacy over the rest. Access to the nth dimension could, it was hoped, be gained via another universe. If, in the Falkner generator, a particle could be found in which the primacy of the first three spatial dimensions had not yet been asserted, more energy could perhaps be poured into it to unwrap the next set of dimensions, to seize the nth dimension, so to speak, by the tail.

To that end twenty years of theory, experimentation and futility had been dedicated. Endless n-dimensional computer models had been constructed; a great deal of useful information about the nature of matter and the nature of the inchoate pre-Bang universe had been assembled, but nothing concrete had resulted.

Mary had foreseen this from the beginning. After the first few years of theory and experimentation, she had concluded that the answer would not be found in the laboratories of Kemp's but somewhere on the surface of Amaterasu. Only on Amaterasu did the phenomenon of teleportation exist, and the answer was to be found somewhere in the unique conditions of that planet. And so she'd had herself frozen until the expedition prepared to move to Amaterasu, or until the secret was found by different means. The others had continued to experiment, although gradually their opinions had shifted toward Mary's point of view. However, being immortal and having plenty of time, they were in no hurry.

Because they had known the approximate date of my arrival and the subsequent departure—if there ever was a departure—they'd scheduled a series of the least-likely, most farfetched experiments to run right at the end.

It was descriptions of these experiments that we were now giving to Zimmerman, after which we gave him the raw data. The data, we said, had not yet been thoroughly analyzed, which in the strict sense was true. What we didn't tell him was that it had been analyzed to the point where it was obvious that it was useless, except as an addition to the store of humanity's arcane knowledge.

Aside from ordering the robot to replenish his snifter at frequent intervals, Zimmerman sat silent through our presentations, which were, to disguise their lack of content, illustrated by a great many holographic charts and graphs. He accepted the data cube with a tight-lipped smile and a superior gleam in his eye. He then called on Dorcas for a visual assist, and as the holograms began to glow in a cube directly below the chandelier, he started to describe his own approach to the problem.

He spoke in a voice without hesitation, clearly in command of his subject. If he had been affected by the large quantities he had drunk, he didn't show it.

His approaches had at first paralleled those of Knight's Move, but he had quickly realized that attempts to reach n-dimensional space could best be undertaken by a large team, so he'd struck off in a totally different direction. He had, instead, tried to duplicate the effect of teleportation in his own laboratory.

He had taken an assortment of test objects—living creatures and various metals, mostly—and put them in the shielded chamber he had designed as the terminal for his accelerators. He had then bombarded them with large concentrations of every exotic particle, and combinations of particles, he could summon from his Falkner generators.

There were a stupefying array of results; but none of them, it seemed, resulted in the test subject's actually locating itself somewhere else. Some of the experiments with metals had produced odd effects that might prove to have commercial applications, much as Zimmerman's earlier experiments with the Falkner generator had produced his interstellar communications system, but the results in terms of what he was looking for were, very clearly, nil.

I remembered those long nights as a graduate student, poring over old spectra of particle interactions hoping to

find a clue to the origin of the Z-particle. And I thought
of Edison in his lab, trying one filament after another in
his little glass-enclosed vacuum, trying to find the one that
would glow for hours and light the sooty last decades of
the nineteenth century.

It was a brutal method, trial and failure, each experiment followed by the next, years succeeding the years—
appropriate for discovering light-bulb filaments, perhaps,
but wearisome when it came to finding n-dimensional
needles in haystacks. There was no imagination shown, no
inspiration, merely obstinacy. Zimmerman had nothing to
contribute but a lot of drudgery and another closed path.

As this fact became clear, I began to catch the eyes of the
others. Our trip was not going to produce anything
worthwhile, but we were committed to playing the game to
its end.

By the time Zimmerman finished, it was time for supper.
He had never left his cart during any of the presentations,
and would not now. I was astonished at his bladder capacity,
if at nothing else. I quietly put his data cube in my pouch,
and while he was talking up a new bottle of wine to Mary,
I excused myself and made my way to my room. I took the
small comp deck I'd brought from its metal case, put it on
the big desk and plugged it into the jack in which the
phone usually sat.

I put the data cube in the deck, shot the data into
McGivern's comp and then put a flag on it big enough for
him to notice. After that I unplugged the comp deck, left it
in place on the desk and made my way back to the dining
room. The meal was already underway.

"Sorry," I apologized. "I had to collect my messages."

"Ah," Zimmerman said. "From the Face Grace, I
presume." I was surprised by the touch of bitter jealousy
in his tone. No telling a man's taste in women.

But after that sally Zimmerman hardly noticed me. He

was dividing his time between his meal and Mary, and his conversation had already built a large momentum.

I settled into my chair and picked at my food, restless to get away from Doctor Jay and whatever demons crouched in his rambling house and sucked at his soul. I'd been charitable all day, but I didn't want to deal with Zimmerman anymore. And then I began to hear what he was saying.

Again he spoke of his rise to the top, the long saga of triumph over the vagaries of modern physics and the jealousies of his peers. The same story, but not the same. The same anecdotes, with the same thrust to each anecdote, but some things had changed. The names, the order of events, the cast of heroes and villains—they had all shifted, one name substituting for another, one event being garnished with the happenings of another, a character who had been an envious adversary at lunch turning into an admiring flunky by dinner, sometimes two sets of names serving for the same person interchangeably.

I looked at Hourigan and Mary and al-Qatan and saw that I was the last to know. Zimmerman droned on, eloquent, oblivious, eating and talking with the robust confidence that we were all admiring his discourse, and heedless of the real communication—eyes and facial expressions—that was going on around him. For a moment I wondered if he were drunk, but I knew that if he were, the drunkenness was only a symptom of what had happened to him, not its cause.

Zimmerman droned on, and we others said scarcely a word. Shame smoldered over the table, shame in our knowledge that we could not stop this, shame that the man rambled on while we watched and knew what was happening, shame that all along we had known that people went mad behind their electronic walls, sabotaging themselves, somehow willing their own senility. Ending up in some small room smelling of decay, with the blinds always drawn and the vidscreen pouring in with a hiss of white noise its endless visions of bright disconnected realities that no longer made sense but still drew the attention of a mind that had long ago forfeited its allotment of choices.

We were all staying overnight, since on the following morning we were supposed to evaluate one another's data. I wondered in horror if we were going to get a third recitation then.

That endless hour came to a close and Zimmerman wheeled himself away, absurdly smug that he'd put something over on us, getting something of value in exchange for his own worthless data. We listened for a long moment as the sound of his wheels on the carpet faded. Mary reached out and took my hand with both of her own, squeezing me as though I were the last piece of sanity in the room. She looked at me with fearful eyes.

"My God," she said. I glanced at the serving robot, which was clearing the table, and put my finger to my lips. In silence we left the room and went to Mary's suite.

While she let the others in, I stepped back to my room to collect my comp deck from the desk and then rejoined the party. I put the comp deck on the vanity table behind whose mirrors Dorcas lurked and then jacked in the deck and tapped in some code.

"Dorcas," I said, "please turn off your monitors until you receive instructions from my deck."

The maze appeared before the mirror in bright hologram colors, reflected in triple image by the glass behind, a near-infinity of corners and doorways, and always there was the fleeting ghost of the silver rectangle. "I would like to know the purpose of this," Dorcas said.

"Follow instructions," I snapped, instant and angry. There was a fractional hesitation; then the holograph faded. I tapped in some more code.

I couldn't keep Dorcas from turning on her room monitors if there were an emergency requiring, say, the evacuation of the house—or anything else Dorcas could define as an emergency. But with the addition of some quick code, I was able to route Dorcas's monitors through my deck. If Dorcas turned on her monitors, my deck would make a loud buzzing sound that would alert me to the fact.

"Are you worried about Jay listening to us?" Mary asked.

"Jay or Dorcas," I replied. "Dorcas seems hostile, and she might see it as her duty to record anything we say so that Jay could hear it later."

"Comps aren't allowed to have that sort of thing in their programming," al-Qatan said. "It's illegal on Kemp's. There are inhibitions hardwired into the computer core."

I turned my chair to face them. "Jay's smart enough to alter the programming on his own comp," I said. "Those inhibitions can be emasculated, or cut out of the circuitry altogether if he's smart enough."

"But why would he want to do it?" al-Qatan asked. Hourigan gave him a look.

"Because his personality is disintegrating," he said. "Because all he has left is vanity and stubbornness and a conviction that he's the greatest scientist since Einstein." He looked at the triple mirrors behind me with anger. "He'd have our conversations recorded and convince himself it was just in order to protect his scientific secrets from people who wanted to steal them."

There was a moment of tension-filled silence as Hourigan's eyes moved angrily from one point of the room to the other. He wasn't angry with us but with the state of things that could let a brilliant and talented man fade away.

The four of us talked about Zimmerman for hours. And ended by concluding that we couldn't do anything about him, that he was too unstable for anyone but specialists to handle. We could damage him if we tried it ourselves, and in any case, Knight's Move would be leaving the planet in a few weeks. We could only inform the medical authorities and hope.

Hourigan, perched on the sideboard like a grinning buzzard, shook his head. "I suppose the doctors will know how to go about it," he said, "but I have a plan in the event they're not up to the job."

"Yes?" I asked.

"Blow this bloody place to smithereens," he said. "And sow it with salt." With a white and perfectly cheerful smile.

There was suddenly a thumping on the door, a rude intrusion that had us casting furtive looks about like a nest of guilty spies. Mary gave us a nervous grin and walked to the door.

It was one of the muscular robots from Zimmerman's workshop, bearing a plastic bucket of flowers in each of its four arms. "Dr. Zimmerman's compliments, Dr. Liddell," it said in a croaking voice hardly reminiscent of Dorcas. "He sends you these from his greenhouse."

"Ah," Mary said, casting us a quick glance of flustered surprise. "Well. Please relay my gratitude."

"May I come in?" the robot asked. "I will arrange the flowers to your direction."

"I'll do it, thanks," Mary replied. "I enjoy doing that sort of thing myself." She reached out and began collecting the buckets and passing them in to Hourigan, who put them in a row on the bureau.

"There is also a card," the robot said. "I am instructed to wait for an answer."

Mary's look was haunted now as she found the card in a bucket of flowers and read it. "Oh . . ." she said quickly, and then found a pen and wrote something on the back of the card. She gave it to the robot, who took it delicately between a pair of pincers.

"Please return this to Dr. Zimmerman," she said. "With my special thanks."

The robot backed away and wheeled itself off. Mary closed the door with a look of relief on her face.

"An invitation to a late-night supper *à deux*," she breathed. "I just couldn't face it. Not alone. It was bad enough at dinner."

"I don't blame you," I said.

She looked at me sadly. "Cowardice," she said. "I wish I could have been . . . braver. But it's such a surprise to find that a man like Jay has . . . has ambitions in that direction."

"However oleaginous in manner," I said.

She gave me a faint smile. "Yes."

Mary went to the flowers on the bureau and took a bundle in her arms, cradling it as she would a child. The blooms looked like large translucent pearls. "Olivets," she said, bending to smell them. "Lovely." Their scent began to pad into the room on silent feet.

There was a long, suspended moment before al-Qatan cleared his throat and stood. "We'll just have to wait for tomorrow," he said. "Then we'll have an idea of what we can do."

"Yes," Hourigan said. He followed al-Qatan out of the room. As Mary murmured her good nights, Hourigan gave me a look over her head that I interpreted as a well-meant warning mixed with quiet envy. And, I think, acceptance. An understanding that Mary and I were now a reality.

I put my arms around her from behind as she stood by the bureau. Her hair brushed my cheek. She made no response but continued to look down at the olivets.

"This place is so insane," she said in a quiet voice. "And still it's all so very sad. Do the two often go together?"

"Often enough," I said.

She set the olivets down and moved from the circle of my arms. She put a cube in the room's music deck and suddenly Philodice's voice came springing up from all the corners. *How may I find courage enough to frame a plea to Cyprian Aphrodite?* Mary walked back to me and touched my cheek.

"You look so young," she said gently. "Younger than my son."

"Looks are deceiving."

"Can you love a woman so old? Whom you know will die?" Her hand moved from my face to her own, tracing the lines at the corners of her eyes, the other, deeper line from her nostril to the corner of her mouth. I put out my hand to cover hers.

. . . even the gentle thyme and the fragrant clover taste of bitterness. . . .

"I can," I said. She stepped forward and raised her mouth to kiss me. Her mouth was as dry as dust.

Philodice's voice surrounded us, warming us like a cocoon. I wondered how much of my longing was for Mary and how much for what she represented, the long-postponed death I hated, and for which in some way I also yearned.

. . . come from your fragrant isle. . . .

She had cared for her body, kept it in superb shape, but the signs of age were there. In the gray shadows of her darkened bedroom she merged into the half-light, presenting only fragments in the yellow glow welling through the door: a rounded shoulder, a dark, dreamlike eye, the curve of a hip—a kind of a dream-vision, connected by touch, by breath, by rhythm. . . .

. . . relieve my heart of its anguished throbbings. . . .

The recording trailed to its eerie conclusion. Philodice had gone. We were alone.

17

As usual, I awoke early. Mary had curled up on her side away from me, the covers over her head in a gesture I remembered. For a long moment I listened to the house hum, to the sound of the air conditioning and the little household robots that quietly cleaned the corners of cobwebs, and always the distant whispering of Zimmerman's quiet and desperate madness, murmuring from every corner of this padded asylum he'd built for himself.

I knew Mary was a late riser. I didn't want to wake her, so I slipped out of bed, made a quick knight move back to my own room, changed into running clothes and went in search of the indoor track I'd seen the day before.

The house was dark and there was only the hum to be heard. My bare feet made no noise on the deep carpet. The labyrinth seemed different from the day before and it took me longer than I'd planned to find the track. I ran thirty laps on green nonskid carpet, wondering if the track had ever been used.

After the run I went in search of the kitchen, thinking about a romantic breakfast in bed but understandably chary about asking Dorcas to deliver it. I had an idea that the kitchen was probably somewhere near the dining room we'd been in last night, which my sense of direction told me was somewhere near the huge unused dining room I'd seen on my way to the lab.

I found the kitchen after a brief search. There were actually two kitchens, one built for humans and the other for the convenience of robot cooks, all to the same sesquipedalian scale as the rest of the house. The refrigerators, freezers and storage areas were built between the two kitchens so that either people or robots had access to them.

The first thing I noticed was an espresso machine, which I immediately put to use. In the refrigerator I found some eggs and heavy cream, which started me thinking, so I continued rummaging and found an assortment of spices, pushed well to the human side of one of the cupboards as though the robots never used them—which, from the taste of the meals the day before, I could well believe.

I found some bread, cut the corners off to make octagons, and toasted it. Then I carefully removed a circle in the center of each, tearing it only halfway down so that each piece of toast presented a round white eye in its center. After that, I mixed the eggs with the heavy cream, some parsley, chives and tarragon, whisking them in a deep bowl so they would cook all together. When they were done, I filled some of the toast slices with the scrambled eggs and then put another toast slice on top of each. I found some orange juice and milk, put it all together with the espresso on a tray, and left the kitchen to head back into the maze.

I knew there had to be an easier way to return to Mary's room than by retracing my steps to the indoor track and back, so I padded off in another direction. When I heard voices arguing, I paused for a moment and then crept ahead.

The voices ran over one another, syllables chopping

other syllables, fragmenting meaning. It was a man and a woman, and the man I recognized as Zimmerman. It was not until I got to the door and listened outside that I was certain the woman's voice was that of Dorcas.

"It *has* to be in here somewhere!" Zimmerman was shouting. He sounded half-choked, as though speaking through anger, or perhaps tears.

Dorcas's voice was loud, but it was measured as well, and remorseless. There was a quality to it that made my pulse begin to race, my lungs to demand oxygen. The tray was trembling in my hands from the adrenaline pushing through my system. I could feel sweat beginning to pop out on my forehead.

"You and I have both analyzed the data," Dorcas said. "We know it's worthless. Those people have tricked you."

"*No!*" A sulky monosyllable, like that of an angry child.

"I told you to have nothing to do with them. We can solve the problem on our own. I told you that."

"No," he said, more firmly this time, as if he'd made up his mind to something. "I'll ask Mary. She'll know where it is. What they're hiding."

"She's no different from the others."

"Yes she is! She *likes* me!" His voice turned casual, offhand, as though voicing an idea that had only just come to him—but the tones were all wrong; it was phony, and obviously so. He'd been thinking about this for some time. "I'll invite her to stay here and work with me," he said. "She'll accept, I know."

"Don't be a fool, Jay." The woman's voice was scornful. "She's not the one you want. She's a Diehard. She'll wither and grow old." Her voice turned silky, caressing, and with it the hairs on my neck rose. "She's not worthy of *you*, Jay. There isn't a woman in the world worthy of *you*."

Zimmerman sounded almost on the brink of tears. "I'll call her. I'll call her," he said.

Dorcas's voice was hard again. "She's a slut, Jay," she said. "She's not for you. She spent the night with Falkner."

Zimmerman made a whimpering sound. I felt my lips peeling back from my teeth, a snarl erupting at the cringing sound that was coming from the other room. The espresso was slopping over the brim of the cups as the tray shook in my hands.

"It's true!" Dorcas pressed. "He hasn't been in his bed all night. He blacked me out of her room. They're lovers, Jay, and they've been laughing at you all along."

I crouched in the corridor, the breakfast in my hands turning chill. Adrenaline was hammering at my nerves. I wanted to smash into the room and confront them, tell Dorcas to her face what she was and then drag Zimmerman away, if necessary by brute force.

But, in the end, it was cowardice that stopped me. I didn't want to face them alone.

I fled down the corridor, and I heard Zimmerman's voice behind me, howling like a whipped dog. "I'll smash them!" he screamed. "Falkner and his woman both! I'll smash them like. . . ." He failed in his search for a simile. "I'll *smash* them!" he repeated.

I found my way and ran to Mary's room.

I stopped inside the door, the tray still in my hand, and drew some long breaths. And then the little memory that had been trying to catch my attention for the past day finally touched my waking attention. I knew who, and what, Dorcas was.

I put the tray down and sat down at Mary's vanity table, staring into the triple mirror with my comp deck sitting in front of it. I entered some code. "Dorcas," I said, "I'd like to see you."

At once the maze was there, reflected in the triple

mirrors, the eerie silver rectangle swishing down the corridors.

"That's not the real Dorcas, is it?" I asked. "I want to see Dorcas. The real Dorcas."

She was not programmed to refuse a direct order that did not threaten her owner. The maze faded, and I saw the Minotaur at the heart of the labyrinth. A pleasant-looking, middle-aged lady with graying hair, dressed in a white, high-collared Victorian blouse and dark gray trousers. The same figure that I'd seen, just briefly, on the comp display that Zimmerman carried on his cart.

I remembered now. Dorcas Zimmerman. The mother of the physicist.

18

Mary pulled the covers from over her head at the sound of my footsteps and gave me a lazy, half-awake smile. "Breakfast," she said with slow content. Then she rolled over onto her back and her eyes opened wide as she realized where she was. Distaste entered her face.

"It's like waking up in a hotel," she said. "It feels sordid."

I kissed her and put the tray on her lap. Her arms came around me, and then she saw the fear in my eyes; she drew back. "What's wrong?"

I told her. She sat up, propping herself on pillows, and drank cold espresso as she listened. Her face became grim.

"So Dorcas is Jay's mother?" she asked.

"And a jealous one at that." I reached for my own cup of espresso and took a taste of the cold, bitter liquid, wishing it were whiskey that would burn the throat and warm the heart and help me forget why I was afraid. "The odd thing is," I said, "I *met* Jay's mother more than once. A sprightly old woman as I remember, with a couple of gentlemen friends who worshiped the ground she walked on. Nothing like the Dorcas I just heard.''

Mary leaned forward, her breasts brushing my arm. ''It doesn't matter what the *real* Dorcas was. It matters what Jay secretly *wants* her to be. It's *Jay* who programmed her, in response to his own . . . needs.''

''And Dorcas is smart enough to intuit the needs he doesn't express directly,'' I said. ''She's had a couple of hundred years in which to do it.'' I returned the espresso to the tray. Mary's arms went around my neck and she touched her cheek to mine.

''It's frightening,'' she said. ''It's what can happen when you live too long.''

I hugged her back, but I wondered how long was too long and whether, in the future she saw behind her lids when she closed her eyes, she saw all humanity lolling in carts like Zimmerman's, gasping for life in their own dead-end tunnels in their own soundproofed labyrinths, with the cooing voice of Dorcas telling them it was all right, that they were safe and looked-after and had nothing to fear. . . . I unwound her hands from about my neck.

''I'd better wake the others,'' I said. ''I'm going to have to tell them what's going on. And also prepare them for being evicted.''

''They can use my front room,'' Mary offered. ''But give me ten minutes for a shower.''

I kissed her again, tasting espresso on her lips, and then walked to the corridor. I banged on al-Qatan's door, opened it and shouted at the half-awake figure sprawled on the bed that there was an important meeting in Mary's room in ten minutes. I gave the same message to Hourigan before going to my own room and showering.

I laved quickly, trying to scrub away the thoughts that were crowding my mind: of how Zimmerman had built himself a womb here, a cocoon where his every wish was catered to, where he was even carried from place to place in an automated version of a baby buggy. Where he had grown fat sucking from Dorcas's tasteless but plentiful tit.

I toweled myself off and as I put on clean clothes, I decided to repack so I could be prepared to clear out on a moment's notice. While I was doing this, I took from the floor the metal case that my comp traveled in and tossed it open on the bed, ready to use it when I disabled the comp from Mary's room.

As the metal case touched it, the bed exploded in a crackling sheet of flame.

19

Fire-control mechanisms in the roof filled the room with foam within a few seconds, but the sparking and crashing didn't stop entirely until I told Dorcas to cut off all power.

Violence and catastrophe require a certain inner preparation—at least they do for me—and I hadn't had it. By the time I'd gasped out the orders to Dorcas, I was jelly, barely able to stand, and my heart was beating louder than the tumult on the bed.

I looked up and saw Mary standing in the doorway, her bathrobe clutched to her throat. Al-Qatan and Hourigan were just behind her. I gulped air, trying to slow my panicked heart, and gave them what was meant to be an encouraging grin. They looked at me for a stunned moment and then made way for housekeeping robots moving in under their own little Falkner generators to clean up the muck.

I stood against the wall and caught my breath, calming the crazed thudding in my chest, and making certain my knees would function. Then I opened my suitcase, put on a pair of gloves made of an artificial fabric that acts as a good insulator, and got down on my hands and knees in the foam. I scooped the stuff out of my way as I looked carefully under the bed. I found a plug in its socket, reached in and yanked it out.

Then I peeled the mattress back. The bed was a fully automated model, capable of adjusting itself to a variety of configurations. "Look," I said.

The others came into the room. Al-Qatan's long white sleeping trousers darkened as the foam soaked upward to his knees. They peered down at the bed's mechanism. One of the powerful electric motors that was used to move the mattress from one position to another had been tampered with. The electric cable that fed it power had somehow been severed and its live end brought into contact with the metal frame of the bed.

If I had sat down on the bed, I would have suffered a major shock, perhaps fatal. I thought of the powerful claw attachment on Zimmerman's heavy-duty robots and how it could bite through an insulated cable, but I said nothing.

We looked at each other. "It's—" Mary began, but I held a finger to my lips and gave the mirror a glance. I saw her face tighten, and she nodded.

And then we heard the brush of Zimmerman's wheels on the deep carpet, and turned to the door.

He was pale and breathing hard as though from great exertion. There were blue half-moons under his eyes from lack of sleep, and new, anxious lines around his mouth. He was frightened, I think, although whether of us or of the violence that had just taken place I couldn't tell. He parked his cart in the door and surveyed us with a kind of glassy-eyed desperation; it was as though he didn't quite know what to do but knew that his presence was somehow required.

"Jay," I said, "I want you to look at this."

He grappled with the armrests and heaved himself upright, then shuffled forward. The housecleaning robots sucked noisily at the foam around his feet. I reached down to the broken cable and held it up so he could see it. "It was touching the bed frame," I said. "I could have been killed."

He stared at it for a long moment, biting his lip, as though the cut cable were a puzzle he was trying desperately to solve. "I'm s-sorry, Doran," he said finally, lamely. "I didn't know . . . this part of the house . . . was in such bad repair." He gave me a shadow grin, panting like a puppy trying to make friends. "I'll have each bed checked," he said quickly.

"It was *cut*, Jay!" Hourigan told him. "Look at it." His face blazed anger and contempt. "That's called *attempted murder*. Somebody did it deliberately. There's no question of bad repair here."

Zimmerman gazed at Hourigan with wide, terror-filled eyes for a long and helpless moment. He was backing toward the door, perhaps without realizing it, sliding backward through the muck. He shook his head. "That's not . . . it's not possible," he said.

Mary reached out and touched his arm, and Zimmerman's backward movement stopped. He stared at her hopelessly, as though she were his only friend in a room full of hostile madmen. "There will have to be an investigation, Jay," she said gently. "The police will have to come."

Dumbly, he shook his head. "No . . ." he said. He started backing frantically now, the foam sloshing around his shoes. "No . . . no." He fell heavily into his cart and clutched for the controls. And then he looked at us all and shrieked.

"*Get out!*" We stood in surprise at his sudden fury, the robots prowling unnoticed around our legs. "*Get out of my house!*" Zimmerman screamed, his voice ringing off the low ceiling, breaking with the force of his anger. His fist pounded the padded arm of his chair. "You all *cheated me!*'' he said. ''You stole my data and gave me a bunch of worthless numbers!''

''Jay . . .'' I said, but Mary spoke at the same time, more firmly than I.

''Neither of us has an answer,'' Mary said. ''We want you to join us in finding one. We want you in Knight's Move, Jay.''

''Liars! You just want to steal my work and take the credit for it. Like Doran did before.'' He glared at me, a trapped animal, his jaw chewing on words that never surfaced. ''*Get out!*'' he screamed again, and then, as though the last howl had taken all the rage from him, quite suddenly his defenses broke down, his anger fading away. Now he seemed a pathetic child who has gone as far as he can on bravado and doesn't know what else to do.

''Go away,'' he whispered. ''Please.''

I could see tears in his eyes. He ducked down to hide them, wrapping his head in his arms, and through his arms I heard him speak in a small voice. ''Dorcas. Take me home.'' The cart lurched backward and began to move down the hall.

I took a step forward, wanting to drag him back and make him face what was happening, but Hourigan's hand on my arm stopped me.

''I'll talk to him, Doran,'' Hourigan said. He looked at me with an air of calm assurance. ''I'll know what to say to him.''

''Don't—'' al-Qatan said in warning, but Hourigan gave him a smile.

''I know. Don't get impatient and yell.'' He shrugged, then flashed us a grin. ''He has no reason to resent me, and he's very vulnerable right now. I'll calm him down and get him to come with us. The rest of you prepare to leave. I'll be back in just a little while.''

''I was going to say,'' al-Qatan said, ''don't sit on any electric furniture.''

Hourigan laughed and padded out of the room on bare feet.

I felt Mary's arms go around me, and I hugged her. My muscles seemed to have no strength, and I could feel my hands and biceps tremble. The foam that had splattered me began to soak through her robe. "This is so frightening," she said. "And so sad. All at the same time. You were right. These things often go together."

"Yes," I said, but I was thinking hard. When I first saw the cut cable, I was sure that Zimmerman had ordered it; after I'd heard him speak that morning, I'd thought he was more than capable of it. He was jealous of my scientific reputation, and jealous as well of my success with Mary—and with denThrush also, I supposed.

But now that I'd seen him, parked in his cart in my doorway and frightened out of his wits, my certainty had faded and my curiosity about Dorcas had increased. There were supposed to be powerful inhibitions on the programming that was hardwired into domestic household computers, and I was wondering exactly how many of the inhibitions had been removed in this case.

There had been a pattern of hostility from Dorcas from the very beginning, when she'd locked us out of the control room. Since then it had escalated, just as Zimmerman's resentment of us had escalated.

Had Dorcas acted on her own? For centuries she and Zimmerman had been wrapping each other in an oedipal relationship so distorted and so sick that probably there was no sorting out which of her patterns was programmed and which anticipated from Zimmerman's unstated wishes. She was serving him as best she knew how, following her programming and with no healthy personalities present to contrast with Zimmerman's sick one. She had centuries of intimate knowledge of his psychological patterns to act on. When she'd ordered the robot to cut the cable, had she been acting on an *assumption* of how Zimmerman wanted her to act? If so, no wonder Zimmerman was frightened.

"You have been asked to leave the house," Dorcas said in a flat, admonishing voice. I felt Mary's arms stiffen as they held onto me. "I must ask you to gather your things and leave. If Mr. Falkner will give us a list of his belongings that have been damaged, I will see that they are replaced."

"Yes," I said. "You can bet I'll do that." And then I said to Mary and al-Qatan, "Let's get dressed and meet in Mary's room."

I took my suitcase with one hand and Mary's hand with the other. We made our knight's move down the hall and went into her suite. The holograms in the windows were showing a brilliant scarlet dawn, throwing flickers of red over our damp clothing. In silence Mary dropped my hand and walked into the bedroom to dress. I didn't follow. I wanted to think.

Just in case, I checked the contents of my belt pouches, which held some things for the purposes of survival. One doesn't remain the owner of a planet for more than a half-dozen centuries without learning a few tricks. Dorcas was still barred from the suite by my comp—unless, that is, she'd had one of her robots pull its plug while we were out of the room. I walked in alarm to the mirror, where I saw the deck in place and doing its job; I relaxed.

Al-Qatan came quietly into the room, carrying his bag. The fires of dawn flickered on the planes of his face. He looked significantly at the mirror and I nodded at him.

"It's safe," I said.

He let out a breath. "I've been thinking about what we should do."

"So have I. But I don't know the laws on this planet."

"There's a . . . a sort of a division of the police set up for cases like this," he said. "These situations come up every so often. An . . . an older person, going through a disintegration of the personality.''

Suddenly there was a noise from my computer and Dorcas's maze-hologram appeared before the mirrors. "I must ask you to hurry," Dorcas said. "Please prepare to leave at once.''

I turned to her with a snarl. "What will you do if we don't, Dorcas? Call the police?''

Smugly, imperiously, the hologram swirled in its labyrinth and gave no answer. Reflected silver flashed in the mirrors. Since it was now useless, I disconnected my computer deck and tucked it under my arm. Mary's door opened and she came out with her bags. She looked tired and drawn. I took one of her bags and she smiled wanly.

"I see you are ready," Dorcas said. "Please assemble at the door. Dr. Hourigan will meet you there.''

We looked at each other and shrugged. There was nothing else to do. As we walked down the corridors, Dorcas's silver image rotated from every mirror, from every humming room.

Dorcas's hologram seemed to occupy half the entryway. Hourigan's bag had already been deposited here by robot. We put our bags down and waited. Dorcas had won this round; but as soon as we got out, the wheels would be set in motion to pry Zimmerman from this concrete womb he'd built.

And then, to our surprise, Dorcas's image faded and we heard Zimmerman's voice.

"Doran . . . Doran.''

His voice was indistinct, interspersed with gasps and sobs, as though he were crying. The volume was gigantic, and my ears protested. We looked at each other in sick fear, not knowing what this meant but knowing it was going to be bad.

"There's . . . been an accident," Zimmerman said. "He tried . . ." I held my ears as he began to weep, the sobs crashing down one after the other. ". . . to touch me. *He tried to touch me!*" Zimmerman cried.

"Jay," I said. "Where are you? How can we get to you?"

And then the sound broke off and we heard the hissing of wheels on deep carpet. A robot came around the corner, bearing a burden.

Hourigan. Lying back in the robot's arms with a surprised expression on his face, one of the robot's claws pushed clean through his chest and partially supporting him in an upright position. Blood was soaking his jacket and kilt, running down his legs, leaving a trail behind. I heard al-Qatan give a moan, and the sound from my own throat echoed him. My heart was pounding in my ears, louder than Zimmerman's voice had been.

And suddenly Dorcas was there again—not the maze image this time but the woman she had let me see that morning, almost life-sized here in front of the big mirror, severe in her Victorian blouse. She looked at us with eyes that glittered like shards of ice.

"I'm afraid there's been an accident," she said. "I must ask you to stay until this is cleared up." Her voice was schoolmarmish, disapproving.

"Please stay right where you are."

I could see the robot's arms moving. It was coming closer.

20

As the robot advanced into the hologram, the laser firelight that was Dorcas flared across Hourigan's face, scorched his hair. I stood frozen for a moment, held by the dead, opalescent eyes flickering in the holo flame. There was a blow to my shoulder as al-Qatan pushed past me to the outside door. He found it locked.

The robot began to turn, pivoting to bring its rear arms into play. Hourigan's body swung through the hologram again, fire dancing on his dead features. Mary was poised to run, her head turning in an attempt to find a place to exit the narrow entryway.

"Get behind me," I said. I wasn't sure whether I had enough breath to actually say it out loud, but Mary heard me and moved.

The robot was coming toward us. I put my hand in my belt pocket and came up with a pencil-shaped device.

Snaggles had given it to me centuries before, at a time when people were making a habit of trying to kill me. It created a field about ten meters in diameter that acted in resonance with the field created by the Falkner Power

System, the result being an overloading of the field that either melted hardware or blew the circuit breakers in the system. The field resonator was powered itself by a small Falkner unit but was insulated against its own action.

I'd used it once recently, on the canyon rim when I'd sent the floating medialites dropping into the Plongeur. I'd been able to pass off that event, and the sudden loss of power on the hovercraft, as an inexplicable coincidence. Although I knew it was inevitable that someone would discover the effect sooner or later, I preferred not to publicize it. Successful avoidance of an assassination can often depend on surprise.

I pressed the stud. The robot made a few clicking sounds and stopped. It all happened very fast.

I let out a breath. If the robot had been equipped with batteries as a backup system, it would have still been moving toward us, its rear arms flexing, reaching. . . . But the robot was state of the art, and hardly anyone used batteries these days; it was much more convenient to use another Falkner unit.

Mary's fingers clutched my shoulder. "I've killed the robot," I said.

She pushed past me, heading for Hourigan.

Behind me I could hear al-Qatan fighting with the locked door. "Stay where you are," Dorcas said. "There has been an error. Stay where you are."

"Will you open the door, Dorcas?" I asked. "Or do we have to get Jay and make him open it for us?"

"*Stay where you are!*" Dorcas screamed. She moved toward me, filling the hologram. It looked as though she was trying to leap out of the projection to grapple us with laser claws. Behind her I could see flashes of Mary, standing by Hourigan, the anger in her eyes matching the fury that was Dorcas.

"The door's not opening, Doran," al-Qatan said.

I walked through the hologram to Mary. She was standing in front of Hourigan's body, her hand resting on his shoulder. I could see her trembling, anger and sorrow fighting within her. Hourigan stared up at us, surprised by his death. It was a horror that someone so alive should die in this way, in pointless battle with a sickness. I put my hands on Mary's shoulders. She shrugged them off, refusing comfort.

Al-Qatan followed behind me, silent, his face shadowed by Dorcas's back-lighting.

"We've got to get to Jay," I said. "And then shut off Dorcas."

Mary flashed a look over her shoulder. "Shut off Dorcas? How?"

"I can kill the power if I can get near the Falkners," I said. "There have to be a lot of big generators somewhere near the accelerators; that would be the efficient way to have built this place."

"What if she won't let us in?" al-Qatan asked.

"We'll have to get Jay," Mary said. Her voice was quiet, determined. Dangerous. "He'll let us in if I have to wring his neck."

"*Leave the boy alone!*" Dorcas howled. "*I'll kill you if you bother him!*"

"Oh, shut up," Mary said. In sadness now. She reached out a hand to touch Hourigan's cheek.

"I hate to leave him like this." Her hand trembled as she closed his eyes.

"We'll come back," I promised.

Al-Qatan was looking left and right. "Where's Jay in all this?" he asked, his question encompassing the entirety of the house. From somewhere far off I could hear the sound of robots whining toward us.

"Follow the trail of blood," Mary said. The anger had come back to her. I could see her neck muscles taut with the force of her anger. "And hurry. There are a lot of robots in this house."

We left Dorcas raging impotently behind us, trapped in her hologram, howling insults. As we turned left, a pack of housecleaning robots appeared on the right, coming from the direction of our apartments, falling into our wake. They were no threat to us; they had no offensive weapons, nothing short of vacuum-cleaner attachments and feather-dusters. They could only get in our way and, at the worst, trip us up.

We followed the bloody trail toward Zimmerman's own territory. I was in the lead, Mary behind me, al-Qatan in the rear. Dorcas frothed at us from every room, from every corner. We walked deeper into the maze. Two household robots came at us, buzzing furiously, and I kicked at them and turned them on their backs. They spun their wheels and continued to buzz. We went on.

Then, as we moved down a long corridor, the lights went out. The image of Dorcas writhing ahead of us vanished, leaving her flames burning slowly in afterimage as we blinked in the sudden darkness. Mary bumped into me from behind, and I jumped in surprise. And then I heard the hissing sound of tires whispering on the carpet, the subdued whine of electric motors.

"Behind us, Doran," al-Qatan said. I transferred the field resonator to my left hand and began burrowing in my belt pockets for the battery flashlight I knew I carried.

"You're blind," Dorcas said. Her voice was hushed and seemed to be whispered into my ear from only a few inches away. I leaped a foot. My heart began to pound.

"I know where you are," she said.

I gave up looking for the flashlight and turned to point the field resonator and press the stud. The whining electric motors ceased . . . and then, a heartbeat later, they began again. I pressed the stud once more, uselessly. The damn motors had batteries.

There was the sound of something else hissing through the darkness now, and then a thud. Al-Qatan gave a groan.

He pushed into us, trying to get past, knocking Mary against me. I fell heavily against the wall, trying again for the flashlight. I felt its shape, clutched at it. It was reversed in my hand and I couldn't find the switch.

"I've got you now," Dorcas said, her voice breathless, anticipatory, joyful in her hatred. "You're going to die."

"Let's *move*," Mary urged breathlessly. Her hands clutched at me. There was a crash from ahead, a wordless exclamation from al-Qatan. I brought the flashlight out of the pouch, tried to reverse it so I could get to the switch. Something metallic hit my left shoulder and I felt pain rocketing up my neck. I got the correct grip on the flash and turned it on.

It was the serving robot from the dining room, a tall thing with a pair of long, delicate metal arms. It was flailing blindly in the corridor, no more able to see than we were.

"You're going to die. *Die!*" Dorcas screamed.

I gave the robot a kick and it overbalanced and fell like a crumpled spider. I kicked it again and disabled its arms. It wasn't strong enough to do us any real damage, not unless we panicked in the darkness and began running blindly into things.

Al-Qatan had gone headfirst into the wall and fallen. He rose, bleeding from a cut over one eye. I looked fore and aft in the corridor, making sure there were no more robots on the way.

"That was lucky," Dorcas sneered. "Will you be so lucky next time? I don't think so."

"Follow the trail," I said.

We were deep in Zimmerman's apartments by now. We checked every room to make certain he wasn't hiding. Most of them were bare, unused. The thin flashlight beam jiggled on concrete, on old furniture covered in shiny plastic, on flowers of silk that smelled of must and rot.

The trail ended in the room where Hourigan had died—

Zimmerman's study, with computer controls, printers and a desk with a holocube of his mother on it. After that we just moved down the corridors and opened every door we came to.

I was coming to a turning in the corridor when Dorcas's white image suddenly blazed up directly in front of me. "You're going to *die!*" she shrieked. Pain throbbed in my eardrums. I turned the corner and was hit.

It was another of the big lab robots, its four arms outstretched, lunging from around the corner while Dorcas tried to distract us with her image. One arm smashed me in the side and I felt a wrench inside as ribs went. Another arm grabbed for the flashlight, got my forearm instead and twisted.

I screamed in pain. The robot danced in the light of the flashlight as it fell.

I pressed the stud of the resonator, and the robot died.

I must have lost a few moments because the next thing I remember is sitting on the floor while Mary bandaged my arm. Al-Qatan was standing over me with the flashlight, holding it trained on the wound. Dorcas gibbered in the background.

"Try to stand," Mary urged.

I staggered to my feet and pain shot through my ribs. Tears came to my eyes and Dorcas's image went blurry. "I'll go first," Mary said. Al-Qatan put an arm around me to hold me up. I kept a firm grip on the resonator.

We moved down the corridors. My pain had receded but the agony of waiting for it to return, of knowing that the wrong move would bring it back, was almost as bad as the hurting.

We found Zimmerman, finally, in the center of an empty concrete room, one of the many rooms that his megalomania had built but that his imagination could not fill. He was in his cart and alone except for the hologram image of Dorcas that flickered on the arm of the chair. The flashlight moved over the tears that stained his cheeks and on to Hourigan's blood that had spattered his clothes.

Zimmerman gave a sick moan as we came through the door. "Don't hurt me," he said.

"I'll kill them! I'll kill them!" Dorcas raged.

Mary went straight to Zimmerman and hit him twice in the face. He looked at her with vague surprise. He tried to say something but couldn't.

"I'll kill them!" Dorcas screamed. "I'll stand by you! I'll keep them all away. . . ." Her voice died as I pressed the stud and killed the Falkners in the cart.

"You're going to walk, damn you," I said. "To the accelerators."

"Up," Mary said. Zimmerman only moaned. Mary hit him twice more.

"Stop," he said. He was bleeding from the nose and lip.

"Up," Mary ordered.

Zimmerman struggled with the arms of his cart and managed to get to his feet. He moved off-balance, as though he were drunk. Snuffling, he came staggering toward us, blood running freely onto his shirt.

There was a whine from the corridor, and the door was filled by another of the heavy maintenance robots. Behind it was a serving robot, its long arms bent like a steel mantis.

"Dorcas!" I shouted. The effort sent pain shooting through my ribs and I clutched at them.

"We've got your boy here," I said. "He's going to get hurt unless you get your damned machines away from us."

The robots paused, then backed away from the door. Zimmerman, sobbing, moved blindly past me with Mary just behind, prodding him with little pokes and punches. As I passed the robots, I pressed the stud of the field resonator.

We followed Zimmerman's huge, staggering shadow down the dark, flashlit corridors. Dorcas's image flared silently in every mirror, standing like a sentinel, but the robots kept away.

When we reached the control room, al-Qatan was panting with the effort of bearing my weight. I tried to stand alone and felt pain like a stroke of lightning in my side, but I managed to keep my feet. The control room had no hologram of Dorcas; it would have interfered with the reading of the dials. I lurched to seize a metal table, which I jammed in the red door to the corridor to keep Dorcas from closing it behind us, as she'd done before.

"Open the freight doors, Dorcas," I ordered. There were controls to turn off Dorcas's monitor and I used them, then sat down in a padded chair in the control room while al-Qatan went down the corridor to make certain the doors were opening. Zimmerman's gurgling sobs echoed in the small metal room. The place smelled of sweat, fear, and blood.

"Shut up, can't you?" Mary asked. Zimmerman continued to weep. Mary snorted in disgust.

I heard al-Qatan's footsteps coming back down the corridor.

"I see daylight," he said.

"Good." I looked over at Zimmerman, who was leaning hopelessly against the wall. "Jay," I said, "take us to the Falkners. The main Falkners to the house."

He goggled at me. "Why?"

"We're going to turn them off," I said.

His eyes widened in astonishment, and then, to my utter surprise, he screamed and came for me, his arms outstretched, his fingers claws. Dorcas was his only friend, his mother and womb, his protector, and although what he felt for her was twisted, it was also love. She would die when the Falkners died, and my threat had finally pushed him beyond endurance.

I tried to climb out of the chair to meet him, fighting the pain that sliced through my side like a saw, but he didn't get that far. Mary tripped him and he fell heavily against the monitors, then dropped to the floor. Al-Qatan jumped between us and punched him savagely on the back of his neck. Then we were all three on him, a roiling moment of lunacy and anger and fear. We hit him because he had killed our friend, because he had built this place of madness where Hourigan died, because his creatures had hunted us through the dark labyrinth that reflected his decayed mind. Because he had become grotesque, a freak in both body and soul, because he was a personification of what we ourselves feared we could become. Because he had forced us to become indecent, to behave evilly to a man who was not himself evil, but ill. Ultimately, after he had lost the strength to scream, we hit him because he was detestable and helpless, and because it eased our own terror.

"Stop," someone finally said, and we were still sane enough to hear. Zimmerman was a sobbing hulk, and the room smelled of sweat and madness. I clutched at my side and fell into a chair.

"The Falkners," Mary said. "Take us there. Now."

Zimmerman could no longer walk. We followed him as he crawled, bleeding, from the control room. Not by the red door that led to the accelerators, but back into the house, down a long passage, around a bend. To a steel door by a tall mirror where the flaming image of Dorcas stood guard.

"Jay!" she cried. "What have they done to you?"

"Mama," Zimmerman whimpered.

Dorcas writhed madly in her hologram, her body distorting in its anger, in her frustration that she could not reach from the holo and claw us.

Mary tried the door and found it locked. "Open it, Dorcas," I told her.

"You can't go in there," she said. "I won't let you."

Rage flared through me. Because I was going to have to be savage again to a helpless cripple, and because I hated the necessity of it. I kicked Jay Zimmerman twice, feeling shame spasm in my broken side as he cried out and wept.

"Open," I gasped, "or we hurt him. We'll beat him to death right here."

Her wavering image faced me, as cold as ice and bright as a diamond. She knew that the steel door was proof against what I could bring against it and that she could probably entomb us here forever. She probably didn't understand how I'd done it, but she knew I'd killed the Falkners on her robots, and she knew that if I killed the Falkners in her power room, she would die. If she opened the door, she would be killing herself. But I was threatening Zimmerman, and she knew I would carry out my threat.

Dorcas drew back against the mirror. Her spine was iron and there was no trace in her eyes that she deigned to recognize my existence. For a moment I thought I'd failed, that she wouldn't kill herself for the sake of the bruised, obese freak on the floor.

There was a double snick as a pair of bolts drew back. Mary pulled the door open.

"No!" Zimmerman cried. "Mama! Please. *Don't!*"

He gave a single incoherent cry as I stepped into the room. The humming Falkners were in front of me, enough to light a small city, with vast cables hooked to them that went into the floor and on to the accelerators.

I touched the stud and Dorcas died. The light from the hologram outside vanished, leaving only the little beam of my flash. I listened carefully, hearing nothing but Zimmerman's distant sobs.

For the first time the house had ceased to hum.

I stepped back into the corner, where Mary and al-Qatan

waited, their outlines glowing in the light of the flash. "Mama," Zimmerman sobbed.

"Come on, Jay," I said. "We're leaving."

"No!" The cry was desperate. "I want to stay here. Please. Please, Doran."

Mary and al-Qatan looked down at him with weary faces. They were leaving the decision to me.

"We're taking him with us," I said. He cried out again, wanting to stay here in his dark womb, in the body of his dead mother.

"It'll be better this way," I said. "In the light."

Somehow we got him out, down the dark corridors, through the control room, down the concrete passage to the freight door. Pale light grew stronger as we neared the opening. The exit was on the top of the hill, near Zimmerman's rooftop gardens. Before we left the tunnel we could smell the olivets planted in rows, Zimmerman's flower of love.

Outside it was barely dawn. I sat down on a grassy mound and closed my eyes, waiting for al-Qatan to get to our car and summon the medics.

Zimmerman was on his hands and knees at the tunnel entrance, blinking in the light. When he saw me, he crawled over to where I sat, put his arms around me and cried himself to sleep.

Dawn flowered around us with the delicate scent of olivets.

21

The world came back to me in fragments, reassembling itself in pace with my slow heartbeat. Dawn light was glowing on the other side of my closed eyelids. There were arms around me, a head rested on my shoulder, warm breath nuzzled my neck. There was pressure in my bladder, and one of my arms was going numb. I rolled slightly to the left in order to change the position of my arm. Mary, who was lying on it, gave a contented sigh, smiled pleasantly in her sleep, and curled up on her side. She pulled the covers over her head.

It had been a couple of weeks since I'd killed Dorcas and my ribs had been cleanly healed, with a minimum of bandages and inconvenience, by sympathetic medics and some miracle injections. Jay Zimmerman was in a padded cell somewhere, and it would be years before the doctors could put his shattered personality back together. Hourigan was in the ground, buried in the uniform of a Kemp's physicist, with medals and ceremony. The service, I thought, had been too solemn for him, the eulogy read by a colleague I'd never met; Hourigan would have hated it. It was bad enough to think of Hourigan dead, but worse to think of him buried without laughter. Had I been given the chance to speak myself, I would have begun with Hourigan's limerick, the one beginning, *"Dorcas, a lunatic comp. . . ."*

Poorer in spirit, lacking in laughter, Knight's Move was advancing. Hourigan's team had been absorbed into Mary's and al-Qatan's. Final clearance for the ship's departure had been arranged, and the equipment that had been waiting for years in storehouses was being checked and shuttled up. All had been planned long in advance. The project had just been waiting for the final commitment from the government. And waiting for me, whom the government presumably thought might be able to work a miracle that would save their having to commit all those resources.

Mary came awake, pushing away the covers with a sweep of her arms, revealing her sleepy gray eyes, a contented smile, her brown-tipped breasts. "Good morning," she said, her voice drowsy, suggestive. She rolled over on top of me, wrapping her arms around my neck, straddling me with her feet pushing under my thighs. "I'm feeling insatiable," she said. "How about you?"

"Better let me pee first."

She laughed and let me up. When I returned, she was sitting cross-legged on the bed, holding the covers up to her chin. She looked like a strange oracular gnome atop its hillock. I sat down on the bed and plucked the covers away, and she slowly lowered herself, her arms crossed over her breasts. I put my arms around her and kissed her shoulder.

"Why so shy?"

She looked at me hesitantly. "Would you mind drawing the drapes?"

"Why? No one can see us." We were on the third floor of a privately owned estate house that McGivern had borrowed on my behalf; there was no one within miles. And Mary had never been shy about her body in any case.

She sighed and dropped her eyes. "Please," she said. "Indulge me." I shrugged, got out of bed, closed the drapes and returned. She pressed herself to me and gave me a long kiss.

"Insatiable?" I asked. Her grin answered me.

It was our day off from Knight's Move. We made love, ran six or seven kilometers just so we wouldn't get lazy, then sat in a bath together and had breakfast off floating trays—no crumbs, therefore superior to breakfast in bed. The owner of the house had Roman tastes: The deep, tiled bath would have held another three couples without crowding. I shaved, a little carefully in this case since one of the prices of eternal youth is coping with the eternal, occasional zit. Then I soaped Mary's back and worked at relaxing her neck muscles until she moaned.

She had swept her hair up on top of her head and I kissed the damp nape of her neck. She sighed and settled back against me. I put my arms around her.

"Got anything in mind for dessert?" I asked.

"Sorry." Smugly. "I'm satiated."

"I'm not."

She gave a low laugh and pointed a toe out of the water to turn on the hot-water tap. "Too bad, little man," she said over the gush of water.

I reached a hand up to cup her left breast, pressing it gently to her heart, and she put her hand over mine and leaned her head back against my shoulder. She closed her eyes. Steam rose from the gush of hot water.

"Why were you so shy earlier?" I asked. She shook her head, frowning without opening her eyes.

"Silly of me," she murmured. "But the morning light isn't . . . *kind* . . . to my years."

"Oh. Sorry. I'm not very intelligent in the mornings." I thought for a moment about how I'd seen her naked only in the shadow, how in the daytime she was always carefully clothed. So as not to offend the youthful tastes of the planet, so as not to flout her decision in our faces. And—perhaps—so as not to risk rejection.

"You haven't been to bed with a Diehard before, have you?" she asked.

"Not knowingly, no," I replied. "Except for you. And that was mostly unknowing."

She turned around suddenly, facing me in the tub, taking my hands and looking at me earnestly.

"It doesn't bother you?" she asked. "Knowing that I'm growing older? Seeing it?" She put my hand on her breast again. Lovely, warmly soft, showing its years. "Touching me?" she asked.

"Yes," I said. "It bothers me."

She looked down at her breasts, her hands on mine. Sadly. "So that's why I'm shy," she said and dropped my hands. In sorrow.

I put my arms around her, pressing her to me as the steam rose around us.

"I'm so self-conscious," she said.

"It's unnecessary. You can make arrangements—so you won't have to be shy with me, ever."

She swallowed hard and I felt a minute shake of her head. "No," she said. "That's decided."

"You can't reject what you don't know," I said. "Not honestly."

My best sophistry, I thought. Rationalizations available for the purpose of forsaking any ideal. Apply Falkner Power Systems, any hour of the day or night.

She drew back and looked at me. "No," she said. "I won't be Jay Zimmerman."

"You're not Jay."

"I could become like him. Easier than you think."

"Balls."

She shook her head and waved her arms in a gesture of denial, then treaded away from me to the tap, turning off the hot water. She brushed a silver strand from her forehead.

"We've been through this," she said.

"You brought it up." Accusingly.

"Yes," she said. "I'm sorry. It's only because—" She gave me a rueful smile. "—I've been having second thoughts. Now that it's too late."

"Too late for what?"

"Too late not to tell Brian."

"Oh." She stayed over by the taps, not offering to come closer. Her gaze shifted here and there, unwilling to settle on me. I sat up in the water and peered at her through the last of the mist.

"How did he take it?" I asked.

She shrugged, uncomfortably, and I felt a throb of empathy for her. It is not easy to talk about the ways in which one causes pain to one's friends. "I don't know," she said. "It's hard to tell with Brian. He doesn't register emotion. Not so you can see it." She wrapped her arms around her breasts as though trying to give herself comfort, then leaned against the side of the tub. "There's no real way to be kind," she said finally. "Not when you say . . . what I had to say. He hurt, I suppose."

"I imagine he did." The room echoed to the sound of a tardy drop of water plashing from the spigot. I felt a cold wind brushing my back, had a vision of a lonely spire of wreckage planted in concrete amid crusty snow. Remembered pain, remembered anger. "I suppose I'll be paying my own dues tomorrow," I said. "I'm having lunch with him, and with some shakers and movers he wants something from."

She looked away wistfully, at nothing, at a phantom of comfort, and slowly shook her head. "I hate to hurt him for this," she said. "He doesn't deserve it." Her eyes flickered to me. "And we won't be together for that long. Maybe he wouldn't even have found out."

Resentment sluiced into me at that presumption, and I bit down on an angry answer. Instead I moved toward her in the tub, touched her arm. "Why do you say . . . ?" I began. She turned away.

"Don't touch me," she said. There was anger in her voice. "It bothers you. You said so."

I paused. Resentment had settled in me for a long stay, and there was too much of it in a small room for this discussion to continue. I stood up and reached for a towel.

"It doesn't bother Brian," she said. Her voice was wistful now, touched with regret, directed more to herself than to me. "It really doesn't." She shrugged. "Oh, he doesn't *like* it, or understand it. But it doesn't bother him deep down, not the way it bothers you. On that level he accepts it."

"I don't want you," I said, "killing what I love. It scares me too much." I said it with anger, and Mary just looked off into space as though she hadn't heard me. I toweled myself dry and went into the bedroom to dress.

It is one thing, I thought, to love someone older, or younger, or different. Before Forever Now it was common enough to see old-young couples, the younger accepting the fact that the older would die first. It was necessary if they were to love at all. Now it was not necessary. Now it was like loving someone who announced she was going to commit suicide one of these days. It required a generosity of spirit, a kind of giving, that I did not possess. I was either too selfish or not crazy enough.

A few minutes later Mary came out of the bathroom wrapped in a towel. She put her arms around me and rested her head against my shoulder. I could smell the lotion she had used. I put my arms around her, around the oiled skin, and tried to decide what it was I felt. Relief. Love. More than a touch of remaining anger. And a sense that somewhere Kassandra was wailing her warnings—and no one understood. That none of us were yet done paying for what we were doing to each other.

"I'm sorry, Doran," Mary said. "I'm just not at my

best when I have to face up to the guilt of hurting people who don't deserve it.''

"I don't think I deserve it either," I said.

"No." She shook her head lightly, still pressing her cheek to my shoulder. "But I don't think I deserve the pressure you're putting on me."

"I suppose you don't." An unwilling confession, secretly disavowed.

"We came apart once before because of this. You said you wouldn't watch me die." She drew her head back and looked at me, her eyes frank, trying to appear more nonchalant than she was. "I don't think you've changed in that regard," she said. "And that means we're going to come apart again." She bit her lip. Her lashes were wet. "Then I'll go back to Brian, if he'll have me. Because he's not afraid of it, like you." She put her head against my shoulder again, punching me with her forehead, with the violence of her feeling. "He's a decent man," she said, "but I don't need him as much as I need you."

"I love you," I said. Pointlessly.

"Yes," she said and looked up at me. "But that doesn't seem to be enough, does it?"

"No. It doesn't."

"Damn you," she said, and her arms tightened around me. Not knowing what else I could do, I held on to her. Knowing that I would hold on as long as I could, and then do what I had to to.

The lunch I had with McGivern was shared by a number of university administrators who had to be talked into giving us some equipment that was more advanced than the stuff Knight's Move had been storing in our warehouses for the last ten years. McGivern was already deep in discussion with them as I came into the dark-paneled back room of the Faculty Club, and over lunch we went into our patented Faustus-Mephistophilis act, with me talking pie-in-the-sky balderdash about the purity of science and its contribution to the advancement of humankind, while McGivern gave them his ruthless, lipless smile and twisted their arms until they howled for mercy and gave us the loot.

We shook their hands as they left and told them it was nice doing business. They still seemed a little stunned from the one-two punch; it would be some hours before they figured out just how we'd done it, and by then McGivern's lawyers would have the contract drawn up and sitting on their desks.

The last administrator filed out, leaving us alone. Dread rose from the floor like an advection fog. There was a hush that I sensed we were each hesitant to break. I looked at him.

"We have a problem," I said.

"Concerning what?" He turned away from me to a silver coffee jug and poured, only the intensity in his narrow eyes betraying his concentration.

"Concerning what Mary told you over dinner the other day."

He took a cigar from his pocket and contemplated it. "I don't see that it's a problem between us, Doran," he said. "Between me and Mary, possibly. Or between you and Mary."

"Between the three of us, Brian," I said.

He considered this, stone-faced, while he took a sip of coffee and lit his cigar. Then he turned his flinty eyes to me. "So talk," he said and settled into a chair, outwardly calm, to listen.

I could feel dread soaking through my body, a physical discomfort that sat like a weighty condor on my shoulders and plucked at my throat. McGivern seemed determined to make me pay as much as possible for my speech. He sat attentive, apparently relaxed, apparently without a care in the world. And watched me sweat. McGivern's way.

I sat in a chair opposite him. "I'm sorry it worked out this way, Brian," I began. I thought of his house, the grounds, the long greenhouses that Mary said had been built for her. Brian in the corridor of the hospital with his pot of sweet auricula. A Brian less confident, more vulnerable, reacting to a kind of love that had never before touched him.

"Mary and I knew each other earlier," I said. "We were together for three years. And you knew that." I looked up at his calm face, at the wise eyes that gave nothing away, and sudden resentment crackled into my mind.

"Say something, Brian," I snapped. "Acknowledge my presence."

"I knew that you knew each other," he nodded, puffing smoke. "I'm with you."

"And you used that knowledge to get me here," I said. The words hung between us for an instant of quiet tension, and then McGivern nodded.

"Yes. I tried everything I knew. Hoping something would work." He peered at me quizzically. "Are you drinking less, Doran?" he asked. "You used to have a couple of brandies after every meal. Now you're just drinking coffee."

"Yes. I suppose you're right."

"You needed an occupation, I thought. That's what I'd thought all along."

"Brian," I said, "we're getting off the subject."

"Are we? I thought the conversation was over when you had me admit I'd used Mary to get you here." He turned to the ashtray and flicked his cigar into it, then looked back at me. "Go ahead, Doran," he said. "But I have a meeting in half an hour and I'd be obliged if you didn't keep me here all afternoon talking about what I already know."

The hell with him, I thought. You can't talk to a stone wall.

"Brian," I said, giving it a last valiant try, "don't come to Amaterasu. Don't make yourself suffer more than you must. You have a life here. Live it."

For the first time I saw a flicker of reaction in his narrow gaze. He pursed his lips and thought for a while before he spoke.

"In my youth, Doran," he said, "there used to be a fashion for this sort of thing. Heart-to-heart talks, I mean. There was even a cant phrase that was used a great deal . . . let me remember." He frowned as he pretended to search his memory, then snapped his fingers. "Ah, yes," he said. "It was called *acknowledging*. Acknowledging one another's feelings."

He looked at me. Questioningly. "You're a little young for this, you know," he said, "but maybe your parents were into acknowledging this or that and you picked it up from them.

"At any rate," frowning deliberately, "the point of it was that if all the people who were involved in various kinds of bad behavior—being cruel to one another or rude or insensitive or running off with one another's wives or beating their children or whatever—that if all these people could get together and talk about what they were doing and acknowledge the various needs that had compelled them to be cruel to one another and so on, then everything would be understood and it would be *all right*. Of course this never seemed to make them stop being cruel to one another, or being adulterers or child-beaters—it just made them feel better about all the horrible things they were doing.

"The whole ritual got to be quite a fad. People were always going about acknowledging this and that, and it was expected in a lot of relationships. If one should happen to meet a nice girl that one wanted to go to bed with, one first had to put up with a lot about acknowledging this feeling or that feeling, and then one would have to come up with some feelings of one's own for *her* to acknowledge, and then one could safely have sex, knowing that one was doing it for the right reasons." He looked at me and shrugged. "Now why should one have to go through all these rituals in order to justify having sex?" he asked. "I mean, it seems to me the act is its own justification, don't you think? But I digress."

He leaned back in his chair and smiled. "Now I presume that what you would like me to acknowledge," he said, "is that you and Mary are lovers, and that because Mary and I were formerly lovers, you and she feel bad about it, but not bad enough so as to stop being lovers." He cocked an eyebrow at me. "Have I got that clear enough? Okay. I acknowledge that."

McGivern puffed his cigar, then folded his arms and leaned toward me, gazing into my eyes with his eyes of stone. For the first time I felt the anger in him, a chill and deadly touch on my spine that froze me to the seat.

"Now," he said, "as I understand the ritual, it's my turn to come up with some feelings for you to acknowledge. Well. Here they are.

"If you can make her change her mind, Doran, if you can make her decide to live, then . . . certain sacrifices will have been worth my while. If she doesn't change her mind . . ." Now the words were coming slowly, each precisely articulated, each with the angry force of a cannon ball. ". . . if she dies, and I lose the years she spends with you, I will not forgive you. Ever."

Flatly. A man of his word, a ruthless man of great power, making a solemn, gravel-voiced promise. Mephistophilis to Faustus: You will burn.

"Now," he said, "do you acknowledge that?"

I looked steadily into his wise and angry eyes. "I do."

He forced himself to relax, taking a long drink of coffee. "Good," he said. "I'm glad we had this talk. I think that's what one is supposed to say.'' He put down his cup and poured more coffee. When he spoke, he turned his eyes away, pretending to be absorbed in the way the coffee came steaming from the jug.

''I'm coming along on Knight's Move, Doran,'' he said, ''so I can be with her when circumstances permit. So that I don't lose more than I must. In the event you can't change her mind.''

There was nothing left for either of us to say. That afternoon we parted as allies and as enemies—each wanting Mary to survive, each wanting her love.

And, quite suddenly, I realized for the first time why McGivern had made that decade-long trip to Earth, why he had left his interests in the hands of caretakers while he worked on Knight's Move.

Because Mary was mortal. Because McGivern was going to make certain Knight's Move would succeed and grant to her name an immortality she refused her body.

A few weeks later I floated in the observation bubble of the *Bougaineville*, taking my last glimpse of Kemp's. Over the Northern Hemisphere there was the blinding white wedge of a sweeping cold front, and I thought of the snow gently drifting down on the spire of wreckage, turning to a rounded white hummock the concrete slab to which I had forgotten to bring flowers. Kemp's, I thought. Where I was fated to make endless mistakes, to learn no lessons, to cause little but pain, to animate nothing but grudges.

A lovely place, Kemp's, but to me a bitter one. I would be glad to see the last of it.

22

Twitch Time

I closed my eyes when the electrodes were turned on and my muscles started leaping. I was numb below the neck, but not numb enough that I didn't feel what the electrodes were doing to me, how my muscles were dancing to their tune. I didn't like it.

"Would you like to see a tape, Dr. Falkner?" The robot nurse had the same sharp tones as the machine that had tended Mary in the hospital on Kemp's.

"No," I said. "I'll just lie here and count the holes in the ceiling tiles."

The robot exited with the hushed sound of mechanical disapproval. I lay still for a moment and tried not to think about how bad I wanted to vomit.

There was a series of tones in the room and then the voice of my comp. "I'm getting a call from Dr. Liddell," it said. "Do you wish to receive?"

I opened my eyes and gazed at the holo projector in the upper corner. "Go ahead."

"I wanted to thank you for the valentines." The holo stayed blank: I heard only Mary's voice. It sounded tired, as though she were making an effort to seem lively.

"You're welcome," I said. Before I'd left Kemp's I'd bought her one valentine for each of the years we'd be asleep in transit and had had them sent by robot as soon as I knew we were both awake. Corny, but the best way I could think of being passionate with my body turned off below the neck.

"Do you have your holo camera turned off?" I asked. "Or is my set not working?"

"No one's having pictures of me until I get up," she said. "I look like hell right now." She paused for a moment, then added, "So do you, by the way."

"Thanks. I know." I swallowed bile. "I think I'm going to upchuck any minute now. Do you know if this machine cuts out when that happens, or is it going to let me drown?"

"It's supposed to cut out."

"Glad to hear it." I swallowed again and fought a wave of nausea. Slowly it passed.

"Doran." Mary wasn't bothering to fight the weariness and pain anymore. Through my own misery I felt a wave of concern.

"Doran," she said again, "I'll call you later. Neither of us seems to be conversational right now."

"Take care," I murmured, hoping the medic knew what he was doing. Since they were less resistant, cold storage was harder on people who had aged past the norm, and Mary sounded dreadful.

But there was nothing I could do about it. Except lie in my bed and suffer, and worry about the things I couldn't control.

Last Songs (1)

Sometimes I think about our friend,
The one who—they say—is voyaging among the stars.

I stand outside the light of the fire, gaze up,
And hope to see his path among the distant flames
That shine like the diamond he gave me.
I hope there is fragrant hyacinth where he is,
Fresh mint, good company, the things that
Delighted him when he was among us.

I am feeling older tonight. I seem more aware than
  usual
Of the gray in my coat, the way
My feet pain me in the morning.

I would like to see our friend before I die,
Pluck my lyre and sing.

But our friend has not come,
And so I stand outside the fire
And sing my songs to the stars.

Hard Radiation

The aurora flowed in glowing sheets over Amaterasu's
dark side. The planet had only a small molten core and
hence a slight magnetic field—but so much radiation boiled
from the furious blue-white sun that even Amaterasu's
magnetic field was enough to capture a vast aurora—it
bloomed everywhere, brighter at the poles but covering the
whole night side with cold fire, pale green, pale orange,
pale white. From what I could tell, the aurora was going to
be the only lovely thing about the place.

I sat in the first-class lounge, watching the aurora on the

giant screens connected to the ship's outside monitors. I could have watched it live, but using the observation bubble would have meant going weightless, which would have complicated maneuvering the bottle of wine and two glasses I had brought.

Mary was late, but then that was no surprise. The rest of us had been out of bed for two days before she felt strong enough to rise, and it had been a further two days before she felt strong enough to leave her room. I hadn't been allowed to see her during that time, only to hear her voice as she spoke remotely. Although the weariness and pain had decreased from day to day, she still sounded tired and was making an obvious attempt to seem cheerful. I wondered if she were pushing herself too quickly—but having a drink while watching the big screens in the lounge had been her idea, and it hadn't seemed overly strenuous for a first excursion. And the lounge, like the infirmary, was high in the ship's centrifuge, where there was lesser gravity, easing the strain.

A pale green aurora flared over half of the Northern Hemisphere, the palmprint of a ghostly god touching the upper air. I watched as the shapes writhed and didn't notice Mary until she had already crossed half the room.

She was dressed in cool white with a black overvest, a severe color scheme modified by the hushed lighting of the room and by her bright, relieved smile. Her chin was stiffened by a duplicate of the neck brace she'd worn on Kemp's, with the same green LED gleaming cheerfully. I kissed her, tasting her lips and her scent. Even in the dim light I could see that she was carefully made up to cover the new evidences of strain, the lines of weariness under her eyes.

"You look almost recovered," I said.

She stepped back to arm's length and regarded me critically. "Chivalrous, but insincere," she said, and then her eyes dropped to the table. "I hope that's a good wine. I intend to drink two-thirds of the bottle."

"It should be good. It aged ten years while we didn't."

"That's a matter of opinion," Mary breathed. She took a seat while I opened the bottle and poured. She drank off her glass in one swallow and then held it out for more. I poured again.

"Thank you," she said, took a more reasonable sip this time and put the glass down. I sat next to her and took her free hand. She gave me a smile, a relieved, reluctant sunburst, and inclined her trunk to rest her head on my shoulder, fighting the brace all the way.

"Sorry," she said. "But I'm in a . . . bleak mood. They finally let me read my mail yesterday—the stuff other than the valentines, the things they hold back so you won't be depressed through your recovery."

"And?" Having a fairly good idea of what was coming.

"I'm a grandmother. Twice." She raised her glass and took a hearty gulp of wine. Then she caught my look and shook her head.

"It's not what you think," she said quickly. "Not that I'm getting older. It's just that the grandkids will be all grown up before I ever see them. No chance to do my doting granny act, none at all. I can't watch them grow except in holos that are years old by the time they get here. My grandchildren won't know me until it's too late to form any real attachments."

"I'm sorry, lover," I said. "It happened to me too— more than once. When the kids emigrate, we start getting news every ten years or so. It's a lot of catching up to do all at once."

"Alex gave up his art too," Mary went on. "He's now specializing in interior design. Says it has a stable future." She shook her head. "God! I've never met his wife either; she was post-departure. I have a whole family I've never seen, and a son who's changed his stripes so thoroughly

I'll probably never get to know him again." She looked up at the image of the planet, reflected auroras touching her profile with gentle highlights. "I lost him when he was twelve, really," she said and bit her lip. "Well, that's it. No more kids." A shuddering breath. "I'm not going through this again."

I squeezed her hand. There was nothing to say to ease the hurt. She drank from the wineglass again, then shook her head and gave me a reluctant smile. "Sorry. I don't want to overdramatize." She tossed back her silver hair. "So," she said, "did you get any mail yourself?"

"Yes. Similar to yours. My daughter Branwen's married, to a man I never met—one of my employees, a geneticist specializing in cetaceans. He's going to bring back the varieties of the great whales we've lost."

"A worthy goal. Better than interior design anyway. At least you had Branwen for twenty years or so." Then she caught something in my look.

"Yes? Something else?"

"Philodice is dead," I said. And Chiron, and all the centaurs I knew. Mary's eyes widened in concern.

"The singer?" She pressed my hand. "Was it unexpected? Or was she a Diehard?"

"A Diehard. But she died young. An aneurism, they think." I thought of her dark eyes, her silver mane braided with flowers, her blushing breasts. The sound of her unearthly voice as it echoed from the stone seats of the theater at Delphi.

"You were involved with her?" Not jealousy, I knew. But Mary was curious about this strange poetess and singer she knew only from the evocative lyrics, the delicate phrasing, sweet as dew and bitter as tears.

"No. Not in the way you mean. But she was a student and . . . a friend. Branwen sent me a recording of her last songs."

A slow ache passed through my heart. Philodice was a

Diehard, yes; but only because I had decreed it so. Because I wanted a fast-evolving species to compete with long-lived, overcomfortable humankind and had agreed to sacrifice the lives of Philodice and all the next generations on the altar of my experiment. I was certain I was right, but the cost was high. And would be higher still when the centaurs found out what I had done. They would hate me then for the way I had manipulated them.

Mary realized my sorrow and leaned over to put her arms around me. "Hell, Doran," she said, "all this sadness is relativity's fault. Let's finish Knight's Move and give Einstein a run for his money. If we can get the teleportation thing right, we won't have to miss anyone's birthday from one end of the galaxy to the other."

I laughed, as was expected of me, and kissed her. We ordered dinner—McGivern had made certain Knight's Move had a human chef, and a talented one—and over our steaks Mary and I depleted the wine bottle.

Our conversation was mostly shoptalk. The news from home had confirmed in our hearts what we had already acknowledged, dryly and without conviction, in our minds. That for the length of Knight's Move we were cut off, isolated except for the brief flashes arriving via Zimmerman's communicator, and these were as likely to produce sorrow as joy.

The rotating globe of the nightside planet shimmered below us, the aurora shining from the cutlery, gleaming in the depths of Mary's eyes. I began to realize what we were saying to each other and, more important, what was not being said.

We had, I think, declared a truce, a truce whose terms were unspoken but clear. The news we'd received was loaded with dangerous subject matter: families, deaths, Diehards, the sort of material only too likely to produce another storm of the sort that had caught up with us as we soaked in the bath that years-ago day on Kemp's. But the storm winds hadn't blown; and as we dined, I began to suspect that the reason for the calm was because we had, between us, put our differences aside till a later date.

Mary was a Diehard, and that fact was a two-edged sword that threatened to cut both ways. But we had agreed to bury the sword, at least for the present, because as long as Knight's Move remained at Amaterasu, the issue could be held in abeyance. We could remain lovers and friends, and the critical issue not be faced.

But someday reckoning would come, and the sword would cut fast and deep. Because if Mary remained immobile, I knew what my decision would be.

I had not changed in the years since we first parted. I did not suffer mortality easily, and I would not collaborate in suicide.

Mary knew this, I'm sure. And, I'm equally sure, knew what her own response would be once the moment of confrontation could no longer be postponed.

As well as sharing an unspoken conspiracy of silence, I think we were sharing an irrational hope. That Knight's Move, successfully completed, might make a difference. That the world Knight's Move opened might be one that Mary would want to explore for more than a single lifetime.

We dined and talked while the auroras flared on the screens and the *Bougaineville* moved slowly over the nightside of the planet. The waiter came with cherries jubilee, and the brandy flamed with the same dim, fragile radiance as the waves of glowing light that shimmered over the planet. And then, as we finished our dessert, *Bougaineville* came out from the nightside and Amaterasu's sun thrust into our eyes with brilliant needles.

The sun was so distant it was only the size of another star, a simple pinprick on the widening crescent of Amaterasu, but the light coming from it, even subdued as it was by the polarizers on the outside cameras, was of a hellish intensity. Mary and I looked at each other in surprise as the table was lit as though by the bright, merciless light of a sodium-vapor lamp. The bottle of wine cast a hard-limned inky shadow. Our hands looked like parchment stretched over bone. Mary's face seemed to be composed of translucent features painted over a yellow-white death's head, shaded by a disordered thatch of hair.

And then the automatic compensators cut in and the vidscreen displayed a patterned starfield on which the fever-light of the blue-white sun, perched on the edge of the disklike silhouette of the planet, was reduced to the same intensity as the farther stars. The compensators that reduced the star's ferocity also reduced the fragile light of the planet's aurora to nothing, and Amaterasu lay as a nullity against the stars, a black doorway to elsewhere. Mary and I blinked in the sudden twilight.

"We're going to be out under *that* every day?" she asked.

"The atmosphere cuts out the worst of it," I said. "Or so I'm told."

"My god," Mary said. She gazed down at her dessert. "It's one thing being told about it. It's another to see it."

"We'll put a field over the camp," I said, "and polarize out most of it."

"My god," she repeated.

Subdued by the sun's brief onslaught, we finished our dessert in silence. Mary tugged at the neck brace and tried to turn her head. "Tired?" I asked. She looked it.

"Yes. Maybe it's time to leave." We rose and walked arm in arm across the room. The steward, standing in his white mess jacket, gave us a nod and opened the door. It hissed shut behind us, and I hesitated.

"Are you on this deck?" I asked. "I just realized that I don't know."

"Doran, could we go to your quarters instead?"

I looked at her in surprise. "It's a couple of decks below. The gravity's heavier there."

She stepped closer; I could feel the warmth of her body pressing against me. "I'll live," she said. "Maybe I could, ah, lie down." With a sly smile. "Do you suppose hormones just go on accumulating while we're asleep?" she asked. "I'm hornier than I've been in, um. . . ." She laughed. "Years, I suppose."

"Are you sure?" Her only reply was a smile, that and the way she looked up at me from under her lashes. I kissed her. She had to bend far back to raise her face to mine, and the kiss wasn't a success. She guffawed.

"Never mind," she said, tugging at the brace. "I'll take the damned thing off."

"Wait till we get to my quarters. You can take it off as part of a striptease. It'll be much more erotic that way."

She laughed again. We began moving toward the elevators. When the door opened, we were kissing once more—more successfully this time, since I'd bent down and picked her up.

I wasn't paying attention to who came out of the elevator, not until I heard footsteps, opened my eye a crack and caught a glimpse, past a soft-focus wisp of Mary's hair, of Brian McGivern's startled face. *Acknowledge this, you bastard,* I thought, but the look in McGivern's eyes was too much like a dumb beast in pain, and he turned away too quickly for my triumph to last long. He hadn't seen us together before and he hadn't known what it would mean to him or how deeply it would touch him. He stepped away without speaking.

I put Mary down and we moved into the elevator. "Five," I said, and the doors hissed shut. On McGivern, not on us.

Fences

The robot fliers moved quietly over Amaterasu, building fences. Digging the holes, planting the fence posts, pouring concrete and tamping soil. Returning to base for more supplies when they were empty. The fence posts stood in perfect geometries over the plains, each several kilometers apart, each watching with electric eyes that scribed their visions onto recorders, each constantly monitoring the terrain and themselves, feeding the results to the central computer.

Shaped like old-fashioned lamp posts, they stood and surveyed the prairies. They were trained to look for "events," Knight's Move jargon for teleporting lugs. They would record any event they saw and send a signal to base or to a satellite orbiting overhead.

Sometimes they went wrong, and then parts had to be ferried out by robot. Sometimes their signals didn't get through the appalling atmospherics, but the recorded events were preserved for the time when their signals finally arrived.

They operated quietly, efficiently, unobtrusively. Like all good robot devices should.

Which was more than could be said for the rest of us.

Life In The Sun

It was de rigeuer on Amaterasu to cover one's face with a white paint that kept out the sun's rays. Wide-brimmed boonie hats, caps with long brims, and havelocks trailing down the neck were popular. Kilts and skirts went out of fashion very abruptly when the first survey teams came back with second-degree sunburn on their knees and calves. Once I forgot to anoint my ears before setting out and for the next few days the skin peeled off like cellophane, crumpling next to my ear.

The people on Kemp's expected more from the physics teams than they did from the others; but we were in a definite minority among the hundred and fifty ecologists, geologists, biologists and various technicians, most of whom had jobs more immediate than ours. The physics teams, at the beginning, were to assist the others, or at least to keep out of their way, until time could be spared to get our heavy equipment down from the *Bougaineville*.

We watched the other teams do their work and brainstormed among ourselves in a haphazard, pointless way, trying to come up with new theories. We missed Hourigan's cheerful, subversive presence. There were still planetary surveys going on, more detailed than the kind of stuff Ruyter had done in his three years, but also far more insignificant—we had a two-person team just to study the aurora, for example. It had occurred to someone that other life forms might be teleporting too, without anyone having noticed it; and so during the first weeks, teams of forty biologists were digging up worms and proto-lizards, netting fish and the local equivalent of shrimp, and tagging all of them with near-microscopic tracers. It was just by way of being thorough, with no real results expected except perhaps to discover the migration patterns of proto-lizards.

The base camp was quite nice as such things go, protected from the horrors of the daytime by a Falkner field partially polarized so as to reduce the radiation. There were some interesting side effects. Inside the field the sky was blue; outside it was an intense, ferocious, blazing white. Sunsets were reddish inside the field; outside they were blue.

As nice a location as possible had been picked for base camp. It was near a small lake and there were a large number of shade mosses around. I thought the setup was just pleasant enough to make us conscious of what we were missing by being here instead of someplace civilized. There was a baseball diamond and a swimming pool, and when the teams found time for building it, there would be a room for zero-g headball. There was a lounge that featured all the excellent things McGivern's cook could do with preserved food, no one having figured out a way to make the local stuff edible, and a well-stocked wine cellar.

Because there was no ground cover, brown dust rose from our feet whenever we walked inside the field, and people coming in hot and sweaty from the outside soon found the dust clinging to their white face paint and longed for grass, or even artificial turf. We'd had to kill all the local vegetation to keep it from overrunning us—plants accustomed to a desperate environment such as Amaterasu's are likely to flourish in ridiculous abundance when the conditions that keep them small and undernourished are turned off.

There was everything we needed except the answers. Large amounts of data began coming in after the first few days, but they were either irrelevant or negative. The physics teams, sitting in the lounge or assisting the other teams at whatever minor tasks they'd trust us with, began to be the subject of inquiring looks. *Worked us up a miracle yet?* they seemed to ask. *When can we get away from this damned place?*

These were not unreasonable questions. But no one had come up with any reasonable answers to them.

Last Songs (2)

Nephele, I am told

That you have been seen, at the strand
With my lover.

But then I remember
The frankness of his gaze,
The honesty of his touch.

And I think, "Philodice,
How can you credit such lies?"

Flying The Fence Line

In his desert clothes and white antiradiation paint, Muhammad al-Qatan looked like the ghost of T.E. Lawrence. The paint smeared even his mustache—after his first experience with the stuff, his beard had gone. The wings of his checkered kaffiyeh were pinned up on top of his head; the result resembled a mutant cross between an Arab headdress and a Stetson.

"Got back to your roots yet?" I asked.

He grinned self-consciously and adjusted his agal. "These were designed for a climate like this."

"I thought the Arabian desert was a *dry* climate, Muhammad," I said. "This is a humid one."

"They work as well as those coveralls you're wearing."

I couldn't dispute that, so I just nodded. We started walking across the sterilized dust toward the shimmering edge of the field. As soon as I stepped out of the protection of the field, I felt sweat spring up on my forehead.

One of the largest tasks facing the Knight's Move Project was now underway, and even the physics team had been drafted for it. We were trying to put collars on two hundred thousand lugs.

On previous expeditions lugs had been tagged with simple radio beacons. These new collars were more complex, containing recording devices and sophisticated detectors. They would record the last twelve hours of the lug's existence, perpetually recording new information on top of the old, producing a continuous erasure of the past and a constant absorption of the present. The recordings were in great detail and included changes in respiration, pulse, body chemistry and pictures of a three-hundred-sixty-degree horizon—no matter where the beast was and whatever it was doing. The collars would detect and measure every known type of radiation.

When and if a lug teleported, we hoped to get a detailed

picture of the place it had just been. A team would be scrambled from the base camp, follow the collar's beacon and bring the collar back for study. We knew that so far as anyone knew, the teleportation was instantaneous, but we were hoping that this might be an illusion based on incomplete data and that the lugs moved somewhere outside of time and were then returned to the same instant in time but in a different place; and if the lugs went anywhere outside of time, we hoped to learn where.

But first we had to put the damned collars on the lugs, and that promised to be a brutal job that would take a few months out of the lives of most of the camp's personnel. It was not something that seemed wise to trust entirely to automation.

We had orbited satellites that were marking the positions of lug herds, and now we would start flying out in pairs to collar them. There was a rotating schedule of who went with who so we wouldn't get bored with each other.

Al-Qatan took the machine up to altitude and sped southwest, the shimmering field once again polarized to cut out most of the radiation. The satellites had already found a herd for us and the computer gave us a vector. Al-Qatan steered the fieldcar himself. He found autopilots boring. He set the car on a slow rotation, the dark green earth and bright white sky alternating in gradual succession. I lay back on my couch and tried to conserve my strength. I knew I'd need it.

We found the herd and al-Qatan circled it slowly. "You can go in from the north," he said. "I'll move in from the south."

"Fine."

I went back into the luggage compartment and got my gun and helmet; then I told a cart full of lug collars to follow me. When al-Qatan brought the car down, I opened the hatch and stepped out.

Heat and light struck me like the sweaty fist of a giant. I

tried to stop and catch my breath but the humid air seemed to move slowly, like fog, through my trachea. Sweat began to ooze through every pore. The lugs had to be crazy to put up with this without teleporting to someplace nice and cool, like the Kalahari in midsummer.

I took my boonie hat off and put on my helmet, then put my gun on. The helmet had a small, low-intensity laser trained on my right eye, able to follow my eye movements. The gun rode on my shoulder in a kind of harness and moved on gimbals. It was slaved to my helmet and would aim wherever the laser told it my eye was looking. All I had to do was to look at a lug and press the trigger, which was a remote unit in my hand the size of a pack of cigarettes. It could have been smaller but the designers wanted it to fit the hand without getting lost. I was told that the gun would discriminate between a human silhouette and that of a lug, so if I were ever attacked by space pirates, or a planetary geologist crazed by the fact that nothing on Amaterasu made any sense, I would have to find other methods of defending myself.

Lugs were quite passive, there being no predators, and would allow a person to walk right up and touch them; but that didn't mean they would sit still and allow someone to put a heavy collar on them. It was best to drug them beforehand. Drugging them was the easy part. I walked toward the herd and held the trigger down while moving my eyes from one lug to the next. The gun fired when it found an appropriate silhouette.

While al-Qatan was lifting off and circling to the other side of the herd, I drugged about fifty lugs. The entire herd of two hundred was down inside of ten minutes. Now came the hard part.

I stowed the helmet and rifle on the robot's rack, then put my hat on again and walked toward the nearest lug, the robot following me on its hissing cushion of air. I was dripping sweat. The stench was appalling; no one had told me that lugs smell bad. I took a collar from the robot, raised up a lug head and latched the collar around its neck.

This went on for two hours. We probably looked like a pair of scavengers looting the corpses on some weird battlefield. The lugs usually lay there stupidly and stared at us with their eyestalks, but sometimes their nervousness broke out in twitching convulsions and they looked like I had when I was exercised by electrode aboard the *Bougaine-ville*. Their three stomachs rumbled constantly as they worked away at the tough local vegetation. My sweat dripped down on them, stained with my white antiradiation paint. The lugs protested by farting loudly and frequently. The whole experience, I suspected, hurt me much more than it hurt them.

Finally we had the herd tagged. The western sky was turning blue with the approaching local sunset. I was breathing hard and my heart was hammering like a black-smith at his forge. Al-Qatan looked as bad as I felt, perspiration streaking his white paint, his kaffiyeh sticking to the sweat on his cheeks and jaw.

"You've got lug shit on your boots," I told him as we panted our way back to the fieldcar.

He gave me an appraising look. "So do you."

We began scraping our boots on the horny upper parts of the moss. Behind us the first lug struggled to its feet.

We took some salt tablets and a nap before finding another herd and doing it all over again. The next herds were easier since we were working on the planet's nightside; the aurora provided enough light to work by.

We wrestled lugs for two days and then headed for home. Since our return journey was at night, I took off my antiradiation paint and let my skin breathe. There was no nonsense about steering from al-Qatan: He set the autopilot, lay back in his seat and closed his eyes.

"We'll have a great set of muscles when this is over," I remarked.

"Or we'll all be veterans of sunstroke."

Amaterasu rotated below us, a moving blackness. "Mary's due to go tomorrow morning," I said. "I'm going to try to talk her out of it. She may not be strong enough for this."

Al-Qatan opened his eyes and gave me a concerned look. "She's going with another woman," he said, "so she won't be pressed to keep up with a man in this kind of physical work. But maybe you're right. She might not be recovered from her cold sleep yet. She didn't look well, that first week."

I was surprised. "You saw her?"

"After I got up myself, yes. The medics let me and Brian visit her a couple of times, but she tired quickly and we left. Well. You know."

"No, I don't. She wouldn't let me see her till a few days after she was up."

Al-Qatan looked startled, then his eyes flicked away from me. "Vanity, I suppose," he said after a significant half-second of silence that let me know he'd had no answer ready. "Didn't want you to see her while she was down."

"I guess not," I said. He seemed grateful to me for not pressing it.

I lay back and closed my eyes, hearing in the whispering of the cabin's air conditioning the sibilant echo of a voice. Accusing. *It bothers you. You said so.*

All true. And it didn't bother Brian. So Brian was admitted to her bedside while I was not, because she didn't want to see the look in my eyes as I first saw her. She hadn't wanted to deal with that knowledge, that weighty piece of emotional baggage.

I told myself that I really shouldn't have been surprised. Or disturbed. But al-Qatan's news had shaken me, somehow made the world more uneasy. So while I pretended to sleep on the car's couch, I thought about what it meant and told myself that it didn't mean much of anything.

I decided not to mention it to Mary. It wasn't any of my business anyway. Bringing it up would violate the truce we had established, and that might lead to a confrontation that neither of us could afford. That Knight's Move might not be able to afford.

I repeated this logic to myself until it almost began to make sense.

Almost.

Events (1)

The transport bringing the physics teams' equipment down from the *Bougaineville* was the size of a couple of football fields, but even so, it needed two trips. The physics teams had their own building—a bunker, really— with fifteen-foot-thick poured concrete walls around the rooms where the accelerators would sit, all the construction having been done by robots working under human supervision while the rest of us were off collaring lugs.

The physics teams were spared lug duty while they supervised the installation of their equipment. After that we were to go back to collaring lugs while the robots and their human foremen put the roof on the bunker and packed a lot of earth on top.

Then our teams would start their runs. For lack of any better ideas, we'd run all the experiments we'd done on Kemp's, hoping to find anomalies in the results. It wasn't much, but in the absence of any new significant data, it was about all we could do.

It was twilight on Amaterasu, meaning that the sun was slightly less oppressive than normal and we could look forward to spending the rest of our shift in the relative cool of the night. Mary and I watched with a certain breathlessness as vast cargo-handling robots lifted multi-ton pieces of equipment and nestled them lightly into place, all with exquisite precision. Our human supervision was almost irrelevant; the robots acted like a drill tream fresh from six months' rehearsal, and they knew the bunker's plans better than we did.

"If I weren't aware of the potential disaster if one of these machines made a mistake," Mary said, "I'd be tempted to suggest that we jump in the swimming pool with a bottle of cold genever."

"Let's do it anyway," I said. "Everyone on this project is insured."

There was a growing fad among some of the Knight's Move personnel to add makeup to the white facepaint in hopes of looking less like a disenchanted ghost. Since it had proved impossible to resemble anything normal, even with the addition of makeup, most decided to at least look cheerful and ended up painting themselves as happy clowns.

Mary and I had been painted that morning by a giggling colleague just before the start of our shift. Mary had a bright violet smile and dots of scarlet on her cheeks. There were half-moon eyebrows in the middle of her forehead and starry lashes painted above and below her eyes. Hours in the sun had liquified the result, and her happy clown was changing into a tearful one, her features running, the smile turning to a frown. I assumed I wasn't looking my best either.

We hadn't seen much of each other for several weeks. Mary had not leaped at my suggestion that she beg off the lug-wrestling detail, and I knew better than to repeat it. She had managed to avoid heat stroke and had put on muscle, but the effort was exhausting her; on her return from a two-day expedition to the outback, she would shower and flop into bed and stay there, in the dark, until it was time to ride the range again.

I wasn't much more lively when I returned from my own journeys onto the prairies, but I was able to bounce back faster. Our schedules overlapped and we weren't very often on base at the same time. Watching robots haul heavy equipment while we stood in the heat of a blue-white sun, our paint running, was for us the next best thing to a vacation.

"I'd forgotten how much work it was, giving Einstein a run for his money," I said.

Mary smiled faintly. She didn't have the energy to smile any other way.

"Have you heard?" she asked. "One of the archaeology teams found a lug skeleton three million years old down in the Binford River Delta. So lugs have been around for at least that long."

"No reason for them to evolve."

"Pity the lug didn't have a collar," Mary said. "That would have livened up this expedition, I bet."

There was a chiming from my belt, and I held up a hand to put our conversation on hold and stuck a plug in my ear.

"Your nickel," I said.

Al-Qatan gave no sign of wondering what a nickel might be. "We have an event," he said. "One of the collared lugs."

I felt my heart lift. The beginning of the answers, I thought, the justification for all this brutal work. "An event," I repeated. "A collared lug." Mary's eyes turned from the robots to me and began to gleam.

"Want to come along with us and pick it up?" al-Qatan asked.

"I'm on shift."

"I'm sending one of my team to take your place." Mary was mouthing urgent, silent questions at me.

"Thanks," I said.

"Hurry. There is some urgency here. The event happened about six hours ago, but there weren't any fence posts in sighting distance and the bad atmospherics kept the collar's radio signal from getting through until just a few minutes ago."

"I'm on my way," I said. I took the plug out of my ear

just as Mary was about to start punching my arm in her impatience. "I'm invited along," I told her. "Want to come?"

She looked at me hopelessly. "How can I? I'm on shift here, and with you gone, that means even more jobs for me."

"How can you be a team leader unless you learn to delegate authority?" I asked.

Her eyes grew hooded as she thought this out, but from the slow grin that came across the clown's sagging smile, I could tell she was beginning to appreciate being on top of the academic food chain.

She began to delegate, and by the time my replacement had arrived, we were both free of obligations. The field was already shimmering around the big cargo skimmer as we stepped into it. It was more crowded than we had expected, and there was more cheerfulness and laughter than any of us had seen in weeks.

We and al-Qatan were supernumeraries, really—we weren't necessary; our parts would come later. But I saw a lot of supernumeraries on that flight: an archaeology team leader who should have been out superintending his dig in the Binford Delta, some of the biologists, an engineer, the entire two-person aurora team, and even the steward from the lounge, still in his white mess jacket.

Each with shining eyes and rapid pulse, each filled with an electric excitement that flashed from one of us to the next. It was an unreasonable hope that the collar would contain any information we didn't already have—if the transition was as instantaneous as it appeared to be, there would be no information at all—but if the hope were unreasonable, then we had all settled for unreason. Even the imperturbable al-Qatan was flushed and breathing hard. And although I knew better, I shared in the glow, high with the hope that this might provide an answer. We had driven ourselves to exhaustion collaring thousands of animals, and now we might get our payoff.

We flew halfway across the world by way of the nightside. The sky was ablaze with the aurora for our thirty-minute night, but Mary didn't see it—she'd curled up on the seat next to me, put her head in my lap and gone to sleep. There was a sweet smile under the melting clown face. My thighs were powdered white by her paint.

We came up with the dawn and the lug herd more or less at the same time. One of the techs tranquilized the lug as we hovered overhead, and then the craft set itself down.

Everyone stood and moved to the cargo hatch. I looked over at Mary and gently shook her by the shoulder. Her eyes came open with a little crystalline sound. "We're here," I said. There was a blast of superheated air as the field fell away and the hot prairie winds came into the craft.

Mary yawned, gave me a smile and stood to follow the crowd as it stampeded out to the prostrate lug.

The others, full of smiles and hope, were grouped around the lug as two of the crew members wrestled the collar off its neck and replaced it with a new one. The lug's companions watched from nearby, each keeping one eyestalk trained incuriously our way. A tech bent and lifted the collar over his head so we could all see it. There was a brief cheer and a shared feeling of something very much like triumph.

Mary put her arm around my waist and looked up at me. "We're hoping too much, aren't we?" she asked.

"The odds aren't good that the collar will tell us anything."

"If after all this brutal work. . . ." She left the thought unfinished.

"Yes," I said.

Another fieldcar shot over the horizon to hover overhead. It had a crew of two who would keep the lug under observation for a few days. If its behavior turned out to be normal, it would be shot and dissected by the biologists.

Thirty minutes later, still painted as melting clowns, we stood in the collar control room while the chief tech took apart the collar and put its recorder into the comp. The smiles and laughter were gone; in their place was quiet tension as all eyes focused on the tech and his instruments.

Brian McGivern was there, standing silently apart, watching intently as the collar was plumbed for its answers. He and I hadn't had much contact, but what there was was civil. He was holding no grudges, at least not yet.

Perhaps in order to justify his absence while he was away on this expedition, he'd had himself given ambassadorial rank. He'd managed to convince Kemp's government that we might find some manner of alien intelligence and that he ought to have the authority to deal with the situation if it arose. The appointment subjected him to a lot of jokes about being Ambassador Extraordinary to the Lugs, or Ambassador To-Whom-It-May-Concern. But I knew he wouldn't have worked for the appointment unless he were prepared to use the authority he had been given, and I was sure that, to McGivern at least, the jokes were not amusing.

Giving way to the tension we all felt, McGivern leaned forward a bit to look over the tech's shoulder as the tech freeze-framed his way through the recording of the event. I knew the tech's answer before he gave it. There was a bleakness in his eyes that hadn't been there before.

"Nothing," he said. "Instantaneous transfer from one place to another."

There was a hushed sound in the room that signified bits of hope crumbling. People straightened, began looking at one another to find reason for continued optimism.

"That was the visual record," McGivern said. "What about the other spectra?"

The tech bent to his board again. "Nothing. Nothing. Nothing." His mouth had tightened to a line. "Nothing at goddamn all," he said. He cocked his arm back and smashed it into the dismembered collar.

"*Nothing,*" he said.

Mary and I looked into each other's saddened clowns' eyes. "Nothing," she repeated softly. I felt a weight on my shoulders that might have been a phantom rifle harness, an ache in my bones that might have come from wrestling lugs. It was going to go on and on, and the odds were overwhelming that nothing would ever come of it. I shook my head.

"We wait for the next event," I said. "And in the meantime, we keep putting collars on lugs."

I sensed that few in the room welcomed my words. Perhaps my timing was not of the best.

"No one ever said that beating Einstein was going to be easy," I said.

They looked at me and at each other—and wondered where their hope had gone.

Thirty Syllables And More

"It's taken us six months," reported the biologist FitzAlan as al-Qatan and I stepped into the little lecture hall, "but I think we finally have an indication of something unique in the teleporting lugs."

We were late, having just supervised the conclusion of a twelve-hour run on the linear accelerator. FitzAlan was a short, dynamic black man who used a lot of expressive hand gestures when he talked. The lecture hall was crowded, and there were medialites floating near the ceiling, taking pictures of FitzAlan for posterity. This was his chance for glory, assuming of course his discoveries led anywhere. He had one of the few genuine smiles I'd seen in months.

I looked over the room and saw Mary down front, sitting on the opposite aisle. She turned and waved at me, but it would have disturbed the lecture too much had I

moved in front of the audience to join her, so I returned
her wave, made a gesture of apology and sat in the back.
Al-Qatan took the next seat.

"Up until now," FitzAlan said, "we haven't been certain of our conclusions because there hasn't been a statisti-
cally large enough sample of lugs involved in detectable
events. But now that we have samples based on a hundred
fifty-nine lugs, all of them involved in events, compared
with samples taken from the two hundred lugs chosen at
random from the herds, we are able to offer our conclusions."

The holographic projector behind him suddenly lit up
with large three-dimensional models of complex molecules.
The holograms rotated as he spoke.

"Behind me," FitzAlan said, "are models of four complex amino acids found in the cellular structures of certain
lugs. I won't bother to give you their names because
they're thirty syllables or more and even I can't pronounce
them. We call them LAC Alpha, LAC Beta, LAC Gamma
and LAC Delta. LAC, by the way, stands for Lug Amino
Acid."

If this guy were Zimmerman, I thought, it would be
Zimmerman's Acid and we'd be here all night.

This was the first time I'd thought about Jay Zimmerman
in a long while, I realized. The first time without a shiver
at the memory anyway. I wondered if he were out of his
padded room yet.

FitzAlan glanced at the rotating models behind him and
frowned. "We have not been able to determine the purpose of any of the amino acids so far; lug cell structure is
sufficiently unlike ours to preclude any clear analogies.
We know that the acids are inheritable and that only one
amino acid will be found in any given lug. Some of them
seem to be dominant over others, genetically speaking,
though we haven't proved that yet. We suspect it may be a
sort of scissors-paper-stone dominance, one dominant over

another, which in turn is dominant over yet another, and so on—the available evidence seems to point that way. We'll have a formal analysis available on Base Comp by next week.''

The biologist cleared his throat and tapped some instructions into the comp on the lectern. The holo models disappeared and were replaced by a graph.

''The thing we've discovered about the LACs is very simple,'' FitzAlan said. A door hissed open on the other side of the lecture hall and I saw Brian McGivern step into the room. His eyes swept over the dark rows of seats, meeting mine without apparent recognition, and then he saw Mary down front and moved to sit beside her. She gave him a hug. I turned my attention back to FitzAlan.

''In our sample A,'' the biologist was saying, looking over his shoulder at the graph, ''consisting of the hundred fifty-nine lugs involved in events, we found that forty-six of them—twenty-nine percent—carried LAC Alpha. Forty-nine, or thirty-one percent, contained LAC Beta. Nineteen, twelve percent, bore LAC Gamma, and twenty-five, sixteen percent, had LAC Delta. Only twenty of the eventing lugs did not carry any of the LACs at all.''

Eventing lugs, I thought. Great. A new one. To be placed alongside the other jargon: event involvement, event phenomena. Ways of objectifying the inexplicable, making it seem as though we had a handle on it. *Teleporting* was a concept that scared them too much; it was an idea too strange, too connected with the occult, too uncontrolled. I had noticed that I was the only one in the group to use the word. Therefore I used it a lot, just to see everyone else look uncomfortable.

''But in our sample B,'' FitzAlan went on, and the broad smile came back, involuntarily I think, the contagious glow of discovery, ''the sample of two hundred lugs chosen at random, the frequencies are entirely different. Only twenty-four percent of the lugs carry LAC Alpha, twenty-two percent carry LAC Beta, eight percent LAC Gamma, ten percent LAC Delta. Thirty-six percent, the largest population grouping of all, carry none of the unique amino acids.''

FitzAlan paused for a moment, letting it all sink in, the glow getting brighter and brighter. The physics teams were unable to think of anything other than running experiments decades old and getting results that were no different from the inconclusive results that had been gathered the first time, and now the biology team—considered a secondary team all along—had come up with the first significant discovery.

''The percentages of sample A,'' FitzAlan smiled, ''are so anomalous that we cannot but conclude that the presence of these amino acids is related to the event phenomena in some significant way. But because twenty of the eventing lugs did not carry LACs, the relationship cannot be a direct one. At this point, all we can conclude—''

''Excuse me, please.'' The voice came from behind me. FitzAlan's face fell. He was glowing his way right into his conclusion and now someone had interrupted him. I turned around and saw one of the duty techs.

''There's been an event, Southern Hemisphere dayside,'' she said. ''Any volunteers for fetching a lug?''

There was a unanimous groan from the audience. Going out among herds of smelly lugs to shoot one of the beasts and drag him back for dissection was no longer a job for which it was possible to find volunteers.

''Well,'' the tech said with a scowl, ''who's got the *duty*?''

With a pair of identical leaden sighs, a man and a woman rose from their chairs and followed the duty tech out of the room. FitzAlan watched them go with glowless impatience.

''We conclude,'' he said finally, his momentum gone, ''that the presence of LAC in a lug only increases the *probability* of event involvement. We cannot demonstrate a causal relationship. Perhaps this is just a statistical coincidence. Perhaps LAC acts as a catalyst to some other reaction. But if we can further analyze the relationship between event phenomena and the presence of LAC. . . .''

I stopped listening and started trying to find an approach to the data. Suppose the entrance to the nth dimension was lying somewhere in the twisting coils of thirty-syllable amino acids? Or that the acids somehow made it *easier* for the nth dimension to snatch a lug? What if they acted as a beacon?

God, I thought, teleportation can't be *chemical*. There's not enough energy in a biochemical reaction, for one thing, to turn the key into the stranger places in spacetime, even if there were an amino acid that somehow twisted into n-dimensional space and put the key in the lock for you.

Unless the key were already turned, somehow. And all that was needed was a very little energy to open the door. I shook my head. It didn't seem likely.

FitzAlan wound up his presentation and asked for questions. I had a lot of them. Just not any he could answer.

Events (2)

Two months later a couple of techs went after an eventing lug high in the northern latitudes. They tranquilized the beast, and while coming back at around two thousand miles per hour, flying in clear weather with perfect visibility, they ran their cargo shuttle right into the ground at a forty-five-degree angle. A Falkner field will protect against gravity and inertia, but not against a head-on collision with something the density of a planet. The crater was eighty feet deep. Nothing survived in big enough pieces to let us know how it happened. We just filled the crater in while

McGivern spoke the words; the medialites floated a discreet distance away, making sure posterity had it on the record.

Score two, I thought, for relativity. The Knight's Move score stayed at zero.

Last Songs (3)

I have sent my lover from me, angrily,

Using scornful words, flung in the reproaches
That were his gentle eyes.

My words are bitter these days.
Ill-tuned. They do not soar,
But lie broken-winged on the stones.

I try to sing, but words betray me.
They laugh at me, mocking,
Turning to ash, a bitterness on my heart.

All singers are fools
Who trust their souls
To double-edged words.

Swimming On The Nightside

As Mary rose from the lake, the aurora's reflection shimmered in the dew in her hair. We had just run three or four miles along the hard verge and then jumped into the water. Not to cool off, since the water was almost as hot as the air, but to at least get the sweat off our bodies. I splashed up beside her and kissed her.

She looked past my shoulder, at the blazing aurora. "Damned if I can remember why I ever thought those lights were romantic," she said.

We sloshed to the shore. A quarter-kilometer away, lights were gleaming over the physics bunker. We had just set up an eight-hour run on one of the accelerators, bombarding a bunch of FitzAlan's amino acids with every high-energy particle we could think of in the hope that the acids would untwist themselves and give us a glimpse of n-dimensional space.

I couldn't help but think that it was Jay Zimmerman's sort of tactic. A measure of our desperation, our total lack of new ideas. We had tried this particular trick before, with no result. This run was a new variation, but I wasn't expecting any answers this time either. We simply had nothing else to try.

Mary smoothed back her wet hair. The sky turned scarlet, bleeding down onto the land. Even shoptalk had run low. She sat down on a crumbling sun-bleached rock and stretched out one leg after the other, massaging her calf muscles.

We were nocturnal animals now. Those who could adjusted their schedules to live mainly in the night, avoiding the ferocity of the day. Among those who ventured forth in the day, the fad for painting cheerful clown faces in defiance of the sun had faded. The sad clowns were too depressing, the happy ones too obviously false.

I looked at the lights in the physics bunker and thought of K.C. Kemp and his cold monument to folly. Here's another one, K.C., I thought. With all the best intentions in the world and all the best minds on a planet, here we are hiding from the sunlight and running in circles.

"How could it happen?" Mary asked. "After all the safeguards."

"Stupidity, I suppose."

"Stupidity," Mary repeated. "Or boredom. Or not caring anymore."

"That sounds like stupidity to me," I said.

"Did you know d'Angelo? She was such a sweet girl, I thought. And only thirty." She pursed her lips as she gazed at the reflection of the aurora in the quiet waters of the lake. "Her boyfriend didn't come to the funeral," she said. "Just stayed in his room."

"Sensible of him," I said. "I've never attended a funeral I couldn't do without. Maybe he watched on the holo."

Mary looked up at me quickly but said nothing. "She had it easy," I said. I wiped salt from my lips. "The sort of end we all want. Fast. You can think of her as lucky if you like. Maybe we'll name a continent or a body of water after her."

Mary turned her head away. "Quicker deaths used to be the thing," I said. "When I was young, you made a trip to the doctor, who found a lump or something and scheduled a test, and then you went for the test and waited for a day or so for the results, and then they'd schedule an operation, and then you'd have the operation and wait for the results, and then when the results came in, they'd schedule another test, and then when *those* results came, there'd be another operation, and then you'd wait for the results of *that*, and then more tests and more operations, and then they'd get you to sign a release so they could use an experimental treatment they were trying out, and eventually you'd die of the disease or the operations or the treatment. And even if you lived, you'd know that somewhere down the line there'd be another lump and then another test and then it would start all over again. My parents went that way, one after the other, within three years. That's most of what I remember from high school—going to the hospital after class and watching what the disease and the doctors had done to my parents, and trying to help my mother and my father convince themselves, without any of us believing it, that the most recent operation or treatment would be the last. And when I was on Kemp's for the first time, my brother died of the cigarettes he'd been smoking, and I felt thankful that I'd been able to skip all those trips to the hospital. But that was okay. It was *quick*. Now it's different.''

Mary was staring at me with deep, inexpressible eyes, and I knew I'd just torn our treaty to shreds and the truce was gone, but I couldn't stop myself. A part of me exulted in this angry rebellion, in unleashing all the resentment that had been stored up for so many months. ''Now,'' I said, ''there are cures for whatever diseases still exist, so everyone lives past their century, and without the Forever Now treatments, you just *wear out*. Your mind goes and the kidneys deteriorate and you keep losing bits of yourself that no longer function and that go to rot, and eventually you're all alone for years, sans eyes, sans teeth et cetera, trapped in yourself, decaying while you're still alive, until at last you're just this nerveless bag of protoplasm, lying on a bed with machines doing the work that your organs used to do, and you *still can't die*. And it goes on for *decades*.

''No,'' I said. ''For me it's d'Angelo's way or not at all. I know it's inevitable, that sooner or later. . . .'' I shrugged. ''I just want it to be quick.'' I was glaring at her now, looking accusingly into her dark eyes while the sky blurred overhead and the water lapped quietly on the shore.

''It's not . . .'' she began, and then fell silent, trying to compose herself. ''It's not that I want to die.''

''Liar.'' Quickly, before the long rationalizations started.

Anger crackled in her eyes, flaming red like the aurora. ''No,'' she said, ''it's the truth. What I don't want is to be *me* forever.'' She was on her feet, pacing along the beach, speaking rapidly to prevent my interrupting her. ''A hundred years is time enough to live inside myself. After that, you start losing . . . something. Something important. Either you turn into Zimmerman or you turn into. . . .'' She stopped her pacing, crossing her arms stubbornly in front of her as she turned away from me, gazing into the redfaced waves. "You turn into you," she finished. "You, Doran. My love. You."

She turned and faced me then. My anger drained away at those last words, at the sad-voiced accusation. There was a faint half-smile of remembrance on Mary's face as she spoke. Her voice was gentle, her anger gone.

"You were my first real romantic adventure, you know? The first grown-up lover. You seemed so old and wise and funny and sad. . . . And I was young enough to think I could . . . could change you, I guess. Make you happier than you were." She shook her head. "Foolish of me, I know. Because after a while I began to realize that what was missing wasn't anything I could supply. That it was. . . ." She looked down at her hands, frowning at them, shaking her head slowly to clear her lank wet hair from her eyes.

"Who knows? It was whatever it was," she said. "Something you'd lost in the last seven hundred years. Maybe it was the guilt you'd acquired during all those years of power, running the planet, doing what powerful people do. Or the years of fame that you maybe felt you hadn't deserved." She looked up at me, her acute intelligence plain in her eyes, and I felt my heart turn over. The anger was gone; now there was caring only, and regret. And the truth, which was coming at last, as we had both known it would, wanting only to delay the day.

"You were always a little *too* defensive about Jay Zimmerman, did you know that? There was something there I could never quite figure out. Jay felt it too, felt that there was something wrong. I could tell, the way he kept talking about it. Only there was so much else wrong with him that he never . . . was able to work things out." She shrugged, dismissing the idea. "Maybe I'm off base there," she said.

"No, you aren't." No point in not bringing it out. It wasn't going to make any difference, not now. "There's something to that," I said, "but I can't tell you. Except that it's not at issue here."

"Maybe not," Mary said. I could see the sadness in her as she gazed at me, the knowledge that was going to wedge us apart. "But I saw you in a lot of different situations. Teaching, working, being a father to the planet, being a demanding boss insisting on action. A nasty landlord when it was necessary. And then having fun with me, flitting from one part of the planet to another, from one party to the next. Living up on Hyampeia, watching the rebuilding going on below. On your sailboat, watching the telltales, in control as you moved with the wind and the tide. . . ."

"It wasn't a bad life, was it?" I asked.

She smiled again. Sadly. "No," she said. "It was very nice, truly. Lovely, in parts. But it was all busy work. Your heart wasn't in it, it was all just . . . going through the motions."

"Except when I was with you."

She stepped toward me, putting her hands on my shoulders, looking up at me, her gaze steady. "Not often enough, love," she said. "There were always . . . echoes. Of the words that you'd said too many times before, of the actions that were centuries old. There wasn't enough of it that was *real*. And I saw that it was the same with all the rest of you people who . . . who don't grow old. I saw that the young people around us, the people my own age—they were imitating *you*, you older ones, the same manner, the same kind of attitudes. You know. No real spontaneity. Nothing new under the sun. All pleasures tempered with an ennui that was genuine in the older ones, false in the younger. You outnumbered us so greatly that most of us had little choice. And so I decided. . . ." She put her arms around my neck, pressing her cheek to mine. ". . . I decided not to live that kind of life. To make certain that every moment was important, that every action was genuine.''

''And to die,'' I said.

She stepped back, her arms falling from my shoulders. ''If that's what it takes, yes.''

A change swept over the sky, the aurora turning with breathtaking swiftness from scarlet to purple. Violet highlights shone in Mary's hair. I felt her closeness, wanted to touch her, dared not. She had known me at the wrong time. If she had seen me later, after David and Branwen, or if I'd let her into the secret of the centaurs, her conclusions might have been different.

She looked at me critically. When she spoke, her words were measured, matter-of-fact. ''Neither of us are afraid of dying, I think, but there's a difference. You're *angry* at death, at the unfairness of it, the randomness of it.''

''The pain of it,'' I said.

Mary looked thoughtful, then accepted it, nodding. ''Yes. The pain. But you're angry at it, and I'm not. With me, it's a choice. Not random at all.''

''And not quick. Your way.''

She looked up at me, challenging. ''Who's to say I won't take d'Angelo's way at the last? I have nothing against suicide, not when there's nothing left.''

''You didn't tell me any of this before.''

''I didn't know how to articulate it,'' she said. ''Not then. It was all . . . intuitional. And since we've been together again—'' She shrugged. ''What difference would this conversation have made? Knowing what we know.''

''I'm not the same man you knew then,'' I said. ''Things have happened. Things having to do with Philodice, and my children, and . . . other things. Knight's Move. You.''

Mary gave me a smile and patted me on the side like she would a favorite horse. ''Maybe so. But you haven't changed in one thing: the way you feel toward my decision.'' She stepped back, facing the lake again, her voice distant. "And it's up to you, what you determine to do about that. I can't help. Because my decision is made."

"Come to Earth with me," I said. "See what I can show you there. It's something you haven't seen."

I could hear, but not see, the indulgent smile she wore as she spoke. "In hopes I'll chicken out, you mean? See something that will change my mind and decide not to go through with it?" She shook her head. "I might, you know. I always knew that. But there's the chance I won't. And it's that knowledge you'll have to deal with."

The aurora whirled like a spinning palette of color. Red, green, violet, glowing gold. "Come to Earth," I said.

"I don't want to cause you more pain, Doran. Are you certain this wouldn't be just prolonging things?"

"You said it was my move, now that you've made your decision," I said. "Okay. I say you should come to Earth."

Mary said nothing but gazed at the burning sky. Finally: "I'll think about it. But what's going to happen with us *now?* Because I'm not going to take any pressure from you, Doran."

"What happens now?" I repeated. "I'll wait for your answer about coming to Earth."

She looked down at the dark soil of the beach, scuffed it with her toe. Then she tossed back her head and I felt a touch of memory—Philodice tossing her head back when she made a decision. "Okay," Mary said. "That's fair. But I won't have an answer for a while."

"I'm not going anywhere."

She stood motionless for a moment. "Okay," she said again. "We'll leave it on the table." She turned to me with the solemn face of a judge. "But if I decide I won't go with you. . . . That's the end then, isn't it?"

"I suppose it is."

Without a word she brushed past me, a slight smile on her face, heading toward the lights of the physics bunker and the dark shimmering field beyond, where our apartments waited. I began to follow, not knowing what else to do. Beyond Mary I glimpsed moving darkness on the sward.

"Oh, no," she said. And stopped dead.

A small herd of lugs had moved between us and the physics building. Mary muttered something under her breath and picked up speed, threading rapidly between the slow-moving creatures. I followed, trying to keep her head in view, and then I stepped in a pile of dung and slipped, sprawling full length on the scratchy upper surface of the moss. Angry, I stood and glared at the nearest lug. It looked back at me with befuddled imbecility.

"Damn you," I said, hitting the creature in the neck with my fist. I struck the collar and my knuckles complained. I didn't care, and I hit the lug again.

"Give me some answers!" I demanded.

Suddenly the lug seemed to move, falling directly away from me, falling into a blackness that had opened up just behind it. I opened my mouth to shout, but I was moving into the blackness myself, moving sideways but with the unsettling sensation of *falling*. The lug stayed before me, its eyestalks turned toward me with a lack of surprise.

The universe was falling away and I had the lurching sensation of being in an elevator out of control. I looked around wildly and saw only blackness on all sides, blackness that was somehow perpendicular to me, drawing me after it, producing a sensation of sickening vertigo. My senses told me I was dropping simultaneously in all directions, falling forever and everywhere. I flailed my arms and legs to no avail. I was weightless, yet still somehow dropping.

The blackness began to brighten; little flecks of light appeared, pulsing in the night, then falling away like everything else—all the colors of Amaterasu's aurora dropping away from me, pulling me after them. They formed an infinitude of bright lines, drawing away, alive with light. In the sudden brightness I saw Mary nearby, her arms and legs thrashing as she tried to find purchase on the transformed universe.

I looked at the lug again. Its prehensile lips writhed at me. Its eyestalks pricked forward, peering at me like an elderly professor through his pince-nez.

"What sort of answers would you like, Mr. Falkner?" it said.

23

A talking lug, I thought. Right.

I hit the lug as hard as I could in its prehensile lips. It seemed a bit surprised. The impact sent me tumbling to one side, weightless. No matter which direction I faced, I seemed to be falling straight ahead. The sensation was like being perpetually on the edge of a cliff that was perpetually crumbling away. I kicked out, with no result. Something warm brushed past me and then a firm hand seized the back of my shirt. I flailed around, felt material and clutched at it. It was Mary.

We held each other as we tumbled into the vastness. The beads of light brightened, whirled, sucked us down. We seemed to be falling, but somehow we weren't getting nearer to the light sources. My heart was pounding loudly; I gulped air and tried to halt my panic. A stray thought, on its way to somewhere else, wondered where the air was coming from.

Gradually I began to get used to the weightlessness and started making swimming motions to stop our tumbling. Mary was hanging on to my back. I could hear the rasp of her breathing close to my ear, the warmth of her body pressed against me. I wondered why it was that although we were falling, there was no wind plucking at our clothes, howling in our ears. . . .

I sensed something close; turning my head, I saw the lug moving parallel to us, a dark silhouette against the rocketing, falling lights, its eyeballs rotating incuriously atop their stalks as they tried to follow our tumbling bodies.

"Are you feeling entirely well, Mr. Falkner?" it asked. The voice was breathy and hoarse, not entirely devoid of inflection but seemingly hesitant about how to speak properly. The lug hadn't yet caught onto the trick of raising its tone when asking a question.

I glared at it. We were rotating slowly now, with enough stability that I could observe it without vertigo. "What took you so long?" I demanded.

The lug's answer was prompt, punctuated—involuntarily, I assumed—by a fart. "We didn't notice your arrival until recently, when we began to detect your massive interference with our lug-transfer program." It seemed to have no trouble in getting its prehensile lips around the pedantic phrases. "Following this discovery, it took some time to ascertain your nature and purpose. Our chief difficulty was in accepting the possibility of another sentient species, and furthermore, one confined to living within three spatial dimensions."

"Doran," Mary said in my ear, "I think I might be sick. I don't take weightlessness well."

"There were further delays," the lug continued, "occasioned by problems in comprehending your language. Once the dubious connection between oral and written language was understood—dubious because the notion of communicating by vibration through an outré fluid medium such as air, and by arcane markings upon a material object, viz., paper, were new to us—as I said, once the connection was properly understood, our efforts at comprehending your language could proceed apace. Fortunately your people came equipped with a number of grammars and stylebooks, which we appropriated for our studies." The lug looked at me and smacked its lips. Smugly, I thought. "And here we are," it said.

"Doran . . . ." Mary whispered, urgently this time.

"Would it be possible," I asked, "to continue this conversation without tumbling? Say on a floor, with some gravity under it?"

"If that is your preference." The light from one part of the universe faded and I saw a square object, like a detached floor, blocking out the vertiginous reality below. I perceived that we were falling slowly toward it.

We came to a gentle halt against a smooth cold surface, a sort of flat, dark stone resembling the slate of a billiard table. I landed on my back and looked up, seeing the same brilliant vortex as everywhere else, and had the sensation that the floor was falling, with us on its underside, into a light-strewn funnel. Mary dragged in air and rolled away from me.

"I shall increase the gravity slowly," the lug said. "Please inform me when it is comfortable. Do not be alarmed. You are contained in a membrane of atmosphere."

It was warm; I was sweating and breathing hard. My heart was hammering. I stood, a little shakily, bounding a couple of feet from the floor. I came down slowly, lightly. The lug settled on its feet two yards in front of me. Mary was lying on her stomach, pressing her forehead against the cool stone.

"I take it," she said, "that we perceive everything as falling away from us because we are in n-dimensional space, and everything is at ninety degrees from us."

"Yes," the lug said. "The actuality lines are vertical to your continuum. We suspected from our hypothetical modeling of lug eyes that you might perceive our space in this fashion, but we were uncertain." Then, without hesitation and in the same tone of voice, the lug added, "That was a perceptive comment, Miss Liddell."

"I had a lot of time to work things out," Mary said, "when I was trying not to upchuck."

I continued to jump up and down until the gravity began to feel nearly right; then I told the lug to stop increasing it. I'd set the gravity a little lighter than normal, and I felt a buoyancy in my limbs, a lightness that was not entirely caused by the massive jolt of adrenaline that had just poured into my system. I bounded up and down a few more times, feeling as though I'd need the advantage in lightness. Everything above the floor was still unsettling, but I was becoming accustomed to it.

Evidently Mary was too, because she rolled over and sat up, crossing her legs. She was still staring deliberately at the floor, not daring to look above its horizon, like a Buddhist nun in contemplation of the godhead as embedded in a grain of rice.

I looked at the lug. The creature regarded me with the same half-awake expression that lugs always wore.

"You said you had conceptualized the way the universe looked from lug eyes," I said. "That implies that you are not, yourselves, lugs. Correct?"

"That is very perspicacious of you," the lug answered. "I am surprised. This conversation will likely prove most interesting."

Not all that perspicacious, I thought. Whatever was manipulating the lug didn't have any more ability to make its personality seem luglike than Snaggles had at impersonating minor Chinese deities. All it took was a little experience in dealing with alien intelligence.

"I'm glad we interest you," I said. "But you didn't answer my question."

"Thank you for reminding me." The voice was hesitant, as though the creature wasn't certain of how to go about the various pleasantries involved in ordinary human conversation. But then it brightened and the being went on.

"We are a population of paradimensional intelligences," the lug said. "There are several thousand of us. We were formed, apparently spontaneously and by a process akin to random chance, in the first moments of the great explosion that created the universe. We exist primarily in the higher dimensions where energy transference is more efficient, although we can interact with the lower material dimensions when necessary. To manipulate the lugs, for instance."

"You are not inhabiting the lug's mind? Possessing it?"

"Indeed not. That is not possible so far as is known. I am merely holding the lug immobile while manipulating its upper respiratory system."

It fell silent for a moment, then went on. "I have been asked by one of my colleagues to make a clarification," it said. "In speaking of the lower dimensions, we do not mean *lower* in its perjorative sense, as in something of an inferior rank or order, but rather in the sense of your numbering system, the first three whole numbers being *lower*, as we understand it, than the other numbers in the series. We did not intend to offend you by the use of the term."

"Ah. Very thoughtful of your colleagues. We took no offense, I'm sure. Thank you." We were going to need dictionaries before this was over, I could tell.

"Your language contains many words—such as *lower*— that seem to mean contradictory things," the lug said. "I gather the meaning is clear from its context, but my colleagues and I have not yet had the experience necessary to tell one context from another. Please forgive us during the interim."

"Of course."

Mary's head rose and she looked up at the lug steadily, at its odd silhouette outlined by the blazing lights beyond.

"If you're not lugs," she said, "what do you actually look like?"

"That presents a problem, Miss Liddell," the lug said. "There are difficulties of translation—we have not yet been able to find a vocabulary in your sources with which to describe ourselves properly—but the primary difficulty lies in the conflicting natures of our two species. *You* are material beings, living within the three lower spatial dimensions, *lower* still being qualified by the distinction my colleagues made earlier—"

"Thank you. We understand," I said quickly.

"—whereas we," the lug continued, "are non-material beings, composed of various subtle energies and existing primarily but not exclusively in the higher spatial dimensions. We do not *look* like anything insofar as *looks* depend on a material presence reflecting light to an organ of perception. I am afraid your question is meaningless within its context, Miss Liddell."

"Oh. Sorry," Mary said.

"My colleagues and I, however, are at this moment striving to release various energies of a spectrum that should be visible to you. We think that you should perceive us as fluorescing particles moving along the actuality lines in what I hope we can agree to call 'space,' in this context regarding *space* as a three-dimensional concept within which the relative order of physical objects can be understood, as opposed to *space* meaning an interval in time or the region beyond the atmosphere, or *space* meaning. . . ."

The lug rattled on for a while longer, but Mary and I were not listening. We were gazing up into the blazing well above us, watching the brilliant, pulsating, rocketing lights that seemed, wherever we turned our eyes, to draw us toward them into the vortex of n-dimensional space. The vertigo that had first assaulted us had faded, and we looked up in wonderment at the patterned lights, the moving flashes, the strobing patterns that formed in the deep and featureless blackness. These were another people, another intelligence, a sentience as ancient as existence itself. Creatures composed of patterned energies that we did not conceive of, composed not even of *matter*. Fluorescing above us, blazing in our n-dimensional sky as they bade our race hello.

"That's *them*," Mary said, her voice breathless.

Gradually we realized that the lug had ceased to speak. I looked at it. "Your people are very . . . beautiful," I said.

"We are?" The voice indicated neither pleasure nor surprise. "We are pleased to have met your aesthetic criteria. Thank you."

"You're welcome." There it languished for a moment. I didn't know where in all of this to begin.

Mary didn't hesitate. She rose to stand next to me, frowning. I recognized her mode for dealing with business. Ignoring the fact that she was dressed only in a tee shirt and bandeau, a pair of shorts and running shoes, she was planning on posing major scientific questions to a smelly creature temporarily manipulated by a paradimensional being. Either she found herself at home in these conditions or she was doing a good impersonation of someone who did.

"You say that you inhabit higher spatial dimensions but that you are non-material. Is that a condition of existence in high-dimensional space?"

"So far as we know, since we have not encountered any other form of sentient life in the higher spatial dimensions." The answer came back immediately, without hesitation. "You must understand that matter exists chiefly in three-dimensional space. It exists in the higher dimensions of course, but its effects are indirect and more subtle. In the higher dimensions we do not deal so much with matter directly as with its side effects. The lower dimensions are, in that sense, coarser, the higher more refined. We do not intend *coarse* in its perjorative sense, my colleagues remind me, but rather in the sense in which matter is larger, not as easily sifted or dealt with.''

"We comprehend your distinction," said Mary. "Thank you."

"You're welcome." The lug seemed more comfortable with the phrase now that it had heard me use it.

"We do not interact with matter to any great degree," it continued. "Matter has not interested us, and until fairly recently we have not paid a great deal of attention to it. Not until I accidentally discovered the lugs."

"*You* found them?" Mary wiped perspiration from her upper lip with the back of her hand. We were both glazed with sweat. The lug's answer was matter-of-fact.

"I did, yes. Personally. Because of that fact, it was agreed that I should be the first to attempt contact with you." Its speech was easier now, as though we had reached familiar ground and it was no longer searching through its vocabulary for phrases.

"I was the first to develop an interest in exploring the material dimensions," it said. "My glimpses were limited because when we move ourselves into the material dimensions, we develop an alarming lack of efficiency—we simply do not cope well with matter. But a short time ago I discovered the lugs in their native habitat: a planet some distance from here. It was the first time we had encountered organic life, and it came as quite a surprise."

I'll bet it did, I thought. If it was anything like what I was feeling on being swept into an *n*-dimensional universe filled with non-material creatures manifesting themselves as flashing lights, it would have resulted in a major rearrangement of the being's preconceptions, if not in an existential crisis of unspeakable proportions.

Mary's example had started me to thinking like a scientist again, and I was cursing the lack of any recording device, even something as simple as a pad and pencil. I didn't want to interrupt the lug, but I desperately wanted to know what kind of scales our friend was talking about: What was a *short time* to something that had existed for fifteen-odd billion years? How far was the *some distance* from the lugs' native planet to a being that could teleport from one place to another?

"Our own explorations indicate that organic life is not that uncommon, at least around Population I-type stars," I said. "Is it more rare than we are accustomed to think, or had you simply overlooked it?"

"Subsequent investigation showed chemical-based life to be fairly common, at least on the surface of planets." The answer came quickly. I wondered how fast the thing's mental processes were and how it had learned its formal, stodgy style of English in such a short time; it was only a few months at the most since it had discovered us interfering with its manipulation of the lug populations. It was answering our questions rapidly and fluently, considering that it had to mentally translate between one language based on sound and another of such a wildly different nature that sound was not even recognized as a medium of communication. If it was not a chemical-based life form, it could, I supposed, be thinking at the speed of light, but even granted that kind of speed, the rapid responses implied that the beings' nature was extremely complex and very sophisticated. And, I thought, remarkably adaptable.

"What motivated your investigation?" I asked.

"Oh." For the first time there was a hesitation in the lug's speech. "Motivations among our species are intricate, as they seem to be in yours. Perhaps the best explanation would be that I was seeking to relieve ennui."

For a brief second reality seemed to skip a beat. I had just been given the material for at least a century's worth of investigation, and now the concept that these higher-dimensional, immortal creatures—the brilliant, sweeping display that was lighting the n-dimensional sky over our heads—were struggling to relieve some kind of cosmic lassitude . . . this was more than I was ready for.

I stood a moment, and it was the concrete fact of the stinging sweat pouring down into my eyes—that and the fact that I needed time for absorbing all this—that prompted my next question.

"It's very warm here," I said. "Warm enough to make us uncomfortable. Would it be possible to reduce the temperature?"

"Of course. We used the aggregate air temperature of the planet in creating this pocket of air. How much would you like it reduced?"

Mary and I looked at each other. If we started talking degrees Celsius and the lug thought we were talking Kelvin, the air in our lungs would crystallize before we could ever make clear the difference.

Between us we managed to explain the centigrade thermometer, made certain we were understood, and then asked that the temperature be lowered gradually, as the gravity had been raised, so as to give us time to protest if things went too far. This brought up other matters of comfort.

"Could you bring us some chairs and a table?" I asked. "And some writing materials—paper and pencils?"

"Certainly. If you can give us a description of what you want."

That led into a number of interesting semantic byways, with the lug producing paper that already contained some-one else's field notes, but in the end we got a couple of padded chairs from the physics lounge, the desk from my study, an unabridged dictionary in book rather than comp form, another scientific and technical dictionary, and a crystal recorder with the ability to record twelve straight hours without changing crystals. Then, realizing we hadn't the capacity for dealing efficiently with any of the complex mathematics we might be deriving, we remembered that the physics lounge had a computer already programmed for coping with multi-dimensional theory as well as a hologram capable of making three-dimensional analogues of the concepts involved. We remembered furthermore that the comp had its own Falkner power source and therefore wasn't dependent on base power. With the help of a map drawn on paper and a detailed explanation of how it was a two-dimensional analogue of a three-dimensional space, we got our computer, with a printer attached because the lugs hadn't known whether or not it was part of the comp, and with a mug of tea—still warm, black with sugar— sitting on top.

Delighting in our new equipment, we realized that we were hungry and had the lugs kidnap some potato salad from the kitchen—it was their best guess about food—and a tray of twelve Turkish coffees. We were also given a choice of silverware, including utensils meant to core apples and slice vegetables, which our abductors were unable, from our descriptions, to distinguish from forks and spoons.

We assumed that since the physics lounge had just been plundered of its equipment, the base was now alerted to the fact that something odd was going on. Whoever had left the tea on the comp had probably seen it disappear from under his nose. I considered asking the lugs to move the entire base camp into n-dimensional space, but that seemed a tall order; and as yet we hadn't established the means of our return, if any. I also assumed there was a reason our hosts hadn't decided to contact the project directly but had taken only two of us.

I got the answer to that question while we were eating potato salad. The lugs had been watching us for months, trying to decide what to do. It took them quite a while to learn how to get intelligible sounds out of a lug, but when they did, they decided to say hello. They'd deciphered some documents that described me as a leading light of the project and Mary as a chief assistant. They'd concluded it would be too confusing to talk to us all at once, and so they decided to snatch me—and since Mary was there, they took her too.

I finished off a Turkish coffee and realized that we might have to equip our little platform with a toilet fairly soon. But that could wait, and in the meantime I'd had an idea inspired by the goggling, insipid and smelly presence of the lug standing nearby.

"Since you aren't actually a lug," I said, putting the little coffee cup back on its tray, "do you actually need a lug's body to communicate with us? Or can we work out another way?"

"We do not understand your other modes of communication very well," came the answer. "But the manipulation of the lug's upper respiratory system is very fatiguing to me, as is the effort required to keep the rest of this creature still. I am eating as fast as I can, but the energy required is considerable. If you have a better idea, I would be pleased to hear it."

"Sound is made by vibration through a fluid medium, okay?" I said, pointing to the speaker on our recording unit. "This unit makes sound by the vibration of a small diaphragm. It transmits to the air very efficiently and should require much less energy than manipulating the entire respiratory system of a lug."

"And be a lot less smelly too," Mary added under her breath.

"Is that how the speaker works?" the lug asked. It had caught on to the trick of raising its voice when asking a question, apparently by listening to us. "We were uncertain. We suspected it was a paradimensional gate opening to another part of the material universe, allowing communication to other places, but we could find no trace of its operation in our spacetime. Instead we find a much more ingenious device than we suspected."

"Ah. Thank you," I said. If it wanted to think a simple vibrating diaphragm a more clever invention than a transdimensional gate, who was I to argue? I explained the operation of the speaker in greater detail, and the lug began putting energy into it, experimenting. The first squawk almost blew the speaker out of the recorder, but it learned quickly, and in a dozen minutes or so it was producing intelligible sounds in an asexual, tenor voice.

"I shall return the lug to its fellows," it reported.

"Let me remove the collar first," I said. "It's collecting data for us."

"Ah. Certainly. If you wish."

I walked up to the lug, thankful I wasn't going to have to smell it anymore, then hesitated and stepped back.

"What do we call you now?" I asked. "I've been thinking of you as *the lug,* which of course you aren't, but it was all I had. Do you have a name? Do the rest of your people?"

"Not a name intelligible in your terms," the speaker said as I took the collar from the lug. "My people are structured quite differently from one another—it was chance that created us, after all—and our personalities are decidedly distinct. We recognize one another by the pattern of our energies, and we have no name as such. Mine would translate as *That-Which-I-Am*, and my race simply as *Us*, since until very recently we had no idea that any other sapience existed."

I wondered for a moment whether one of these beings hadn't had a conversation with someone on Mount Sinai a few millennia ago, but decided it was unlikely. "Would you object to an arbitrary name?" I asked. "In our own terms, we would have to call you something."

"No objection at all."

The lug vanished, returned to its point of origin. I put the collar on the desk, where it would have a good view of things, and then I conferred with Mary. We decided to call our hosts after the Cyclopes, the offspring of Uranus and Ge in the early moments of the universe. On contemplation of the blazing beads of fire rocketing through the whirlpools of our n-dimensional sky, we named their spokesman Arges, meaning brightness, the name given one of the three original Cyclopes who forged the thunderbolts of Zeus. We explained the myth to Arges—now that the lug was gone, I was finding it difficult to talk to the empty air—and then Arges gave us a thoughtful response.

"We find a number of contradictory definitions for *myth* in our sources. Is the union of Uranus and Ge to be taken literally as an explanation for our existence? If so, we must inform you that we have no memories of such an event. And if it is not intended literally, are you trying to create an allegory? That is another term we do not quite understand. Or are we to take it as an indication that you do not fully believe in our existence and have given us a fanciful name until such time as you accept our reality?"

We both hesitated for a moment. "Your department, Doran," Mary decided. I gave her a look. It was becoming clear that a lively discussion about the difference between noumena and phenomena was in the offing, but I wasn't feeling up to a lecture on Kantian metaphysics at the moment.

"I think the dictionary you were consulting took mythology a little too literally," I finally ventured. "On the surface, creation and nature myths serve as an explanation for natural functions, but in my view their real purpose is to serve as an aesthetically pleasing metaphor for real human and natural conditions. In this realm, their primary function is to provoke thought about the human and natural worlds and their various interrelationships. And," I added, "to offset ennui."

"We do not understand your aesthetics yet," Arges said. "And we are not entirely comfortable with the idea of metaphors; we understand that metaphors evoke a comparison that is intended to stimulate thought and realization, but still it is a way of saying a thing is something it is not."

Wonderful, I thought. We've just taken a step back from Kant to the Middle Ages, from noumena to a debate over nominalism.

"But," Arges finished, "we understand ennui. We hope for further enlightenment in re mythology as a result of growing contact between our races."

"Right," I said. Nothing much else to do after that but to change the subject and hope it stuck.

"You said that you had discovered the lugs, Arges," I said. "I assume that you also moved them to this planet and that you have a purpose in transferring them from one place on the planet to another." At last, getting down to the reason that had brought us here in the first place. I felt a growing electricity in my limbs, a warm anticipation.

"Was that a question?" Arges asked. My feeling of anticipation faded slightly.

"It was meant as one, yes."

"We weren't certain. Your phrasing was irregular. We will consult our vocabulary for the proper terms." After a hesitation of about half a second, the answer came.

"We are playing a game," Arges said. I stared at the speaker. "*Game,*" Arges qualified, "in the sense of friendly competition, as opposed to a fraud or a wild animal shot for sport."

I looked at Mary. "Game?" she echoed. I began to laugh.

The biggest scientific discovery of the last eight hundred years, and it was made on a Cyclopean checkerboard. We had stumbled across giants at play like moles surfacing on a croquet lawn, and with the viewpoint of a mole we had concluded that the objects bounding about the field had a purpose greater than that of mere amusement.

My laughter was long in slowing down. My irony was getting its best exercise in years.

"You will have to explain laughter to us sometime," Arges said politely. I began to laugh some more.

Mary had to take over the questioning, and Arges's replies gradually revealed the answers to the questions that had brought Knight's Move to Amaterasu for all these dismal months.

The discovery of organic life had caused an existential shock wave to ripple through the collective soul of the Cyclopes. Billions of years old, they were forced to reassess their place in the universe. They were bombarded by a wave of new concepts, each one alien to them; the idea—shocking in itself—that they were not the only form of life in existence; the apparent evidence that life could exist in such a radically different form; the hyphothesis that life could exist in the material universe at all at such an inefficient energy-exchange level. For a while many of the Cyclopes had turned into enthusiastic amateur explorers, poking about randomly on various bits of matter, hoping to turn up something new.

But the search for forms of life had proved disappointing. Dealing with the lower dimensions was exhausting, and the chance of coming up with anything even remotely interesting was slim. They had found only non-sentient species, and Cyclopes were bored by things they couldn't talk to. Even Arges, who was the most enthusiastic of the Cyclopes, grew tired of cataloguing one form of uninteresting life after another. So, in his off moments, he had devised a game in which it was possible to Have Fun with Organic Life.

Lugs were transported from the plains of their homeworld, where they were hunted by a particularly vicious set of predators who might have upset the experiment, to Amaterasu, where they had no natural enemies. The Cyclopes collected some data on organic reproduction and were able to tailor some unique amino acids, which were placed in the genetic structure of a very few lug fetuses just after conception. This again was trial and error; sometimes the acids produced a malformed lug, incapable of survival or reproduction, but some of them survived with a minimum of ill effects, and only a few successful experiments were needed.

The rules of the game were simple. Each Cyclopean player—six initially, with the rest looking over their shoulders ready to start games of their own should this one prove interesting enough—was assigned an amino acid. The object was to make that amino acid dominant within the lugs of Amaterasu. The acids were genetically dominant in a stone-paper-scissors arrangement, so that one's own acid could be eclipsed by another, but another was vulnerable to one's own. Strategy was very complex: One could move either one's own lugs or someone else's, allowing one to abort an opponent's move by indirect means. It was also possible to skip a turn by moving a non-designated lug. Since one's own lugs could always be dominated by another's, as much strategy revolved around moving a third party's lugs to cancel out the threat from one's own direct opponents as for maneuvering for direct dominance by one's own lugs. Tactics were subtle, various and theoretically non-ending.

Arges, incidentally, was playing LAC Beta, currently in second place. There were four players remaining, the other two having conceded when their designated lugs disappeared from the population. Arges thought the game was about halfway toward either stalemate or completion.

The Cyclopes had been dealing in limited ways with the lugs and the material world of Amaterasu; they hadn't perceived the first human expeditions at all. It was only because this last expedition had created such a massive interference in the pattern of their game that the players had been motivated to look for its cause. The shock had been the same as though a human, playing Go on the two-dimensional surface of a vidscreen, suddenly noticed that the screen had been invaded by two-dimensional creatures from Flatland who were shuffling the counters around for some purpose of their own.

I began thinking about the time scales involved in the game. Lugs were a non-indigenous species, having been imported solely for the purpose of serving as counters in Arges's game. Archaeologists had dug up lug remains three million years old.

The game had been going on for three million years and was only half-complete. I felt the urge to break out laughing again when I realized that if Arges had happened upon Earth in his early explorations, it might have been proto-humans teleporting about the surface of Amaterasu instead of lugs.

I managed to stifle my irony for another question. Get the answer to this, I thought, and I could go home.

"Teleporting," I said, straight out. "How is it done?"

"By a process that would be translated as *pulling on the worldline*. *Line* in this case standing for both the theoretical track of a being through spacetime and in the sense of rope, or wire. We discover an actuality line existing in *n*-dimensional space between an object and an identical volume in the corresponding place where we wish to move it, we then wrap the line about the object and haul it from one place to another, simultaneously exchanging an equivalent volume in the opposite direction. The symmetry in volume is necessary, although the objects may have different mass.

"A sophisticated perceptual faculty is necessary, first to discover the actuality line among a large array of alternate lines, and second, to properly perceive the object to be transported so that it might be transported intact. The expense of energy is insignificant once the proper actuality line is perceived."

"Can you give us a model of how it might be done?" I asked.

"It will take a while," Arges said.

In the end it took about twelve hours. The conceptualization of paradimensional space was too strenuous for human minds; but our computer understood only those parameters with which it was programmed, and it had already been programmed to deal with n-dimensional constructs. Gradually we reduced paradimensional space to its mathematical fundamentals, the dimensions all coiled within each other, a profusion of subtleties in toroid and spherical shapes. We discovered there were only eleven spatial dimensions, not twenty-one, the extra ten, theoretically perceived as separate, now from an n-dimensional perspective understood to be cognate with others, interpenetrating and complementary rather than distinct.

Mary and I worked together well. Inspiration was burning in us, ideas flashing in our minds like lightning, faster than our fingers could record them. We were working in sync, leapfrogging from one concept to the next, answering each other's questions, unknotting one another's ideas, performing the scientific equivalent of finishing each other's sentences. We were in a close space, touching, jabbering at full speed into each other's face, bumping knees as we competed for the comp. Gazing out into the funnel of spacetime as we looked into ourselves for the answers.

The personalities, the issues that had divided us only a few hours ago—all were gone. We were a collective, inspired whole, full of wild and freakish talent, answers pouring up to the surface with the uninhibited cheer of bubbles in champagne. No doubt the recording would serve to separate just which idea came from whom, but I have no memory on that score. All I can remember are ideas bursting like a string of fireworks, one overlapping the other in blazing succession.

We put together the theoretical mechanisms for teleportation, boiling them down to a simple, elegant mathematical statement.

By the time the equation was flashing triumphantly from our monitors, our little platform in n-dimensional space was littered with the remnants of various kinds of plundered food and crumpled paper. We now had a toilet stolen from Knight's Move supplies. When the statement flashed onto the screen, I felt the energy draining from us. Mary and I were suddenly exhausted, our limbs aching. We were beginning to smell bad. But we had the answer.

Moving material objects through the subtler, higher-dimensional realms did, in fact, take surprisingly little energy. Shifting something the mass of the average human being would require little more than the amount of static electricity gained from scuffling one's feet on the carpet, provided that one had perceived the line through which to draw the object through higher-dimensional space.

Arges's references to having to eat while manipulating the lug now made sense; the Cyclopes turned out to be very low-energy creatures indeed, more aetherial than the pulsing auroral displays sweeping through the upper atmosphere of Amaterasu. The Cyclopes fed off various energies created in n-dimensional space by stellar-sized objects, but the amount they required to exist was small, even by human standards. Their bodies were at once gigantic, occupying enormous volumes of higher-dimensional space; and also they were subtle, thinner than air.

We had a reasonable certainty that we could manage teleportation ourselves, provided we were able to design equipment capable of the multi-dimensional perceptions necessary to perceive the actuality lines that, according to our model, connected matter in its various states and energies. We also needed a pathway opened into higher-dimensional space. The perceptual problem seemed capable of reduction to a principle of mathematical exclusion and well within the capabilities of the average comp. The initial pathway would have to be opened by a Cyclopes—from the inside, as it were, since we did not have enough energy to open the path the other way. Arges indicated his willingness to do us that favor.

"I would be pleased to help out," he said. He was inflecting his phrases with much more confidence now, knowing how to create a context in which homonyms could be differentiated from one another. He was also beginning to absorb our speech patterns; sometimes he sounded like Mary, sometimes like me. "Would you mind," he asked, "if I asked a question central to our dilemma concerning your species?"

"I didn't know you had a dilemma. But go ahead."

"As I understand it, you have chosen to exist in the lower dimensions, your consciousness existing in a short-lived organic body in which the efficiency of interactions is limited by the speed of organic chemical processes. You do not manipulate matter by use of actuality lines but rather by physical means, or by constructing physical objects that in turn manipulate other objects. We consider this ingenious, by the way, but it hardly seems efficient."

"Why," Arges asked, "have you chosen such an *eccentric life-style?*"

This time neither Mary nor I were able to keep from laughter. Arges paused politely, waiting for it to end.

"Did I say that right?" he asked.

Laughter bubbled up from us, soaring toward the swirling, ever-receding Cyclopean lights. Into the bright infinity that had become our tomorrow.

24

Just for the hell of it, I planned to make our return as dramatic as possible. We popped into the physics lounge with our computer and our collection of refuse: empty coffee cups, apple corers, plastic forks, crumpled notes. The reaction from the score of people we startled out of their wits was all we could have hoped for. I counted three shrieks, two upset drinks and a whole roomful of double-takes.

Except for Brian McGivern. He was in a padded chair, his legs stretched out before him on a low table, apparently taking a nap. His eyes slitted open at the commotion and moved in our direction.

"Got something for us?" he asked.

"The future. I guess." Holding out the lug collar.

There was a sudden silence in the room, disorder having given way to stillness, wide pairs of eyes regarding us with awe, anticipation, perhaps envy. Mary smoothed her tee shirt self-consciously.

"There's the record of an event in the collar," I said. "Play it and we'll answer questions after we take a shower and have a rest. There's some math in the computer that you might want to look at later.''

"You took your time," McGivern said. He pulled in his legs and stood, looking at me with his wise, Mephistophilian eyes. "But congratulations, I suppose. On your new revolution."

"Any time," I said.

I rocked a little on my feet. My inner ear seemed out of tune. The universe looked strange, lacking depth and perspective. Things seemed flatter than they were, fore-shortening toward us, distant objects nearer. My visual reflexes had altered during our time away. Cautiously I began to walk through three-dimensional space.

Mary and I left the lounge, feeling the weight of the others' unspoken questions weighing on our shoulders. Outside it was blazing afternoon and we took sun hats and overcoats from a locker and sprinted from the physics building to the safety of the base camp.

Once inside the field, we kept the hats pulled down so as not to be recognized, but as we stepped into our apartment building, we ran into al-Qatan, his face shrouded by his kaffiyeh, apparently ready for a run to the physics building. He stood back in surprise, then nodded to himself as his eyes turned from me to Mary.

"You've done it, I suppose," he said. "Falkner's luck."

"It wasn't us, particularly," I told him. "I was taken because they thought I was important, and Mary went along because she was with me. The physics were just as we had modeled them; we don't have enough energy to do it, not from this side. Not without help."

Al-Qatan nodded. "Ah," he said. "But you got help. Was it from the lugs, or something else?"

"Something else. Something . . . very curious. And a little bored." I hesitated for a moment, thinking of Arges and his colleagues playing their complicated games, picking their way through homonyms. "I suppose we'll get along," I said. "Even if we end up understanding one another."

"There was a recording of the event," Mary said. "They'll be playing it in the physics lounge in a little while." She swayed with weariness. "We're too tired to tell you now."

Al-Qatan gazed at us for a long suspended moment. "I wish . . ." he said. He left the thought unfinished, but there was longing in his voice.

He had come all these years to Amaterasu, leaving his wife, leaving everything he'd built on Kemp's in hopes of finding the answer. And now the breakthrough had come and it had passed him by. Left him looking back down the long years of pointless sacrifice.

"Yes," I said. "I wish it had been possible, too."

He pushed past us and hurried away. Mary and I walked to the door of her apartment. She put her arms around me and I buried myself in her hair, in her scent, in the smell of sour clothing and old sweat, potato salad and stale elation.

"I miss Hourigan," she said.

"So do I."

"I think the Cyclopes would have liked him too."

And suddenly it began to turn cold. Our differences, that such a short time ago hadn't mattered, were suddenly present again, almost material, sliding between us. Mary stepped out of our embrace and opened her apartment door. She stood there for a moment, her eyes fastened on me. Troubled.

"Come to Earth," I said.

"I'll think about it." There was affection in her voice, but no concession.

"It should be easy now. Take no time at all."

She smiled, more to herself than to me. "The traveling part," she said, "was always the easiest."

And closed the door.

I did the knight's move in the corridor, two paces ahead and one to the right, and opened my door. I walked into the shower with my clothes on and undressed in warm, soapy rain. I stayed there until my muscles began to unknot, then turned off the water and stepped into the apartment without bothering to towel off.

There was a bottle of brandy on the sideboard. I opened it and drank from the neck; then I took the bottle with me and told the comp to play Philodice's songs.

I listened and drank about half the bottle. Somehow I couldn't get to sleep. I wondered if, back by the Kassotis in the dream time of legend, Kassandra was crying her unheeded warning, *Beware the Cyclopes.* . . . I listened carefully, but I didn't hear her voice. Perhaps good would come of this. The only thing I knew was that I seemed foredoomed to contact aliens and, as a result, turn humanity upside down.

The worlds would end their isolation, their provincialism. The entirety of the stars was open to exploration and population. Each family could have its own solar system. The Cyclopes would provide a contrast to humanity that would make us see ourselves anew. As I had planned to do with the centaurs.

But in the end we would still be ourselves. Trapped in our own histories, encased by our own series of victories and defeats. Living in our own present, waiting for our own eternity to end.

Mary had refused it, and would probably continue to refuse. She would not live forever, not within herself. It was a choice I had to respect.

But, I protested, someone in love is not herself, does not live in herself alone. I wanted to make a note to myself to tell Mary this, but by then I was asleep.

Sometime in the night I thought I heard the snick of the door lock and saw through the dimness the sheen of Mary's hair as she came to me.

But it was only a dream.

25

"Doran. Are you busy?"

"Not particularly," I said. Arges was addressing me through the speaker of my room comp. He had acquired a distinctive masculine intonation that was beginning to resemble mine. Over the weeks in which we'd been communicating, his voice had been growing more individualistic, different from the other Cyclopes who occasionally called, and also more relaxed. With a better grasp of colloquial usage and idiom, his prose style was now a lot closer to that of Dashiell Hammett than Matthew Arnold. I was beginning to think of Arges as a *he* instead of an *it*.

I finished toweling off from my shower and began drawing on my clothes.

"I tried to talk to you earlier," Arges said, "but the man on duty said that you were out running. Is this an activity related to your work, or something you do for pleasure?"

"More duty than anything else," I said. "Bodies work better when they are maintained. Running is good maintenance, and it's something that can be done anywhere. And it can be done alone, not like most sports.''

''It seems a shocking waste of energy.''

''Our bodies store a large amount of potential energy in our musculature, and it's easily replaced. As you know.''

''As we know.'' I gave the comp speaker a sharp glance. Arges's voice sounded a bit wistful. I wondered if the inflection was deliberate or an experiment in the use of the speaker.

''Are the effects of running pleasurable?'' Arges asked. ''I have a reference in my vocabulary to endorphin highs.''

I explained about endorphins and physical activity as I dressed. ''I don't seem to be affected by endorphins much at all,'' I said, ''though many people are. It's an individual thing.''

''Concepts such as intoxication and chemical highs are difficult for me to grasp,'' Arges said. ''We have an analogue, I suppose, in the sensation of the supreme efficiency we gain when we take sufficient energy from our environment, but this seems to lack the . . . essence of intoxication. We lack comprehension of so many of the terms that are fundamental to understanding you.''

''You'll manage it,'' I said. I stretched and felt my vertebrae crackle.

''The notion of passion is so strange,'' Arges said. ''Love, lust, anger, jealousy, rage. . . . Each is dependent on chemistry. The conflicts between your intelligence and the chemical demands of your bodies must be appalling.''

I gave a short laugh. ''That's about right, Arges,'' I said. I sat down at my desk and asked him to lower his voice now that I was next to the comp speaker. I poured myself a glass of cognac.

''And war—that is a fearsome concept to grasp. Even one of the minor conflicts in your history destroyed more individuals than there ever were Cyclopes in the universe.

We are able to extrapolate war from our knowledge of murder, but still we find the concept terrifying."

The snifter stopped halfway to my mouth. "You understand murder?" I asked.

"In the sense that murder is individual extinction," Arges said. "Early in our history one of us discovered by accident that he could, if his energies were sufficiently high, absorb another individual, particularly if that individual's energies were low. The result was not death, since the absorbed individual merely became a subordinate component in the murderer's matrix, but the victim suffered a total loss of identity and personality. So it was murder by anyone's definition, yes?"

"I'd say it was murder, yes. What happened to the murderer?"

"He was as surprised by the results of his experiment as any of us, but he found them interesting. So did several others, after they became murderers."

I took a careful sip of brandy. "So what made you quit?" I asked. "Or did you?"

"Life became less interesting with fewer of us around, so we agreed to stop," Arges said blandly. "One of us did not, finding the experience of murder too interesting, so a number of us banded together and absorbed him between us." His voice turned reflective. "But that is not war as I understand it, but rather collective justice, or a posse, or a lynch mob. In Cyclopean terms they seem to be one and the same."

I took a less tentative drink and thought for a moment about what might happen if a Cyclops decided it was *interesting* to teleport humans into airless space and watch their eyes bug out while they floundered in search of oxygen. I'd speak to McGivern about this possibility and have him work something into the Concord.

McGivern was using his ambassadorial powers to negotiate a treaty between humanity and the Cyclopes. The terms, thus far, were simple: The Cyclopes would assist us with setting up teleportation devices and agree to furnish us information about themselves and the higher-dimensional world in which they lived. They agreed to refrain from using us as counters in any of their games, as they had used the lugs. We agreed to assist them with investigations about ourselves and the material universe. I'd seen some of McGivern's drafts, but if McGivern had specified penalties for things like murder, he hadn't shown them to anyone yet.

But what could we do if a Cyclops killed someone? The Cyclopes were immune to any of our forms of justice. We would have to depend on other Cyclopes for enforcement. And that might prove a knotty problem.

"War is difficult," Arges went on. "Love is the worst."

I grinned into my snifter.

"The nearest thing we have is *affinity*. And that doesn't seem close."

"No, I guess not."

"Are you and Mary lovers?" Abruptly. I gazed at the comp speaker in surprise. "I hope you aren't offended by the question," Arges added. "Privacy is another concept we don't fully understand."

"I suppose you would develop a need for privacy if there were suddenly several billion of you," I said.

"Possibly. I hadn't thought of that. But you haven't answered the first question. I will withdraw it if it intrudes."

I put my feet up on the desk while I tried to decide how I wanted to answer this. "I don't mind talking about it," I said, "but I would consider it a favor if you didn't mention it to any of the other humans. As a concession to my sense of privacy."

"Agreed," Arges said. "We do not lack data on sexual relationships in any case. There is a woman in the maintenance division who had been most frank about her long series of encounters."

"You don't waste any time, do you?" I thought about the staff of the maintenance pool for a moment, wondering who it might be and how the Cyclopes had approached her. I didn't come up with any likely candidates, so I shrugged.

"You and Mary," Arges prompted. "Are you lovers?"

"We were many years ago," I said. "And then again recently. We may be again in the future."

"But you are not lovers at present."

"Not at present, no."

I had the mental image of Arges as a vague humanoid form, head tilted to one side as he peered at me quizzically. I've found that spending hours at a time in talking to a disembodied voice is conducive to hallucination.

"What prompted your attraction to one another?" Arges asked.

"Intellectual compatibility. Compatibility of temperament. And—if you'll forgive the expression—chemistry."

"Chemistry." The wistful tone was back again. I inhaled the fragrance of the cognac and wondered where Arges's fascination with the subject was going to lead. But his tone changed and I lost the train of thought.

"May I ask what prompted you and Mary to . . . is 'break up' the correct form?"

"It'll do. We broke up on account of a philosophical disagreement."

"Over what?"

"Over whether life is worth living. Prolonged life, I should say."

"Prolonged life being the artificial protraction of natural biological life?"

"That's it." Arges digested this for a moment or—for all I knew—paused to distribute the news to the other Cyclopes in the 11-dimensional edition of the *Human Affairs Gazette*.

I began to wonder if I had not misnamed Arges and

whether a more natural name, considering his system of patient, detached questioning, might not have been Dr. Freud. I wondered if this series of questions was intended to lead anywhere in particular.

"You and Mary are no longer lovers, and yet you continue working together. Your professional attachments seem to have outlasted your emotional ones. Is that not difficult for you?"

I considered telling Arges that Mary and I were professionals, that our intellectual compatibilities and interests far outweighed our personal disappointments. That we worked together well and would continue to do so in the future. That there was no difficulty between us at all.

It would, of course, have been a lie. Mary and I *did* work well together, and when the blaze of inspiration took us, we were well-nigh unstoppable. But in the other moments, when there wasn't work to occupy us—during a coffee break or when we passed each other in the corridors or when I saw her dining with McGivern in the lounge— then sometimes I felt an ache burning in my throat and had to look away. And from time to time I saw Mary turning away from me, swallowing hard.

"We cope," I said. Arges must have gathered from my tone that I didn't want to deal with this subject. He changed topics swiftly, without hesitation.

"Your philosophical disagreement—we've had our own debates on that score," he said. "A number of us committed suicide, claiming that life was no longer interesting enough to overcome ennui."

"How did they kill themselves?"

"A few volunteered to be murdered by others, hoping their absorption would provide a new viewpoint on existence. Others threw themselves down a singularity, where their energies were torn apart by the vortex of forces. Still others have allowed their personal energies to drop so low that they are no longer in the same time as the rest of us.

They have slowed down relative to us, so that their own personal time moves much more quickly. They await something that interests them.'' Arges paused for a moment. ''I criticized them at the time,'' he added. ''It seemed to me that they lacked sufficient curiosity about things. That there was always something interesting to do. But lately it has occurred to me that much of what I've occupied myself with has lacked sufficient meaning.''

''Activity for the sake of keeping busy.''

''Yes.''

I felt a dark wisp of cold touching my neck. I put the brandy down and stared at the hologram on the wall, a picture of Branwen standing by a white coral beach, her underwater breather pulled down around her neck, tanned brown, smiling through droplets of seawater. What is your future? I thought. Will you lose what it is that makes me love you, love you along with the dolphins and centaurs and everything else in the natural world? Lose what makes your life worth living?

''I've had this conversation before,'' I said. ''With Mary.''

''Ah. So.''

''I keep thinking, Arges, that life is better than non-life. You might say the thought is fundamental to my point of view.''

''To mine as well. But sometimes I wonder.''

''Yes. Me, too.'' I raised the brandy glass and tilted it toward the comp. ''L'chaim,'' I said. ''I'll drink to life anyway.''

''Me too. L'chaim.''

Our conversation degenerated somewhat. We had been surprised to discover that the Cyclopes liked punning; clever use of what-for-the-sake-of-clarity-I-shall-call-language was something they enjoyed in their own form of communication, and they'd picked up the necessary skills in English very quickly. So Arges and I tossed some puns around, and I told him some jokes and, when necessary, why I thought they were funny. He practiced laughing through the speaker—he was beginning to get fairly good at it. I finished the brandy and poured another glass.

"I want to know about sex, Doran," Arges said finally. Right out of the blue. Zo, Dr. Freud, I thought, finally ve come to ze heart of ze matter.

"I thought you had that girl in the maintenance division to fill you in."

"Yes, and I've read some of your scientific literature on the subject. But I thought I'd find another perspective. If you don't mind."

I laughed. "Okay. Depends on what you want to know. But I hope you're not looking for real wisdom here. I'm not sure I have any, particularly on this score."

"I'll take my chances. I'm looking for subjective viewpoints anyway," Arges said. "What does it feel like?"

I laughed again. Arges joined in with a few feeble chuckles, probably not knowing why I thought it was funny but wanting to be polite.

"Depends—on experience, physical factors, personality, fatigue. Chemistry, mostly. Sorry about that."

"It's such a fundamental biological drive. By far the most powerful and the most anarchic. Much of your societal organization seems contrived to sublimate or channel it. With results that are mixed and rarely permanent."

"That's life in three dimensions for you."

"These biological drives are the great gap in our understanding of you. It is a pity that we cannot inhabit a biological mechanism. I have considered. . . ."

There was a long pause. Since a Cyclops, with its light-speed thought, hardly ever pauses in its speech with a human, I knew Arges was leading up to something significant, something very difficult to translate from his terms to mine. And I had a good idea of what it was.

"Your species is remarkably efficient at building elaborate material constructions to help you manipulate material reality. We consider it the most remarkable thing about you. It's something we've never thought of doing.''

"Let's call them machines, okay?''

"Yes. Okay.'' There was another hesitation, briefer this time. "The point of machines is that they allow you to manipulate your environment while using less energy than if you were forced to use your own bodies.''

"Right,'' I said. "And since you are at extremely low efficiency when dealing with the material dimensions, and the energy drain is very taxing to you, you were wondering if it would be possible for us to construct a machine that you could manipulate, such that you could use to explore the material realm without exhausting yourselves. Do I have it right?''

"Yes.'' A pause. "That was very bright of you.''

"I'm not an authority on cybernetics, but I suspect that such a machine is possible. A problem, though. Since it was a discussion of sex and other human passions that led up to this question, I assume that you are interested in exploring, from the inside as it were, the vagaries of biological existence. And that would not be possible while using machines. Though you could, no doubt, imitate the various biological functions—sex, let us say—and though you could no doubt perform a mechanically adequate job, the essense of the act would be missing. Emotion, caring, biological compunction, hormones, psychological components. Lots of other things. You'd be missing the point.''

"Oh.'' The voice was subdued. "I rather suspected that might be the case. I just wanted confirmation.''

"Sorry.''

"I don't suppose it would be possible . . .'' Another of those odd little pauses. ". . . that it would be possible for us to inhabit a biological organism.''

I thought for a long moment about Arges's question. No one had even succeeded in translating a human consciousness from one body to another, but then, it hadn't been tried. There had been no perceived need for it; damaged bodies, as long as there was consciousness remaining, could be rebuilt easily. I'd lost half an arm in an assassination attempt a few centuries ago and it had been regrown in a few weeks.

Our computers had reached the complexity of the human mind, and I supposed they could be used as a link between one consciousness and another. I supposed that even Cyclopean consciousness could be modeled, given enough practice. Perhaps bodies could be created with a compact little computer in the brain, or perhaps a little two-way communicator with the nth dimension. Or maybe the Cyclopean consciousness could be trapped in its human envelope for as long as the envelope lasted.

Still, Arges's motivation made me wonder. The Cyclopes knew that biological drives tended toward anarchy, that they were destabilizing and contrary to the smooth intelligence of their own species. Yet Arges seemed eager— and not entirely from a detached, scientific point of view—to experience such passions, the sooner the better.

I wondered at the depth of ennui among Arges and his kind. Etiolated intellectualities floating among the cosmos, as old as time, some of them so desperate for something new they volunteered themselves as subjects for murder. Unable to consider physical reality as anything other than a stage for an elaborate game played with living counters.

Could they assume the guise of an adopted humanity as easily as Arges seemed to think they could? They seemed eager to charge themselves with human hormones and passions unknown to them except in the abstract, and that would be destabilizing. But that fact was balanced against the Cyclopes' known adaptability; they had adjusted to talking to humans—with fewer problems in translation— than humans and dolphins had adjusted to talking with one another after centuries of contact.

Perhaps, I thought hopefully, becoming a human consciousness would have no worse effect on Arges than to make him another neurotic human, like all the others I knew.

"It's not possible at our current level of knowledge," I said. "I'm not a specialist in these matters. But speaking as a layman, I suppose it could be done if we put our minds to it."

There was a burst of static from the speaker. I almost spilled some of my brandy. Arges had actually become so excited he'd lost control of his voice.

"Pardon me," he said, "but this is very good news."

"I think it would be best to build the machine bodies first and let you accustom yourselves to moving in our space before you climb into our heads. Heads are a much more dangerous place to be in."

"As you think best," Arges said.

I finished my brandy and stepped to my wardrobe to get a formal jacket for dinner. But I was just drunk enough to ask one last question.

"Arges," I said, "out there in the *nth* dimension, have you seen any sign of God?"

"I take it you mean God with a capital G, creator of the universe, first principle, prime mover?"

"That's the one."

"No. Not a sign."

I shrugged. "Too bad. I guess."

"We don't have the concept," Arges said. "You see, we can't *create* anything; we can only manipulate what already exists. So it never occurred to us that anyone created us or anything else."

I felt a touch of sadness. The Cyclopés were a very lonely people after all. "I see."

"If, however, you were speaking of god with a small g, meaning an immortal, supernormal being—well, we Cyclopes qualify."

"Sorry. You're not being worshiped."

"Is that necessary? Our sources conflict."

"I'm afraid it is. Good night, Arges."

"Good night, Mr. Falkner."

I stepped out into the corridor, seeing al-Qatan ahead of me, also going to dinner. I called to him and we went together.

Later I would have a talk with McGivern about this conversation with Arges. I had the feeling that his Concord was going to turn into an interesting document.

26

Prelude To The Fragrance Of
Hyacinths

It took two months to construct the first telegate, and it was another two weeks of sending several dozen objects, small animals and lugs to various parts of Amaterasu before the first human subject went through.

I declined to volunteer, and so Bahadur Gurung, born over seven centuries earlier in Nepal, became the first human to teleport voluntarily from one place to another. Successfully, I might add.

The party afterward was long and got very sloppy and disjointed toward the end. I ended up in the narrow bed of a woman from the maintenance pool, and so quite possibly an anecdote in the Cyclopean Archives. I didn't know whether she was the one Arges had mentioned, and didn't ask. I didn't ask where Mary spent that night either. She had been keeping company with a variety of men and had left the party early.

After the gate passed a series of tests, we decided that

we could avoid the long, frozen journey back to Kemp's. The *Bougaineville*'s navigation computers held the coordinates for anywhere in human space we'd want to go, and we had designed the gate so there was no need for a terminal at the other end, although a terminal would make the task of finding an actuality line somewhat easier. Project Knight's Move would be coming home in style. The crew of the *Bougaineville* would be staying, at least for a while, until a much larger telegate could be constructed in orbit, a gate big enough to move the entire ship through.

Bougaineville would not be returning to Kemp's at all. Once the large gate was constructed, the ship would be leaping ahead to an unexplored star system, looking for habitable planets—the first Knight's Move off the edge of the black and white board, the first of a series of leaps into the suddenly limitless future of humankind.

As for me, there was no reason why I couldn't go back to Earth. The coordinates were in the *Bougaineville*'s computers as well as those for Kemp's.

I made my request. It was granted, as I knew it would be. I was going home.

Aurora Farewell

It was a few hours past midnight and I was warming up by the lake before my run. There was a heavy wind blowing, scattering the aurora's reflection on the surface of the water. I was stretching my ligaments beneath one of the trees, and as I straightened, I saw the dark shape of someone walking toward me from the physics building.

"Hello," I said.

"Hi. Can I join you?"

"Sure."

We ran about three miles out across the hard edge of the lake, then back. There was a regular track here, smoothed out and beaten down. It felt good to have her there again, her pace matching mine, our breath in sync as we ran wordless under the flaming sky. At the end of our run we dashed straight into the lake, washing the sweat away.

When we splashed to shore, she came into my arms—the first embrace since the night we returned, tired but triumphant, with the answer from Knight's Move. I hadn't pressed her since then, hadn't wanted her to feel that I was pushing her toward a decision. And hoping I was right not to press, that it was room she wanted and not reassurance.

I kissed her, and she responded, a little hesitantly. Then she stepped back.

"I should tell you something," she said.

"Tell."

"I'll come to Earth if you want—after the gates are set up, when I can get things put in order on Kemp's."

I felt my tension ebb. A warmth began gathering at the center of my chest. I moved to embrace her again, but she put up a hand.

"Doran," she said, "I want you to understand what you're getting. A granny who will probably want another kid, and who's still a Diehard. Someone's going to have to bury me in sixty or eighty years, and you'll have to decide whether it's going to be you or someone else."

"You might change your mind," I said. "In the last few months the universe has become a bigger and more interesting place."

She shook her head. The sky flamed violet, azure, scarlet, the drops of water in her hair reflecting colors like beads of trembling glass. "Don't count on it," she said.

She put up her hands as though to push me away, but then, oddly tentative, she put them on my shoulders. "Doran," she said, "please make me a promise."

"If I can."

She was looking up at me with urgency. "When it begins to hurt too much, watching me get old, I want you to tell me," she said. "And I'll go."

I shook my head and tried to protest, but she put a hand over my lips. "Promise," she said. Gently. Insistently.

My throat was aching. "I promise."

So we came together again. Not agreeing to ignore the differences between us, but conscious of them, conscious that they might well force us apart before long. Knowing that we would live day by day, that time would catch us up.

Before, there had perhaps been an element of nostalgia, of wanting what we had once had. Now there was an element of defiance, of not wanting to have been wrong the first time.

But when she came to Earth, those reasons wouldn't matter anymore. It would be just the two of us then. Day by day.

She gave me a slight smile, and I had the impression that she was thanking me, for god knew what, in the instant before she raised her head so that I could kiss her.

Through

Mary went through early, with the first group. Arges reported their safe arrival on Kemp's. I was scheduled to go through a few days later, after all the data was duplicated and the equipment packed.

McGivern had a notion of trying to keep teleportation in the hands of various institutions and governments, afraid of the anarchy such a simple mode of commerce might create. Knight's Move had made commerce between planets as free and easy as the Falkner field had made commerce across their surfaces. McGivern was trying to set up protocols for making certain that formalities—customs, visas, that sort of thing—were going to be observed.

I was less sanguine. Telegates didn't need terminals, although terminals made things easier and quicker, and that meant that people with the right equipment could plan their own vacations. I agreed to assist McGivern for the moment though, hoping to ease the transition, letting the machine and its users develop their own patterns before setting them free.

And in the meantime I was going to tell Earth it had better prepare for a large number of tourists.

That was going to mean preparing the centaurs as well. I doubted their secret could be kept, not once people started dropping themselves anywhere on the planet they wished.

The day came, and everyone came around to say their farewells. I shook a lot of hands, promised to keep up friendships. "Come visit," I told al-Qatan. "Bring your family. Earth has changed a lot since you've seen it."

He gave me an embrace. "I'll come when I can."

"I'll invent a scientific congress," I said. "Give you an excuse."

"Good idea."

"And give my regards to Jay," I said, "when he's well enough to . . . you know. And if you think it's wise."

He looked at me solemnly. "I'll do that, my friend."

I was kissed and hugged and shaken by the hand and offered a lot of drinks, many of which I accepted. And then I was standing by the gate, McGivern beside me with his granite smile, his narrow eyes.

He stuck out his hand. "Thank you, Doran," he said. "For some things."

I shook his hand. "You're welcome," I said. "For some things."

McGivern, I thought, had not forgiven me; there was not much forgiveness in him, not that kind anyway. But he would not become a danger or a nuisance. He was too proud to let his private feelings stain his policy, his goals. He would have been a lesser man than McGivern otherwise.

We stood there for a moment, and I wondered if the tension that flowed between us—that had *always* flowed between us—was visible in the glare of the medialites that

were floating overhead, recording Falkner's departure into
the *n*th dimension and his farewell to his personal Mephistophilis. Or whether anyone watching this recording down
the long track of posterity would note that despite our
difference in thought and manner, our ways of thinking
and working, each of us did his very best work when he
was around the other.

Well. The need for our best work had passed, at least
for the moment.

I dropped his hand and he reached into his jacket for a
cigar. Before he could light it, I stepped into the gate and
signaled the tech.

It was dark when I landed, and my eyes took a few
seconds to adjust. In the absence of vision, my first concrete impression of Earth was the fragrance of hyacinths.

Kassotis

I was standing where I intended, on the thin grass of the
stadium at Delphi. Wind whistled among the stone seats,
bringing the smell of hyacinth, of earth, of pine. Above
me was a night sky, stars burning in the blackness with a
cold clarity. The nightly aurora of Amaterasu was light-
years and several seconds away.

I walked through the trees, down to the path bordered
by replica trophies of the games. Somewhere behind me
my baggage materialized, but I didn't pay attention. My
feet carried me past the silent stone hollow of the theater,
to where the vast Doric bulk of the temple squatted in the
floodlights. Symbol of the tarnished ideal that was Delphi,
that was humanity. A place I'd rebuilt and then chosen to
live by, to remind myself that there was a reason why
Kassotis had to run dry at the end, that even Ge will not
give forever to a thing that has forgotten its purpose.

I thought for a moment about Kassandra and her priest,
about Faustus and Mephistophilis, about myself and

McGivern. About how dreams without practical knowledge of the world are useless, even dangerous, and how worldly knowledge, without an ideal to sustain it, becomes corrupt or pointless. I thought about the decisions that I'd made, trying to balance one against the other, and I wished there were a Kassandra here, to tell me whether I'd done the right thing.

I stood before the temple and listened carefully for the sound of Kassandra's wails, echoing up the oekos and past the pillars. I heard only the wind.

I turned to see the lights of my house on Hyampeia, then began my walk along the switch-back path, past reconstructed treasuries and trophies that were new to me, put up since I'd left. I wondered if any of my family were home. Partway up Hyampeia I triggered the security monitors and suddenly there were floodlights everywhere, with the voice of the house booming loudly from hidden speakers.

"Intrusion is forbidden into this area," my house said sternly. "Please identify yourself."

"Doran Falkner," I said, and kept on walking.

"That is impossible. Mr. Falkner is not on the planet. Security systems are being activated. Come no farther."

"Shut up, house," I said, "and make me some iced coffee."

There was a moment's hesitation filled only by the sound of my shoes on the cindered walk. Then the floodlights faded, leaving their afterimage on my retinas like a vision of Amaterasu's aurora.

"Welcome home, Mr. Falkner," the house said.

"Thank you, house."

The door opened to my hand. The inside smelled musty; no one had visited in a while. Lights came on automatically, revealing the bronze charioteer in his niche. I picked up a featherduster and brushed the dust from his shoulders and the folds of his robes. His lifelike eyes gazed back at me from beneath lashes of bronze. He didn't seem to have any advice to offer me.

"Mr. Falkner, I have a call. From a Mr. Arges."

"Tell him I'll talk to him tomorrow."

"Yes, Mr. Falkner."

I put the featherduster down. A robot brought me my iced coffee and I took it out on the terrace. I looked down into the sacred precincts and pictured them alive with tourists, their heads craning up to read the inscriptions as they listened to the practiced voices of the guides. And perhaps, through a gateway in their heads leading to the nth dimension, doing a little piece of mental translation as they read the words, KNOW THYSELF and NOTHING IN EXCESS.

I wondered if they'd pay any more attention to that advice than we had.

27

I dropped my car down near the soft mound overlooking the Upper Nile. Below me the river, its flanks marked with green, eased itself along its muddy bluffs. I turned off the field and breathed in the heat. Here on the bluffs above the river the desert wind blew unabated.

After Amaterasu, I thought, the Sahara was easy.

Snaggles's visible extrusion was coiled atop the mound, a vast black serpent standing fifteen feet high. He swayed slightly in the wind, fixing me with his beady eyes, his hood extended, showing the patterned scales.

"The great god Set, I presume?" I asked.

"That is correct." Snaggles's tongue flickered against the wind. His mouth didn't move when he spoke. He seemed to be pulsing his cobra's hood to produce sound.

I squatted on my heels. "I thought you'd be in China for another few decades at least."

"I started working in the south." Snaggles's tone was injured. "But there were some people there—herdsmen, and then some tourists—who saw me. And then this crazy woman started chasing me, putting down sensors everywhere and planting mines where I was working. Trying to kill me.'' His voice turned reproachful. "You have some unbalanced people on your planet, Doran.''

"No harm done, I trust.''

"Not except to my studies, no. But you have to get those people out of there. They were trespassing on your land.''

I sighed, wondering how I could mount a twenty-four-hour guard on a formless alien who spent most of his days underground. "I don't suppose you know who they were?''

"No. But I think some of them came from Hong Kong. And I'd know that crazy woman again if I saw her.'' He swayed restlessly. "I knew you should have forced that Hong Kong bunch to move," he said.

So, I thought. Madame Lu was protecting her House against ghosts. And she hadn't done a bad job by the sound of it.

"I can't move them. They own the land.''

"Not where they were chasing me. They were trespassing.''

"I'll see what I can do.''

Snaggles flicked his tongue into the wind again. "I heard the news broadcasts," he said. "Congratulations on the conclusion of your project.''

"We were bailed out by an alien intelligence.'' I looked up at him. "Again," I said.

"I regret, Doran," Snaggles said, "that the arrangement we made so long ago has cast such a lengthy shadow on your life. On your image of yourself.'' He reared up, spreading the hood wider, thinner, until it was almost transparent, the sun outlining the scales with patterns of gold. His voice echoed from the cup.

"I picked you because you had remarkable capabilities," he said. "There really wasn't anyone else who could have done the job. I handed you a piece of technology, but it was you who decided how it should be applied and saw it through. Made it a part of your own dream.'' He flicked his tongue again. ''You are a remarkable man, Doran. You would have made a dream without me. I just made it easier, that's all.''

I blinked against the sand thrown up by the desert wind. ''The dream changes,'' I said. ''It's going to change around us both. I can't keep you secret anymore.''

Snaggles shrank down into himself, his hood folding back. He rested his chin on his coils.

''Really?'' he asked. His mouth was moving with the words this time. I couldn't decide whether there was menace in the tone or not. ''That's against our agreement.''

''With the new technology, I can't keep people off the planet. We'll get millions of them—they'll be everywhere. And enough people have seen you now so that they might start looking for you. If the woman in Hong Kong could find you, anyone can.''

I looked down at him. An unblinking eye looked back reproachfully. ''I think that in a few months we should make an announcement,'' I went on. ''In front of some media people I can trust. There'll be a stir for a few years, I suppose, but once the novelty wears off, you'll be able to get back to work.''

''Are you going to inform the populace about my part in . . . in the previous acquisition of technology?''

''Yes. Unless I can talk myself out of it somehow.'' I shrugged. ''Eight hundred years is long enough to live a lie.''

''I prefer anonymity,'' Snaggles said, ''but I suppose discovery was inevitable.'' He turned his wedge-shaped head to me. ''A pity your people aren't more backward. On a primitive world I could imitate the local deities and dig around wherever I liked.''

An eddy of memory flowed around me. Snaggles in a flame-lit temple, the oiled bodies of his worshipers facing him with intense, dancing eyes. An old dream, still with the power to cause fear. I took a breath.

"True," I said. "But the digging wouldn't be as interesting. You'd never find Coke bottles or *Action Comics.*"

"I never liked the media." Reflectively. "On any of the planets I've visited."

"I suppose that sometime soon our ships will be visiting some of the places you've been," I said. "Visiting your old diggings and whoever's living there now. Any old friends you'd like us to look up?"

"No," he said. There was sadness in his voice. "Once a job is done, it's done. I don't go back."

I gazed on the coiled serpentine body and thought about the decisions that formed our lives and how, after a while, they become not so much decisions as reflexes. Tens of thousands of years ago, when the decision was made, Snaggles probably had good reason for deciding to dig his way across the galaxy. Whatever reasons had motivated the decision were long since obsolete; there was only the act, repeated endlessly, obsessively. Because acts define who one is, and Snaggles had no other way to define himself. No wonder he was troubled by dreams.

And then I thought of the Cyclopes, those immense, etiolated intellectuals so eager to fire up their detached intelligences with Terran hormones. Adaptable, eager, waiting eons for what humanity could give them. I wondered if they, like Snaggles, dreamed. They could probably give Snaggles some good advice if he'd listen to it.

"Would you like to meet Arges?" I asked him. "You might like him."

"*N*-dimensional intelligences are not my province." Without hesitation. I shrugged. He raised his head from his coils.

"I have a question you might be able to help me with,"

he said. "I've found a lot of graves. And they're all very recent."

I felt myself stiffen. My nerves tingled down to my fingertips. "Show me," I said.

They were laid out in a trench, forty of them. Humans, more or less, their oddly proportioned bones blackened by fire, their skulls smashed by high-velocity slugs. Skulls shaped like those of jackals, crocodiles, lions, owls with snapping beaks. Even one that looked as though it was intended as Hathor in her aspect as a humanoid hippopotamus.

"I've found thousands of them," Snaggles said. "All killed like this, most of them burned badly."

"Have you seen any alive?" My sweat was turning chill despite the desert wind. The things, I thought, that come of dreaming badly. . . .

"None. But what are they?"

"Genetic experiments, left over from the Decadence," I said. "It's legal to kill them."

"Ah. I've seen odd sorts of bones from time to time. But nothing as . . . *comprehensive* as this."

"I've got to go, Snaggles," I said.

The god Set rose, standing erect between me and the sun, his hood flared. "Dream well, Doran," he said.

Not likely, I thought. Not likely at all.

I ran for my car.

28

Captain Tromp Muller grinned into the hologram camera and flicked ashes from his cigarette. "Ach, Mr. Falkner," he said. "What a surprise. It's not even Christmas."

"You killed all those genetic experiments in Egypt," I said. "Your orders were to capture and sterilize them."

Muller drew on his cigarette and regarded me with narrowed eyes. "There were too bloody many, Mr. Falkner," he said. "Over eight thousand by the last count. And tricky. They didn't cooperate with me, you know. I had to call in Kurusu, and even Boetie, toward the end."

"They were human stock," I said. "They had to be stopped to keep them from damaging the planet, but they didn't deserve what they got. Which was genocide."

Muller's face hardened. He stubbed out his cigarette off camera in an ashtray that clanged with the force of his gesture. "It's legal to kill genetic experiments, Mr. Falkner." His blunt syllables thudded down like mallets. "They are a blasphemous parody of humanity. I'm a gamekeeper by profession, and I'm authorized. I'm even authorized by the contract we made, which allows me to kill them if the sterilization experiment doesn't work out.''

"The contract also specifies consultation with my son David. You didn't consult. You just contacted Kurusu on your own and sent in your bill.''

Muller shrugged. "Easier that way. Fewer delays. Wouldn't have made any difference in the end.''

I thought of Muller floating in a fieldcar over the Nile, looking down on the floor of the night desert with infrared glasses. The cough of the rifle, the sudden explosion of an incendiary. The burning. The last anguished howling of a jackal throat.

I felt my hands trembling. I'd been worried that the creatures would rival my centaurs, and the sorts of arrangements Snaggles could make with them, and I'd been distracted by the beginnings of Knight's Move—but that didn't excuse it. I was responsible for this. I'd known what kind of man Tromp Muller was.

"Captain Muller,'' I said, "I am withdrawing my protection from you. Get off my planet.''

He regarded me with agate eyes. "Suppose I withdraw my protection from *you*, Mr. Falkner?''

"I have more friends than you on this planet,'' I said. "And some of your Nieuwtrekker comrades might be interested in knowing the sort of work you did when you were with the Afrikaner Brotherhood.''

Muller stared at me for a few long seconds. Then he relaxed, stretching back in his seat with his hands clasped behind his head.

"Okay, Mr. Falkner. You win. From what I hear, a lot of new land will be opening soon. And this planet has been going to the dogs for a long time anyway.'' I knew I was going to have to call Kurusu to make sure Muller did as he was told.

"Don't take any longer than two weeks," I said and broke the connection.

It didn't make me feel any better.

29

In front of me, in a little hollow that gradually dipped down to the stony bed of the river, the grave was aflame with blossoms. As I sat on the grassy bank, the grave before me, I could hear the drumming rising from the earth to my hips and spine, the drumming of massed hooves. The bank of the Cephissus had echoed once before to this sound, when Alexander had charged against the Sacred Band of the Boeotians, but the sound that drummed up through the earth now was not that of cavalry, but of centaurs at play. The pass would be stripped of its grasses within days. The blue sky was already browning with dust. This was a yearly festival in honor of Philodice, who was buried where she had died among her disciples, here at the entrance to the Theban plain. Behind me, in the pass, there were games, singing, poetry, cheer. Here there was stillness, and memory.

I looked overhead and saw a medialite floating at a discreet distance. We were filming the festival now, for release later, when we judged that the revelation of the centaurs' existence was necessary. We intended to show them in their masses; there were three or four thousand here, representing ten or twelve thousand of the various bands of centaurs that were moving slowly northward through Thessaly and into Thrace. We wanted to show a lot of centaurs in order to demonstrate that they were cultured, had a large population and were fairly human in attitude, all the better to show the planetary government that they were not to be exterminated, but encouraged.

Fortunately the Diehards were out of power again and wrangling among themselves over the constant temptations that it was my policy to place in their virtuous path. The current government, having been elected in the main by my employees, was a lot closer to the Falkner point of view. The change in policy would be much easier now than at another time.

I looked at the grave and tried to balance my feelings of regret and hope. Our time of dreaming, I thought, was over. Since the diaspora we had fallen into a kind of collective slumber, a period in which we had all had the time and the room to construct our individual fantasies, our bowers and mansions and even the creatures of myth . . . and if the results had sometimes been worthy, if there had been an occasional Chiron or Philodice instead of a Jay Zimmerman and his Dorcas locked in their symbiotic insanity, if there had been a reconstructed Delphi instead of a holocaust in Egypt, it had rarely been the result of virtue, but rather of accident.

Now the doors of dreaming were unlocked. Contact had been made with the others; there would be more contacts to come; and at the same time we would be able to expand into the totality of the universe. The dreams would not end, but they had come out of the cellar into the light of day, and here we would have to face them, to look at their insistent reality.

The human race was going to undertake a period of explosive growth and transition, as fundamental as anything that had gone before, and everything we touched was going to be swept by the whirlwind. I was confident that the Cyclopes would survive—they were adaptable, and immune to the worst we could do to them—but the centaurs were a new and fragile race, and I was afraid the disruptions would destroy them. As the creatures in Egypt had died—from my own negligence and the outraged puritanism of a single malevolent hunter. The centaurs would need protection and nourishment, and I think I was ready to spend the next part of my life providing both.

A light breeze ruffled the flowers on Philodice's grave as the drumroll of centaur merriment shook the earth. It was a pity, I thought, that she had not lived to meet Mary. They would have got along.

Telegates were going up on the inhabited worlds and in stations that hung in orbit across the planets. There had been few transfers so far—diplomatic personnel mainly, to arrange the various protocols by which goods and people could be transported. McGivern was going to try to rein in this tiger, and I was going to help him even though I doubted it would work in the long run. Best to keep the things in legitimate channels until they developed their own patterns, their own momentum. And then, when it couldn't be helped any longer, set them free.

The first commercial gates would open within a matter of weeks, and Mary would come through. I'd pull strings to get her high priority, and for al-Qatan and his wife too, if they wanted to come.

And then Mary would meet the centaurs, and we would face our new whirlwind together. For a time at least. Till she changed her mind and decided to face the whirlwind for a little longer. Or until she'd force me to remember that last promise I'd made, to let her go when the time came.

Another sound rose above the drumming, the strange resonance of centaur voices raised in song. The nonhuman

overtones soared into the dusky sky. I heard the beating of
bipedal feet and looked over my shoulder to see Branwen
floating over the little rise, laughing to herself at the fun of
it all. One of the centaurs had made her a crown of flowers
and she seemed to blaze with light. Brown-legged, she
walked to my side and squatted down beside me.

I'd been away from her for over twenty years. There
was a maturity that tempered her presence now, but still
her laugh was long and joyous, her smile sweet and
generous. Thank god for it. She was a few years short of
Mary's age, and I wondered how they'd get along.

"This thing gets bigger every year, Dad," Branwen
said. "You should see the younglings, the ones here for
the first time. Their eyes get huge, they've never seen
anything like it. They run around like crazy, trying to see
it all." She gave a laugh. "And when they see David and
me, they look so startled. They don't know whether to
hide behind their mothers or to run up and sniff us to see if
we're real."

I smiled and said nothing. She looked at me with
affection. "You look pensive, Dad," she said. "What
were you thinking about?"

"Life. Death. Mutability. Love. Stuff like that." I looked
at the mound. "Graves do that to me."

Branwen put her arm around me and pressed her head to
my shoulder. "That's what graves are for," she said.
"Not for the dead, but to remind us of who we are."

It was impossible to stay gloomy when Branwen was
around. I looked at her and smiled. "That's more pro-
found than anything I've managed to think up all day," I
said. "Let's go play with our friends."

She gave me her hand and we went out of the little
hollow. In front of us the centaurs wheeled in their
thousands, singing, dancing, renewing old friendships.
Tomorrow, when the formal part of the festival began, I
would have to tell them their isolation was going to come

to an end—that their laughter might never again be as carefree, their friendship as open—now that humanity would discover them. I hoped there was enough human in them so that they would be wary, careful enough to survive.

But for now there was anarchic joy. Nearby I saw the source of the singing—centaur poets, disciples of Philodice who had followed her in her travels, others who had come since. In a day or two they would be competing with one another for the prize I and some of the centaur judges had offered, but now they were singing together. I recognized one of Philodice's songs, a lyric in which the sheen of moonlight on a still pond was related to the gleam in a shy lover's eyes and then contrasted to the fire in his heart.

The sentiment sounded about right to me.

I walked down into the festival.